Beauty in Thorns

KATE
FORSYTH

Beauty in Thorns

VINTAGE BOOKS
Australia

A Vintage book
Published by Penguin Random House Australia Pty Ltd
Level 3, 100 Pacific Highway, North Sydney NSW 2060
www.penguin.com.au

First published by Vintage in 2017

Addresses for the Penguin Random House group of companies can be found at global.penguinrandomhouse.com/offices.

National Library of Australia
Cataloguing-in-Publication entry

Forsyth, Kate, 1966– author.
Beauty in thorns/Kate Forsyth.

ISBN: 9781925324242 (paperback)

Artists' models – Fiction.
Artists – Fiction.
Scandals – Fiction.
Historical fiction.

Typeset in Goudy Old Style by Midland Typesetters Australia
Cover design by Nikki Townsend Design
Cover photographs: main image, Betsy Van der Meer/Getty Images; castle, Irina Mosina/Shutterstock; wallpaper, mahout/Shutterstock; rose, photosoft/Shutterstock
Printed in Australia by Griffin Press, an accredited ISO AS/NZS 14001:2004 Environmental Management System printer

Penguin Random House Australia uses papers that are natural, renewable and recyclable products and made from wood grown in sustainable forests. The logging and manufacturing processes are expected to conform to the environmental regulations of the country of origin.

I wish it were possible to explain the impression made upon
me as a young girl whose experience so far had been quite remote
from art, by sudden and close intercourse with those to whom it was
the breath of life.

The only approach I can make to describing it is by saying that I felt in
the presence of a new religion. Their love of beauty did not seem to me
unbalanced, but as if it included the whole world and raised the point
from which they regarded everything.

Human beauty especially was in a way sacred to them, I thought; and
of this I received confirmation quite lately from a lady ... 'I never saw
such men,' she said; 'it was being in a new world to be with them.
I sat to them and was with them, and they were different to everyone
else I ever saw. And I was a holy thing to them.'

Lady Georgiana Burne-Jones
Memorials of Edward Burne-Jones, Volume I

Part I

Waking the Sleeping Beauty
1852–1856

... a copy of Grimm's Household Stories, sent to us from outside, made us free of fairyland.
Lady Georgiana Burne-Jones
Memorials of Edward Burne-Jones, Volume I

On the eleventh birthday of the little sister of whom I have spoken, Edward took her, as a treat she could quite understand, to see Rossetti, who was very kind to her ... Edward in his encouraging way helped her to make two pen-and-ink drawings which he insisted on calling hers; one was of Christ receiving little children and one of the Prince waking the Sleeping Beauty.
Lady Georgiana Burne-Jones
Memorials of Edward Burne-Jones, Volume I

1

O'er the Hills and Far Away
Winter 1852

'Imagine falling asleep for a hundred years. Would it not be awful?' Georgie Macdonald whispered to her sister.

Carrie gave her a quick, crooked smile, but the shabby young man who sat at Georgie's feet laughed. 'Why? I think it'd be marvellous.'

'Sssh!' Georgie's eldest sister, Alice, pressed her finger to her lips.

Will Fulford, holding high a small leather-bound book, declaimed: 'All round a hedge upshoots, and shows at distance like a little wood; thorns, ivies, woodbine ...'

Georgie tugged at the young man's threadbare sleeve. 'What do you mean? How could it be marvellous to sleep so long? Why, the world would be so different once you woke.'

'That's why.' His grey eyes seemed full of light. 'Just think of it! What new discoveries would have been made, what new inventions?'

Alice glanced at him reprovingly, as Will recited: '... Bur and brake and briar, and glimpsing over these, just seen, high up the topmost palace-spire ...'

'Can you not see it?' The young man whispered. 'A castle all overgrown with roses, and everyone in it asleep for a hundred years.'

He gave her a smile of singular sweetness. His name was Edward Jones, she remembered, called Ted for short. 'A capital fellow,' her brother Harry had said. 'Smart as a whip, but too highly strung for his own good.' He had won an armful of school prizes, Harry had told her, then fainted on the doormat when he got home.

Ted Jones and his friends had come to visit Harry for tea, and did not seem to mind at all having it in the schoolroom so as not to disturb Mama. The day was so cold the windows were frosted over, filling the room with a strange twilight gloom. Everyone had congregated about the coal-stove. Squat as a black goblin, it stood on four widespread legs, the slitted eyes of its grate gleaming orange. It smelt sulphurous, like hell-fires.

A one-eyed rocking-horse gazed sadly out at the sleet pelting against the barred windows. Beyond was a murky landscape of gabled roofs, chimney-pots, factory smokestacks, and church steeples drifting in fog. Georgie's father said Birmingham was the workshop of the world, and she could understand why. All day and night, the air rang with the clatter of trains, the banging of presses, the whirling of cogs, the spray of fiery sparks, the belch of steam. Pyramids of slag on every corner, and the roads churned to mud by heavy wagons dragged by weary horses.

Even the snow fell dirty in Birmingham.

Harry lay back in a sagging armchair, swinging one scuffed boot and stifling a yawn. Georgie's younger brother Freddy lay on the hearth-rug, hacking at a lump of wood with his pen-knife. All the other chairs in the schoolroom were taken up by Georgie's sisters. Fifteen-year-old Alice sat upright, her skirts smoothed down over her knees to make them seem longer. Carrie lay on the only couch. She was eighteen months younger than Alice, and Georgie was eighteen months younger again, the third daughter at eleven-and-a-half years of age. All three girls were darning socks, so as not to tempt the Devil with their idleness.

Agnes was nine and Louie was seven. They sat together on the floor by the window, playing with a wooden Noah's Ark set. Four-year-old Edith was pretending to feed her dolly with a tin spoon. The doll had been made from an old pillow, the eyes and mouth sewn crookedly. All six girls were identically dressed in brown calico frocks under old pinafores, their hair hanging in tight plaits down their backs.

'She sleeps: her breathings are not heard, in palace chambers far apart. The fragrant tresses are not stirr'd, that lie upon her charmed heart,' Will recited.

Ted whispered to Georgie, 'Do you think Tennyson means to say she's snoring, but not so loud she can be heard?'

Georgie laughed, then clapped her hands over her mouth.

Alice said, 'Mr Jones, please be quiet. I want to listen to Mr Fulford.'

'You'll never be in want of an opportunity to do that,' he answered at once, casting Georgie a glance brimming with mischief. She had to bite back a smile in response. Alice frowned at them. Ted returned his attention to the centre of the room, where his friend was saying, 'He travels far from other skies, his mantle glitters on the rocks. A fairy prince, with joyful eyes, and lighter-footed than the fox.'

He has joyful eyes too ...

Even as she thought it, Georgie remembered that her first impression of Ted Jones had been that he seemed long-faced and mournful, unlike her brother's other friends who were all so cheerful. And in repose, listening quietly as he was now, his face did seem sorrowful, like a painting of Christ.

Yet, when Ted had first arrived, he had made such fearsome expressions that he had delighted Louie and terrified Edith. And Harry said he was always sketching wicked caricatures of all the masters at school.

'He comes, scarce knowing what he seeks.' Will paused, then cleared his throat. With an air of embarrassment, he continued, 'He breaks the hedge: he enters there.'

Harry gave a knowing snicker. Alice looked down, colour mounting her cheeks.

Georgie looked from one face to another, sensing impropriety.

Mama would not have approved of young men reading her daughters poems such as this. She only allowed the girls to read books with titles such as *Redemption and Zeal*. Georgie was sure that she would consider Alfred,

Lord Tennyson as morally corrupt as William Shakespeare, whose works were banned in the Macdonald household.

Mama had one of her heads, however. She had sunk into the Slough of Despond after the death of Baby Herbert the year before, and showed no sign of ever emerging. Herbert was the third of Mama's babies to die and indeed it sometimes felt as if she cared more for the dead children than she did for the living. 'I wish you could have seen my boy,' Mrs Macdonald was prone to saying to lady visitors. 'His beauty was so touching to see, so pure and white and cold, like a little marble statue. My only comfort is that he is safe with God now, no longer suffering the evils of this life on earth.'

There's no reason to worry Mama, Georgie told herself. *It's just a fairytale.*

'More close and close his footsteps wind,' Will read. 'The magic music in his heart, beats quick and quicker till he find, the quiet chamber far apart. His spirit flutters like a lark. He stoops – to kiss her on his knee.'

Alice was blushing rosily now.

Will read on. 'A touch, a kiss! The charm was snapt. There rose a noise of striking clocks, and feet that ran, and doors that clapt, and barking dogs, and crowing cocks …' On the rhymes tumbled, quick as dancing feet, and Georgie wanted to clap her hands with the joy of it. Once again Ted looked back at her in quick unspoken sympathy.

Then the poem's rhythm altered once more, slowing into a dreamy lilt. 'And on her lover's arm she leant, and round her waist she felt it fold, and far across the hills they went, in that new world which is the old: across the hills and far away …'

It was the most beautiful thing Georgie had ever heard.

When Will had finished the last stanzas, everyone in the room stirred, as if they too had found themselves held suspended in a spell of sleep. Then a hum of conversation rose.

Ted twisted about so he faced Georgie. With her sitting on a chair, and him cross-legged on the ground, their faces were almost at the same level, for she was a daintily formed child and he was tall and lanky. At nineteen years old, he seemed to her quite grown up, though only the faintest down appeared on his chin and upper lip. His hair was fair and very fine and flopped into his eyes, and every now and again he swept it away with an impatient gesture. His forehead was broad and high, but his face tapered down to a pointed chin, giving him the air of a wise elf.

'Isn't it a wonderful poem?' he said.

'I liked it very much,' she answered shyly. 'Particularly the end.'

'O'er the hills, and far away ... through all the world she follow'd him.'

Georgie nodded. She felt something sharp in her heart. She hardly knew what it was. She felt the same thing, sometimes, singing in church, or when she saw the twilight sky through a filigree of twigs.

'I wish I could write something so beautiful,' she said in a low voice.

'Maybe you will one day.'

She shook her head. 'Papa does not approve of such things. He loves books and has a great many, but they are all of sermons or such things. Books of an *improving* nature.'

'Ah, yes, I know the type. But you shouldn't read just to be improved! Books are meant to amuse and delight as well, you know, and to bring beauty into our lives.'

Georgie could only be glad that her mother was not present to hear him speak so. Mrs Macdonald lived in fear of offending God, who seemed to frown on so many things. *If thy hand offend thee, cut it off: it is better for thee to enter into life maimed, than having two hands to go into hell, into the fire that shall never be quenched ...*

Georgie's whole life was bent and shaped to appease her mother's God. Each day began and ended with prayer. The Macdonald sisters spent the hours between playing hymns on the piano and sewing proverbs into samplers, while Mama read to them from the Bible. The six girls only left the house to attend chapel and temperance meetings, to organise fund-raising bazaars for the missionaries, and to take the Word of God to the downtrodden poor. Once a week they went to Bible Class, where their souls were examined and found wanting, and so they were reproved and exhorted to try harder to guard themselves from sin. It was not easy to make friends with any other girls they met at chapel, or in Sunday School, when all sat meekly under the censorious eyes of the congregation, attending upon the ordinances of God. And since the Macdonald family moved every three years, following their father on his preaching circuit, it hardly seemed worth the effort to try.

Georgie did not know how to say all this to Ted, and so they sat in silence for a moment. Georgie waited for him to excuse himself and go to talk to his friends, standing warming themselves by the stove and talking about cricket.

But Ted fixed her with his intent gaze. 'And do you still think it would be awful to sleep for a hundred years?'

She nodded. 'Indeed, yes, for I'd wake up and everyone I loved would be dead and gone, and the world quite different.'

He spoke eagerly: 'Perhaps it'd be a world where there was no rich and no poor … no prisons or factories or workhouses … no ragged children begging in the streets …'

'That would be a wonderful world,' she agreed. 'But …'

Ted tilted his head quizzically, raising one eyebrow.

'But it'd be lonely, if everyone else I knew was dead.'

'You'd have your fairy prince to kiss you awake.'

Her eyes fell and her fingers twisted the fabric of her pinafore. Her cheeks felt hot. He went on in a rush, 'Besides, all your loved ones would have slept with you and awakened with you, just like the king and all his courtiers in the poem.'

'Well, then,' she said, 'perhaps it would not be so terrible.'

He did not answer. His eyes had darkened and did not seem to see her any longer. 'If I were to sleep a hundred years, there'd be scarcely anyone to miss me,' he said, in so low and gruff a voice she hardly heard him.

She gazed at him wonderingly. 'No-one?'

'My mother died when I was only six days old. My father was so prostrate with grief he could not bear to see me or touch me. He buried himself in his work. There was no-one to care for me. At last they found a housekeeper to look after me … she did her best, but …' His words trailed away.

'I'm so sorry,' Georgie faltered, her heart moved with pity.

'I only saw my father on Sundays, which was the day my mother died,' he went on. 'He'd hold my hand and we'd walk through the town, all smoky and noisy, to the graveyard, where all was deathly quiet … which was worse. And my father would kneel and make me kneel beside him, and he would pray and cry and hold my hand so tight it hurt. I did not like it.'

'But does he not care now?' Georgie asked.

Ted nodded his head slowly. 'Yes. In a way, he cares too much. Mrs Sampson too. All they ever do is fuss.' Suddenly his expression changed. Mischief lit his eyes again. 'Mrs Sampson was always asking me, five-hundred-and-thirty-seven times a day, "What are you thinking, Ted?" So, quite some years ago, I came up with an answer that seemed to satisfy her.'

'Why? What did you say?'

'Camels.'

For an instant, Georgie gazed at him in astonishment, then she broke into peals of laughter. Ted joined in, and his laugh was so free and joyous and wild that everyone in the room looked around, smiles starting to their lips.

Alice swept over, hands on her hip. 'What are you two talking about?'

'Nothing,' Georgie said.

'Just camels,' Ted replied. Their eyes met, and they fell again into laughter.

2

Pretending To Be Drowning
Spring 1852

Lizzie floated in water, pretending to be drowning.

She had to stay absolutely still. If she moved even a little, the bath water rippled and the fabric of her silver-embroidered dress billowed. Then Mr Millais would heave a great sigh. She would hear the scrape of his palette knife, followed by a long silence, in which she knew he was staring at her, measuring her, finding her wanting.

Lizzie could not see Mr Millais. She had to look up towards the windows at the far end of the studio. He had coloured the panes so that the light fell through in shades of green and gold. She had watched those panes slowly darken, a single star pricking out in the sky above the dark geometry of rooftops. She had watched the panes turned to black, and still Mr Millais kept on painting.

The studio was cold, the water in the bath even colder. His mother had lit candles under the bath, to warm the water, but they must have blown out.

Lizzie could not afford to lose this job. She earned seven shillings in an afternoon, just for lying in a bath full of water. In her old job, sewing flowers on hats for twelve hours a day, six days a week, she had earned only nine shillings a week.

Since Charlie's death, her family needed her wages more than ever before.

Her brother had died of consumption. In just a few months, he had wasted away and died. He had been only twenty-two years old.

Lizzie had never seen anyone die before. She had been so cold afterwards. She felt it in her bones, in the hollow of her stomach. She would have liked to crawl into bed and stay there till the bitter winter of his death had passed.

But she could not. She had to help support the family. Her younger sister Lydia was working two jobs, in her aunt's candle shop during the day and sewing at night, helped by her mother and the two youngest girls, Mary and Clara. Her brother Jimmy was labouring with his father in his cutlery workshop, and even poor daft Harry, who was only nine, was doing what he could.

So, two weeks after Charlie's death, with her grief still as sharp as it had been the day her brother had died, Lizzie had written to Mr Millais and told him she was ready to come back and model for him again. He was grateful indeed, for he was keen to finish his painting in time for the Royal Academy Exhibition in April. He had nothing left to paint but her face and figure, having finished the rest of the scene down at the Hogsmill River in Surrey.

'I don't want to waste all that work,' he had told her. 'I had to stay for months, sitting on the banks of that infernal swamp, swatting away the most muscular flies you've ever seen. The farmer who owned the field threatened to drag me before the magistrate for walking over his hay. Then, once the hay was taken in, he put his most ferocious bull in the field, just to punish me.'

Lizzie had laughed, imagining the beautifully dressed young man running away from a bull, his easel and paints and brushes shoved under his arms.

Then Mr Millais had sobered and said gravely, 'But it is you who are the crux of my painting, Miss Siddal. Your face and your hair, and the dress billowing out into the water. All the rest of it is just there to frame you.'

Lizzie knew the painting had already been sold for an astonishing three hundred guineas. She could not let Mr Millais down. If she failed him, she would have to go back to working in that dark little hat-shop, with no hope for any other life.

Ever since Lizzie had found a fragment of a Tennyson verse wrapped about a pat of butter as a little girl, she had loved to draw and write poetry. Her mother had not approved, thinking it a waste of time, and so Lizzie had always done her scribbling, as her mother called it, in secret.

'You're a dreamer,' her mother had scolded. 'Bad as your pa, always building castles in the air.'

Mr Siddal had been raised in Sheffield and trained as a cutler, but was sure he was born to better things. By rights, he said, he should have inherited the family's ancestral home of Hope Hall, in the Peaks of Derbyshire. 'Mr Charles Siddal o' Hope Hall, Derbyshire, sounds right respectable!'

'It's not called Hope Hall anymore,' Charlie would cry. 'It's a coaching inn called The Cross-Daggers, and if we lived there we'd be serving ale to yokels.'

As long as Lizzie could remember, her father had been pursuing his right to the property through the courts. One day, in a temper, Lizzie's little sister Clara had thrown his legal papers on to the fire and her father's dreams had gone up in smoke. After that, the Siddals had no choice but to live in the crowded slums of Southwark, breathing in the stench of the tanning yards every day.

Perhaps, if Clara had not burned the legal papers, Lizzie would be Miss Siddal of Hope Hall instead. Sitting under an oak tree in a silk gown, painting the grand landscape of the Peaks while a butler poured her tea.

Perhaps Charlie would not have gotten sick and died.

One day, Lizzie heard that a delivery of hatboxes was to be made to a well-to-do lady called Mrs Deverell, and had at once begged permission to take them herself. Her employer, a sharp-faced, sharp-eyed woman named Mrs Tozer, stared at her in surprise. Messenger-boys were normally employed for such tasks. Lizzie was, however, one of her best milliners, having a real eye for how to place a silk rose, and so Mrs Tozer had unwillingly given permission.

Instead of a bonnet, one of the hatboxes Lizzie carried contained some of her best drawings. For Mrs Deverell was married to the Secretary of the London School of Design, where women were permitted to take drawing lessons for two hours each day. Lizzie had already been to the school's premises in Somerset House, in the hope of gaining admission, but the tuition cost one shilling and sixpence a month, which was well beyond her means. She was hoping against hope that – if she showed Mr Deverell her drawings – he would find enough merit in them to recommend her and, perhaps, even sponsor her.

It was as unlikely as her pa inheriting Hope Hall, but Lizzie had to try. She was twenty years old already, and life was narrowing upon her.

As she was shown into the drawing-room of the Deverells' grand house in Kew, Lizzie's mouth was dry and the bones of her corset seemed too tight. She showed the bonnets to Mrs Deverell and her daughters, teaching them how to tie the ribbons to best advantage. They were surprised, but pleased, at the extra service. Finally, at the very last moment, Lizzie summoned up enough courage to lift out her drawings and show them to Mrs Deverell, who raised her eyebrows in surprised affront.

'Please, ma'am, forgive me for being so forward,' Lizzie said. 'I didn't know who else to turn to. I know they're not that good, but, indeed, I want to learn to do better.'

Mrs Deverell's air of icy hauteur did not thaw. 'My dear girl, what is the point? A woman cannot become a professional artist. Such a thing would not be seemly. That is why women are not permitted to join the Royal Academy schools.'

'Which is why the School of Design began classes for women, Mama,' Miss Deverell said. She was a round-faced young woman with a profusion of dark ringlets. 'Remember, Papa says the school seeks to find a practical application for an artistic bent. And surely this young woman should be commended for trying to better herself.'

Her mother gave a harrumph that seemed to indicate otherwise. Miss Deverell took up the sheaf of Lizzie's drawings. 'My brother Walter is studying at the Royal Academy. If you like, I can show him your sketches. Perhaps he can give you some advice.'

On the train back to London, Lizzie sat with her gloved hands clenched, her eyes smarting with tears. She deeply regretted the loss of her sketches. She could imagine Miss Deverell forgetting all about them, and the skivvy using them to light the fire the next day.

A few days later, Mrs Deverell swept into Mrs Tozer's millinery shop, a handsome young man by her side. Lizzie stood behind the counter, adjusting the bow on a fetching bonnet of tulle and rice straw. Lizzie quickly put the hat back on its stand. If Mrs Tozer found out what she had done, Lizzie would lose her job and then she'd really be in the suds.

Mrs Tozer bustled forward, begging to know Mrs Deverell's pleasure. The young man came forward, smiling. 'I can see by your hair that you are the girl who visited my mother this week. My sister tells me you have an interest in art.'

Lizzie gave a quick nod, not daring to glance in Mrs Tozer's direction to see if she had overheard.

'Then I have a proposition for you.'

Lizzie's colour deepened.

The young man flushed also, and said, 'That is, I mean to say … I need a red-headed girl … to paint, I mean. I've had the devil of a time finding the right kind of girl. But then my sister told me about your visit and said that your hair was the most glorious shade of copper and that, really, you could easily pass as a boy if we tied it up …'

A swift procession of emotions passed through Lizzie. For a while she lost the thread of his words.

'… I'll pay you, of course, and you can sit at a time that suits you, since I know you're a working girl … I mean, a girl that works … and my sister can sit with us, to chaperone you, I mean, and maybe the extra blunt will be of use to you, in paying for your art schooling, and so on. Because, you know, it just seems like such a stroke of luck! You coming just when I was at my wits' end ...'

'How much?' Lizzie asked.

When he told her, she drew a deep breath and said, 'Your ma will need to come and tell my ma that no impropriety is intended.'

Walter Deverell cast an unhappy look at his mother, who was looking over lace caps and stockings with a very hard-done-by air.

Lizzie said firmly, 'My ma's a stickler for propriety. And don't even think of asking me to take my clothes off, because I won't do it.'

Mr Deverell coloured to the roots of his hair. 'Of course not. I mean, it is better if we can do a life study ... to try and get the drapery right, you know ... but my mother wouldn't allow such a thing anyway ...'

'When do you want me?' Lizzie had said.

That was how she found herself modelling for Water Deverell's painting of Viola, the heroine of Shakespeare's play *Twelfth Night*, who disguised herself as a pageboy to work for the man she loved.

Then all Mr Deverell's friends wanted her to model for them too.

It was intoxicating – and bewildering – to suddenly be sought out by these sophisticated young men, with their quick wit, their easy manners and their strong opinions. William Holman Hunt with his button nose and sudden temper, whom the others called the Maniac. Ford Madox Brown, nicknamed Bruno, who was conducting a not-so-secret affair with one of Lizzie's childhood friends, a plump young woman called Emma. Johnny Millais, who everyone thought some kind of child prodigy for he had been only eleven when he was admitted into the Royal Academy schools. And Dante Gabriel Rossetti, the handsomest of them all, who had tried to kiss her more than once and promised to write a sonnet to her eyes.

Being asked to model for an artist had seemed like the most remarkable chance to be part of a world where the things Lizzie loved most were celebrated. Perhaps, if she pleased them, they would show her some of their secrets. Sitting quietly in one pose after another, Lizzie had watched and listened and tried to learn. They had shown her their sketches, let her look through their folios of the work of great masters, and given her books of poetry to read.

If she failed them, these idealistic young men would no longer wish to paint her. All the beauty, all the poetry, would be lost; the newly kindled light in her snuffed out.

So Lizzie lay in the freezing dark water and focused all her thoughts on Ophelia, the young woman she was pretending to be. Betrayed in love, her mind broken, Ophelia had wandered the water-meadows, singing and gathering weeds and wild flowers. A branch had broken. She had slipped into the river and had let herself sink away. Lizzie imagined her numb despair, the grief that dragged her down like water-weeds . . .

Tears seeped from the corner of her eyes and ran down her cold cheek. It was hard to breathe. The weight of the silver dress dragged at her. Everything ached, her neck, her arms, the bones of her cranium. She set her jaw, and willed herself to stay still.

Lizzie could not go back. She would not go back.

'Johnny, darling, should you be keeping Miss Siddal so long?'

Then a rush of feet, the rustle of silken skirts.

'Johnny! The candles have gone out. Miss Siddal must be freezing.'

Johnny Millais jumped up. 'The time just ran away with me. I didn't realise how late it was . . .'

Water gushed all over the floor as they lifted her out. Mrs Millais wrapped her in an old blanket. Lizzie could scarcely feel the touch of their hands. Tremors shook her from head to foot. Her teeth chattered. Someone chafed her hands. 'Look, her lips are quite blue!'

Johnny gave her a glass of something, but she could not close her fingers about the tumbler. When they held it to her lips, it clattered against her teeth.

'Johnny, what were you thinking? Five hours she's been in that bath!'

Nothing could warm her. Johnny ran for hot water bottles, while his mother struggled to draw off the sodden gown.

'That boy,' Mrs Millais cried. 'He forgets the world when he is painting. It's like he's under a spell!'

Lizzie looked at the painting on its easel. She saw her own pale face gleaming out from the dark swallowing water, the glint of the silver embroidery, the red blur of a poppy floating by her hand. Then, in the configuration of light and shade at the edge of the canvas, she suddenly saw – staring at her – the white bones and dark hollows of a skull.

3

That Lovelorn Maiden
Spring 1852

'If she survives the night, we may be able to save her ...'

The doctor spoke in a low voice, but Lizzie heard him. Clutch of panic at her throat. She struggled up, and saw him pour away a basin of her blood.

'Has she got consumption?' Her mother's voice was tense. 'You know our son died just a few weeks ago.'

'We will need to keep a close eye on her,' the doctor replied. He lifted Lizzie and gave her some laudanum to drink. 'I'll return tomorrow to bleed her again.'

When he had gone, her father came in to Lizzie's bedroom. There was no fire up here in the attic, and so his breath plumed white as he spoke. 'How are we meant t'pay the ruddy doctor's bills? We still owe for Charlie ... and now we don't have owt coming in from Lizzie either.'

'What else could I do?' Mrs Siddal asked. 'Her fever was that high, I was afeared we'd lose her too.'

'We'll ask that artist fellow to cough up some rolls of soft. He can afford it. While we're at it, we'll sue him for Lizzie's loss of income.'

Lizzie tried to raise herself up on her elbows. 'No, no, you can't do that ... what will they think of me? Please, Pa, you mustn't.'

'Don't go upsetting yourself. That artist fellow will soon realise we're not fools to be swindled.'

Lizzie tried to protest again, but slow waves of darkness rocked her away. She wondered: *Does Mr Rossetti know I almost died?*

She drifted in and out of daydreams in which he rushed to her bedside, kissing her hand and saying he could not live without her. She imagined him winding her hair about his hand, unbuttoning her chemise, baring her skin. When she woke, she felt his absence keenly. Lizzie wished she could write to him, begging him to come and see her. But young ladies did not write such letters to gentlemen of their acquaintance.

For the next few weeks, Lizzie was confined to her bed, with mustard plasters applied to her chest and feet, and the doctor coming several times to take a basinful of blood from her veins. Her limbs felt heavy and, when she rose to use the chamber pot, her vision swarmed with tiny fizzles of light. It hurt to breathe.

She was still troubled by a racking cough, only eased by regular doses of Sydenham's Laudanum Elixir. Luckily Mr Millais had agreed to cover her medical bills, though he had politely declined to pay the fifty pounds Lizzie's father had demanded. Lizzie had been afraid that Mr Millais must be angry with her, but he wrote her a kind note thanking her for her work and assuring her that he had been able to finish his painting.

In May, the Royal Academy Exhibition opened. Lizzie insisted on rising and dressing, despite all her mother's scolding. Her black dress was loose on her.

She limped along the cobblestones, her feet sore and tender. The wind cut through her thin coat, and made her breath wheeze in her chest. The sound frightened her. It was too much like the rattle in her brother's lungs in the last weeks of his life.

Soon Lizzie was feeling so faint, she realised she would never manage to walk the three miles to the academy. Digging in her purse, she found a few pence and hailed an omnibus. It lurched over to the curb, and she caught hold of the leather strap and hauled herself inside. The omnibus jerked and jolted over every bump and pothole till Lizzie's head ached, but at least she could rest her weary legs.

Lizzie paid her shilling, and slowly made her way into the exhibition. She looked all through the crowd but she could not see Gabriel anywhere. She asked an usher where she could find the Ophelia painting, and he smiled. 'Ah yes. In the West Room. It's been a dreadful crush, everyone wants to see it.'

Lizzie's heart missed a beat.

'Some people queue up for an hour to see it, then go back to the end of the line so they can see it again.'

Smiling, Lizzie joined the end of the long serpentine file. It moved so slowly, she had plenty of time to view all the other paintings covering the walls from floor to ceiling. When at last she reached *Ophelia*, her breath caught. It shone out of the multitude of gloomy paintings like a window on to a summer's day. Yet it was a summer day overshadowed by the brazen light that comes just before a thunderstorm. Ophelia was caught at the very moment of surrender to her death, her hands relaxing, the centre of her gravity sinking into the shadowy depths. It was mesmerising. And heartbreaking.

'Miss Sid!'

Lizzie spun on her heel at the sound of Gabriel's voice. He was coming towards her, both hands held out, delight on his face. Her face lit up in response. He grasped her gloved hand. 'It's good to see you. I wondered if you would come to see yourself in all your glory.'

'I wanted to see how it turned out.'

'Magnificently, as you can see.'

'It's the heroine of the hour herself!' Walter Deverell said. He and Gabriel had been lounging against the wall, laughing and teasing Johnny Millais as he did his best to respond to the adoration of the crowd.

'Have you ever seen anything like it?' Gabriel said. 'Ophelia is a sensation!'

'Not everyone likes it,' Walter said. 'Did you read the *Times*? I quote! "There must be something strangely perverse in the imagination which sources Ophelia in a weedy ditch, and robs the drowning struggle of that lovelorn maiden of all pathos and beauty."' He laughed.

'Even Mr Ruskin is not wholly convinced,' Gabriel said.

Lizzie looked at him in sudden swift anxiety.

'He called Surrey "that rascally wire-fenced garden-rolled-nursery-maid's paradise",' Walter told her gleefully. 'He must really hate the place.'

'Don't mind us,' Gabriel said. 'We're just teasing Johnny so his head doesn't swell. Everyone thinks you're a great beauty and a perfect Ophelia.'

Lizzie looked up at him in gratitude.

'Johnny said you've been unwell, that you caught a bad cold after your dunking. Are you still fagged to death?'

She shook her head, so glad to see the concern in his eyes that she felt quite light-headed. 'I am much better, thank you,' she answered, smiling up at him.

Gabriel laid his hand on her arm, as if they were not standing in a crowded hall where everyone could see them. 'Johnny should be ashamed of himself, making you ill on his behalf. I'm half minded to call him out!'

Lizzie smiled. 'What, paintbrushes at dawn?'

'He'd thrash me, the way I'm going. Look at him, the belle of the ball, and I haven't a thing to show for all these past months of work. Maybe you're the magic key. Maybe I should whisk you away, keep you all to myself, and see what masterpiece I come up with.'

She looked up at him, meeting his eyes boldly. 'Maybe you should.'

It had been two years since Lizzie had met Dante Gabriel Rossetti. Even his name was unlike any other.

His friends called him Gabriel, as if he were angelic, but she had never known anyone so much of this earth. He loved to laugh, to talk, to eat, to make merry. He had dark wavy hair, worn long over a soft collar, and his eyes were deep set and ringed with shadows. His voice was low and deep and melodious, with a fascinating hint of a foreign accent.

He had been christened Gabriel Charles Dante Rossetti, but he had dropped the prosaic Charles and changed the order of his birth names to better effect. Lizzie understood why. Names were important. Gabriel had convinced her to change the spelling of her own last name, from Siddall to Siddal. He said it looked much more refined that way.

She had first seen Gabriel in the painted shape of a fool, singing, in Walter Deverell's painting, *Twelfth Night*. The sight of him had stirred nothing in her. At that time, she had been indulging in a few foolish daydreams about Walter. But as soon as Lizzie met Gabriel, Walter and all the other young artists simply faded away.

'Your hair,' he had said, 'is the most beautiful I've ever seen. It is molten gold. I must paint you.'

Nobody had ever said anything like that to her before.

Lizzie had always been considered sadly plain. It was not just her red hair, though that was quite bad enough. It was everything. She was too thin and bony, and had too many freckles. But since Gabriel had declared her a 'stunner', his word for a woman of extraordinary beauty, suddenly everyone seemed to admire her.

And Gabriel seemed to have laid claim to her. If any of his friends wanted to paint Lizzie, Gabriel would turn up at their studios uninvited, his coat pocket bulging with pencils and battered old paintbrushes, and draw her too. Then he would offer to walk her home afterwards. Lizzie did not want him to see where she lived, but she strolled through Hyde Park with him, listening raptly as he told her about the great artists he and his friends considered Immortal, and quoted his poetry to her.

'Her hair that lay along her back, was yellow as ripe corn,' he declaimed, while boldly twisting one of her long red-gold tendrils about his fingers. 'I must have known I was to meet you, Miss Sid. I immortalised you in verse before I even knew you!'

Lizzie was utterly enchanted.

When she was with Gabriel, she was able to imagine herself as he saw her. Luminous, intelligent, bold.

He understood what a risk she had taken agreeing to model at all, and understood at once that she had done so because of her love of Art.

'I've never met a girl like you before,' Gabriel said.

She laughed. 'I've never met anyone like you either.'

He tried to kiss her a few times, and she had to turn her face away and hold him off with one hand. 'I cannot help myself,' he had said. 'You should not look so delectable if you don't want fellows to try and kiss you.'

Then his face had darkened. He had demanded to know if any of his friends had tried. Lizzie had thought Walter Deverell might have liked to, but he had never managed to screw up enough courage to try. She did not tell this to Gabriel, though. His mood could change from humour to discontent or anger very quickly. Her denial pleased him.

'One day,' Gabriel said, 'I'll be a great artist, and sell my paintings for hundreds of guineas, and then we'll run away to Italy and live in a castle on an island, and do nothing but paint and write poetry all day.'

'I'd like to go to Italy,' Lizzie replied primly, though her spirits soared.

Lizzie knew she should be guarding her heart as carefully as she guarded her virtue. It was such a strange experience, however, having someone else's attention focused so intensely upon her face, her hair, her figure. She loved the way Gabriel's fingers trembled when she unpinned her hair, how he laughed when she gave free rein to her observations on those she saw around her, and how he never thought she was a fool just because she was female. She had never felt such power.

Could it ever be?

Her father was an ironmonger.

His father had been an Italian poet and a revolutionary, fleeing the despotic rule of the King of Naples in a rowing boat.

Her mother had been born in Shoreditch.

His mother was the daughter of an Italian scholar and translator.

Her uncle owned a grocer's shop in Barnsbury.

His uncle had been John Polidori, Lord Byron's doctor and the author of the infamous story, 'The Vampyre'.

Lizzie was just a shop-girl.

Gabriel was a poet and a painter, and the self-professed leader of a mysterious brotherhood of young men who had decided they were going to change the world with their art.

Surely it was not possible.

But did Gabriel and his friends not scorn the old rules? Did they not want to make the world anew? Surely, in the world that they imagined, anything was possible?

We live but once in this world, Lizzie thought. She had to try to live the life she wanted, even if she risked everything.

4

The Girl Who Unfastens the Door
Summer 1852

Lizzie sat with her eyes closed, a strand of her hair held between her lips, a distaff lying loosely in her other hand. She had sat in this exact pose, not moving a muscle, for what seemed like a very long time.

With her eyes shut, her other senses were heightened. She could hear the flurry of Gabriel's pencil, the rustle of a mouse in the thatch. She could taste the tang of salt in her hair, and smell Gabriel's distinct spicy odour.

On her tongue lingered the bitter aftertaste of the laudanum she had drunk before settling into her pose. She did not want her cough to bother her, disturbing her pose and breaking Gabriel's rhythm.

Outside the bees hummed in the summer garden. This little thatched cottage on Highgate Hill seemed a thousand miles away from Southwark. Gabriel had needed somewhere to stay and work, and some friends of his had given him the use of the studio in their garden. It had one small panelled room downstairs, which Gabriel used as his living space, and a tiny bedroom in the gable above, reached by an outside stair. Ivy grew over the mullioned windows, giving the room a mysterious green cast. Gabriel had set Lizzie in the deep window-seat, so the light struck over her shoulder and touched one side of her face. Beside her, in the shadows, was set an old spinning-wheel.

Lizzie was dressed in a white chemise that laid bare her arms. Her hair hung loose down her back. She was posing as Delia, a woman in ancient Roman times who was waiting for her lover. Gabriel had read her the poem that had inspired his painting.

You too, Delia, don't be shy at deceiving the guard.

Be daring: Venus herself assists the brave.

She favours the youth who tries out a new threshold,

or the girl who unfastens the door …

Lizzie knew she had broken every rule of propriety, coming here to this secluded cottage with a young man. The other artists' studios had been busy places, with Johnny Millais's mother within earshot, or Walter Deverell's sister drawing at her own easel. Here she and Gabriel were all alone.

Tension taut as a copper wire between them.

At last Gabriel laid down his pencil and came towards her. Lizzie opened her eyes and looked up at him. His fingers lifted her hair and arranged it gently so it fell over her shoulder. 'I am almost afraid of trying to paint you,' he whispered. 'How can I catch all this beauty?'

She smiled at him. He bent and kissed her. Lizzie ran her hand up his back, feeling the play of muscles under the silk of his waistcoat. Their kiss deepened. Gabriel's hands began to explore her body through the thin cambric of her shift. She drew him closer. His breath caught, and he stepped away, running a hand through his hair. 'I mustn't,' he said, his voice huskier than ever.

'Don't you want me?' she challenged him.

He looked at her in surprise. 'Of course I want you! But … well, you know I have no money … I cannot afford to marry … and I should not take advantage of you …'

She stood up and put her arms about his neck, pressing herself against him. 'Aren't we trying to disyoke our necks from custom?'

It was a line from a Tennyson poem he had been reading to her, about a princess who had sworn never to marry, so that she would not be the slave or toy of any man.

Lizzie knew it would make him laugh and catch him to her, kissing her again. After that, it was easy. They fumbled at each other's clothes, sometimes laughing, sometimes sighing in surprise. Their bodies seemed to know what to do instinctively, each new discovery unlocking another secret. Afterwards, he rested his head in the curve of her shoulder, his breath rapid and uneven. Her fingers played with his hair.

'Lizzie, darling,' he whispered. 'I've wanted to do that for so long.'

She gave a soft murmur in response, kissing his bare shoulder, stroking his back.

When he lifted away from her, fastening his trousers, his fingers suddenly stilled. Sitting up, she saw a reddish stain on the white linen. She pulled the chemise down, tucking the stain out of sight.

'So ... you've never done it before either?'

When she shook her head, he looked troubled.

'We've discovered it together.' Her voice cracked with the intensity of her feelings. 'Isn't that the best way?'

Gabriel kissed her tenderly, then rose and - half-naked - found his pencil and sketchbook and began to draw her again. He filled page after page with her image, looking up only to ask her to move her chin a little to the left, or to bite her lip a little harder. Every now and again he rushed over to kiss her again.

Lizzie sat, her lips curved, her hands relaxed. She did not speak, or sigh, or shift her weight, or ask for a break. She did not want to break his intense concentration on her face, her lips, her eyelids. She wanted him to keep drawing her forever.

At last it was time to leave, and Lizzie put on her grey dress and bonnet. There was a moment's difficulty when she realised that she must ask him to pay her for the afternoon's sitting. She hesitated, not wanting him to think of her as some kind of harlot, wanting money in payment for her body. Gabriel had the same moment of realisation, and turned red.

He laid out the usual fee, busying himself with his palette and easel while she tucked the money away in her purse.

Gabriel toyed with his paintbrush. 'I think I am ready to start the watercolour now. Can you come early tomorrow? And stay late?'

Lizzie did not want him to think of her as too easy a conquest, so she answered a little coolly, 'I might have things of my own to do.'

He looked up in sudden jealousy. 'You aren't going to see Walter, are you? I know he wants to paint you again.'

'I might be.'

'Don't go, Lizzie. I need you here.'

Her heart melted. 'All right. I'll come then. But only if …'

'Only if what?' His voice was wary.

'If you'll teach me to paint.'

Light kindled in his eyes. 'Gladly!'

The long summer weeks passed by, and each day Lizzie and Gabriel were easier in each other's company. When she was not modelling for him, they read side by side in the window seat, or talked eagerly of art and poetry. Gabriel gave her a sketchbook, and Lizzie drew pictures of girls in loose dresses, drawing, reading, day-dreaming, girls who looked just like her.

'Do you think I should go to the Academy of Design? They have life-drawing classes there.' Lizzie pressed her hands together hopefully. She felt she needed to ask him, for it would mean that she could not model for him as much, and Gabriel did not like it when she modelled for anyone else.

He looked up from his easel. 'Oh, I don't think so. Places like that do nothing but strangle your creative freedom. You'll learn more puttering about here, with me to help you.'

Lizzie nodded, trying not to show her disappointment. She had so badly wanted to take lessons and learn properly, with other women who wanted to be artists. But she could not afford to do so without Gabriel's help, now that she was no longer earning much through her modelling.

One problem was that Gabriel was not the most committed of teachers. If an idea for a poem struck him, he would wander off and start writing. Or he would go in search of a book, and Lizzie would find him standing and reading a quite different book half an hour later.

He also liked to show her by example. One day he seized her sketchbook and, with just a few swift strokes, transformed her stilted drawing into something full of life and drama. He then gave it back to her, grinning.

'I can't do it! It's no use.' Lizzie had thrown her sketchbook down.

'Rubbish,' he answered. 'It takes a lifetime of practice to learn. You are a few years behind me, that's all. The more you draw, the more your fingers will remember.'

So Lizzie drew until her fingers could scarcely be unlocked from around her pencil.

She had never been happier.

'I draw better when I am hungry,' Lizzie said, not looking away from her easel.

'You've scarcely eaten a thing all day,' Gabriel protested.

She shrugged one shoulder. She could not explain to him how clear and pure her head felt when her stomach was hollow. It was as if the world clicked into sharper focus. Her body was all bone and sinew and nerve, like an artist's body should be.

'I could send out for a pie.' Gabriel drew her back against him, sliding his hands down inside her bodice. She had abandoned her corsets, unable to bear the way they constricted her movements when she painted, and so had made herself a dress that was easy to fasten and unfasten. Gabriel thought she had done it for him.

Lizzie pulled away. 'I don't know how you can eat those pies. How do you know what's in them? Haven't you heard those stories about a barber who kills his victims and cooks them up in a pie?'

'That's just a penny dreadful.'

'Still, it could be cats or rats …'

'Or bats. I get the idea. It needn't be a pie ...'

'My mother will be angry with me if I miss dinner again. She likes the family to eat together.' Lizzie looked out the window and realised how late it was. She jumped to her feet, shoving her paintbrush into a jar of turpentine. 'Oh, Gabriel, why did you let me paint so long. I must fly!' Hurriedly she unrolled the sleeves of her dress. 'Will you tidy up for me? Where's my coat?'

'Are you sure I cannot walk you home?'

Lizzie shook her head. 'There's no need. I'll hail a cab.'

Gabriel looked troubled. He pulled out his purse. 'Let me give you some money for it.'

She took it awkwardly, kissed Gabriel goodbye, and hurried down to the street. A hansom cab clopped past, the driver sitting up behind the cabin, shrouded in his greatcoat against the fine mizzle.

Lizzie did not hail it. She began to walk, as swiftly as she could, with the weight of her skirts hampering her legs. Her basket banged against her hip. It was filled with her sewing, which she worked at quietly while Gabriel drew her. She had given up her job at the millinery shop, but earned what she could by sewing fancy work for a Southwark dressmaker she knew.

She had to earn some money somehow. Gabriel did not like to think of her modelling for anyone else, and it was hard to ask him for money now that she shared his bed.

She passed an apothecary. Lizzie's steps faltered. She stood for a moment, hesitating, then hurried inside, paying two shillings for a small brown bottle of laudanum. She hid it in her pocket, then rushed back out on to the street. *Only if I cough*, she told herself. *Or if I can't sleep.*

It was a long walk. The domes and spires and chimneypots were black against a fiery sky. Puddles gleamed with uncertain light, restless beneath the pricking rain.

The lamplighter was already making his slow way from gaslight to gaslight, his pole over his shoulder. As he lifted his wand high, Lizzie heard the hiss of the gas. Then a bright golden star bloomed, making the darkness thicken.

At last, Lizzie saw the hulking shape of the Deaf and Dumb Asylum, and knew she was almost home. She paused to catch her breath and smooth down her mud-fringed skirts. Her father was outside his shop, in his long canvas apron, fastening the shutters over the windows. Steel dust glittered in his hair. 'Ye're late,' he said. 'Get lost, did ye?'

'I know. I'm sorry. Mr Rossetti was that keen to finish a bit of work while the light was right.'

'Did he pay you owt extra?'

'Of course. A little. My omnibus took ever so long coming home. A horse fell on the hill, and the traffic was a nightmare.' Her cheeks warmed, and she avoided her father's eye.

'Well, get yeself in. You know the night air ain't good for ye.'

'Yes, Pa.'

Lizzie went through the shop, the tools and blades shining faintly in the light of her father's lantern, which he had set on the cracked wooden counter. She could hear the clanging of tools from the workroom out the back, where her younger brothers were finishing up the day's work.

As she climbed the steps to their rooms, she felt tired and heavy-limbed. Her mother was stirring a pot that hung from a tripod above an open hearth. Lizzie's stomach roiled at the smell.

Mrs Siddal turned around, her red hair frizzing out from her head in the steam. 'Where you been, Lizzie?'

'Working. I got held up on the way home. A horse slipped and fell.' Lizzie found it easier to lie to her mother than to her father.

'You hungry? We're just about to eat.'

'I've eaten already. Mr Rossetti fed me.'

'What did you eat?'

'Mutton pie.'

Her mother grunted. 'Better fare than you get here, I suppose.'

'No, that's not it. He was sorry for keeping me so late, and wanted to make sure I had some supper.'

'As long as you ate. Coming to the meeting?'

Lizzie lifted her basket. 'I've still got work to do.'

Her mother looked displeased. 'The state of your soul needs work too.'

'I know, Ma. I'm sorry. But if I get it done quickly, then Mrs Tweedale will be pleased with me and give me more work.'

Her mother took off her apron and hung it on a hook, and tidied her hair in an age-spotted mirror that hung from a beam. 'There are some nice young men that come to the prayer meeting. Proper workers with proper wages. It'd do you no harm to come along and be nice to them every now and again.'

'Yes, Ma. Maybe next week.'

Her mother began to slice the boiled corned beef. It was red and rough, with a thick rim of yellowish fat. Just the smell of it made her feel sick. Lizzie went into the sitting-room and picked up her sewing. As soon as she heard everyone leave, she pulled out a sketchbook and a pencil, and began to draw. Her fingers felt stiff, though. After a while she tore the page out, scrunched it up and flung it on the fire. Flames leapt up hungrily, and then sunk away again into a dull glow.

You've got to practise, practise, practise, Gabriel told her.

All Lizzie did was practise, and yet her drawings remained rigid and lifeless. Perhaps she just did not have the talent. When Gabriel was only six, he had amazed the local milkman by his drawing of a rocking-horse. Lizzie was sure that no-one would be amazed by any rocking-horse she drew.

Her hand slid into her pocket and touched her bottle of laudanum. *A few drops won't hurt*, she told herself.

In a daze, she drew until she heard her family's boots on the stairs. Then she hid her sketchbook away, and pretended she had been sewing.

The Siddal family went early to bed, to save lamp oil. Lizzie lay in her lumpy bed, listening to her sister's breathing. Her whole body thrummed with tiredness, and every now and again one of her legs would twitch, startling her from a doze.

There was a sick knot of anxiety in the pit of her stomach. Tomorrow was Saturday. Mrs Siddal would be expecting Lizzie's pay packet. Lizzie had managed to save only a few coins. Gabriel was very relaxed about money.

When he was short, he borrowed some from his brother or his friends. When he had a windfall, he spent it. He thought her very working-class, she knew, counting every penny.

If only he would marry her! Then she would be free of her family, free of all these worries over money, free to do as she pleased.

She crept out of bed and fumbled through the darkness to where her coat hung on its hook. As her fingers closed around the little bottle in its pocket, she felt a pang of fearful guilt. Laudanum was not cheap, she should be saving it for emergencies. But her head throbbed, her tongue and mouth were parched, and her stomach felt like a knotted tangle of string.

Lizzie tipped the bottle and drank it down.

One evening, Lizzie was nestled into Gabriel's side, listening to him read Tennyson, when someone banged the front door open.

'Gabriel!' a man's voice shouted. 'Where are you? It's devilish dark in here. Care to join me at the pub?'

Gabriel pushed Lizzie aside and jumped to his feet. She scrambled up also, cheeks scorching. For a moment, the three of them stood there. No-one spoke, though the young man stared at her in curiosity. Lizzie realised that Gabriel had no intention of introducing her to his friend. Embarrassment turned to shame.

One did not introduce one's friends to one's mistress.

She picked up her skirts and fled.

As Lizzie hurtled down the steep hill, tying the ribbons of her bonnet, tears flooded down her cheeks. She felt like such a fool. No wonder Gabriel never took her out to meet his friends. Lizzie had thought it was because he wanted to keep her all to himself. She had not minded, existing in a kind of happy dream where she had pretended that the little thatched cottage was their home, and Gabriel was her husband, and they were building a life of art and love together.

It was all a sham.

She could not stop the tears from falling. The wall of Highgate Cemetery loomed over her in the lingering summer dusk. She ducked into the shadow of its arched gateway, and pressed herself against cool stone, hiding her face in her hands.

At last the storm of tears passed. Lizzie looked through the chained bars at the graveyard beyond. She could see dangling willow leaves, marble obelisks, stone angels.

Lizzie knew she would return in the morning, with her sketchbook and her pencils, and pretend she did not mind.

For she had come too far now to turn back.

5

The Winged Life
Spring 1853

One of her lover's treasures was a handwritten manuscript of William Blake's poems and pencil sketches, which Gabriel had bought for ten shillings from an attendant at the British Museum.

He had, of course, borrowed the tin from his brother.

Blake painted angels and demons and ghosts. Lizzie could understand why Gabriel was so fascinated by him. The same images haunted his paintings too. The poems, however, clanked with manacles and chains and locks, particularly in relation to marriage. One poem read: *Why should I be bound to thee, O my lovely Myrtle-tree? Love, Free Love, cannot be bound, to any tree that grows on ground ...*

Lizzie realised Gabriel shared Blake's view of love and marriage just as he shared his fascination with the ghoulish and ghastly. It was troubling to her. She had thought Gabriel's objection to marriage was simply a wild young man's reluctance to settle down too soon. She was beginning to realise that it went much deeper than that. Gabriel seemed to truly believe that love should be given freely, without any constraints of conventional morality. Another little poem of Blake's said: *He who binds to himself a joy,*

Does the winged life destroy; But he who kisses the joy as it flies, Lives in eternity's sun rise.

Lizzie was afraid that she had gambled away her virtue for nothing.

One day, Gabriel came wandering into the studio, a note in his hand.

'Bruno's been caught in the parson's mousetrap! I'm to stand witness for him and Emma next week.'

Lizzie looked up from her easel. 'What? You mean Bruno is to marry Emma!'

She had known Emma as a girl; their mothers had been friends. Emma had given birth to Bruno's daughter, Cathy, a few years earlier. It was Cathy who, with her lisping attempts to say Gabriel, had given him the babyish nickname Guggums that he and Lizzie now each called the other.

Bruno kept Emma and little Cathy in a few rooms on the outskirts of London, visiting them three days every week, but keeping their presence in his life secret from all but a few very close friends.

'I suppose he feels he must do the right thing,' Gabriel replied. 'There being a baby and all. And he seems happy enough. Just devilish short on tin, poor old chap. He's only keeping a step or two ahead of the bum-bailiffs, and hasn't any money for paint. That's no way to live.'

Lizzie took a deep calming breath. 'But surely it makes better sense for them to live together, rather than Bruno paying for two establishments?'

'He'll get no work done at all with a wife and baby in the house.'

'They can model for him. Make sure he doesn't paint all night in the cold.'

Gabriel looked uncomfortable. 'Guggums … darling … you know I can't afford to get married. I have even less tin than Bruno. My father's going downhill awfully fast, and not earning a bean. My poor old mother and Christina are fagging over some kind of school in the country while poor old Maria is teaching Italian to idiots. And my brother William has taken some filthy job with Inland Revenue – when he has the soul of a poet! I've thought about getting a job too, honestly, I have. I went and applied for a job as a railway telegraphist, but I couldn't do it, Lizzie.'

Gabriel had come to kneel before her, holding both her hands in his. He kissed one, and then the other.

'I know you understand that, dear heart. You wouldn't want me to be a telegraph operator, would you?'

Lizzie shook her head, unable to help a smile.

'So you understand? It would be wrong of me to think of myself now, when my father is so ill and everyone in such a worry. It's different for Bruno, he hasn't any ageing parents or ailing sisters to worry about. He can marry when and whom he likes. It's different for me. I owe my parents such a debt of gratitude, they've supported me for so long. I need to knuckle down and get a decent painting done, and start earning some tin myself. Then things will be different, I promise.'

'All right,' she said with a sigh. 'Only … Gabriel, you do love me, don't you? You do want to be with me?'

He had turned her wrist so he could kiss the thin blue veins that pulsed beneath her white skin. One hand slid around her waist, drawing her closer. 'I adore you. You are my own dearest Guggums.' He drew her face down and kissed her.

Lizzie lived in fear of her parents finding out. Every day drew the coil of deceit a little tighter. One day she trudged home wearily in the dusk, and came up the stairs to find her mother waiting for her. Lizzie's stomach keeled over.

Her mother stood up and silently held out her hand.

'I'm sorry … I haven't any coins … Mr … Mr Rossetti has not paid me yet.'

'What? You're out all day long, and come home without a penny to show for your troubles?'

'Mr Rossetti is just a little strapped for cash at the moment. And you know he sometimes gives me painting lessons free of charge, in return for me modelling …'

'And what use is that? It doesn't put food on our table. I was against this modelling business from the start, you know I was, but you told me it would bring in extra coin for us all. You must tell this Mr Rizzetty of yours that you won't be coming back, and then you'll go to Mrs Tozer and beg her pardon and ask her for your old job back.'

'I won't! You don't understand, Ma ...'

'I understand all too well,' Mrs Siddal responded. 'You fancy yourself in love with this rackety painter fellow, and hope you can bring him up to snuff. Well, men like him don't marry girls like you, Lizzie, and you should know it. You need to find yourself a good solid down-to-earth man who'll turn a blind eye to your past in return for a warm bed and lots of children.'

'But that's not what I want!' Lizzie pleaded. 'Ma, please ... I have a real chance here to do something with my life ...'

'I won't have it. It's not respectable. Either he makes an honest woman of you and marries you, or you get a proper job and look about you for a man that will.'

'He can't marry me.' The words burst out of her.

'Why not?'

Lizzie's cheeks burned. 'He's poor ... he can't afford a wife ...'

'Then tell him to get a proper job so he can.'

'You don't understand.'

'Indeed I don't.'

'His art is everything to him.' Lizzie stumbled to explain. 'He has such big dreams ...' Her mother's contemptuous snort goaded her on. 'And his pa's sick and cannot work anymore ... and his ma is so burdened with grief and worry, he cannot bear to add to her trouble ...'

'And why would the news that he was about to marry be such a worry to her? I would have thought she'd be glad to see such a rattle-pate settling down.'

Lizzie's eyes fell. 'His parents don't approve of me ...'

'Well, I don't approve of him. These artists are all loose fish.'

'He's not! Ma, please. He says he will marry me just as soon as he can.'

'Well, until then, I forbid you to see him again. If he wants you, he can come with a ring in his hand.'

Lizzie stood motionless, her pulse thudding. Then she shook her head. 'No. I can't leave him. I'd die without him.'

She turned and went blindly towards the door.

'Where are you going? I'm not finished with you!' Her mother's voice was shrill.

'I'm finished with you.'

'I tell you now, if you walk out that door, you won't be welcome back here again!'

'I've never been welcome here,' Lizzie said, and put on her coat and bonnet and opened the front door. Her mother slammed it shut behind her.

It was dark outside. Lizzie ran away down the road, shoulders hunched against the sharp wind. She remembered all the many small cruelties of her childhood. Forced to sit at the table for hours, staring down at the congealed mutton chops on her plate till her stomach was lurching, and still her mother would not let her leave till every last disgusting mouthful was choked down. Being made to sit alone in her freezing attic room to read or write or draw, because her mother thought such things a terrible waste of time. Never being good enough, no matter what she did. She remembered how her Sunday School teacher had once complimented her on how smart she was, and her mother had said, 'Smart's no use at all, shame she's so plain. Looks are the only thing that'll help a girl get on in this world.'

Tears ran down her face. Lizzie blotted them away with the back of her gloved hand. She could not regret walking out, but she had no idea what she was to do now.

It would be wonderful if she arrived at Gabriel's place and he swept her into his arms and said, 'Bother what they all say! Let's get leg-shackled.'

But Lizzie knew it would not happen.

She sighed. If only Gabriel could have the same kind of success as Johnny Millais. But somehow he never seemed to finish a painting, or publish a poem. Mr Ruskin had championed both Millais and Holman Hunt, but paid little attention to Gabriel, who had failed to get anything ready in time for the Royal Academy exhibition again that year.

She walked on towards Blackfriars, where Gabriel and his brother William had taken rooms together. Though William paid for the apartment, he was rarely there. Lizzie could only hope he would be absent again that evening. Although she had not yet met Gabriel's brother, she was sure that he disapproved of her too.

It was frightening being out alone at night. The gas-lamps only made the shadows deeper, and the fog muffled sounds so she could not tell if the drunken singing and unsteady footsteps she heard were close or far away. A cat yowled eerily somewhere in the darkness.

As she approached Blackfriars Bridge, Lizzie's steps slowed. She was beginning to regret the impulse that had driven her out into the night. Her mother would never forgive her for her defiance, and her father would feel shamed in the eyes of his congregation, having a daughter who chose not to live under his protection. They would all think that Lizzie was a fallen woman, and expect her to end up on the streets.

The buttresses of the bridge were all carved to look like pulpits, a nod to the monastery that had once stood here on the banks of the River Thames. She could not look at them as she passed by, feeling as if preachers stood there, glowering down at her and finding her wanting.

Gabriel's rooms were in an apartment block in Chatham Place, looking down on to the Thames. She could see a light shining out of his windows, and felt both a giddying relief that he was home and sharp anxiety that he would turn her away.

He loves me, she reminded herself. *It's only because he fears he cannot be married and still be free to do his art. If I can just show him that he need not be afraid ... that I too have an artist's soul ...*

Gabriel was surprised to see her, but he opened wide the door and let her in. His small apartment was crowded with old furniture draped with Persian shawls, and lay-figures in strange postures. Books and papers were piled higgledy-piggledy everywhere, and paint-mottled blue shirts lay tangled with a gold-embroidered robe.

'Gugs, what are you doing here? What's wrong?'

She told him, hands clasped in desperate hope.

'You must stay here with me, dear heart,' he said at once. But the next moment her spirits were once again dashed as he said, 'But it wouldn't do for you to stay for more than one night. Where do you plan to go?'

'Oh, Gabriel, why can't I just stay with you?'

He looked uncomfortable. 'Whatever would my landlady think? She'd be horrified. And it took me so long to find these rooms, I don't want to lose them.'

She turned away, taking off her bonnet and laying it on the table. 'Of course not. Whatever would you do then?'

He did not notice the faint trace of sarcasm in her voice.

'And the thing is, Gug, I've got a party of fellows coming over tomorrow night for a pipe or two and a chinwag. You won't want to be here for that, I know. So we'll need to find somewhere for you to stay fast.'

Lizzie said tonelessly, 'My aunt may let me stay a while. She and her husband have always been kind to me, and they know what Ma can be like.'

'That sounds like a good plan,' Gabriel said, pleased. He came and took off her damp coat, kissing the back of her neck and then drawing the pins out of her hair so it fell heavily down her back.

'But for now, you're all mine,' he whispered. 'And we have the whole night together. Let's leave tomorrow to look after itself.'

6

Grimm Tales
Autumn 1853

The sound of knocking on the front door roused Georgie from her book of fairytales.

She waited a moment, expecting the cook to respond, but there was no plod of feet and grumble of complaint, only a new round of vigorous banging.

'I wonder who it could be?' Georgie asked.

'We aren't expecting anyone, are we?' Carrie sat up, clutching the cloth soaked in camphorated oil that had been folded across her chest.

Georgie jumped up and ran down the hall, unbolting the door and opening it wide.

Ted Jones stood on the doorstep, a pile of books in his arms. He wore a pair of narrow purple velvet trousers, and a soft collar with a floppy scarf.

He smiled down at her. 'Hello, Miss Georgie.'

'Mr Jones,' she answered shyly. 'I'm sorry, but everyone's out. There's just me and Carrie at home.'

He looked disappointed. 'That's a shame.'

'You can come in and wait, if you like. We could have some tea.'

His face changed at once, joyously. 'That would be lovely, thank you.' He followed her back down the hall and into the drawing-room. It was overcrowded with furniture – a chaise-longue, two fat red chairs, a battered piano with decently clad legs, and a great many crookedly sewn samplers with texts from the Bible all over the wall.

Carrie was lying on the couch, and she struggled to sit up and put her feet to the floor.

'Don't get up, Miss Carrie,' Ted said. 'You stay just as you are.'

She lay down again gratefully. The exertion had cost her strength, and she began to cough, hiding her mouth behind her handkerchief.

'I'm so sorry you're not any better.'

'Thank you,' she whispered.

'It's a great worry,' Georgie said. 'We all thought she'd be hale and hearty by summer.'

'I'm sure I'll soon be well again,' Carrie said. 'It's just that my chest hurts so much when I breathe.' Her voice was raspy.

'It's my job to look after her while Mama is out,' Georgie said. 'I have to give her camphor on a sugar lump every twenty minutes, and rub her chest with turpentine and camphor oil.'

'That explains the strong smell in the room,' Ted said.

'I hope you don't mind it,' Georgie said anxiously. 'It's good for Carrie, it helps her breathe.'

'I don't mind one bit. I've had a chesty cough myself. It will help clear it for me.'

'I'll just ask for some tea. You can entertain Carrie for me while I'm gone.' Georgie ran to the kitchen to cajole a pot of tea and some oatcakes from the cook, then returned to find Ted drawing a quick caricature of Carrie with her feet in a steaming mustard-bath, a poultice on her head, and camphor fumes emanating from her. As Georgie came in, he swiftly added a little drawing of her in her pinafore, her arms piled high with boxes and bottles of remedies, a harried expression on her face.

'Oh no, that's not me at all,' Georgie said. 'I'm very happy to look after Carrie. I've been reading stories to her.'

'What stories?' Ted asked, presenting the sketch to Carrie with a little bow.

'I got a new book of fairytales for my birthday.'

'It was your birthday? I'm sorry I missed it. How old are you now? Twenty-seven?'

'Thirteen.' Georgie blushed, even though she knew he was teasing her.

'A perfectly wonderful age. I often wish I was still thirteen. What stories were you given?'

'Grimm tales from Germany. Look, aren't they beautiful?' Georgie picked up the leather-bound book, opening the pages to show Ted its delicate black-and-white drawings. 'This is my favourite story, the one about the princess who sleeps for a hundred years. Do you remember when we heard the poem?'

'I do,' Ted answered, gazing down at the drawing of the sleeping princess surrounded by roses, the prince leaning in to kiss her. 'What a jolly sketch. I wonder who did it.' He looked at the title page. 'A chap called Wehnert. I've never heard of him. I like the way the rose briars make a window frame.'

'So do I,' Georgie said.

The cook came bustling in with the tea tray, and Georgie busied herself playing mother. As she passed Ted a cup and saucer, he said, 'Will you read me the story? I only know it from the poem. Carrie, you won't mind hearing the story again, will you?'

'Oh, no,' she said. 'I love hearing them. Georgie reads so well.'

'I like to do all the different voices,' Georgie explained, and began to read. '"In olden times there lived a King and a Queen, who lamented day by day that they had no children …"'

Ted leant his chin in his hand and watched her, his eyes dreamy. When she came to the passage when the frog in the queen's bath told her that her wish would be fulfilled, Georgie put on a deep bullfrog's voice, and Ted laughed in delight. Half a page later, she reached the scene where the slighted fairy arrived at the feast, in a rage because she had not been invited. Georgie said, in the cracked voice of a malevolent old woman: '"The Princess shall prick herself with a spindle on her fifteenth birthday and die!"'

Then, when it was time for the twelfth fairy to try to avert the curse, Georgie affected a high, sweet voice: '"She shall not die, but fall into a sleep of a hundred years."'

On she went through the story, acting out all the parts with aplomb. When she had finished she gave a little bow, and Ted and Carrie both clapped.

'Well done,' Ted said. 'You do read beautifully.'

'It's a wonderful book to read aloud,' Georgie said. 'Much better than *The History of Little Goody Two-Shoes*.'

'I have made a new friend at Oxford,' Ted said. 'He loves to read aloud too. He has been reading me *The Lady of Shalott*.'

'What is his name?' Georgie asked.

'William Morris, but we all call him Topsy because he has such a head of triumphant black curls, just like the little girl in *Uncle Tom's Cabin*. I met him during my first week at Oxford, though I'd seen him the year before when we did our matriculation. We sat next to each other, and I remember him because he was so quick to answer all his questions, and so decisive in the way he threw down his pen and folded his paper.'

'Are you enjoying Oxford, Mr Jones?' Carrie asked.

'You mustn't call me Mr Jones. That sounds like a grocer. Call me Ted. Everyone does.'

Carrie went pink. Georgie said, 'Mama would not like us to be over-familiar, Mr Jones.'

'Then let us cut the difference. How about you call me Mr Edward?' he answered.

'Very well. If you are sure. So, can you tell us about Oxford, Mr Edward?' Georgie said, greatly daring. 'Is it very wonderful?'

'I thought it would be, but I was sadly disappointed at first. Maybe I was homesick. I had such dreams of changing the world. I wanted to found a Brotherhood of Galahad. You know, to live by the rules of chivalry. But all the fellows at Oxford were only interested in rugby and rowing and drinking and, well, in girls. I was utterly wretched. If it had not been for Topsy I'd have been in despair. But things are better now.

We have somewhere jolly to stay, and we've got the old Birmingham set there, who all like poetry and art and the stuff I like . . .'

As he spoke, Georgie encouraged him with little smiles and murmurs of encouragement, and he began to talk more easily, his eyes glowing, his hands sketching in the air.

Then the front door banged open, and in came the rest of the family with a great roar of conversation, and a lot of boot stamping and door slamming. They had been to a prayer meeting, and were all hot and thirsty. Mr Macdonald retired to his study, and Mrs Macdonald to her bed, but the children all crowded into the drawing-room, talking nineteen to the dozen. More tea was called for, and oatcakes, and Ted found himself mobbed by small girls wanting him to read them stories.

Georgie wished them all to the Devil.

The train snorted steam. A long shrill whistle.

Georgie peered out the window, searching for Ted's face, but all she could see was great clouds of smoke. She yanked up the window, and put her head out, unmindful of smuts. At last she saw him, thin, eager, waving his handkerchief enthusiastically. She waved back, and his face lit up in that sudden sweet smile that never failed to wrench her heart.

The train jerked into motion. She kept waving, kept smiling, leaning so far out of the window she was in danger of falling. Then the station dissolved into the black, swirling smoke, and she fell back into her seat, pressing her gloved hands to her eyes.

Her mother sat opposite her, lips moving in silent prayer, her hands gripping her carpet bag. Carrie was propped up on cushions, coughing into her handkerchief. Alice held Edith on her lap, holding her firmly against the sudden jolt as the train began to move. Freddy had his head craned out the window, Louie struggling to see past him. Agnes had her face pressed against her mother's sleeve. She was weeping quietly.

Georgie was close to weeping herself. The Macdonalds were moving to London. Mr Macdonald had been given the Seventh London circuit.

It meant another new start, another new congregation, another severing of ties to friends and familiar places.

It had been an exhausting month. Mrs Macdonald had had a Spasm, and spent days in bed with smelling salts and her Bible. Mr Macdonald's thousands of books all had to be dusted and packed up, and all their furniture sent off in a bullock cart. Many tears had been shed, mostly by the girls, but also privately and shamefacedly by Freddy, who had made many friends at his Birmingham school.

'It's so unfair,' he had cried. 'Why must we always be moving?'

'I must go to the people to minister to their needs,' his father had said. 'Is it too much to ask that we sacrifice our own comfort in the godly harvest of souls? The Reverend John Wesley rode more than two hundred and fifty miles on horseback, and gave sermons in fields and brickyards and prisons. Always he resolved to be more lowly. Should I do any less?'

'I suppose not,' Freddy had muttered, abashed.

That afternoon, while packing up her father's study, Alice had found an old envelope containing one of Mr Macdonald's most precious relics. A dusty lock of Charles Wesley's hair. With a shrill laugh, she had cast it into the fire. 'See! A hair of the dog that bit us!'

Then she had gripped Georgie's hand and sworn her to silence, shocked at what she had done. They could only hope their father would believe the sacred lock of hair lost in the move.

Georgie's parents had had to decide what to do about Harry. Eventually he had been left behind in Birmingham to continue his studies there, living in lodgings. The cook and parlour-maid had been laid off, after refusing to travel to London. The rocking-horse had been given away.

Ted Jones had come up from Oxford to say goodbye. He had drawn a caricature of himself as a tall, thin, disconsolate figure, waving a handkerchief and weeping, as the Macdonalds charged off happily towards the capital, depicted as a cloud of smog out of which a few landmarks peeked. He had given it to Georgie, then taken her hand and said, in his solemn way, that he hoped he would see her again soon. Georgie thought it unlikely. He lived in Birmingham and attended university in Oxford. Whatever would bring him to London?

The train gained speed, rattling along the railway lines. Through the dirty window, Georgie saw glimpses of smoke-stacks and steel-mills, windows glaring red. Tears filled her eyes. She bent her hands down over her eyes, not wanting anyone to see. The train raced into a long dark tunnel.

Silently she grieved at the leaving of him.

7

The Shadowed Wood
Spring 1854

Gabriel and Lizzie wandered along the beach. The sea was the most extraordinary range of colours. *Cobalt teal*, Lizzie thought. *Turquoise. Cerulean blue. Ultramarine.*

Such wonderful words for blue.

'Just breathe that sea air!' Gabriel said. 'It must be helping you. Do you feel you need to go to the infirmary?'

She shook her head. Lizzie hated doctors. They tapped her chest and listened to her breathing, felt her pulse, looked at her tongue, then stared at her with frowning eyes. They were always concerned by how thin she was, and thought that perhaps she too had consumption, the disease that had killed her brother. They asked her to cough, and cough again. They asked her if she was hot and feverish at nights. Lizzie told them she was cold all the time. One doctor told her that she had early signs of tuberculosis, which skewered her with terror. Another said she had curvature of the spine, which was a puzzle as Lizzie's mother had always insisted on perfect posture. All said she needed to be fed up on beef tea and calf's-foot jelly, the very thought of which made her gag.

So Gabriel had paid for her to come to Hastings, though Lizzie thought it a sad waste of time. She would much rather be in London, painting.

'Really, I'm feeling fine. Particularly now that you are here.' Lizzie pressed Gabriel's arm.

It had been a difficult few months for him. First his grandfather had died, and then his father. Professor Rossetti's death had not been a shock. He had been ill for a long time. Lizzie thought that Gabriel was more relieved than grieved. His father had not been an amiable patient, and had scolded Gabriel constantly for his failure to make something of his gifts.

Lizzie unfastened her bonnet and swung it from one hand. Long tendrils of red-gold hair blew about her face. 'You look like Botticelli's Venus,' Gabriel told her. 'Except with far too many clothes on.'

Laughing, he drew her profile in the sand with the tip of his walking stick, hair twining out like honeysuckle. A wave rushed up and foamed over the top of one of his shoes. When the wave retreated, it had wiped the sand clean like a child's school slate. 'Here lies one whose name was writ in water,' Gabriel quoted. He shook his damp foot. 'My shoes are not made for walking on the beach. Do you feel strong enough to walk up on to the hill? I've heard you can see for miles from up there, even all the way to France on a clear day.'

'If you'll help me,' she said.

'I'll carry you if I must. It'd be like carrying a little bird. I know you say you are feeling better, Lizzie, but indeed you are very thin. Are you eating properly?'

She looked away from him. 'Oh, yes. That is … I don't much like the food my landlady serves up. It's all pies and puddings and plum heavies. I feel I'm in danger of turning into a pudding myself.'

'No fear of that,' he answered, rather grimly.

The hill was steep, and Lizzie was soon short of breath. Gabriel moderated his own eager stride to her feebler step, and helped her over the stile.

A tunnel of hedgerows led to green meadows and a wide view of the shining sea. A kestrel rode the wind. Lizzie watched, marvelling at the bird's swift effortless wheeling across the sky, its shadow flitting over her face as it crossed the sun.

At last they reached the cliff's edge. There was a natural seat made of a great slab of sandstone. Smiling, Gabriel perched beside her, leaning his hat against his knee. Lizzie's heart made its presence known within her, like an over-wound clock.

'I've heard of this place,' Lizzie said, looking about her. 'It's called the Lovers' Seat. There was a girl of good family, who fell in love with a sea-captain. Her parents would not countenance the match, and so they used to meet here in secret. Eventually they eloped, and were very happy together. So now they say anyone who becomes betrothed here will find happiness in love.'

She felt, rather than saw, the stiffening of Gabriel's body.

They sat in awkward silence for a long moment. Then Lizzie stood. 'Shall we go back?'

'If you like.' Gabriel's voice was cool.

They walked back through the meadows. Lizzie's throat felt as if a choker had been fastened too tightly about it. When they reached her lodgings on High Street, she gave Gabriel her hand and said good night.

'Do you not want to have some supper?' he asked in surprise.

She shook her head. 'I'd like to rest now.'

'So when will I see you?'

'In the morning. Are we not going to see your friends? I will see you then. Good night.'

His face softened. 'Good night, my dear. Sleep well.'

Alone in her own small room, Lizzie undressed and stood naked before the mirror, turning this way and that to observe herself. She could see the knobs of her spine, her sharp shoulder blades like tiny wings, the deep hollows beneath her collarbones, the protruding lines of her ribs. She looked down at her hands, translucent skin stretched over bones and tendons and veins. The feeling of constriction in her throat increased until she could hardly breathe. Lizzie hid herself in her voluminous nightgown. She drank down her usual nightly dose of laudanum, and climbed into bed. The mattress was hard and lumpy. She lay flat and straight, and put her hands on the hollow of her stomach.

She thought of the kestrel, and its mastery of the wind.

She thought of her brother, begging her not to forget him.

She thought of dying, and leaving no trace of her presence in this world.

Eventually she slept, a little.

'She sits so still!' Anna Mary exclaimed. 'Really, she is the perfect model.'

Lizzie let her lips curve a little. Her body was heavy and loose, her hands upturned on her lap. Her tongue still tasted the delicious sweetness of the laudanum.

'How can you stay motionless for so long?' Barbara demanded.

'I just think,' Lizzie said. 'There is always so much to think about.'

She looked out at the garden again. She and Gabriel and his friends were sitting on the terrace of an old farmhouse not far from Hastings. Built of red brick, the house had a steep red-tiled roof and tall chimneys. Behind the house was a quaint wooden barn with a tucked roof like a nun's wimple. The only sounds were the distant lowing of a cow, and the twittering of birds.

The house belonged to Barbara Leigh Smith. A young lady of twenty-seven, she wore a plain brown dress without a single flounce or knot of ribbon, cut short enough to show her sensible brown boots. She looked more like a farmer's wife than an heiress. Yet Gabriel said she had more tin than she knew what to do with. Her grandfather had been the famous reformer and abolitionist William Smith, who had inherited a fortune made from the proceeds of sugar and spice plantations worked by slaves. He had spent his life campaigning fiercely for their freedom, and his granddaughter had inherited his revolutionary fervour as well as a good portion of his wealth.

Her cause was for the liberation of women, and she was hard at work on a pamphlet that outlined, in plain language anyone could read, the stupidity of England's laws regarding what they called the fairer sex.

Barbara may have been rich and well connected – she was related closely to both the Nightingales and the Bonham-Carters – but she was nonetheless an outcast from polite society. She was illegitimate. Her father had refused to wed her mother, because he believed that marriage was a state akin to slavery. So although Barbara and her siblings had been brought up with every luxury money could buy, she would never have a coming-out ball, never be issued with vouchers to Almack's, never enter the Royal Enclosure at Ascot, never tread in the divots at a polo match, and never, under any circumstances, be presented to the Queen.

Barbara's mother had been a milliner, and Lizzie was sure that was why Gabriel had chosen to introduce them. At first Lizzie had been cold and stand-offish, hurt that Gabriel should choose this way to rub her face in her lack of marriageability. But Barbara was simply too forthright and too kind-hearted to stand on ceremony with, and Lizzie had found herself thawing under the warmth of her interest.

'She looks just like an angel,' Anna Mary said. 'And the colour of those irises against her hair. I wish I had time to paint her.'

'You'll have to come back,' Barbara said to Gabriel. 'We'll paint all morning, have lunch, then go for a tramp in the afternoon.'

'That's hardly fair to Lizzie,' Anna Mary exclaimed. 'She's an artist too, she'll want some time for painting.'

'I will sit for you if you will sit for me,' Lizzie said. 'You'd be a lovely study.'

Anna Mary flushed, and looked down in pleasure. 'Why, thank you.'

Barbara snorted. 'I notice no-one asks me to sit for them.'

'But I'd love to draw you too,' Lizzie said. 'Your face is so strong, and yet so full of warmth and kindness. I think I'd like to draw you as a queen.'

'I have often thought that,' Anna Mary cried. 'A queen from days of yore …'

'In battle armour and a sword. I see it now,' Gabriel said lazily. He was lying on the grass, his hands bent behind his head, the sketch he had done of Lizzie lying beside him. Lizzie wondered if Anna Mary and Barbara found it as disheartening as she did, watching him produce something so full of life, so quickly and easily.

'Though I do not think I have the talent to do you justice,' Lizzie said to Barbara. 'I'm not good at heads.'

'I am sure that's not true,' Barbara said. 'Gabriel says that you have a natural genius, only wanting some tutoring to allow it to flower.'

'He is just being kind. I have all the longing and none of the ability.'

'All of us are afraid of that,' Anna Mary said. 'Us women, I mean. It is such a struggle for us, when every moment we spend drawing and painting is seen as a waste of time, and an indulgence of our vanities. And, of course, they will not let us take classes like the men.'

'You're better off without them,' Gabriel said. 'All the Academy does is stifle your creativity and try to make you draw slosh. Slosh, slosh, sloshetty-slosh.'

'Easy for you to say,' Barbara objected in her forthright way. 'You at least had the chance to learn from the masters. We have to fumble our own way forward, without anyone to help us or set us straight.'

'That's true of all of us artists,' Gabriel objected.

The women all glanced at each other, silently acknowledging the obtuseness of men and the peculiar difficulty of being a woman in a world that thought they were little more than children.

Both Barbara and Anna Mary had gone to art classes, however, even if it was not at the Royal Academy. They could afford canvases and paints and paintbrushes, and did not need to worry about how they were going to pay their rent.

What a difference money makes, Lizzie thought. *They think they struggle being women. They have no idea what it is to be both a woman and poor.*

'Well, it's wonderful to leave the hustle and bustle of London, and have some peace for a while,' Anna Mary said. 'We plan to do nothing but draw and read and walk on the Downs, don't we, Barbara?'

'Yes, I'm determined to be the most selfish cove imaginable, and refuse to do a thing I don't want to do. I have this grand landscape in my mind's eye that I simply must work out.'

Barbara turned to Lizzie. 'So are you working on anything new?'

'I've been working on a drawing of a scene from one of Robert Browning's poems,' Lizzie told her shyly.

'Capital! Which one?'

'"Pippa Passes".' Lizzie's cheeks warmed. 'I'm drawing the scene in which Pippa walks past the ...' She hesitated for a moment, then continued, 'the women gossiping on the steps.'

'Barb, she's done a fine job of it, and I'm thinking it'll be perfect for the next Folio.' Gabriel turned back to Lizzie and said eagerly, 'We've founded this club, to share ideas and drawings among us. The theme for the next round is "Desolation". I'm doing this drawing of a young woman on the streets who is found by her old sweetheart, and Johnny Millais is doing something about a Roman soldier abandoning his English lover and Anna Mary is doing a sketch of a poor flower-girl, all cold and alone.'

'To illustrate Job 30:19,' Anna Mary said. '"He hath cast me into the mire and I am become like dust and ashes."'

'I'm doing a landscape of a windswept quarry by the sea,' Barbara interrupted. 'Really, much more desolate than all these fallen women.'

'How can it be?' Lizzie cried. 'A lonely landscape is not a living thing. It's only desolate when it reflects the misery in the heart of someone who looks upon it. What can be more desolating than to give yourself to someone you love utterly, and to be abandoned by them, left ruined and without hope?'

Gabriel and the two women stared at her. Anna Mary leaned forward and gently touched Lizzie's hand. 'Well said, my dear. You are absolutely right. Barbara, I think it would be a wonderful thing to include Lizzie's drawing in our folio.'

'Excellent,' she answered. 'Send it to me when you can, Lizzie.'

The maid brought out a tray of sandwiches. Gabriel loaded up a plate for Lizzie, saying, 'You've hardly touched a thing, Gug. You need to eat and build up your strength. Tell her, Anna Mary.'

'He's right,' she answered at once.

Lizzie looked down at her plate in dismay. But with all three watching her, she could do nothing but smile and lift one of the sandwiches to her mouth and take a bite. The bread stuck to the roof of her mouth; the cucumber felt slimy and foul. She managed to swallow it down. Still they were all watching her. She forced down another mouthful, trying not to gag, then laid down the rest. 'I don't much like cucumber sandwiches,' she said apologetically.

'You need to eat meat,' Barbara said, and passed her a sandwich thick with rare roast lamb. Lizzie valiantly chewed her way through it. After a while, conversation started up again and they stopped watching her so intently. Lizzie dropped bits of her sandwich under her chair, and hoped the ants would come and carry it all away.

When Lizzie thought no-one was paying her any mind, she stood up and excused herself, going to find the outdoor privy. She found it a little hard to walk across the lawn; her legs felt rubbery. She did not need to force her fingers down her throat. The thought of that lump of half-raw meat rotting away in her stomach and the foul smell of the privy were enough to make her vomit straightaway. Her gullet burned with acid; her eyes stung with tears. It took her some time to compose herself, rinsing out her mouth with water again and again, and pressing damp fingers against her cheeks and eyes.

When she walked back through the garden, it was to see Gabriel and Barbara sitting alone under the oak tree, their backs turned to her, their heads bent close together. Her heart knocked. She just knew they were talking about her. Lizzie crept across the lawn and stood in the shadow of the oak's trunk, listening.

'I would have thought you of all people would not be promoting the institute of marriage,' Gabriel was saying. 'You're the one who wrote that women lose all rights once they are married, even that over her own body.'

'Which is absolutely true,' Barbara replied hotly. 'But the alternative is no better. You think I don't know? My father would not marry my mother because it went against all of his principles, and so my mother was thought a whore, to live with a man and bear him children out of wedlock.'

'But …' Gabriel began.

Barbara cut him off. 'You think him brave and noble, no doubt, but my mother suffered terribly from the shame, and so do I and all my brothers and sisters. You think I don't care, because I'm rich and that gives me a measure of freedom most women do not have. But I do care, I care very much. Just remember … Miss Siddal is poor. She has no rolls of soft to cushion her against the censure of the world.'

Gabriel said, a little shamefacedly, 'I know. It's just … my mother …'

'You think your mother disapproves of her because she has worked as an artist's model, which makes her easy game in the eyes of the world. Well, that is true, but the only way to make her respectable is to marry her. Your mother is a good Christian woman, I know. Surely she would forgive you for marrying a woman whom you have ruined in the eyes of the world? And just look at the poor girl! She's wasting away. Clearly she's not long for this world, any blind fool could see that. Marry her, look after her, give her what happiness you can.'

Gabriel huffed out a deep sigh. 'It's just that I loathe and detest any kind of domesticity. The very thought of the parson's mousetrap …'

'Lizzie is not going to expect you to get a job in the City and hire a footman. She wants exactly what you want. To paint, to write, to be together without being cut by those she knows.'

'I suppose you're right. And I do love her.'

'Then make her happy.'

A tremulous smile curved Lizzie's lips.

Then she heard Anna Mary's quick footsteps coming towards her down the path, and at once stepped out from behind the tree. She did not want to be caught eavesdropping. Gabriel stood up at the sight of her. 'I might show Lizzie your woods. I've heard they're very pretty.'

'That would be lovely,' Lizzie said demurely.

They walked hand in hand through the meadows and into a copse of silver birches. A haze of blue lay over the ground, and Lizzie cried aloud. 'Look! Bluebells. Aren't they beautiful?'

'I've never seen so many.' Gabriel turned about, looking at the bluebells that stretched in all directions. Thunder muttered overhead, and then there was a faint patter of rain on the leaves. He caught Lizzie's hand and they ran, laughing, to shelter.

It began to rain hard. The wood was shadowed and dark.

Gabriel put his arm about Lizzie and drew her close.

'Gugs, I'm sorry if I've made you unhappy. You know I love you.'

She searched his face with her eyes.

'So I'm thinking ... we could get married if you like?'

'If you like? Are you mad? Of course I like!' Lizzie threw her arms about him.

'We need to wait for the mourning period to be over. For my father, you know. My mother wouldn't want us to marry before then.'

Lizzie looked at him in sudden anxiety, but he was kissing her and so she closed her eyes and kissed him back.

A year of mourning ... she could wait that long ...

8

Owt for Nowt
Spring 1855

Anxiously Lizzie looked at her reflection in the mirror. She was wraith-pale, hollow-cheeked.

'Are you coming?' Gabriel called. 'We'll be late. Not that I mind, particularly, but Mr Ruskin is a stickler for punctuality.'

'I'm coming!' She pinched her cheeks for some colour.

Almost a year had passed since Gabriel had promised to marry her. In a matter of weeks, he could lay aside his black gloves.

Yet he had not spoken again of marriage. Lizzie did not like to press him. It had been such a contented year, working side by side, helping each other. Gabriel had been struggling to develop his painting of a fallen woman found by her former sweetheart. Lizzie had worked on her drawings. Her best work had been a pair of lovers listening to gypsy women playing music, with a small angelic-looking child standing with one hand on the gate, as if about to swing it open. The man in the drawing looked like Gabriel and the woman looked like Lizzie, as they did in all of her work. She had no-one else to model for her.

Her drawings were getting better. Lizzie could see that. Yet that gap between what she imagined and what she created was still so great, it seemed impossible that she could ever bridge it. Gabriel lavished her with praise, but she doubted his clear-sightedness. It seemed as if he saw her, and all she did, through a haze of golden light.

Though perhaps Gabriel was right, and it was Lizzie who saw her own work through a self-distorting lens. For Gabriel had shown her drawings to John Ruskin a few weeks earlier. He had liked them. Indeed, he had bought a whole sheaf for thirty pounds, promising to have them splendidly mounted and bound together with gold. Lizzie had never earned so much money in her life. It was more than she had been paid in a single year as a milliner.

Now she was going to meet John Ruskin and his parents, who were the ones who really held the purse strings. Mr Ruskin had sent a carriage for them. It was a black, glossy brougham, and driven by a straight-backed man in spotless livery. Lizzie was too anxious to relax back against the cushions. She had chosen her most demure grey gown to wear, and her cleanest gloves. Even Gabriel looked tidy, his black cravat tied in a most conventional knot. He put on a great pretence of being at ease, lying back against the cushions, but Lizzie could tell he was as tense as she was.

'Did you know Ruskin's parents read all his mail?' Gabriel said. 'Can you imagine? My mother would die of shock if she read any of my letters to my friends.'

Lizzie smiled, but her lips felt stiff. She looked out the window. She had never seen such large, grand houses. Her stomach knotted.

The horse trotted through a set of iron gates, held open for them by a man who touched his hat, then brought the carriage around a sweeping drive to draw up in front of a tall Georgian mansion. The driver opened the carriage door, and Gabriel handed Lizzie down.

By the time they had mounted the few wide steps to the portico, the front door had been opened by a footman in dark livery, who bowed them through to the drawing-room. Every inch of its walls were covered with paintings.

'Turner,' Gabriel whispered to her. 'Ruskin loves him.'

Lizzie did not answer. Her attention was focused on the three people waiting in the centre of the room. The two men were almost identically dressed in dark coats of sober cut, their sandy hair parted and neatly brushed to one side. The elder man had a white linen stock folded about his neck; the younger man's neckcloth was of cornflower blue silk. They rose as Lizzie approached them, and inclined their heads in greeting. The woman remained seated. She was stout, and wore a black silk gown with a white cap over her severe iron-grey hair.

'Good afternoon, Mr Rossetti,' the older man said. He had a fierce pair of eyebrows, grey and sprouting. 'Good to see you again. How are you getting on?'

'Very well, thank you, sir,' Gabriel answered. Lizzie had never heard him sound so subdued.

Mr Ruskin turned his attention to Lizzie. 'Miss Siddal, welcome. We have heard much about you. Please be seated.' As Lizzie chose the hardest, most uncomfortable-looking chair, he introduced his wife and son. Lizzie smiled politely, and said all that was expected of her, even as she covertly examined the man who had paid so much for her drawings.

John Ruskin was around thirty-six years of age, tall and thin and a little stooped, with a mouth marred by a small scar. He looked stiff and uncomfortable.

Sympathy stirred within her. The previous summer, John and his wife, Effie, had caused the biggest scandal in years. She had left him, charging him with impotence. Their marriage had been legally annulled. It was rumoured that Effie and Johnny Millais were in love and intended to wed, which had shocked Gabriel terribly. He could not understand how Millais could be so ungrateful, when Ruskin had been such an important supporter of them all. The good news, though, Gabriel had said ebulliently, is that Ruskin and Millais were no longer on speaking terms, and so perhaps the rich art critic would be looking for someone new to patronise.

John took her hand and bowed his head over it politely. He scrutinised her closely, still holding her hand. He seemed to like what he saw, for he drew up a chair and sat, uncomfortably close beside her, still staring at her.

As Lizzie turned her attention to Mrs Ruskin, she was aware of John's eyes on her face, then examining her slim form. It made her feel uncomfortable, but she kept her back straight, her voice well-modulated. She was pretending to be the kind of girl that usually visited rich ladies and gentlemen, with a maid to serve them tea in gilded teacups.

'So, my son informs me that your father is a watchmaker,' Mrs Ruskin said. 'A fine profession for a man. They say that God is like a watchmaker, and the cosmos like a great machine created and wound up by Him to tick towards the Final Judgement.'

'Yes, indeed,' Lizzie replied faintly. Her father was not a watchmaker. He was just a humble ironmonger. She glanced at Gabriel, who gave her a sheepish grin. She flushed slightly and looked away. Gabriel was always embellishing and exaggerating, yet for him to do so about her family made her feel as if she was complicit in a lie. Yet she could not contradict him.

'What do those watchmakers say, heh?' Mr Ruskin interjected. 'Perfect is near enough? A good philosophy for any of us.'

'Yes, sir,' Gabriel replied. 'Well said.'

'And I believe your family frowns upon you wishing to pursue art,' Mr Ruskin went on. 'That is a shame, indeed, a great shame.'

'But perfectly understandable,' Mrs Ruskin said in her ponderous way. 'They must have wished for better things for you.'

Lizzie bowed her head. She knew better than to try to defend herself.

John came to her rescue. 'Perhaps they do, Mother. However, it is a sin to deny such a God-given gift as Miss Siddal's. Particularly when so much else is denied to her due to her sad delicacy.'

Her breath stopped. John had spoken aloud her own secret fears. Lizzie had seen her brother dwindle away till he was nothing but a scarecrow. Now she was as gaunt. It was no consolation that the doctors said her lungs were too clear, her skin too cold. Lizzie had seen her brother die. She knew the white disease was eating away at her flesh. She knew she too would waste away to nothing.

Gabriel ran one finger inside his black neckcloth. 'If Lizzie would just eat a little more … keep up her strength.'

John was staring at her with that strange, intent look again. It reminded Lizzie of the look Gabriel got when he went hunting in the flea markets, and found a particularly fine piece of rare china for a bargain price.

Mrs Ruskin sniffed. 'I hope that Miss Siddal has not fallen into the disreputable habits of those other rackety artists. I was most distressed to hear that Mr Millais thought nothing of painting on a Sunday!' She spoke the name of Johnny Millais as one might speak of the Devil.

'Indeed, I have not,' Lizzie said, in a voice of mild affront. 'My mother would never permit us to do anything on a Sunday, not even sew our samplers. She was most strict on the subject.'

'A worthy rule,' Mrs Ruskin said with approval. 'I wish that more would follow her example. We never permitted our boy to do anything but read the Bible and study his catechism.' She looked fondly at John, who looked down at his hands, his expression difficult to read. Lizzie wondered if his Sundays had been as long and dreary as hers had been. As if reading her thoughts, John looked up and met her gaze. Lizzie looked away. He did not do the same. She wondered at him, so stiff and formal, yet not knowing enough not to stare a girl out of countenance.

Gabriel was soon bored, and rose to inspect the paintings. Mr Ruskin joined him, and they were soon deep in a discussion about Turner's brushwork. Lizzie longed to join them, but she sat and drank her tea, and listened to Mrs Ruskin, who was giving a long lecture on the evils of modern society. To Lizzie's surprise, John did not join the other men, but stayed and listened to his mother too.

By the end of their visit, Mrs Ruskin had mellowed sufficiently to promise to send Lizzie a gift of some powdered ivory for her to mix into jam and eat. 'It will do you the world of good,' she promised.

When John said goodbye, he held her hand too long. Again she was discomfited, and yet unwilling to snub him when she knew how important his patronage was.

In the carriage on the way home, Gabriel was exultant. 'He adores you, Guggums! Oh, you were perfect.'

Lizzie smiled, but she felt uncomfortable. She had to remind herself that John Ruskin had bought all her drawings before he had ever met her. He had obviously seen something in them.

But she could not help wondering if he was so interested in her because she was dying.

The next day, John Ruskin dropped by the studio. He told Gabriel that he wanted to either buy every drawing or painting that Lizzie produced, or to pay her a regular quarterly allowance. He offered one hundred and fifty pounds a year. It seemed like a fortune.

Lizzie felt she had to turn it down.

'Don't be so high in the instep, Gugs,' Gabriel said. 'It's a brilliant offer.'

'But ... what does he want in return?' Lizzie said uneasily. Her father had always said: *you don't get owt for nowt.*

'Only to help and support you. He called you a noble, glorious creature,' Gabriel said. 'Oh, I knew they would love you!'

Lizzie chewed at her lower lip. She did not like it. Not least because Ruskin had spoken to Gabriel about his plans, instead of to her. She had not even been consulted. She remembered that glint of possessiveness in Ruskin's eyes.

The next day a letter was delivered, addressed to Miss Siddal. Lizzie cracked open the seal and read it, Gabriel watching her anxiously.

'*The world is an odd world,*' John had written. '*People think nothing of taking my time from me every day of my life (which is to me life, money, power, all in all). They take that, without thanks, for no need, for the most trivial purposes, and would have me lose a whole day to leave a card with their footman; and you, for life's sake, will not take that for which I have no use. You are too proud. You would not be too proud to let a nurse or friend give up some of her time, if you needed it, to watch by you and take care of you. What is the difference between their giving time and watchfulness, and my giving such help as I can? Perhaps I have said too much of my wish to do this for Rossetti's sake. But if you do not choose to be helped for his sake, consider also the plain hard fact is that I think you have genius; that I don't think there is much genius in the world; and I want to keep what there is, in it, heaven having, I suppose, enough for all its purposes. Utterly irrespective of Rossetti's feelings or my own, I should simply do what I do, if I could, as I should try and save a beautiful tree from being cut down, or a bit of Gothic cathedral whose strength is failing. If you would be so good as to consider yourself as a piece of wood or Gothic for a few months, I should be grateful to you ...'*

It was an extraordinary letter. Lizzie read it over and over, always returning to the lines: *I think you have genius ...*

How could she turn down such a generous and life-changing offer? It was all her dreams come true.

As soon as she could, Lizzie went to an art supply shop and bought her own paints and brushes and palette; Bruno took her, as Gabriel owed them too much money to show his face there.

Then Bruno and Gabriel took her to have tea with Mrs Rossetti, and her two long-faced daughters, Maria and Christina. They looked like crows in their black dresses. She tried to pretend that she was the sort of girl that Mrs Rossetti would approve of – demure, devout, docile – yet she felt as though that thin, upright woman saw straight through her and did not like what she found.

Mrs Rossetti asked no questions about Lizzie's family and frowned when she coughed into her handkerchief. Her back stiffened as she noticed the many small attentions and affections that Gabriel lavished on Lizzie, and she only stared in cool surprise when Lizzie – who knew she was a pious woman – talked about her own parents' piety. Lizzie became uneasily aware that perhaps her mother's idea of God was not the same as Mrs Rossetti's.

She retreated into silence, as Gabriel became ever more effusive. The two sisters did not help. Both were stiff and cold and very, very polite.

Then Gabriel proudly told his mother about John Ruskin's offer of sponsorship for Lizzie. Instead of being pleased, as he had expected, Mrs Rossetti was affronted. It was clear she thought Lizzie a very-lower-class-kind-of-girl. To be paid to model was bad enough. But to be paid to paint!

As Gabriel silently walked her home in the swiftly falling dusk, Lizzie imagined the conversation in the austere sitting-room she had just left. *I never thought that Gabriel would become entangled with such a common girl . . . and that hair! The Devil's colour . . .*

The days passed, and with it the anniversary of the death of Professor Rossetti. Gabriel began to wear his ox-blood red cravats and flowered waistcoats again. But no word of marriage was uttered.

And the letters from John Ruskin to Lizzie kept coming.

'I should like you to go to the country immediately. The physician who you consult . . . may recommend south of France or Italy . . . if you were my own sister, I should plead hard for a little cottage in some sheltered Welsh valley . . . try and make yourself as simple a milkmaid as you can . . . only draw when you can't help it . . .'

Lizzie had no intention of seeing any more doctors. She was far too busy playing with all her new paints and brushes. She thanked John politely but ignored his advice. A few days later, he wrote:

'Forgive me for pressing you to do anything you do not like . . . I hold it of the very highest importance that you should let Dr. Acland see you . . . You shall be quite independent. You shall see no-one. You shall have your little room all to yourself. Only once put your tongue out and let him feel your pulse . . . I am so certain it is the best and happiest thing for you that I have taken upon me . . . to get your lodgings for you ... Please therefore pardon me, and get ready to go to Oxford, for every day lost is of importance. Could you get one of your sisters to go with you on Monday?'

Once again, Lizzie tried to rebuff him politely, but John Ruskin was not a man to take a hint. He came to visit her and Gabriel at Blackfriars, criticised the way she held her pencil, and told her that she must give up drawing scenes inspired by poetry and stories, and concentrate on drawing in a dull way from dull things.

Lizzie had been hard at work on a drawing inspired by one of Gabriel's poems about a young woman who melted a waxen effigy of her faithless lover on the morning of his wedding to another. She could not help being hurt when John told Gabriel that he was allowing Lizzie to wear herself out with fancies. Nonetheless, she listened to his advice and tried to sketch a scene set in the milliner's shop, the dullest subject she could think of. The result was just as boring as the subject.

John wrote to her that same day:

'You are a very good girl to say you will break off those disagreeable ghostly connections of yours. I do hope you will be able to go to Oxford on Saturday. I have asked Rossetti to write and tell Dr. Acland if you will. The Doctor will let you see a little sea, if you tell him you like it ... I know it is difficult to be cheerful when one is ill. I could sit down to-day and cry very heartily ...'

Lizzie did not know how to withstand him. Unhappily, she agreed to go to Oxford, to see the doctor he recommended. All she wanted was to be left alone to draw and paint and write her poems, while she still could.

Oxford was as awful as she had expected. Everyone bothered her greatly, and made arrangements on her behalf, and would not let her work. She was expected to make visits and leave cards and go to church and eat in company and enjoy being shown black beetles under microscopes; and Dr Acland was always pressing her to eat more meat and drink more milk, two things that Lizzie particularly hated. The doctor was puzzled by her, she could tell. She was so thin, as if she were wasting away, and yet there was no sign of any consumption in her lungs or bones. In the end he decided that her illness was the result of 'mental power long pent up and overtaxed', and told her that she must have a complete rest. No reading, no writing poetry, no drawing, no painting, no late nights, no exertion of any kind.

It was more than Lizzie could bear. 'I won't! Don't you see? I'd rather die!'

It only made the doctor even more certain that she was a hysteric.

John wrote to her again:

'The difficulty is to keep you quiet, and yet to give you means of passing the time with some degree of pleasure to yourself. You inventive people pay very dearly for your powers. There is no knowing how to manage you.'

Still there was no sign from Gabriel that he intended to make good his promise to marry her. As summer turned into autumn, and plans were made to send Lizzie south for the winter, she began to work secretly on a new poem, writing on any old scrap of paper she could find:

Slow days have passed that make a year,
Slow hours that make a day,
Since I could take my first dear love
And kiss him the old way . . .

9

Men Will Be Men
Winter 1855

Lizzie leaned on the wrought-iron railing of her tiny balcony and gazed out at the sunlit green lawns of the Jardin des Tuileries. She could not believe that she was here, in Paris. It was a dream come true.

John Ruskin had told her she was to head straight to the south of France, where he expected her to moulder away in some tiny village with nothing to look at but old men in berets and donkeys. *Paris will kill you or ruin you,* Ruskin had written. Lizzie did not care. She had bought a train ticket to the French capital and booked herself into the most expensive hotel in the city. She had spent her allowance on flounced silk dresses and a cage crinoline, the latest rage at the court of the Empress Eugénie. She had dragged her chaperone, Mrs Kincaid, huffing and puffing through the entire Exposition Universelle, gazing at all the artworks and inspecting the Empress's extraordinary imperial crown, made with more than two thousand diamonds. She had drunk champagne on the Avenue des Champs-Élysées, in the shade of the flowering chestnut trees, and seen the emperor driving out with his beautiful mistress, the Countess di Castiglione.

Yet the longer she was away, the lonelier Lizzie had become. So she wrote to Gabriel and begged him to come and join her in Paris. He had written back to say Ruskin had forbidden him to come, but Ruskin could be damned. Gabriel was on his way. Lizzie could not wait to see him. She had left him a note with the concierge, with nothing in it but her room number. It made her feel quite scandalous.

A soft tap on her door. Lizzie hurried to open it, her new crinoline skirt swinging. Gabriel stood on the other side, looking more handsome than ever in a pale flowered waistcoat and his favourite plum-coloured velvet jacket, pockets bulging with pencils and paintbrushes as always.

He smiled at her and stepped into her arms, kicking the door shut behind him. Lizzie melted into his embrace.

'I've missed you so much,' she breathed, when at last he lifted his head away. 'I'm so glad you're here.'

'Ruskin is furious with me.' Gabriel grinned at her, and tossed his hat on to a chair. He unwound his muffler and began to unbutton his coat.

'Sometimes I think he's trying to keep us apart.' Lizzie sat on the edge of the bed, unfastening her shoes.

'Maybe he's in love with you himself.' Gabriel shrugged off his waistcoat.

She grimaced. 'Or with you.'

He laughed. 'If so, he has a very strange way of showing it. He comes by every few days and sticks pins in me. Repaint that head, he says. Take out the green in that flesh. Keep your room in order and go to bed early at night. He's worse than my father ever was, for at least Papa never came to my studio and tried to tell me how to paint!'

'He's furious that I'm still here in Paris. He keeps writing and telling me that I must leave at once. I'm pretending I've never received his letters.'

Gabriel came to sit beside her on the bed. 'Have you missed me?' he murmured, kissing the side of her neck.

'Horribly,' she answered. 'Oh, Gabriel, why must I be here with that awful old woman instead of with you? She's always telling me I must not exert myself. When I am here! In Paris! I have longed all my life to come to

Paris, and she and Mr Ruskin between them are insisting I must leave, and go somewhere quite remote and boring.'

'We haven't the tin to visit Paris by ourselves,' Gabriel said. 'Ruskin was furious when I said I was coming. He wouldn't advance me the money, though I begged him. I had to paint a new picture to get the funds. I've never painted anything so fast, and I have to say it's quite lovely, even though it only took me a week.'

Lizzie sighed in envy. How she wished she had his easy facility with the paintbrush. She was certainly not getting any chance to improve her skills, with Mrs Kincaid snatching away her sketchbook and brushes whenever she saw them.

Gabriel began to twine Lizzie's hair around one finger. 'I painted the story of Paolo and Francesca da Rimini. You know, from Dante. I did one panel with them discovering their forbidden love for each other and kissing, and another with them consigned to the flames of Hell, but not caring much because they have each other.'

Lazily Gabriel began to undo Lizzie's dress. 'Just what is this contraption you are wearing? How on earth do I get you out of it?'

For ten days, they deliriously rediscovered each other, escaping Mrs Kincaid as much as they possibly could. It was winter, and very cold. Although it had not snowed, it rained nearly every day, bright leaves swirling down in the wind like scattered coins.

One day, Gabriel came to meet her with a note clutched excitedly in one hand. 'We've been invited to meet Mr and Mrs Robert Browning!' he cried. 'They're in town for the exhibition and wish to know if we'd like to take tea with them.'

Lizzie caught her breath in excitement. She loved the poetry of both Robert Browning and his frail wife, Elizabeth Barrett Browning, and was smitten by the romance of their love story. Robert had admired Elizabeth's verse and written to her, they had corresponded clandestinely for a year and a half, and had eventually eloped to Italy where they now lived in exile. Lizzie was hoping she could show Mrs Browning some of her own poems, which she carried rolled in a sheaf and tied with ribbon.

It was a raw, cold day, and Lizzie found it hard to get warm in her new dress. The wind seemed to whistle up underneath her crinoline, making it sway and bounce. Her feet were cold, her bones were cold. She had wrapped herself in a new paisley shawl, but it might as well have been gossamer. She took a few quick drops of her laudanum while Gabriel was giving directions to the coachman, and then a few more while the coach rattled over the cobblestones, to warm herself, and ease the ache in her body. Gabriel was so busy peering out the window and pointing out to her all the sights of Paris that it was easy to dose herself a few more times. At last, she felt warm and relaxed and euphoric. She had to clutch at Gabriel's arm for support once they alighted. He teased her for buying such silly silk slippers. She laughed, clutching at him again as she almost slipped on the damp cobbles. He held her close, smiling, but his glance down at her was puzzled and a little anxious. She pressed her gloved hand against her mouth to stop herself laughing again.

They were taken in to meet the famous poet. Mr Browning was a small slight figure, with loose waving brown hair and a grizzled beard that clung to the edge of his narrow chin. He rose to greet them, smiling, and begging his wife's excuses. 'She is unwell, I'm afraid. You know her health is most easily upset.'

Gabriel shook his proffered hand heartily, and then the poet turned to Lizzie. As his gaze met hers, his whole demeanour changed. His body stiffened, his eyes sharpened. He glanced quickly at Gabriel, then drew Lizzie to sit down. 'You will want to rest now, Miss Siddal,' he said, and indeed Lizzie's body was soft and boneless, her mind wandering away. She heard snippets of their conversation, as if from a far distance. She was too fascinated by the play of flames in the fireplace to listen too closely. She heard the words *opium eater* and *my wife* and *be careful.*

For a while, she rested between the worlds, thinking strange and far-reaching thoughts, then slowly she came back down into her skin. Her tea was cold and unpleasantly scummed. She wrinkled her nose and pushed it away from her. To her surprise, Gabriel was rising to his feet and thanking Mr Browning. Lizzie rose too, feeling light and unsteady.

He said goodbye, and she managed to say, 'I am a great admirer of yours, Mr Browning.'

'Thank you,' he answered. 'Please, take care of yourself, Miss Siddal.'

Suddenly Lizzie wanted to weep. She wanted to tell him that she was already marked for death, the inexorable machinery of fate taking her, tick by tock, step by stumble, ever closer to her grave. All she could do was try to hook herself into immortality with her words, her faint pencil scratches, her awkward daubings. If she could have found the words, she thought he might have understood. But her tongue was thick, her throat seized up, and so she only smiled and mumbled something.

Gabriel was looking at her oddly. She leant her head against his shoulder, but it was stiff and unyielding. When at last they made it back to their hotel through the first blow of snow, he helped her to her bed and then left her, to retire to his own. He insisted she go on to Nice, as Ruskin had commanded. He went back to London, leaving her alone with Mrs Kincaid, who seemed to watch her with suspicion-sharpened eyes, and told her to eat all her food, and stop with her silly fancies.

One day, Lizzie found her store of laudanum had been taken from her. She wrote to Gabriel, begging for more money, so she could replace it. Those days were hard and cruel. She refused to go down and sit with Mrs Kincaid at dinner. Instead, she ordered a tray to her room and then hid the food, so her plate would go away empty. Sometimes she got so hungry she ate the food, but the thought of it rotting within her distressed her so much she had to get it out, somehow. Her knuckles grew red and raw.

At last the money came, though Lizzie was so weak and dizzy it was an ordeal to go and fetch it. The man at the post office seemed to stare at her as if he suspected her of the worst kind of felony, and indeed Lizzie was trembling so much she was afraid she might faint. At last the money was in her hands, and she could go in search of an apothecary, and more bottles of laudanum. She could not wait to go back to the privacy of her room. She stood there, in the crowded shop, and tore out the cork with her teeth, and drank down most of one bottle, heedless of who might see. Then it was a strange, dark wandering journey back to her room, afraid of all the eyes that watched her.

She wanted Gabriel. She wanted to go home. She was tired of living in hotels, with no-one but that hard-faced suspicious-eyed woman for company. It did not seem to make any sense. She was not getting any better, but then she was not much worse either.

John Ruskin wrote and told her she must travel on to Switzerland, but Lizzie ignored him. She had to get back to Gabriel. He had hardly written to her lately, and she felt uneasy.

It was such a joy to hear English spoken at the docks, and to see green English fields and grey English skies and rows of neat English houses and then, as her train rattled towards the capital, glimpses of smog-bound English chimneys. And it was wonderful to be back in Gabriel's arms.

At first, all seemed well. But then Gabriel said she could not stay with him, that she must find lodgings for herself. That hurt. She could not understand why he did not simply marry her and find somewhere they could live together. So many of his friends had married. Johnny Millais, Charley Collins, Arthur Hughes.

She and Gabriel began to quarrel, over silly little things. He did not like her drinking so much laudanum. He complained about her spending so much time with Bruno's wife, Emma. He piled her plate high with horrible food like fried eggs and kippers and sausages, and grew angry with her when she pushed her plate away. And he was always too busy with his own affairs to give Lizzie the lessons he had promised her. Her frustration and disappointment made her sharp with him. He was cold and unkind in return.

Lizzie felt as if the world had shifted somehow, while she was away.

It was Emma who told her. She and Lizzie had known each other for a long time, and had grown closer since Emma had married Bruno.

'I don't know what's wrong with him!' Lizzie cried one day, after Gabriel had slammed out in a temper.

Emma had hesitated, then said, 'Lizzie, my dear girl, I don't quite know how to tell you ...' Her round, sweet face was troubled.

'What?' Lizzie asked, stiffening.

'He's been going around a lot with that Annie Miller girl, you know the one. She modelled for the Maniac's painting of the girl who got a conscience.'

Lizzie nodded. She had heard of Annie Miller. She had been a barmaid Holman Hunt had picked up somewhere. Lizzie vaguely remembered that Holman Hunt had decided to educate her and save her from the streets with the intention of marrying her himself one day. He had then gone off to the East, leaving Annie Miller to amuse herself.

'All the boys have been mad for her,' Emma said, pouring them both a stiff finger of gin. 'She went boating with Fred and dined out with George. Even William Rossetti took her out!'

'What about Gabriel?' Lizzie demanded.

'He took her dancing,' Emma confessed. 'But I'm sure it meant nothing. She was modelling for them all. You know what it's like with artists and their models.'

Her voice trailed away as she saw the look on Lizzie's face. 'I'm sorry,' she said at last, simply. 'I thought you should know.'

Then, as Lizzie dropped her face into her arms and began to sob, Emma put her plump arm across her back and tried to comfort her.

'He loves you, Lizzie, you know he does. It's just . . . you've been away so long! And men will be men, you know.'

10

The Sleeping Princess
Winter–Summer 1856

Georgie sat by the window, where the light was best, and drew the curve of Louisa's cheek. Her younger sister heaved a sigh and kicked one leg irritably.

'Please be still, Louie,' Georgie said, her pencil poised in the air. 'It's impossible to get you right if you keep wiggling around.'

'I'm bored,' Louie announced.

'You could always go and help Mama with the darning.'

Louie sighed again, louder. 'Can't you read me a story?'

'I can't read and draw at the same time,' Georgie answered, putting pencil to paper for a few tentative strokes. 'But if you sit still just a few minutes longer, I will read you a story at bedtime tonight.'

Louie accepted this philosophically, and turned her gaze back to the street.

Something caught her attention. She leant forward. 'I say … isn't that Mr Edward?'

Georgie dropped her pencil and jumped up. She bent to see out the window. Walking along Walpole Street, wearing a disreputable jacket and a soft hat, was Ted Jones. He had a leather portfolio tucked under one arm and a broken umbrella held aloft, flapping wildly in the breeze.

'Oh it is! It is!' Georgie flew to the mirror and checked herself, smoothing back her chestnut-brown hair and pinching her pale cheeks to bring some colour into them. She then ran around the room, tidying up. Louie watched her, grinning. They heard the knock on the front door, then a few moments later the sound of feet. Georgie sat down and spread out her skirts as prettily as she could, then picked up her pencil again. When Ted was shown into the room, she was delicately adding a few strokes to the paper.

'Hello, Mr Edward,' Louie said. 'I'm being immortalised!'

'Hello, Miss Louie, Miss Georgie,' Ted answered. He looked damp and wind-blown, the hems of his trousers wet and muddy. 'Look at you both, all grown up.'

'I'm ten now,' Louie said self-importantly.

'And Miss Georgie is old enough to put her hair up.' He sounded sad. Georgie touched her hair self-consciously. She was almost sixteen now, and had let down her skirts and put her hair up at her mother's insistence, when she had started taking art lessons at the Government School of Design a few months previously.

'You're dripping on the carpet,' Louie said.

Ted looked down at his wet shoes. 'It's very miserable out there.'

'Come in and get dry.' Georgie got to her feet, coming forward a little shyly. 'Would you like some tea?'

'I'm gasping for it,' he answered.

'Louie, would you mind ...' When her little sister looked inclined to argue, Georgie jerked her head imperatively and Louie got up with an exaggerated sigh and went out of the room.

'I have not seen you in so long,' Georgie said, coming to stand near Ted, who was warming himself by the fire.

'You know I went away last year with Topsy ...'

'Where did you go? What did you do?'

'We went to France to see all the cathedrals and the abbeys and the art. It was glorious. We went to the Louvre – I couldn't miss that! Topsy covered my eyes and led me up to a painting by Fra Angelico. When

I opened my eyes, such a shaft went through me – I knew that was what I had to do. I had to try to paint like that ...'

He was excited, restless, pacing up and down on the hearth-rug. Georgie listened quietly, her hands clasped together in her lap.

'It's changed everything for me, Miss Georgie. Topsy and I ... we spent most of one night walking up and down the shore at Le Havre, just talking. That was when we decided that we just had to do it ...'

'Do what?' she asked, when he paused to poke the fire into life again.

'Give up everything ... do what we really want to do ... to begin a life of art ...' His thin face was flushed, his grey eyes alight with fervour. 'Topsy means to design things – houses – cathedrals, maybe ... and I will paint. And we will try to make the world a better place, through our art.'

'I think that's wonderful.'

'Do you? Do you really?' He came to sit down beside her. For a moment she thought he meant to take her hands. But then he drew back. 'I'm so glad. Everyone thinks I am crazy. I've told my father. He wants me to be a bishop. Such a respectable thing to do. I have disappointed everyone by giving up so much respectability. But I cannot do it. I've tried, Miss Georgie, I really have. Doubting, doubting, doubting all the while – so anxious to do well – and yet I just can't – I can't do it ...'

'Then you mustn't,' she said gently.

He had been growing agitated, but at her words he took a deep breath and looked at her.

'I don't believe in it anymore ...' There was agony in his voice.

'Neither do I,' she said quietly.

He was surprised. 'You don't? Why?'

Her colour had risen, but she looked at him steadfastly. 'Did you know that ... that Carrie died? Last year, in the spring?'

'Oh, Miss Georgie, I'm so sorry!' He reached out impulsively and took her hand.

Georgie looked down, trying to hide the sheen of tears in her eyes. Her throat was thick.

It had been the most awful day of her life. Georgie and her sisters had spent hours kneeling by Carrie's bedside, praying for her. Carrie had lain on her bed, her face flushed with fever, her breath sucking in and hissing out.

Georgie had prayed with all her might. *Please, God, don't take her away. I'll do anything. Please don't let her die.*

It was no use. Carrie had begun to cough and had been unable to stop. Mrs Macdonald lifted her up. Blood gushed from her mouth. Mrs Macdonald began to sob. Georgie rushed to Carrie's side, putting her arm about her, holding a handkerchief to her lips. Carrie had coughed again, splattering Georgie's face with blood.

She had been dead within the hour.

I will never forgive you, Georgie had told God.

She tried to explain to Ted, whose fingers were still clasping hers. 'Everyone keeps saying that Carrie has gone to a better place, that she is better off dead. I cannot believe it. I will not believe it. Surely it is life that is important? She was so young, the same age that I am now. I have so much I want to do. I want to see the world ... I want to create something lasting and important ... I want ...' She looked down, crimson-cheeked.

He looked grave. 'I want all those things too. So you understand why I must give up this idea of being a parson and try to do what I truly want to do? Be a painter?'

'Oh, yes. I understand perfectly.'

'And you do not think less of me?'

She raised her eyes to meet his gaze. 'Oh, no, I think more of you.'

He flushed. 'I knew you would understand, I knew you would.'

They sat in silence for a moment. Georgie was acutely aware that Louie would be back any moment with the tea-tray and the moment of confidences would be past. Greatly daring, she leant forward. 'What do you need to do? Do you know anything about being an artist?'

'Nothing! Nothing at all. I'm twenty-two years old and I have never met, or even seen, a painter in my life. I know no-one who has even been inside an artist's studio. But I'm hoping ... I've come to London to try to meet someone. I've seen some of his work and it has all the *feeling*, all the *meaning*, of what I want to do. His name is Dante Gabriel Rossetti. I am hoping he will advise me.'

Georgie made a small sound of encouragement.

'There was this one night in Oxford,' Ted went on. 'It was winter and I had gone to see the burial place of Fair Rosamund. At Godstow Abbey, you know. It was the most beautiful evening. The sun was going down and the sky was all lit up with golden light, and I could see it all reflected in the river, like in an old bronze mirror. In my mind's eye, I could see what it must have been like in the days of Fair Rosamund. The knights on their prancing horses, with hawks on their wrists and dogs at their heels, and the fair ladies in their flowing dresses and tall hats with veils. It was like I was seeing ghosts from the past, so vividly real, I was afraid my head would burst. Then I heard the shriek of a train, and its great plume of steam as it clattered along the lines, and I was brought back into this world – that I cannot convince myself I have to live in – and I felt such an urge to capture it all. These dreams and visions I have, they burn in my imagination. I feel I must paint them, I must!'

'Then you will,' Georgie answered, and clasped his hands more tightly.

The air rang with the sound of bells.

Dressed in her Sunday best, Georgie walked slowly out of the chapel, surrounded on all sides by her sisters. The congregation was talking with admiration of her father's sermon. 'He made Hell seem so real you could find it on an atlas!' one old man said.

As Mrs Macdonald led the way onto the thoroughfare, Georgie lifted her eyes. Her gaze met Ted's. He was standing in the window of the lodging-house opposite. A quick half-smile flashed between them, then Georgie lowered her gaze demurely and walked away down the street.

Ted had moved to live in Sloane Street, a narrow cobbled road that resounded all day with the clop of horses' hooves and the clatter of iron-rimmed wheels. It had two great advantages. It was dirt cheap; and it was directly opposite the chapel where Mr Macdonald preached each Sunday. Georgie could only hope it was the latter reason that was the more compelling for Ted.

It was hard to tell. When asked, he only replied: 'I looked at two thousand, eight hundred and forty-five rooms, you know, but two thousand, three hundred and seventy-four had only one sitting-room, and of the remainder, only two hundred and forty had a bedroom, and of the one hundred and thirty left, they had such viragos of landladies I dared not stay there, so that left only six places in all of London, of which I liked this one the best.'

Ted had given up university without achieving his degree, and was working hard at learning to become a painter. He had no money, and was always choosing paints and brushes over food, so that he seemed more thinly drawn and highly strung than ever. His boots had holes in them, his patched coat hung from his angular shoulders, and his trousers were worn thin at the knees, but he did not care. Ted was the happiest he had ever been.

Ned, Georgie reminded herself. He was not to be called Ted anymore. His teacher and idol, Dante Gabriel Rossetti, thought Ted was the name of a country bumpkin. Mr Rossetti had decided to call him Ned instead, and so everyone else had to follow suit.

Ned, Ned, Ned, Georgie repeated to herself. She had to make sure she got it right.

Not just his name had changed since Ted ... Ned ... had met Mr Rossetti. His speech had exploded with a whole host of new words. Beautiful girls were called 'stunners'. His lodgings were his 'crib'. Everything was spiffy or cheesy or jammy or ripper. He said Will Fulford was 'spoony' over Alice. And the events of the day were always defined by Ted's tinlessness. 'Got no tin left,' he'd say sadly. 'Do you want to walk by the river?' Or, if his father had managed to scrape together some money to send him, he'd say, 'Tin's in! What shall we do?'

He took Georgie to see the Royal Academy exhibition, where she saw *Scapegoat* painted by William Holman Hunt, a rather disturbing picture of a sacrificial goat in a desert landscape that Ned assured her was drawn from life in the Dead Sea in Israel; *The Blind Girl* by John Everett Millais which was one of the most heart-rending paintings Georgie had ever seen, depicting a poor blind girl who cannot see the beauty of the double rainbow in the sky; and *April Love* by Arthur Hughes, showing a young woman turning away from the bereft figure of her lover, huddled over her hand.

'Topsy's nobbled that one,' Ned said. 'I had to go and deliver the cheque. You should've seen Arthur's face! Topsy's so lucky. He has so much tin he can buy any painting he wants.'

He made a restless jerky movement, which Georgie had come to recognise and dread. Ned was, mostly, the most delightful of companions, full of a puckish humour and a sense of wonder and delight in everything he saw. But sometimes a darker mood would possess him. It seemed as if the world wounded him. Georgie could only do her best to protect him from it.

One day Georgie came home from art school, only to be called into her mother's room.

'Your young man has asked for your hand,' she said. 'You are not yet sixteen, and so he knows he must wait. Your father and I feel this must be your decision. Do you wish to marry him?'

Georgie could only smile and nod, even as her heart turned cartwheels.

'You are both in God's hands,' her mother said. 'Let us pray.'

Kneeling by her mother's side, her eyes closed, her hands pressed together like a child, Georgie could not keep the smile from curving her lips.

It seemed that their love had been written from the beginning of the world.

Being betrothed was such a strange and special place to be. It meant she could put out her hand and touch Ned's, and not fear she was being too forward. It meant they could talk, and not be remarked upon.

The day after their engagement, Ned came with his arms full of all his favourite books. Georgie understood she had been admitted into the inner chambers of his heart.

One evening he even drew her close, and kissed her mouth, and muttered something in her ear before he fled. Georgie went to bed in a daze, unable to sleep, feeling such joyousness within her she felt it must burst right out of her skin, like a butterfly from its chrysalis.

Ned took Georgie and Louie, an eager chaperone, to meet Mr Rossetti. He lived on the river, near Blackfriars Bridge. Georgie had never seen such a place. Dirt, cobwebs, paint set hard in scatters and splatters of vivid colour, books laid face-down with broken spines, sketches on any old scrap of paper, costumes cut from old rags, tarnished jewellery, food-encrusted blue-and-white platters, wooden lay-figures, crumpled fabrics, pagan idols, old easels, paintings, sketches, drawings, studies, pinned and stuck and discarded everywhere. Many had the same face: a young woman, vulnerable, downcast, longing.

'Call me Gabriel,' he said with a smile. 'All my friends do, and I'm sure we are going to be great friends.'

Gabriel had the most beautiful compelling voice, full of charm and mischief, and he spoke with such confidence and authority one felt he must be right about everything. He allowed them to watch him paint. Not a single hesitation, not a moment's pause. It was humiliating, to see how easily designs sprang from his fingers. Georgie wished her fingers were as deft and sure.

The sun began to melt into the Thames. The stink from the river was extraordinary, but Gabriel did not seem to notice. Louie grew tired and fractious. It was her eleventh birthday, and she had hoped for treats. Ned gave her paper and some pencils, and they set themselves to draw.

'Close your eyes, Georgie,' he said. 'Pretend you are asleep.'

She obeyed. She thought she would always obey, gladly.

When at last Georgie was permitted to open her eyes, it was to find that he and Louie had drawn her as the Sleeping Princess of the fairytale she so loved.

It was beautiful enough to make her cry.

Part II

Of Blessed Memory
1856–1862

Many commissions from (the firm) were waiting for Edward; amongst them one for coloured tiles which proved a welcome outlet for his abounding humour, and in this form the stories of Beauty and the Beast and Cinderella took at his hands as quaint a shape as they wear in the pages of the Brothers Grimm of blessed memory . . .

Lady Georgiana Burne-Jones
Memorials of Edward Burne-Jones, Volume I

1

Gorge
Winter–Summer 1857

Ice rocked against the embankments. Lizzie just could not seem to get warm. She huddled her coat closer, her sketchbook under her arm.

A young woman bounded down the steps towards her, hat swinging from one hand. Tight yellow ringlets hung on either side of her face. At the sight of Lizzie, she gave a mocking sideways smile, then, laughing, went racing away.

Lizzie slammed the door of Gabriel's apartment behind her. 'Who was that?'

'Who?' Gabriel looked up from his easel, startled.

'That girl I saw leaving.'

'Oh. Her. That's Annie Miller.'

'What was she doing here?'

'Modelling for me, of course,' he said. 'What else?'

'Exactly what I want to know!' Lizzie marched over to his easel. It held a drawing of Annie with her hair cascading over her shoulders. More drawings lay littered on the table.

Lizzie seized them and tore them into pieces. Gabriel tried to stop her, but she ran to the window and flung the torn shreds of paper into the wind.

'Are you mad?' he cried. 'That's hours of work!'

'Hours spent with her instead of me!'

'But I can't paint only you, Lizzie. I'd never get any commissions.'

'Are you saying that's she's prettier than me?'

'No. Of course not. But I need … a variety of forms and faces …'

'Do you want to break off our engagement? Is that it?'

'No, Lizzie, of course not.'

'Prove it,' she cried. 'Come and have tea with my mother.'

It was time to leg-shackle him, Lizzie thought bitterly. She had put up with his excuses long enough. It was time that he made good on his promises.

Even if that meant she had to face her mother again.

On the day of the tea party, Lizzie spent the morning cleaning her tiny sitting-room. She knew her mother would notice the faintest speck of dust.

Gabriel came early, looking uncomfortable in a starched collar. He had brought a fruitcake. Lizzie cut it up and arranged it on a plate. She had made chicken sandwiches, and bought some ginger buns, which she knew her mother liked.

Mrs Siddal and Lydia arrived, escorted by Lydia's young man. The usual business of taking off coats and hats and shaking out umbrellas helped ease the first awkward moments. Lizzie found it hard to look at her mother, and even harder to speak to her, but Lydia and Gabriel kept up a genial flow of small talk. Lizzie even managed to force down a few mouthfuls of her sandwich, which was far too dry.

'Should've put more butter on it,' Mrs Siddal said.

'Yes. Sorry.' Lizzie offered around the fruitcake.

'Don't hold with fruitcake,' Mrs Siddal said. 'They put alcohol in it.'

Gabriel had just taken an enthusiastic bite. He put down his slice and chewed his mouthful behind the shelter of his napkin, while Mrs Siddal tasted the buns and then stated they were sadly lacking in ginger.

At last, the winter afternoon began to darken and Lizzie's brother James arrived to escort Mrs Siddal and Lydia home again. He had always thought Lizzie showed a sad want of conduct, and so he did little more than nod his head at her in greeting.

Just then, a knock came on the front door. Anxiously Lizzie went to open it.

It was Bruno, looking as shabby and untidy as ever. There was paint under his fingernails and crumbs in his beard. He was surprised to find Lizzie's sitting-room full of people, but shook hands all around warmly enough and gave Gabriel a clap on the shoulder.

'I'm glad to find you here, old chap,' he said. 'I've been wanting to speak to you about this idea we've had of setting up house with some of the fellows. Ned Jones is keen, and so is Topsy Morris, and you know he's got the tin to help us fund it. He might have found a place big enough to suit us all, but the thing is ...'

'Perhaps we could talk about this later,' Gabriel interrupted.

'But we need to get things settled if we're not going to lose the place,' Bruno plunged on. 'And it's only got a few double bedrooms. Emma and I will need one, of course, and so will Ned and his girl. And the thing is, Hunt is bound to want one too, he's still as mad as ever about Annie. And I was thinking ...'

'Annie Miller?' Lizzie said. 'You want to go and live in the same house as *Annie Miller?*'

'Well ... no ...' Gabriel floundered. 'It was just an idea ... and I obviously thought you and I would want one of the bigger bedrooms ...'

Mrs Siddal had been listening with a look of deepening horror. Now she stood up, utterly scandalised. 'You are just as shameless as I expected,' she told Gabriel. 'As for you, Lizzie, I have never been more shocked. I think it's high time we left. James, if you please.'

She swept out of the sitting-room, Lydia following close behind and looking scared. James opened the front door for them, then turned to say, 'Just what kind of rackety company are you keeping, anyway, Lizzie?'

'It's not like that ...' Lizzie faltered. 'Really ...'

'Brazen hussy!' Her brother shut the door with a bang.

Lizzie turned to stare at Gabriel, who at once rushed into an explanation. Of course he had meant to tell her, but he knew how she felt about Annie Miller and so he thought he would wait until he found out if Annie and Hunt were set on the idea and then of course it really depended on whether or not Hunt still wanted to marry Annie which was not set in stone by any means and then, if Lizzie was willing, well then perhaps when the two of them were married they could join all the others and really it could be a capital scheme as they would choose a place with a big old garden and lots of light where they could all paint and think how much tin they would all save …

Lizzie could not speak at first. She felt like she was swallowing a ball of hot iron. The tears and words came together, hot, angry, unstoppable. Bruno edged out the door, muttering apologies. Lizzie hardly realised he was gone. All her rage was focused on Gabriel.

Eventually he left, slamming the door behind him. Lizzie paced the floor, her angry thoughts spinning. What must her mother have thought? She felt sick with shame.

Lizzie went into her bedroom and pulled out the chamber-pot she kept under her bed. Kneeling beside it, she jammed her fingers against the soft tissues at the back of her throat. She gagged once or twice, then her stomach emptied itself in a gush of foul-smelling vomit. She sat back on her heels, wiping her mouth, feeling the usual giddy relief. After a moment, she did it again, till there was nothing left in her stomach to throw up.

Then Lizzie ate everything she had in her larder – the heel of bread, the wheel of cheese, cans of sardines, an old bruised apple. She knelt over her chamber-pot, and shoved her fingers into her throat till the food she had eaten came rushing out again.

When there was nothing left within her but bitter bile, Lizzie crept through the dark house to empty her chamber-pot in the outside privy. She could not bear the thought of going back to her rooms, the landlady peering at her through the crack of a door. So she hid her chamber-pot under a pile of black wet leaves, and began to walk through the dark streets towards Hampstead Heath. The rain came and went in gusts.

Lizzie walked without direction or intention, her wet skirts tangling about her legs. Once she tripped and fell to her knees, grazing her palms in the gravel. A faint line of light appeared in the east. She saw that she had come almost to the Browns' small house on the far side of the heath. Her steps quickened till she was almost running. When Bruno opened the door, she half-fell into his arms.

'Look at your eyes! What have you done?' he cried.

Lizzie looked at herself in the hall mirror. The whites of her eyes were poppy-red. She had burst all the blood vessels around the iris. She hid her face in her hands.

'What's wrong? What's happened?'

'You … Gabriel … my mother …' Lizzie could not form a sentence. She felt hot and cold all at once.

'I don't know what to do,' Bruno said helplessly. 'Emma's not here. I'll send for Gabriel.'

'No, no!' Lizzie cast herself down on a chair, sobbing.

He knelt beside her, patting her awkwardly. 'I'm so sorry, I had no idea that my visit would cause you so much distress.'

'You … he …' Lizzie could not catch her breath.

'You cannot stay, Lizzie,' Bruno said eventually, after a long time trying to comfort her. 'It's just not seemly without Emma here. I'm sorry, but I have to take you home.'

She got up. Her legs were weak, and her head was hot and heavy. When she put out a hand to support herself, she saw it was filthy and bleeding.

Bruno had no money for a hansom cab, and neither did she. They had to walk, Bruno doing his best to support her. Lizzie managed to get herself to bed. It hurt just to lie still. Her own bones bruised her.

Days passed. Emma came to nurse her. At first she brought her baby boy with her but its thin wailing drove Lizzie to distraction, and so she had to leave it at home. When Gabriel came shamefacedly to visit, Lizzie fell to the floor in a faint. Emma pushed him out and would not let him back in. After he had left, Bruno spoke through the door. 'I've lent him ten pounds,' he whispered. 'He's gone to buy a special licence. You'll be married this weekend.'

But of course they were not. Gabriel spent the ten pounds on something else. Bruno had to apologise again. He said he must have mistaken Gabriel's intentions. But Lizzie knew the truth. Gabriel did not want to be tied to a creature like her.

Lizzie refused to eat. She could not even think of food without remembering that terrible night, when she had gorged and purged till her throat was stripped raw. It had been a kind of madness. She could not let it happen again.

'She hasn't eaten in two weeks,' Emma told Bruno. 'If this goes on, she'll die.'

At last, in desperation, Emma wrote to Lizzie's family. Lydia came in a hansom cab. Doctors were called. Murmured conversations over Lizzie's head. She did not listen. It took all her energy just to breathe. She was lifted and carried out to a carriage. It rattled and jounced for miles, hurting Lizzie with every jerk. Lydia told her they were going to a spa in Matlock Gorge. Lizzie didn't care.

It took them several days to reach the spa. The journey exhausted any reserves of strength Lizzie had left. Lydia wept and wrung her hands, sure that Lizzie was going to die.

The carriage began to descend a steep road. It seemed they were descending as deep as hell. Yet the deeper they went, the colder it grew. Lydia had to get out and walk behind the carriage, to ease the burden for the horses. No-one tried to make Lizzie walk. It was like she was dead already. The carriage her coffin.

At last she was settled into a room. They wrapped her in eiderdowns and stoked up the fire. Lydia helped her sit up against her pillows and brought her some paper. Lizzie wrote to Gabriel, telling him she never wanted to see him again.

Then she wrote to John Ruskin, thanking him for his kindness and refusing his allowance.

She would never paint again.

*

'Anyone would think I was trying to make you eat broken glass,' the nurse complained. She went away and brought the doctor, a bearded man with a gold watch-chain stretched across an ample belly. He took Lizzie's wrist in his hand, and pinched her skin. The white mark of his fingers did not fade.

'You are malnourished,' he told her. 'It happens sometimes in young women who overstrain their nervous energy. You must have complete bed rest, with no stimulation. No letters, no visitors, no novel reading. A few drops of laudanum morning and night, to check your hysterical tendencies, and abundant feeding ...'

But Lizzie did not want to eat. She wanted to need nothing. Not love, not art, not food. The doctor frowned and said something in a low voice to the nurse. She returned a few minutes later with a brown wooden box. The doctor opened it and showed Lizzie the contents. A rubber hose. A gigantic syringe.

'This is a feeding tube,' he told her. 'If you do not eat, we put the tube up your nose and down the back of the throat so you cannot spit it out. And then we pump gruel into you. It is not pleasant.'

So, unwillingly, Lizzie swallowed down the beef tea and claret jelly and milk custards they insisted on serving her six times a day. All her little tricks – hiding food under her fork, dropping it under the table, spitting it out into her napkin – were of no avail. The hard-faced nurse recorded every mouthful. The more she resisted, the more they made her eat.

Each day she grew a little stronger.

By the time the gorse was turning the dales golden, the doctor thought she might be permitted to read her letters. She was given a pile, most of them in Gabriel's distinctive hand. After a long moment she opened the first.

She could hear his voice in her head as she read. He begged her pardon, and asked after her health. He was sorry, he wrote. He had never meant to upset her so. After a while, the letters became less contrite and more like himself, filled with tidbits of news and details of his work.

The last letter was only thin. Gabriel told her excitedly that Bruno had organised an exhibition of Pre-Raphaelite art and wanted to include some of her paintings. Gabriel thought she should show the self-portrait she had done in oils, plus the best of her drawings and watercolours. *You must let me hang Clerk Saunders too,* he wrote. *Ruskin agrees it is the best of your work and hopes we can sell it for you.*

Lizzie stared down at the letter. Her paintings were going to be exhibited. Strangers would see them. Her heart was beating very fast and her palms were damp. She did not know if she was excited or frightened. The two feelings were often akin for her.

Lizzie got out her suitcase and began to pack.

The doctor was not pleased. He thought she should stay another month at least. But Lizzie was adamant. She must attend her first ever exhibition.

It felt strange to be back in London. The brown smear on the horizon. The choke of coal smoke. The clatter of carriage wheels on cobblestones. Crowds of people hurrying about their business, faces shuttered. The feeling of being invisible.

The gallery was opened for a private viewing the evening before the official opening. Lizzie could not eat a bite all day. Her body thrummed with nerves. Tonight she would see Gabriel for the first time in almost three months. Lizzie did not know what to expect. Would he be cold and remote? Or would he be sorry?

As Lizzie walked in, a little murmur arose from the crowd. She held her head high, one hand holding up the loose folds of her gown. She saw that her face and form were everywhere, in Gabriel's drawings and paintings. As brightly coloured and crowded as stained glass windows, they glowed from the walls.

Here and there were hung her own small canvases. Lizzie thought they compared favourably with some of the other artists' work. Her brushwork was much looser and freer, but her use of colour was good and she had managed to catch something of the emotion of each scene. Her main fault was the stiffness of her human figures. If only she had been able to take life drawing lessons at the Royal Academy! How else was she supposed to learn?

Then Lizzie saw Gabriel. He turned, and looked at her. His eyes lit up, and he held out one hand.

Lizzie walked over, and put her hand in his.

'Let's celebrate!' Gabriel cried, a bottle of champagne in his hands.

Lizzie's heart quickened with hope. She gazed at him, her hands pressed together at her breast.

'The exhibition is going to New York!'

Lizzie was conscious first of a stab of disappointment. She had thought Gabriel had meant at last to marry her. But then the words penetrated her brain, and she felt a new surge of excitement.

'Really? I cannot believe it! My paintings too?'

'One of them. *Clerk Saunders.*' Gabriel grinned at her excitement. 'It's a Yankee friend of Ruskin's. His name is Charles Eliot Norton, and he's from Massachusetts.' He pronounced the word in an exaggerated Yankee drawl. 'He came to the exhibition and liked what he saw, and made a selection to take back with him.'

'My painting is going to America.' Lizzie marvelled at the very idea.

'Let's drink to rich Americans!' Gabriel popped the cork out the window, then poured out two frothing glasses. Lizzie clinked her glass with his and drank deeply.

'Norton has commissioned me to do a watercolour for him, of any subject I like,' Gabriel said nonchalantly. 'He's paid me fifty guineas for it.'

'Fifty guineas! Oh, Gabriel, we're rich.'

'He wrote an essay for *The Atlantic Monthly* in which he said my paintings were among the best the age had produced.' Gabriel poured more champagne. 'And Coventry Patmore has sent me his review of the exhibition. He said my contributions were the main interest of the whole exhibition.'

'Did … did he mention me?'

'Oh yes.' Gabriel tossed Lizzie the article, then came and stood behind her, kissing the back of her neck. He unpinned her hair and let it unfurl down her back, then began to unbutton her dress. Lizzie ignored him, all her attention on the article. Gabriel, Bruno, Johnny Millais, William Holman Hunt and Arthur Hughes were all mentioned in the opening lines. Her name did not appear. She scanned the rest of the article quickly. Finally she found her name, in the very last paragraph. She read it with breathless eagerness that turned quickly to horror.

'Look what he said! "Her drawings display an admiring adoption of all the most startling peculiarities of Mr. Rossetti's style." Startling peculiarities!'

'Oh that's just his pompous way,' Gabriel said. 'Don't let it worry you.'

Lizzie twisted away. 'He said *Clerk Saunders* did not please him! Oh what if the American man reads the article? He might change his mind about taking it to New York.'

'He won't change his mind.' Gabriel smiled at her reassuringly.

She paid him no heed. 'No-one will want to buy my paintings after this! He said my self-portrait was a promising attempt. *Attempt!*'

Gabriel grabbed the paper from her. 'It's not that bad, Lizzie. Look, he said a *very* promising attempt. And he said the other paintings deserve more notice than he has time to give them.'

'He had time to give you five paragraphs,' she said.

'Well, yes, but ...' Gabriel's voice trailed away as he saw the look on Lizzie's face.

'All of London will read it. They'll all think I'm a bumbling amateur who had the gall to think I could paint. I'll never get another exhibition ... I'll never be able to sell a thing ...'

As she spoke, Lizzie paced back and forth ever more wildly. Suddenly she paused, her gaze caught by Gabriel's trunk that had been brought up from the lumber-room. It was half-packed with clothes and books. 'Are you going somewhere?' she asked in a very different tone of voice.

'Well, yes, actually.' Gabriel's gaze slid away from her. 'Some of the fellows have got up a scheme to paint some murals on the walls of the Oxford Union's debating hall.'

'Oxford? You're going to Oxford?'

'Just for a while, Lizzie.'

'How long?'

He twisted his glass back and forth between his long, paint-stained fingers. 'I guess it'll be two or three months.'

She did not speak. Her silence agitated him.

'You know I get seedy if I stay in London over the summer. The smell from the river ... I thought you'd be away yourself. You seemed to like that last place all right. You could go there again. I've got that money Norton gave me ...'

'I thought we were going to use that money to get married,' Lizzie said. 'You said we would.'

'And we shall. When I get back from Oxford.'

Lizzie moved towards the door like a sleepwalker, picking up her bonnet as she went. Her hair still fell loose over her shoulders.

'Where are you going?' His voice was sharp.

'To pack,' she said. 'If I'm to go back to Matlock Gorge, I'd better get ready.'

2

A Rare Beauty
Autumn 1857

Janey crossed the King's Head yard, carefully carrying a jug brimming over with ale. She did not want to spill a drop. Her mother knew exactly how much liquid her jug carried.

It was mid-afternoon, and the blue sky was softened with spindrifts of high clouds. The leaves of the trees were golden. The streets were full of laughing students in long black gowns, returned to Oxford for the Michaelmas term. It would not be long, Janey knew, before the laughter and high jinks turned to white-faced anxiety as exams loomed. But for now, the students were full of exuberance. Janey would have to keep well out of their way if she did not want the ale spilled.

'Look at that girl!' a young man's voice cried. 'Have you ever seen such hair?'

Janey ducked her head lower. Many people commented on her hair. It was dark and heavy. Impossible to comb smooth. She tensed, expecting another unkind comment about her height or her raggedness.

The young man surprised her, however. 'What a stunner! We have to show her to Gabriel. He would adore her. What a Beatrice she would make!'

Janey glanced up. A shabby young man with fair floppy hair and pale eyes was leaning over the balcony rail. He was with two other young men, all with tankards in their hands. They seemed too old to be students.

They cheered and raised their tankards to her. Embarrassed, Janey hurried away. Her mother would be wanting her ale.

Janey carried the jug down Holywell Street towards St Helen's Passage, the alley where she had been born. Locals called it Hell's Passage. Narrow and dark, it led to a small cobblestoned yard with a cesspit in the corner, protected only by a cracked wooden cover. A gutter in the centre of the alley oozed foul-smelling slime. The smell was so awful it was hard to walk past without gagging. Small shacks made of old bricks and packing cases had been built against the walls. Clothes-lines hung with ragged shirts hid the sky. An old woman sat on a doorstep, smacking her gums, her twisted hands fumbling at a piece of leather she was attempting to cut into shoe soles. A dirty child with a swollen stomach and bare feet stood wailing nearby. His mother shouted at him to shut up.

Janey stopped outside one of the shacks, and pushed open the makeshift door with her hand. The only light came from a single rushlight stuck in a cracked saucer. Her mother lay on a pallet, covered by a filthy blanket. She wore nothing but her chemise and a pair of old stays, stained to the colour of tea. The tiny room stank.

'Where ye been?' Annie slurred. 'I been waitin' and waitin'.' She sat up and groped for her tin cup. 'Fill me up, there's a good girl.'

Janey bent and poured the ale. Her mother's hand shook so badly, the liquid sloshed on to the bed. Annie smacked Janey hard across the ear. 'Mutton-head! Look what ye did.'

'I'm sorry,' Janey whispered. She filled the cup to the brim, then set the jug down on the floor beside the pallet. 'Are ye hungry? I brought ye some bread.'

'I might have a peck at it later.' Annie slurped at the ale.

Janey put the dark heel of bread, wrapped in a cloth, on the floor next to the jug. She picked up some clothes and hung them over a line made with a length of old twine.

'Stop with yer fussing, ye know I can't stand it. Got any stub?'

'Nay,' Janey answered. 'Ye know I don't get paid afore Sat'day.'

Her mother reared up, seizing her arm. 'If I find ye're lyin' to me, ye'll meet wi' it, that I swear.' Roughly she searched Janey's pockets, then put one hand inside her bodice, to make sure she had not tucked any money inside her stays.

Janey pushed her hand away. 'Told ye.'

'Any more cheek fro' ye, an' ye'll get the back o' me hand.'

'I need t'get back to work.' Janey stoked up the fire, then picked up the empty jug to take back to the inn.

As she passed through the pub's yard, she saw her father harnessing a carthorse to the brewer's cart. A hullocking man, his black hair was curly as a ram's fleece. He had a way with horses, and people whispered it was the gypsy blood in him. Janey did not know if it was true. She did not look like an English girl, though, with her wild, black hair and long nose.

'Hi, Da.'

'Hi, Janey.' He hesitated then said, 'How's yer ma?'

'Same as ever.'

He looked down at his boots, then slipped his hand into his pocket and drew out a two bob bit. 'Here ye are, Janey. I know it's yer birthday this week. Get yerself summat nice.'

She accepted the coin in surprised pleasure.

'Got a tip from a rich young cove,' he explained.

He went back to work. Janey went into the pub, fingering the coin in her pocket. A two bob bit wasn't enough to buy a book, which is what Janey really wanted. She had not been able to read much since she had left the local parish school, five years earlier, at the age of twelve. She had loved the afternoons sitting sewing with the other girls, one invisible stitch after another, while her teacher Mrs Leigh had read to them aloud. The little classroom so small and snug, the kettle singing on the hob, and the stories unfurling themselves in the quiet. Janey had loved those stories so much, Miss Leigh had let her stay back after class, and read on herself, as much as she was able. Janey would have given all she owned to never have to leave that room, that moment.

But of course she had to.

It was no use longing for a book of her own. Her mother would just tear out the pages to light the fire. Janey could have bought herself a new collar for her dress. But it'd be hard to keep it nice in that hovel. She could buy herself a cake. A couple of bites, though, and it'd be gone.

As she went about her work that afternoon, scrubbing floors and black-leading the fireplaces at the pub, Janey's mind kept returning to the bright little coin in her pocket. She could not take it home, else her mother would find it and take it. She had to spend it today.

She stood up and dusted off her apron. Her eye was caught by the jar of spills on the fireplace. Furtively she sorted through the narrow twists of paper, hoping to find a poem or a story that she could smuggle out.

She found a playbill for a show that was to play that night at a temporary theatre set up at the old gymnasium on Oriel Street. Tickets were a shilling a head. Janey crumpled the playbill in her hand. She had never been to the theatre, though she had watched Punch and Judy shows and other performances in the street during the St Giles Fair. She had often wondered what it would be like.

As soon as her shift at the pub was done, Janey hurried to Oriel Street, where she purchased two tickets to that evening show. Her heart was thumping hard with dread and excitement. She hid the tickets in her bodice, and went to find her sister, who worked for a laundress on Merton Street.

'But what'll we wear?' Bessie demanded, as soon as she heard the news.

'We'll have t'wear our Sundays,' Janey answered.

'But they're so old an' shabby.'

'It's all we got.'

Both girls had only two dresses. Their everyday frocks were grey and much-mended. Their Sunday dresses were kept for best. Janey's was made of faded blue wool, with a wide plaid trim at the hem and cuff. She had trouble finding dresses to fit because she was so tall. Bessie's was brown cotton calico printed with tiny white flowers. Both dresses were cut very simply, without flounces or frills.

Janey lied to her mother and said she had found the tickets lying in the street. Her mother was not happy. She complained the whole time the girls washed in the bucket and drew on their dresses.

'Go an' have a dram an' a pipe at the pub,' Bessie suggested. 'Mr Whittaker ain't there, his missus would be glad o' a bit o' company.'

Annie brightened at once. She had lost her job at the pub, having turned up to work drunk once too often, but the publican's wife was an old friend and could be relied on to turn a blind eye to Annie's unpaid bills.

A steady stream of people made their way to the old gymnasium. Most were local workmen and their wives, but there was a smattering of more genteel people, the women dressed in silk crinolines and the men in top hats and fringed white scarves. There were also a great many young men, moving in packs, and ogling the girls. Most were university students, but there were others in rough tweeds and flat caps as well. Janey and Bessie kept close together, hurrying from one gas-lamp to another, until they were safe in their seats in the gallery.

The lights had been dimmed and the curtains drawn back to show a scene of a country village, with a windmill and a church and various rose-covered cottages. A gypsy was walking along with a parcel tied up in a handkerchief, while a young man pretended to pitchfork straw.

At that moment, two young men began to push their way along the chairs lined up in front of Janey and her sister.

'Pardon me, did I tread on your toes? If you could just let us through.'

They collapsed into the seats directly in front of Bessie and Janey.

'That was close,' one said.

'I would've been annoyed if we'd missed the show, Gabriel. Why must you always be late?'

Janey recognised both the voice of the second speaker, and the name that he pronounced. It was the slender young man with the floppy hair that she had seen in the pub's yard. He looked to be around twenty-two, and was wearing a pair of purple velvet trousers and a dark coat with darned elbows. The man named Gabriel looked around thirty, and had black hair that curled over his collar. His coat was rich plum-coloured velvet.

His voice had been beautiful. Deep and musical. It had just a hint of something foreign about it. He looked foreign too. His skin was as swarthy as Janey's, and his hair as dark. His eyes were shadowed, with a deep horizontal dent between them as if he was always frowning in concentration.

On stage, the young man with the pitchfork had begun to sing.

'Good God, Ned, what have you inflicted upon me?' Gabriel cried. 'It's a music hall number.'

'Sssh!' said the woman in the feathered hat.

'Sorry, Gabriel,' Ned said with a laugh. 'It's the only show in town.'

'Why, oh why, did I leave London?' Gabriel mourned. 'To think I could be worshipping at the feet of Miss Herbert at the Royal Strand right now.'

'There might be a stunner in this show too, Gabriel. Look, there's a girl come on now.'

Janey returned her attention to the stage. A plump girl in a print frock and a frilly little apron had come on stage, coyly twisting a strand of her improbably golden hair. She carried a long-handled feather duster in one hand, and was singing as she dusted the roses.

'I'll lay you a monkey that's a wig,' Gabriel said.

Janey laughed, then pressed both hands over her mouth.

He turned and looked at her. Janey tucked her hands together in her lap and pretended not to notice him. 'But here's a rare beauty under my very nose,' he said. 'How did I not see *you* before?'

Janey coloured hotly, sure he was mocking her.

Ned had turned to look too. 'That's the girl we saw today, at the inn. I knew you'd adore her, I told the others so. What a coincidence to find her sitting right behind us in the theatre!'

The woman in the big hat made more shushing noises, and the old gentleman said coldly, 'Excuse me, sir, if you would be so good ...'

'I endeavour to be good as little as possible,' Gabriel answered.

'Quiet, sir! Watch the show,' another man said.

Gabriel shrugged and returned his attention to the stage, but every few moments he would steal another glance at Janey. Bessie grinned and dug her sister in the ribs. 'Wait till he sees what a Long Meg ye are on yer feet,' she whispered. 'He won't think ye're such a looker then.'

'Sssh,' Janey said.

On stage, the girl with the golden hair was singing:

Whenever you marry, soon you get sorry
When poverty hasn't a pound,
Hearts'll be sinking when no money's chinking,
And love soon fall to the ground.
Advice I give to each fond lass
Say 'No' to every man.

'Excellent advice!' Gabriel clapped loudly. The girl heard him and turned his way, smirking and dropping a little curtsey.

The show rolled on, with sailors dancing with village maids, and an evil miller plotting to burn the hero's ship and wreck his wedding. Gabriel kept up a running commentary that made Janey bite her lip so she would not laugh again. The people around him grew angry and flustered, but he had an air of supreme unconcern.

At last the play ended, and the house lights came up. At once Gabriel twisted about in his chair.

'You are the most beautiful girl I have ever seen. I must paint you,' he said to Janey.

She stared at him dumbly.

'Will you come tomorrow to my rooms? We are staying at number 13 George Street.' He took out a card and a little silver pencil from his waistcoat pocket, scribbled the address on it, and presented it to her.

Janey's face was burning. She ducked her head, twisting her hands in the cloth of her dress. After a moment Gabriel pulled the card back.

'We mean no disrespect,' Ned said. 'We are artists, painting murals on the walls of the Oxford Union's debating hall. Mr Rossetti here is one of the most famous artists in London. He needs models to sit for him … to be painted by him.'

'I be mortal sorry, but I can't,' Janey whispered. They exchanged quick glances at the sound of her accent. Pulling Bessie up, she hurried away down the aisle between the seats.

'Are ye crazy?' her sister demanded, as they pushed through the crowd towards the street. 'Ye might've got some stub out o' them.' She looked back towards the two artists, who were following them. 'An' one o' them is right handsome.'

'They didn't want to *paint* me.' Janey quickened her pace, tugging at Bessie's hand.

'O' course not. Who would?'

'I ain't no dolly-mop,' Janey said fiercely.

'Ma's right. Ye're too nice. S'pose it was all that schoolin'. Well, ye're a dummel. Bet he'd pay a tuppence for a quick screw in the alley.'

Janey only tried to get through the crowd faster. Bessie was right, she knew. She was too nice. A girl like her had no call to go dreaming of love, and trying to keep herself clean for it. Once she started standing on street corners, though, begging gentlemen to take her up against an alley wall, she'd lose all chance of anything else.

'Please, miss … just a moment!'

Janey hurried on, but felt a hand catch at her sleeve. Bessie stopped and turned, pulling Janey around with her.

'Ye're wantin' summat, gen'lemen?' Bessie asked, hand on one hip.

'Please don't be afraid,' Gabriel said. He stepped closer, his hand on Janey's arm. She could feel the heat of it through the fabric. 'I must paint you. You are a queen, a goddess.'

Janey felt something shift deep within her. To have such things said to her!

The other one said, 'You need not fear that we will be too forward or risk your reputation in any way. We are both betrothed to be married.'

Janey looked up quickly at that. Gabriel did not look best pleased at his friend's words. He fixed his eyes on her. 'Please let me paint you. I shall make your face the most famous in all of England.'

Janey hesitated.

'We shall pay for your time, of course,' Ned said.

'How much?' Bessie demanded.

When they told her, Bessie dug her elbow into Janey's side. 'Lawks-a-mussy!'

Janey was startled. For a moment, she was sorely tempted. It was a lot more money than she earned with her sewing and her scrubbing. But it felt too dangerous. She had seen desire in a man's eyes all too many times before. Growing up in the same room as her mother and father, and spending her childhood begging on the streets, Janey had no illusions about sex. She had seen it and heard it and smelt it most days since she was a babe.

But Gabriel was not like the men she knew. He came from a different world. She did not know the rules of that world. And Janey feared for her heart. Bessie might be happy to have a quick tumble in return for a threepenny bit, but Janey knew it would never be that easy for her. Since she was a little girl, she had always taken things hard. Why should love be any different?

Janey shook her head. 'I be mortal sorry,' she said again. 'I can't.'

'If you change your mind ...' Gabriel said, and offered her the card again. She took it, and pushed it into her pocket.

Gabriel took Janey's hand, bowing low over it.

'I will see you tomorrow, I hope.' Then he turned her hand, peeled back her glove, and kissed the hollow of her bare palm. It shook her like a bolt of lightning. With a mischievous grin and a wave of his beaver hat, he and his friend disappeared into the crowd.

Janey stood, motionless. Her palm was tingling.

Bessie was agog. 'What a swell. Ye'll let him paint ye, won't ye, Janey? If paintin' is what he really wants.' She giggled.

Janey shook her head. She drew out the card in her pocket and, without looking at it, tore it into a dozen tiny pieces.

3

The Swell
Autumn 1857

It was too much to hope that Bessie would keep her trap shut.

All the way home she sang: 'Janey's got a swell, Janey's got a swell.'

'Please don't tell Ma,' Janey begged, but her sister only tossed her head and said, 'An' why no'? She'll be reg'lar raw to think o' all that stub ye could've got.'

'That's why,' Janey whispered.

Bessie told their mother as soon as they got through the door. Annie gave Janey a back-hander across the face. 'Ye think ye're goin' to get a better offer? Think again, ye numbskull! A girl like ye ain't got that many chances. Ye think I got yer father by actin' all coy? Nay! I had him in me bed in the first ten minutes I knew him, then had him to the church as soon as I had a babe in me belly.'

'An' look how well that turned out,' Janey said.

Her mother slapped her again. 'Watch yer cheek! Ye ain't too big to put over me knee ...'

'I think she is!' Bessie gurgled with laughter, and earned herself a clip over the ear.

'So listen up, ye dummel! Ye go an' give that swell what he wants tomorrer an' then ye bring back the stub to me, do ye hear? An' ye do what ye can't please the man, for I can promise ye now, there ain't that many out there that'll want a great hummocking lass like ye.' Her mother gave her another sharp slap, for good measure, then lay back down on her pallet, in high spirits at the thought of all the money Janey would earn the next day.

Her cheek and ear stinging, Janey took off her good dress and hung it on the peg, then unhooked her stays. Once she was dressed only in her chemise, she lay down on her pallet, turned her back and pulled her tattered quilt over her head. Bessie was humming one of the songs from the show as she unrolled her stockings. Janey pressed her fingers into her ears. Her eyes smarted with unshed tears.

It was almost her eighteenth birthday, and her mother wanted her to mark it by selling her body to some foreign gent.

Janey supposed she may as well start selling what some swells simply took for free.

Janey washed herself as best she could in a bucket, and put on a clean chemise. She forced a comb through her heavy crimped hair and pinned it back. She needed a great many hairpins to keep it up. Then, dressed in her Sunday frock, she walked to George Street. Her steps lagged. She kept her arms crossed tightly about her ribs.

It was another warm autumn's day, with the domes and spires of Oxford gleaming in the sun. Pigeons hopped everywhere. When Janey was a little girl, she had often netted a pigeon for their dinner pot. In the darkness she would climb up the walls and creep over the roofs, looking for the birds roosting along the ridge. They would hear her coming and start to flap their wings and squawk. Janey would leap on them, seizing their warm bodies in her hands, trying to keep free of their raking claws. Their little hearts would drum frantically against her fingers. She would have to wring their necks, quick, before pity overcame her.

Her heart was drumming that fast now.

'Just make sure he pays ye!' had been her mother's only birthday wish for her.

Janey's steps slowed.

'I say! It's you.'

Janey turned at the sound of the voice. It was Ned Jones, the tall young man with the floppy fair hair.

'Gabriel will be so pleased to see you. He was gutted when you didn't come. Gutted.'

'I be sorry … 'twas my Ma. She was a-feared …'

'I understand. I can't tell you how many other mothers feel the same. We are always trying to reassure them we have no ill intent. Would you like me to come and speak to your father? I would not like him to be uneasy about you.'

Janey did not know what to say. Nervously she dipped her head, and took him to the stables at the King's Head. Ned said all that was proper, astonishing Robbie Burden whose daughters had been out working and begging in the streets since they were bairns. Robbie frowned, grunted something, and turned back to his work currying a fine bay with three white hocks. Ned looked startled, but took the grunt as agreement.

'Well, then … I guess that's all right,' he said to Janey. 'Gabriel's at the Oxford Union now. It's only a few minutes' walk away. Will you come?'

Janey nodded. Gripping her hands into knots, she followed him along the street. They turned at Cornmarket Street, and soon wended their way through to Frewin Court, where the Oxford Union had their debating rooms.

'It's sort of a place where fellows can go and argue about things you're not allowed to talk about in the colleges,' Ned explained. 'An acquaintance of ours built the library there, and Gabriel thought it was just crying out for some paintings on the wall. So here we are. For most of us, it's our first real commission. Well, sort of. We aren't being paid. But it could lead to bigger things. And in the meantime, we're having such a jolly time.'

Ned gave Janey a smile of pure joy. She gazed at him in amazement. He seemed so young and so naïve. She wondered if her brother might have turned out like this, if things had been different. Will was a good four years younger than this lanky artist, but he looked much older and harder.

They came into a sunny garden with a linden tree scenting the air sweetly. Ned gestured towards a grand building made of red brick, with a steep slate roof with windows shaped like flowers cut into it.

Ned led her inside the front door, and into a long oblong chamber. It had a high vaulted ceiling, with scaffolding built up to it. Paint-stained dust sheets covered the floor and were draped over the lower walls. In the centre of the room was the most extraordinary fireplace Janey had ever seen. It was double-sided, with two hearths facing either half of the room, but it did not have a chimney. Janey could not think where the smoke could possibly go. The flat marble top was crowded with tubes of paint, empty soda bottles, teacups, and jars of dirty water stuck with paintbrushes.

The upper wall was set with ten bays, each pierced with two flower-shaped windows. Janey could see shapes and colours had been laid in patterns in some of the bays, with here and there a figure or a face or tree taking shape. Tall double windows lined the far wall. It was gloomy inside, though, as the glass had all been whitewashed.

Young men were busy mixing paint on their palettes, standing at an easel and sketching, or up on the scaffolding, painting the ceiling. They had all been laughing and talking, but as Janey came in they fell silent, drawing close to look at her. She felt uneasy, and gripped her skirt with both hands.

'Fellows, this is … why, forgive me, I do not know your name!'

'Janey,' she whispered. 'Janey Burden.'

'Miss Burden, let me introduce you to the fellows.' One by one, Ned went around the circle, naming each of the artists.

'This fellow with the grand beard has the equally grand name, John Roddam Spencer Stanhope, to match his grand lineage. We call him Roddy, though. He is painting Sir Gawaine and the Damsels, and so he'll be extra pleased to see you since he doesn't have any damsels to paint.'

Roddy bowed his head in greeting. He was a handsome young man, with a magnificent dark beard. His clothes were very fine, and he seemed older than the youthful Ned.

'This is Val Prinsep.' Ned indicated a tall, well-built youth dressed in a loose white cotton shirt, the sleeves rolled up to the elbow and revealing burly, brown arms. 'He's our ox, the one we call on to heave anything about.'

Val nodded at Janey, his eyes bright with curiosity.

'The one up on the scaffolding is John Hungerford Pollen. He's helping out with some of the decorative work on the ceiling.' A tall man with an austere face bowed to Janey, then turned back to his work.

Ned then gestured to a smiling young man with abundant dark hair, eyes as bright as blackberries, and cheeks ruddy with good health.

'This is Arthur Hughes. He's the only one of us who really knows what he's doing. He had his first picture hung at the Royal Academy when he was only seventeen, so he's rather an *enfant terrible* ... or rather, he was, for as you can see he's quite old and stout now.'

'My wife feeds me too well,' Arthur replied, with a smile. 'You don't mind if I get back to work, do you, Miss Burden? For I have a hankering to get back to her as soon as I can.'

He returned to his painting, whistling, and Ned whispered, 'He married his favourite model, the most beautiful girl called Tryphena Foord. They're so ridiculously happy, we had great trouble getting Arthur to come.'

Janey stared at him in amazement. One of these artists had married his model? She had never imagined such a thing.

At that moment, the door banged open and Gabriel came in. 'All is well! We have sandwiches, so none of you need faint and fall off the scaffolding.'

He stopped short at the sight of Janey. So too did the young man behind him. He was not much above middle height, with a tousled mop of exuberantly curling hair, wearing a grubby shirt buttoned awry. His arms were full of soda bottles and brown paper packages.

'You came,' Gabriel said simply. He walked towards her, both hands held out. 'I am so glad. I need you. No-one else could possibly be my queen, once I had seen you.'

Janey did not know what to do with her hands. It did not matter. Gabriel reached her side, untucked her hands from her skirts, and held them in both of his. 'Please, come and sit.'

Janey sat where he directed her, on a wooden stool drawn up near the whitewashed window. Gabriel took her face in his hands, turning her towards the light. 'Did I not say she was a wonder? The most stunning of all stunners.'

The young man with the curls was motionless, staring at her.

'Miss Burden, this is my dear friend William Morris,' Ned said. 'We call him Topsy, on account of his hair.'

'And because he grow'd and grow'd,' Gabriel said with a grin.

Janey did not understand what they meant. It was obviously some kind of joke.

'Have you met all the fellows?' Gabriel said. 'Seven of us again. It's a new Pre-Raphaelite Brotherhood.'

Ned and Topsy both glowed with pleasure at the remark. 'Better get back to work,' Gabriel said. 'Ned, I won't need you to sit for me now that my Stunner is here. You can go and work on old Merlin.'

Reluctantly the two younger men left him, taking sandwiches and drinks around to the others, then climbing up the scaffolding to work at different bays. Topsy was painting what looked like sunflowers, while Ned was working on what seemed to be an old man with a long white beard.

Gabriel brought over an easel, and dragged some pencils out of his coat pocket.

'If you will just sit still for me, I will do some studies of your face,' he told her. 'I am painting a scene from *Le Morte d'Arthur*, and was racking my brains about what to do about Queen Guenevere. I did not want her to be golden haired. I am so tired of painting golden hair. Besides, she was a tragic Celtic queen. Her hair should be dark and heavy, her eyes blue and full of sorrow. As soon as I saw you, I knew you would be perfect.'

As he spoke, his pencil was flying over the paper. Curious, Janey followed the movement of his hand with her eyes. 'Sit still,' he said. 'Look down, as you were before.'

Janey tried to remember how she had been sitting. He came to stand beside her, taking her face in his hands and tilting it to the side and down. 'Perfect,' he said, low and intimate in her ear, before going back to his easel.

Janey was flushed and breathless. She sat quietly, staring at a blotch of paint on the floor.

'Do you know the story of Queen Guenevere?' he asked.

She shook her head, then remembered she had to stay still. 'Nay.'

'I've only just read it. Ned and Topsy are mad about it, and showed it to me. It's perfect for a series of paintings like this.' Gabriel began to tell her the story. Janey listened, entranced. Swords in stones, and wizards trapped in hawthorn trees, and a queen who loved her husband's bravest knight, and a quest for the cup said to be used at the Last Supper and able to heal all ills. She had never heard anything like it.

When Gabriel reached the end of the story, he said gently, 'I have done enough for today, thank you, Miss Burden. You can stand up now and stretch. You must be stiff, you have been sitting still so long.'

Janey stirred and stood up. To her amazement, the long room was lit now by candles. A fire had been kindled in the fireplace. Topsy and Ned were toasting bread and cheese on long-handled forks, and Arthur was heating up a jug of spiced wine with a hot poker. The smell was delicious.

'Come and have something to eat and drink,' Gabriel said. 'I was so eager to draw you, I have been a very bad host.'

Janey hesitated, but he smiled at her, holding out his hand to her. She took it and let him draw her closer to the fire, before pouring her a cup of the mulled wine.

No-one had ever pulled out a chair for Janey before, or served her with a courtly bow. No-one had ever told her that she looked like a queen. She felt quite dazzled and off balance.

Gabriel passed her toasted bread, brown and bubbling with cheese. Janey ate hungrily. In moments it was gone, and Gabriel made her some more. He watched her eat every mouthful. Janey was aware she should not eat with such gusto, but she was hungry and the food was good. She ate till she was bursting, and still Gabriel urged more upon her. At last she had had enough. She shook her head, smiling, and wiping her mouth with her sleeve. Gabriel sat back with a sigh, gazing at her with his large, dark, melancholy eyes that seemed to want to devour her.

Arthur poured her some more of the hot mulled wine, then went to play some card game with the other artists on the other side of the double-fronted fireplace. Janey knew she should go home. It was getting dark outside. But she was so warm and comfortable, and the thought of having to return to the evil-smelling hovel she shared with her mother and sister filled her with dismay.

'Topsy, read us one of your grinds,' Gabriel said, stretching out his boots to the low flames.

'Topsy's a poet,' Ned told Janey. 'One day he'll be a great name, like Tennyson or Wordsworth.'

Topsy went red. He pulled a handful of crumpled pages out of his coat pocket. 'This is just what I came up with last night,' he said. He looked at Janey shyly. 'It's called "The Defence of Guenevere", and is told from the point of view of the queen.' He began to read in a loud voice:

> I was half mad with beauty on that day
> And went without my ladies all alone,
> In a quiet garden walled round every way;
> I was right joyful of that wall of stone,
> That shut the flowers and trees up with the sky,
> And trebled all the beauty to the bone ...

He read for a long time, but Janey did not weary of it. When at last he laid down the closely written pages, Topsy looked expectantly at Janey. 'Did you like it?'

She nodded. When his face fell, Janey tried to find the words to explain what she had felt. She laid one hand on her heart. 'It hurt me, here.'

Topsy's face lit up.

'I write poetry too,' Gabriel said. 'This is the poem I wrote for the painting I'm doing of Lancelot and Guenevere.' He stood up, lifted high one hand, and dramatically intoned:

> Lancelot lay beside the well:
> (God's Graal is good)
> Oh my soul is sad to tell
> The weary quest and the bitter quell;
> For he was the lord of lordlihood
> And sleep on his eyelids fell.

'Is "lordlihood" even a word?' Topsy asked.

'It is if I want it to be,' Gabriel answered loftily. He turned to Janey. 'I never knew such a fellow for churning out poems! Just because he got a degree from Oxford, Topsy thinks he knows all there is to know about words. He's not quite so skilled with the paintbrush, though. He was meant to be painting *How Sir Palomydes loved La Belle Iseult with exceeding love out of measure, and how she loved him not but rather Sir Tristram.* But we have renamed the piece *Sudden Indisposition of Sir Tristram, recognisable as Collywobbles by the pile of gooseberry skins beside him*, for the poor man is so green.'

He laughed, and Ned joined in. Topsy's ears turned red, but he did not retort. He only gazed at Janey. 'I could paint better if I had you as my model. Your beauty would make the whole thing glow. Will you sit for me too?'

'If ye like,' Janey replied shyly, then saw that Gabriel was frowning at Topsy.

'Hang on, I saw her first,' he objected.

'Actually, I did,' Ned said. 'But such beauty cannot be confined to just one canvas. It must be shared with the world.' He gave Janey the sweetest smile, and bent forward to refill her cup.

4

One Sweet Hour
Autumn–Winter 1857

Humming to herself, Janey hurried along Broad Street. Her skirts billowed behind her in the wind.

She caught a glimpse of her reflection in a shop window. For a moment, she did not recognise herself.

It was partly her new dress which she had bought at the markets. It was also, however, because she was standing tall. Gabriel had told her so many times that she looked like a queen, Janey was beginning to walk like one.

For the first time, Janey believed she might be beautiful.

If one did not think there was only one kind of beauty.

Janey kept walking, thinking about this. All her life, she had thought that one had to be small and fair and dainty to be pretty, like the Queen when she was young. Attractive women had smooth pale hair, soft round cheeks, rosebud mouths, little white helpless hands.

Yet what if a woman was allowed to be tall and strong and capable? What if a man did not mind a woman who could meet their gaze straight on, or even look down on them? What kind of world would that be?

It was not the world that Janey now lived in.

But perhaps these passionate young artists, with their old-fashioned ideas of chivalry and their odd notions of beauty, were trying to create a different world. If so, it was a world Janey wanted to belong to.

Topsy met her at the entrance to the courtyard, and took her basket from her. 'I've bought the most wonderful book,' he told her. 'Can't wait to show you. It's an old medieval missal. Got the most marvellous paintings in the margins.'

He drew her into the dimly-lit hall, and cleared a space on the fireplace to show her an ancient parchment book. Each page had been decorated with vivid images of monks with tonsures and brown robes, working amidst trees and flowers and beasts.

'It must be right old,' Janey said in wonder.

'It is,' Topsy agreed.

'Look at the little mousen there! Ain't they sweet?' Janey cried, then silently cursed herself. She should have said mice. That's what educated people said.

Topsy did not laugh at her. He just said gravely, 'And see the cat? Waiting to pounce? The monk who drew it must've had a cat of his own. Don't you think? To get its posture so right.'

'It must've cost a mortal lot.'

'Well, yes. But I've got rather a lot of tin, you know. And what's money for, if not to save beautiful old things like this that might otherwise be lost?'

Janey gazed at him in amazement. Topsy did not look rich. His clothes were rumpled and stained with paint, his stout boots were scuffed, and his sleeve was missing a button. Janey had always assumed that Gabriel was the rich one. Yet she remembered now that it was always Topsy being sent off to buy new paints, or to fetch them supper, or to pay the boy who served them.

'I buy a lot of their paintings too,' Topsy said, nodding at the other artists busy about their easels. 'I bought Arthur's painting *April Love*. I bought five of Gabriel's. Paid two hundred guineas for the lot. Bought one of his friend Bruno's too. Fellow is awfully hard up. Paid forty guineas for it. I also bought Ned his own copy of *Morte d'Arthur*. Poor chap was going into a bookshop each day to read it. Too poor to buy it. So I bought it for him.'

'Ye're right kind … I mean, very kind.'

'I'm rich. They're poor.' Topsy spoke gruffly. The tips of his ears had turned red. 'Got something else to show you.'

He found a large parcel, tied up with twine. He tried to undo the knot, lost patience, and ripped it open. Two dresses slithered out. Both were of medieval design. One was pale green with long hanging sleeves, lined with tapestry. The other was made of rose-patterned brocade, with gilt-buttoned red sleeves that turned back to show the black silk lining.

'For you.' He could not look at her.

'They're beautiful.' Janey caught them up, thrilled.

'Costumes. For the paintings.'

Holding the dresses up against her, she stammered some thanks.

At that moment, Gabriel came in from the side-chamber. His plum velvet coat was wet through, and he was trying to dry himself with an old towel. Janey was surprised. It had not rained that day.

She looked at him questioningly. Gabriel said, with an annoyed look, 'Some students thought it'd be a lark to drench us all with buckets of dirty water. Apparently they took exception to our noise.'

Janey went to him swiftly, taking the towel from him so she could mop him dry. 'Ye'll catch yer death!' She began to tousle his damp curls. She was so tall, he did not need to bend his head to her. She could smell the scent of his skin. Something fresh like lemons. He met her eyes. She let her hands fall and stepped away, feeling that familiar confusion he always aroused in her.

'They are right, though. Those students. It is noisy in here. And I should get changed. Though I can't be fagged to go home and then come all the way back again. Miss Burden, would you mind very much if we worked back at my lodgings today?'

'Nay,' she answered uncertainly.

'Good,' he answered, and picked up the pale green medieval dress. 'Shove this in your basket, and let's be going.'

Janey did as she was told. As Gabriel led her out of the debating hall, he shot a look of triumph back over his shoulder at Topsy, standing forlornly by the fireplace, his arms full of rose brocade. Janey looked back too, apologetically.

'It's freezing out here,' Gabriel cried. 'Let's get you somewhere nice and warm.'

The words were innocent enough, but his tone made them suggestive. Janey followed him along, her heart beginning to thud again. They reached George Street, and he showed her into their rooms with a flourish of his hat.

It was a terrible mess. Books piled haphazardly, clothes everywhere, dirty plates and cups on the side tables, pages covered in sketches on the floor and pinned to the wall. Gabriel showed no signs of embarrassment. He flung his hat on the couch, and began to loosen his stock. Janey tensed.

'I'll just go and get changed. That's Ned's room there. Do you want to put on old Topsy's dress? Then I can do some studies of you.' Gabriel pointed out a door to her, then went, whistling, into another room.

Bewildered, Janey changed into the green medieval dress. It clung to her figure in a way the fashions of the day did not. She could not wear her stays underneath. She felt her old awkwardness return. When Gabriel came out, dressed in trousers and a loose shirt, he stared at her. 'You look beautiful.' His voice was rough.

Janey stood, waiting, sick with anxiety, but Gabriel only pinned some fresh paper to the easel, and began to draw her. Janey hung her head, not understanding why there was such a lump in her throat.

'You always looks so sad,' Gabriel said. 'Do you not want to sit? Just throw all that stuff on the floor. Wouldn't you be more comfortable?'

Janey sat and looked down at her hands. What was wrong with her? She should be glad he did not want to touch her. She had been dreading the day.

She remembered he was betrothed. 'What she like? Yer girl?'

Gabriel's smooth swift strokes came to a halt. He looked at her quickly, then looked away, colour mounting his smooth olive cheek.

'Is she pretty?'

'Not pretty,' Gabriel said after a moment. 'Striking. Unusual.' He began to draw again, more slowly. 'She was very beautiful once. Before …'

He spoke so soft Janey could hardly hear him. 'Before?' she repeated.

'She's been ill. We thought she was sure to die … oh, so many times. We all thought she had consumption. Her brother died of it … and she got so thin and weak … but the doctors say it's not consumption.'

Janey's elder sister Mary had died of consumption. She remembered the hacking cough, the flushed cheeks, the bones protruding through her skin.

'Then what is it?'

Gabriel shrugged. 'No-one knows. Dozens of doctors, and they all say different things. She has no appetite. If only she could keep some food down! When she can eat, she regains some strength … but even the thought of food makes her ill.'

Janey felt sharp pity for her. How awful, to be sick all the time. To always be wondering when you'd die.

'I love her, I do,' Gabriel whispered, after a long silence. 'But … I get so tired of her always being sick. She's like … like a succubus.'

Janey did not know what that meant. She looked at him enquiringly.

Gabriel gave a tired laugh. 'I cannot explain. She clings on to me with all her strength, but … well, in other ways she's as cold as ice. We've barely touched in months, and when we do … I feel she's enduring me.'

Janey did not know what to say.

'Enough of Lizzie!' he said with an effort. 'I am here to escape it all. Please let's not talk about her. Let's talk about you. I want to know everything about you.'

Janey swallowed. Her hands fidgeted together. 'There's naught t'know.' He started to protest, and she summoned a smile for him. 'Really. I'd much rather ye told me more about what ye're paintin'.'

His face lit up. At once his hands began to sketch shapes in the air. 'I'm painting Sir Lancelot. You remember. The lord of lordlihood. He wants to enter the chapel of the Holy Grail, but he cannot. He has sinned because of his forbidden desire for the queen; he is not pure enough. So he sleeps and he dreams of Guenevere. She stands before him in the boughs of an apple tree, in her green dress. Above him hangs his shield with a snake writhing upon it. On the other side will be an angel. Ned's been sitting for Lancelot. He really does have the face of some kind of medieval knight, don't you think? And there should be lilies ... and wings of flame ...'

Janey listened, enraptured. Once again the hours sped past. Then Ned and Topsy came home. While they made tea, and teased Gabriel, Janey quietly tidied the room.

'It's not much of a place,' Topsy said to her apologetically, as she piled all the books neatly, largest to smallest.

She looked at him in amazement. They each had their own room, and shared a sitting-room and a small square of cobblestones where they could sit in the sun and read. Janey longed with all her heart for a place half as small.

That afternoon she sat and sewed on missing buttons, while Gabriel and Ned sketched her and Topsy read aloud from *Le Morte d'Arthur*.

She had never felt so content.

The next few weeks flew past. Topsy wrote poetry and painted sunflowers, Ned drew caricatures of his friends and wrote long letters to his own little Stunner, waiting for him in London, and Gabriel drew Janey again and again.

One day Topsy came to the debating hall in a state of high excitement. He had drawn up a design for a medieval helmet, and a long jerkin of small linked metal rings that he called a surcoat. He had taken the design to a forge near the castle, and the smith had made them for him. Topsy hurried behind a screen to try it all on. He looked like a king out of a painting, Janey thought admiringly, when he came out. The surcoat reached his knees, and he had drawn up the hood so it framed his face. Everyone clustered around him, fingering the fine work of the chain mail.

'Put the helmet on,' Gabriel said.

With some difficulty Topsy pulled it over his head. Gabriel promptly slammed the visor down so he could not see. Topsy tried to lift it, but could not manage it. Then he tried to take the helmet off, only to find it jammed on the chainmail hood.

Dancing about, bellowing with rage, Topsy tried to drag the helmet off, while all his friends stood by and roared with laughter. Janey came to his rescue. Holding on to the rim of the helmet, she pulled one way and Topsy pulled the other, until at last the helmet came free. Topsy fell back on to his bottom, the mail ringing like a hammer on a horse's shoe.

Grinning, Gabriel helped him up. 'How ever did they fight in all that?'

'They would have had squires to help them get it off and on,' Topsy growled, very red in the face.

'I think you made the helmet a little too small,' Ned said, his face still alight with amusement.

'It's not the helmet that's too small, it's Topsy's head that's too big,' Gabriel said at once, making them all laugh again.

Janey thought they were unkind, but Topsy took all the teasing in good part. He put the helmet down, but wore the surcoat all day, even to climb up on to the scaffolding to work away doggedly at his painting of Sir Tristram (whose face, Janey had to admit, was rather green).

The paintings were progressing slowly, since so much time was spent talking, telling jokes and playing pranks on each other. The artists began to call their project 'The Jovial Campaign', in mimicry of the battles of medieval knights. Gabriel was the acknowledged king, and all the other artists his faithful followers. They laughed at his jests, adopted his way of speaking, and tied their stocks in the same careless knot.

Both Gabriel and Ned had a talent for caricature, and soon little cartoons of Topsy were sketched in the dark corners behind the beams or scratched into the whitewash that covered the windows. There were also many sketches of a small rotund animal that looked rather like a beaver without a tail.

'It's a wombat,' Gabriel explained to her. 'The most absurd and comical of all God's creatures. They have one in the zoo at Regent's Park, and I go and visit it whenever I'm in town. Did you know it has a sort of big pocket in which it carries its babies? Only it carries them backwards. So when one goes waddling past, you can see the baby's dear little face sticking out underneath the mother's ... ahem ... tail.'

Janey did not know whether to believe him or not.

Friends often caught the train from London, delaying the work even further. They sprawled about the debating hall, playing cards or arm-wrestling, or dressing up in Topsy's armour so someone could paint them. Sometimes they clambered up the scaffolding, a brush in hand, to splash some paint around.

'Are they all artists too?' Janey asked.

'Some of them,' Gabriel said. 'The others just wish they were.'

Janey was never invited out to lunch but she often ate supper with them, sitting around the fire, listening to Topsy read out the latest stanzas of his poems. He was polishing them up in the hope of finding a publisher, and would often stop mid-sentence to change a few words, or add in another syllable. He had an astonishing ability to come up with rhymes at the drop of a hat. Janey had never heard the like.

One day a burly figure with an immense wiry beard arrived to spend the day. His name was Brown, but everyone called him Bruno. He had a gruff way of speaking, and stared at Janey with beetling brows. His presence had a dampening effect on everyone. Even Gabriel was quiet, and barely looked at or spoke to Janey the whole time his friend was there. Janey was hurt, but Ned told her afterwards that Bruno's baby son had died only a few months earlier.

'Bruno was utterly devastated, and Gabriel too. He was little Arthur's godfather, along with Lizzie ...' He stopped what he was about to say, adding uncomfortably, 'So you see, we're all very sorry for poor old Bruno.'

Janey nodded. It must be very awful to lose a baby. But she wished Gabriel had explained it all to her, and not been so cold. She was afraid Gabriel's friends must think her a figure of fun, dressing up as a queen and playing pretend like a maundering child.

A few days later, Janey went to the hall as usual, only to find Gabriel had not turned up to work that day. Ned told her he had received a letter that had worried him.

'Does he ... does he no' need me fer today?' Janey asked anxiously.

'I'm sorry, I don't know,' Ned said, standing with one hand on the ladder, his other holding a palette of freshly mixed colours. 'I would think not. Perhaps you can enjoy the day off.' He smiled at her, and began to climb the ladder up to the roof.

Janey looked about disconsolately, not knowing what to do. After a moment, she tied on her bonnet again and went out into the raw November day. Everything was grey and damp and blackened with soot. A hansom cab trotted past, splashing her with cold muddy water. Shivering, tucking her gloved hands into her sleeves, Janey hurried along Cornmarket Street. She passed the church of St Michael at the North Gate, and came to a halt at the corner. Broad Street was to her left, leading the way back to Hell's Passage. George Street was to her left, leading to Gabriel.

Janey turned left. Her steps quickened till she was almost running. She came to the door of the lodging-house and knocked timidly. The landlady let her in, recognising her with a grunt. She looked disapproving, as always. Janey went to knock on Gabriel's door.

He looked tired and dispirited, his eyes shadowed and his curls rumpled. He let Janey in with a muttered apology. His trunk stood in the centre of the room, and clothes hung out the sides.

'I'm so sorry, I have to go,' he said. 'I have just heard from Lizzie. You know ...' His voice trailed off and he sank down into a chair.

Janey gazed at him in dismay. 'Is she sick again?'

'She says so. I can't help feeling she's heard some gossip about you, and is malingering.'

'Gossip? About me?' Janey's heart gave a weird hard thump.

He smiled at her wearily. 'Of course. Lizzie is friends with Bruno's wife. I knew as soon as I saw him that word would get back to her about you. Lizzie is very jealous. It doesn't matter that I haven't laid a finger on you, much as I want to.'

He wanted to? A tumult of emotion rushed through Janey. She did not speak, but just gazed at him, her hands clenched tightly before her.

Gabriel looked down at his own hands. He had tried to scrub them clean, but paint was still embedded in his cuticles.

'I wish I did not need to go!' The words burst from him. 'I wish I could stay here with you, Janey.'

He dropped his head into his hands, his fingers writhing through his hair. 'But I can't, I can't. I have to go to her. What if she died? I would never forgive myself.'

Janey went to him, and knelt before him, taking those restless, long-fingered hands in hers. 'I know ye have to go. But does it have to be right now? Couldn't … couldn't ye give me just a li'l space o' time?'

Gabriel looked down into her face. She raised herself up so she could press her mouth to his. He groaned and gathered her to him.

All Janey had ever wanted was someone she could love. She knew Gabriel could not stay. She knew he loved another. She knew she'd be sorry in the morning.

But she did not care.

She wanted just one sweet hour.

5

Victuals and Squalor
Winter 1857

Mrs Macdonald lay on her bed, propped up on pillows, clutching her smelling salts.

'It strikes me to my very heart,' she said. 'To think that this house, which has seen such deep sorrow, will soon be the home of a stranger!'

'Never mind, Mama,' Georgie said, bringing a cordial in a little glass to her mother's lips. Her mother drank it down, then dabbed at her eyes with her handkerchief.

'My dearest Carrie died, in this very room, on this very spot, and soon I shall never see it again. How many times have I dropped to my knees beside this bed, in agony, begging God for the strength to submit to his will and endure this loss that still wrings my heart?'

'Many, many times,' Georgie said.

'Yes, you are right. Many, many times. And now someone else will kneel here to pray and feel nothing of my anguish.'

'Perhaps it will be a good thing ... to start afresh?' Georgie ventured.

Her mother was horrified. 'How can you say such a thing? This room is sacred in my eyes ... this is the very last place on earth that her dear presence brightened ...' Mrs Macdonald began to weep again.

Her dutiful daughter dipped a clean handkerchief in lavender water and passed it to her.

Georgie was secretly delighted at the idea of moving from this narrow, damp house, nestled cheek by jowl with a dozen other houses just the same. Her father's new posting was in Marylebone, only a few blocks away from Regent's Park. Georgie and her sisters would have somewhere beautiful to walk every day. Best of all, it was only half an hour's walk away from Red Lion Square, where Ned was renting rooms with Topsy. Once they moved, she could perhaps see him several times a week. Her heart sang at the thought.

She had hardly seen Ned in recent months. He had been in Oxford with Topsy and Gabriel, painting some murals. Plump letters arrived several times a week, describing in humorous terms the fun and games they were getting up to and stuffed with caricatures of Topsy, tearing his hair out in rage.

As her mother sighed and laid the damp handkerchief over her eyes, Georgie sat down and drew one of Ned's letters out of her pocket. She had read it so many times it was already beginning to be worn at the creases.

I have from now till breakfast to write to you in, and I have no idea what now is, for after the most elaborate directions for being called early, which were strictly attended to, I turned over and dozed away like a pig and now I expect my usual morning tormentors, Rossetti and Pollen, who come in at about 8 o'clock to insult me – laugh at me, my dear – point the finger of scorn at me, address me by opprobrious names and finally tear blankets and counterpanes and mattresses and all the other things that cover me, from my enfeebled grasp …

Georgie smiled. How clearly she could hear Ned's voice in his written words. And each time she read the words 'my dear' a little thrill ran over her.

Her mother sighed heavily and lifted up the handkerchief. Georgie hurriedly hid the letter in her apron pocket.

'Why, oh, why must we be always moving?' Mrs Macdonald complained.

'That is the lot of a minister's wife.' Georgie was so glad that Ned had chosen a different vocation.

'I suppose I must be grateful that my poor dear Carrie was saved from the vale of tears that is this world,' Mrs Macdonald said tremulously.

'Yes, Mama,' Georgie answered, her thoughts far away.

Ned stayed much longer in Oxford than he had expected, and Georgie missed him constantly. Life was so drear and drab without him. It seemed to rain every day, and the new house in Beaumont Street was old and very draughty. There was nothing to do but practise the piano and watch for the postman.

A week or so before Christmas, however, he sent Georgie a note saying he was back in town and begging her and her sister Louie to come to tea. Mrs Macdonald was soothed and cajoled into giving permission, and Georgie brushed her straight hair till it shone and scrubbed at her face with a rough flannel to bring some roses into her pale cheeks.

She almost didn't recognise Ned at first. He was thinner than ever, and had grown a wispy beard and moustache. She hesitated a little on the threshold, but then he smiled at her and took her hand, and she knew him again.

Ned leant out the door to call down the stairs. 'Mary, can you bring us quarts of hot coffee, pyramids of toast, and multitudinous quantities of milk?'

'Yes, sir,' came the distant response, and he grinned and shut the door, leading them into the studio.

It looked as if a whirlwind had gone through it, with bits of medieval armour lying tumbled next to costumes and strange bits of jewellery. Easels stood about the room, to catch the best light at different times of the day, and canvases mounted on wooden frames were stacked against the walls. One elastic-sided boot lay in the middle of the floor, and a stand full of swords and spears was doubling as a hatstand. Books were piled haphazardly everywhere.

'Don't mind the tumble and rumble and jumble,' Ned said, waving his hand at the mess.

'Oh, I don't,' Georgie responded quite truthfully. She found it fascinating.

'Your beard looks like a goat's,' Louie said.

He stroked it thoughtfully. 'I think it makes me look like an artist. They are all very hairy, you know.'

'I do know! You sent all those cartoons of your friend Mr Morris. He has a lot of hair.'

'He does indeed. He is most unnaturally and unnecessarily curly. You should have been there one afternoon in Oxford. We managed to get him to sit still on the pretext that Bruno was going to paint him, but all the while Arthur Hughes was crouched behind him, quietly tying all his hair into knots. You should have seen his rage when he was at last allowed up and ran his fingers through his mop, like he always did!'

Louie regarded him rather dubiously, and said that surely Mr Morris must have felt Mr Hughes knotting his hair.

'You would think so,' Ned answered. 'But we had asked Tops to write us a poem while he was being painted, and so he was frowning furiously and gnawing the end of his pen and so had no attention left over for Arthur.'

'I would so like to meet Mr Morris again,' Georgie said wistfully. 'I saw him that one time at the Royal Academy exhibition, and he was so engrossed in the paintings he hardly noticed me at all.'

'Well, that's why you're here,' Ned said. 'Or one reason at least, apart from wanting to see you. I was thinking I might give a party. Gabriel is coming home to see his mother for Christmas, and Top is swinging past for a few days too, to see a chair he has designed for our apartment. I thought it'd be fun to have a shindig. But I'll need your help. I've never given a party before.'

'Neither have we,' Louie said at once. 'Unless you count temperance meetings.'

Ned looked at her in horror, then turned his gaze on Georgie. She laughed a little ruefully, and said, 'I'm sure we can help, though, Ned. What sort of party do you want to have?'

'One with all my friends, and something to eat and drink, and maybe some music. And I thought perhaps your mother might let you and your sisters attend?' He spoke hesitantly. 'It won't be a bachelor fling. I was planning to ask Bruno – Mr Brown, you know, and his wife, Emma – and Arthur Hughes and his wife, Tryphena, and maybe Gabriel's sisters would like to come too.'

Georgie felt a warm glow of pleasure. At last she was to meet some of Ned's friends!

The chair was extraordinary.

Huge and dark and medieval in design, it looked like something out of a fairytale. Georgie stared at it in awe, and wondered at the imagination that could conceive of such a thing.

Ned dashed off quick notes to everyone, inviting them to the party, and Georgie helped him address the envelopes, while Louie licked the stamps. He wrote to Bruno: *'Come tonight and see the chair, there's a dear old fellow – such a chair!!! Gabriel and Top hook it tomorrow, so do come. Hughes will come, and a Stunner or two to make melody. Come soon, there's a nice old chap – victuals and squalor at all hours, but come at 6.'*

Georgie very much liked being called a Stunner. Her most secret fear was that Ned would fall in love with one of the beauties that smiled out of so many of his friends' canvases. She thought it would just break her heart.

The guests began arriving promptly at six o'clock, and soon the room was crowded. Georgie met so many new people, her head was in a whirl. Arthur Hughes and his beautiful wife, Tryphena, who had hair the colour of a new guinea. The two Misses Rossetti were dowdily dressed, with dark severe hair, long sallow faces and large eyes of quite remarkable beauty. Ford Madox Brown was a bluff bear of a man with a great spreading beard and a kind, rather ponderous manner. His wife, Emma, pretty and plump, had a forced brightness about her and went straight to the hot gin punch, serving herself three glasses in rapid succession. Georgie remembered that Emma had lost two babies that year; her ten-month-old son, Arthur, and her unborn child a few weeks later. She tried not to judge her too harshly.

Georgie, of course, drank nothing but water. She had handed out far too many temperance pamphlets in her time not to be aware of the evils of alcohol. Ned was always making jokes about it, and liked to pour her water from a great height so it came into her glass with a sparkle and froth to it.

Topsy was there already, of course, but he paid Georgie as little attention as he had the first time he had met her. He was looking pale and drawn, she thought, and remembered that Ned said he had fallen head over heels with a girl he had met in Oxford. 'Being in love doesn't suit Topsy,' Ned had remarked mournfully. 'He's in the devil of a temper.'

Georgie had a taste of his temper a little later in the evening, when they all sat down to supper. The maid Mary had made them roast beef, which was rather dry and leathery, followed by plum pudding, which she had boiled in a bag in the old-fashioned way. It was rather small, Ned not having had much money for ingredients. Morris was furious. He impaled the pudding upon his fork, waved it about and bellowed at the top of his voice, 'Mary, do you call that a pudding?' When Mary popped in, wiping her damp hands on her apron, he hurled the offending pudding at her. She ducked, and the pudding crashed into a jug and smashed it to the ground.

For a moment there was a stunned silence, then Ned began to roar with laughter. Most of the men joined in, though Miss Maria and Miss Christina looked horrified, and Emma stared blearily into her punch glass.

Mary straightened up, picked up the hot pudding with her hands protected by her apron, and said cheerfully, 'It'll be fine if I dust it off. An' an extra serve of brandy custard will help fill up the corners fer you, Mr Morris. I know ye're a hungry feller.'

'He is indeed,' Ned said and slapped Topsy's belly.

Gabriel had not arrived in time for supper, but he came soon afterwards, dressed in his old plum velvet jacket with a purple scarf knotted loosely about his throat. His eyes were shadowed, and he seemed in an ill humour too. Called upon to admire the grand medieval chair, he said merely that it looked as if it were sturdy enough to bear Topsy's weight without breaking, then asked whether the odd box at the top was meant for keeping owls in.

Georgie played on a piano hired for the evening, then she and Alice sang old French songs. Everything passed off swimmingly, with Topsy's temper much restored by the extra-large serving of pudding and brandy custard.

As everyone was gathering up their coats and hats, ready to depart, Bruno took Gabriel's arm and shook it, asking gruffly, 'Well? How is Lizzie, old man? Could you not have brought her for the evening?'

Gabriel's face darkened. 'She's been ill, Bruno, terribly ill. The doctors are in a quandary. She just can't seem to keep any nourishment down.'

'Ah, I'm sorry to hear that,' Bruno said.

'So when are you two going to tie the knot?' Emma demanded, her words slurring just enough to be noticeable.

'It has been a while,' Bruno said apologetically.

'Four and a half years,' Emma said.

'Yes,' Gabriel answered after a moment. 'It has been too long. Far too long.'

'Maybe in the spring, then?' Bruno asked. 'When Lizzie is feeling better.'

'Maybe.'

Bruno flashed a smile at Ned and Georgie. 'Don't take a leaf out of Gabriel's book, Ned, and leave it too long! Marry this pretty lass just as soon as you can. You'll love being a married man, I promise you that.' He gave Georgie a flicker of a wink, then supported his wife's tottering steps out the door.

Gabriel scowled, thrust his fists into his pockets, and went out after them.

Georgie was blushing and smiling. Ned took her hand. 'I knew that they would all love you. Old Bruno was so interested in your wanting to paint. He said you can go to his studio and have lessons if you like. Isn't he a grand old fellow?'

Georgie agreed, in a little glow of happiness.

Ned drew a little closer, bending to whisper. 'And I've started to get a few commissions now, Georgie. I do so look forward to the days when we can be together and learn everything there is to know about art and life and love ...' His voice dropped on the final word, and he coloured. 'I imagine us living in some round tower by the sea, you and me, and maybe Topsy, and Louie ... painting and singing ...'

He moved even closer. Her heart pitter-pattering, Georgie daringly lifted her face for his kiss.

6

I Cannot Paint You
Winter 1857–58

Janey grieved for Gabriel with all of her heart.

She lay on her pallet, weeping till it felt as if her eyes would fall right out of her head. Days passed, and not even her mother's kick in the ribs would rouse her.

Eventually she had to get up, if only to try to find some way to make some money. She took in some sewing, and helped the laundress next door with the washing.

One day, soon after Christmas, there came a great hammering at the door. Janey thought it was probably the bum-bailiffs come again. She wished them luck finding anything to sell. Her mother yelled at them to go away. The hammering came again, louder.

Annie got up, shuffled to the door and opened it, swaying on her feet. 'Wha' you want?'

'I . . . I am looking for Miss Burden.'

Janey jolted upright. It was Topsy. Here in Hell's Passage.

She scrambled up, pushing back her great mass of tangled hair. She rushed to the door, thrusting in front of Annie who yawned and shambled back to her bed and her bottle of gin.

'Wha' is it? Wha' do ye want?'

He stared at her with shocked eyes. 'I wondered why you did not come and sit for us anymore.'

She shrugged. 'Gabriel's gone. I didn't think I'd be wanted no more.'

'I want you,' he said, very low.

She gazed at him with sombre eyes, afraid of his meaning.

'I made a mess of my mural. Val said my queen looked like an ogress. I want to try again. With you.'

Still she did not speak.

'I swear to you my intentions are honourable.'

After a long moment, she nodded her head. 'Just give me time to get ready.'

As she quickly washed her face and pinned up her hair, Janey imagined Topsy standing in the alleyway, smelling the cesspit, hearing the wailing of the sick baby next door, looking at the ramshackle huts with their make-shift roofs and crooked chimneys, and the sad collection of rags hung out to dry on the washing strings. She was so ashamed she could not speak to him once she came out. She followed him back to his lodgings, her eyes hot, her head bent.

Topsy was as quiet.

He wanted to paint Janey in the rose brocade dress. Once again, she was pretending to be a tragic queen, in love with a man who was not her husband. Her name was La Belle Iseult. She wore a garland of rosemary and convolvulus on her head, and was in the process of clasping a golden girdle about her hips, as if she had just risen from bed.

Standing there, the golden belt in her hands, Janey was acutely aware of the sensuality of her pose. She felt the weight of Topsy's gaze on her.

When Gabriel drew her, he had worked swiftly and surely, telling her old stories or quoting poetry to her, so all she had to do was stay still and listen, caught in a spell of enchantment.

It was very different being painted by Topsy. He cursed, he stamped about, he tore at his hair with his paint-stained hands, he groaned, he kicked over a brass jug, kicked it again. Sometimes he stood still for ages, trying to compose himself. When Janey said his name, he did not respond. It was as if he had slipped away to another place for a moment.

He could be rude and bearish at times, yet he was also unfailingly kind. He bought her an orange one day, after she had mentioned she had never tasted one, and peeled it for her. He passed her a small segment, bursting with juice. The taste of it was a revelation. Janey ate it greedily, then another, trying to think what it tasted like. Sitting with the sun on your back on a hot summer's day. Orange hawkweed growing out of a crack in a churchyard wall. The sound of singing in a hayfield as women raked the mown grass into piles. The glint of a new sovereign.

Topsy watched her face as she ate, pleased. The next day he brought her half-a-dozen oranges in a string bag, and she was able to eat one whenever she wished.

He did not find painting easy or joyful. Janey thought he only painted because Gabriel had said all poets must paint. What Gabriel said was law for Topsy.

It was bitterly cold. Snow flumped down all over Oxford, making it seem pure and clean. The icicles in the trees gleamed golden with light from the gas-lamps, and the sound of angelic singing drifted over the college walls. Janey wondered why Topsy stayed in Oxford. 'Ain't ye got no family?' she asked.

'Gosh, yes,' he answered. 'Far too many of them.'

'So don't they want ye home for Chris'mas?'

He was silent for a moment. 'I'd rather be here. But I will need to go soon.'

His words made Janey feel sad. She stood silently, the rosemary wreath on her head slowly withering.

On Candlemas Eve, everyone set lighted candles in their windows so that the city shimmered as if with fairy lights. Janey set a rushlight in the tiny window of her mother's shack, imagining that she was lighting a beacon for Gabriel to find his way home to her. But the rushlight burned down to ash, the days kept slipping away and still he did not come.

Ye're a dummel, she told herself. *Just stop lovin' him.*

But she did not know how.

Topsy was brusquer and kinder than ever. For Christmas, he had bought her an illustrated copy of Tennyson's poems, with woodcut drawings by many artists, including Gabriel and his friends Millais and Hunt, who Janey had not met. She thought it very beautiful and treasured it, though Topsy wondered why she would not take it home with her, leaving it in his rooms.

'To keep it safe,' she said.

Gabriel had given her a small pencil sketch he had drawn of her, dated and inscribed with what she thought must be Latin, as she had seen similar on the walls of old churches. She had kept it hidden away inside her mattress, afraid that her mother might burn it for warmth, or smear it with her dirty hands. She took it out now and slid it inside the book of poems, at a drawing by Gabriel of a woman on her knees praying, love letters scattered about her. Janey felt she knew what the woman in that poem felt.

Topsy had told her kindly that Gabriel was in Derbyshire with his betrothed. It was impossible not to wish that Gabriel realised he loved her instead, and came rushing back to sweep her off her feet and marry her. She even hoped, in her most secret heart, that Lizzie would die and release Gabriel. Janey was ashamed of these thoughts, and steadfastly pushed them away.

At least she had the memory of their brief time together to sustain her.

Spring came, and all the trees in the colleges budded with new leaves. The air was bright with birdsong. Janey was so restless she found it hard to sit still. Topsy took her out walking, telling her stories about his days in Oxford as a student, and how he had first met Ned. He did not ask about her childhood here. Janey thought he probably imagined it all too well.

One morning Janey went out to the forest to pick a bunch of sweet violets. She put them in a vase by the fire, in the sitting-room that was now as neat as a new pin, and smelt their delicate fragrance as she stood posing for him. She hoped that they masked the smell of the slum on her skin, which no amount of scrubbing ever washed away.

That afternoon she was making herself a new collar for her dress when Topsy stopped by her chair. 'You should embroider some violets on that. It'd look pretty.'

'I don't know how to do that,' Janey confessed. She had only ever been taught to do plain sewing. Hems and buttonholes and suchlike.

'Here, I'll show you.' Topsy went into his room and, most surprisingly, came out with a little basket full of coloured silk threads, scissors, a fat pink satin pin-cushion, and a round wooden frame which he unclasped and fitted Janey's linen collar within. He deftly threaded a needle with purple silk, put a dainty silver thimble upon his thick forefinger, and began to make tiny smooth stitches upon it. Slowly a small flower began to take shape upon the linen.

It made Janey smile to see the tiny needle in his big rough paw. 'I ain't never seen a man sewin' afore!'

'I like it,' Topsy said. 'It's a dying art. The architect I worked for here in Oxford had an interest in old embroideries done for churches. His sister was a fine craftswoman. She taught me. Nowadays so many things are made badly by machines. I like the idea of making beautiful things, slowly, with the hand.'

He showed her what he had done.

'I'd like t'do that,' she said shyly. 'Make beautiful things.'

'Here, I'll show you. The trick is to lay the stitches together as smoothly and closely as you can.'

Soon they were sitting side by side, heads bent close, Janey bursting with pride as a violet bloomed from the sharp point of her needle. The next day Topsy gave her a sewing basket of her own, filled with dozens and dozens of embroidery silks like a rainbow come to earth, and a book of embroidery patterns. Janey found that she loved nothing more than to sit quietly, carefully laying one colour down next to another, one stitch after another, till her cloth was alive with pictures.

Topsy's poems were published a month later. He was tense and anxious and mad with joy all at once. He held the little brown book as tenderly as a child, turning the pages – frowning and smiling and tugging at his beard in turn – stroking its leather binding as if it was alive. At last he gave it to Janey to read. She curled up in her favourite chair by the fire, and read it through from first page to the last.

The poems shook her to her core. Spare, strange, urgent, full of passion and fear and longing and heartbreak.

> Ah Christ! If only I had known, known, known;
> Launcelot went away, then I could tell …
> how all things would be …
> moan, and roll and hurt myself, and long to die …

He had looked inside the secret chambers of her heart and seen what she had tried to hide.

Janey could not see the words for the tears that swam in her eyes. She took a deep breath, dabbed them away, and read on, Topsy in an agony of impatience.

She closed the book, trying to compose herself. Topsy gazed at her hopefully. 'They're beautiful,' she whispered. Once again she did not know how to speak of her feelings. 'Ye're a great poet,' she managed.

Topsy turned away. When he spoke, of something quite different, his voice was gruff. But Janey knew she had pleased him.

That afternoon, he asked her to pose for him again. She stood, the golden belt hanging heavy in her hands. Words had been scrawled across the back of the canvas. She took a step closer and bent to read them.

Topsy had written: *I cannot paint you but I love you.*

Janey had been nine the first time a boy had dragged up her skirt and thrust his cock inside her. She had been coming home in the dusk, the few pennies she had earned screwed up in her handkerchief for safekeeping.

He had grabbed her and pushed her up against the wall, his arm across her throat. She had kicked him in the balls, as her brother had taught her, and managed to get a few paces away before he brought her down. He dragged her up, shoved her face into the wall, and had her skirt and chemise up about her waist in a moment. There was nothing she could do but endure, her face knocking into the rough stone again and again.

He was finished quickly enough. He wiped himself off on her skirts, then felt in her pockets till he came across the little hard knot in her handkerchief. He took it and strolled away, buttoning his trousers as he went.

Janey crept home, her face bruised and bleeding, fearful of what her mother would say about her empty pockets. Annie gave her a ringing blow on the side of the head and kicked her out into the night, telling her not to come home till she had got them something to eat. Janey had found herself a dark hole under a stoop and huddled there, crying. In the cold dawn, she had wandered the streets, begging, till someone took pity on her and gave her a ha'penny.

Janey tried to make herself invisible after that, but she was too tall and too arresting. Sometimes it was one of the slum bully-boys, wanting a quick rut. Sometimes it was a customer at the inn, coming across her scrubbing a floor and thinking her fair game. Most often it was a fine gentleman thinking a girl selling flowers on a street corner was also selling her body.

Janey had never really felt safe, not anywhere.

She looked at Topsy. She could not speak.

He knelt before her, taking one of her cold, clenched hands. 'I do love you most terribly. Won't you marry me? Let me look after you?'

She shook her head.

He got clumsily to his feet, and stood at the window, looking out on to the courtyard. 'He will not come back to you,' he said, after a while. 'He has been betrothed to this other girl for years now.'

'I know.'

'I don't expect you to love me like I love you. I know that would be too hard.'

She swallowed, looking down at her hands. So rough and red they were. How could a swell like him want to marry a slum girl like her?

'I cannot stay in Oxford any longer,' Topsy went on, speaking to his reflection in the glass. 'I've been here far too long as it is. But I cannot bear the thought of going away and not taking you with me. I couldn't sleep at nights for worrying about you.'

He halted, and she knew he was thinking of Hell's Passage. 'If you were cold or hungry or in danger … don't you see? If you married me, I could look after you. We could be comfortable together, like we've been these past months.'

They had been comfortable together. She had liked it very much, embroidering pretty flowers, listening to his poetry, drinking a glass of golden sherry with the pot roast he had ordered in from the landlady.

She wondered if he knew that she had given herself to Gabriel. It seemed impossible to tell him.

He had begun to pace, his hands clenched behind his back. 'I'd build you a house … in the country, with a garden and apple trees and roses … maybe we could have children one day ... little girls that look just like you …'

She thought of lying with him. They would be a strange couple. Her feet would stick out past his like her father's did over the edge of his mattress. And he was so broad and square. He'd be heavy on her.

But the bed would be soft and the sheets would be crisp and clean like new snow. And he was a gentle man, for all his bearishness. He would be kind to her. And she'd be safe.

Janey cleared her throat. 'Are ye sure? I ain't yer kind.' She imagined his mother's outrage, the dismay of his brothers and sisters. What would all his friends think? She imagined a long table, set with a spotless white tablecloth, and shining glasses, and gleaming china plates, and rows and rows of silver knives and forks and spoons, and all the people at the table staring at her because she did not know what fork to use. She imagined their faces when she opened her mouth and spoke. She imagined the snickers hidden behind white gloves, the laughing mouths. Topsy would not notice. He did not care what people thought of him. It was because he was rich. He could do what he liked.

But Janey cared. She cared dreadfully.

'You are my kind,' Topsy said passionately. 'Do you not love poetry and art and music and green growing things just as much as I do? Do you think it matters that you are poor? I have money enough for both of us. It's the beautiful shining soul of you that I love, not who your father is or where you grew up.'

A lump in her throat.

He came and took her hands. 'I'd do my best to make you happy, Janey ...'

Tears and smiles together. 'If ye're really sure ...'

'I have never been so sure of anything.'

He kissed her hands, and then he kissed her mouth. She nestled into his arms, with her head on his shoulder, thinking, *He's such a kind man, such a good man. I'm sure I'll come to love him in time.*

7

Running Mad
Spring 1858

Struggling. Screaming. Arms held down. Someone on her thighs. So heavy. Head forced back. Fingers digging into jaw. Cannot scream. Tube thrust into nostril. No! No! Up her nose, down her throat.

Gagging.

'Hold her still!' he ordered.

Cracking of eggshells. One. Two. Three. Four. Five. Six.

Sound of whisking.

One arm free. Grabbed tube. Tried to yank it out. Arm wrenched back. Tube forced deeper. Throat bruised.

Funnel in tube. Glug glug glug. Disgusting.

At last the tube pulled out. Her arms and lower body released. Lizzie twisted away. Gagging.

'If you vomit, we shall be forced to feed you again,' the doctor said.

She swallowed it down. Bitter as wormwood.

'Let her rest now. Feed her again in the morning. Six raw eggs in milk. Then the sulphur water therapy. I shall see her again tomorrow.'

The nurses nodded. Hard-faced bitches.

He went out, and the nurses packed away the feeding tube and funnel. One washed Lizzie's face with icy-cold water and a rough flannel. Another smoothed out the rumpled sheets and blankets and tucked her in so tightly she could scarcely move a finger.

Their heels rapped loudly on the wooden floor as they marched out, in single file, proudly bearing their instruments of torture.

'You may go in now,' one said.

Lizzie shut her eyes. Her throat hurt.

She heard the tentative sound of Gabriel's feet, and smelt the familiar scent of his eau de cologne as he leant over her. 'Are you awake?' he whispered.

Lizzie did not answer. She wondered how much he could hear from the other side of the door. Her screaming and thrashing? The awful glugging?

How could he let them do it to her?

After a while, she heard the faint sound of him sitting down. She stayed motionless, arms restricted by the tight bedclothes. She imagined all the raw egg and milk roiling in her stomach. Once again she gagged involuntarily. She forced herself to swallow.

Lizzie had tried to do without Gabriel, she really had. She had spent the summer with her cousins in Sheffield, going to chapel like a good girl, visiting ancient bedridden aunts, helping out with the darning. She had expected Gabriel to come and find her, begging her pardon and taking her home. Yet the months had slipped away.

She had some money. The rich American had bought her painting of *Clerk Saunders* for thirty-five guineas. She had a horrible suspicion he had only bought it to be kind, for the art critics in New York had singled out her painting for particular abuse. One had said it was 'Pre-Raphaelitism run mad'.

Those words bothered her. Sometimes Lizzie was afraid that *she* was running mad. People looked at her strangely. Made excuses for her. 'She's delicate,' her aunt Sarah would explain to visitors. Lizzie found it hard to manage with so many people worrying over her all the time. She asked if she could have a tray in her room. That made them think she was stuck up. But Lizzie could not bear to have people watch her eat. She fed most of it to the mice and the birds in the garden.

When the winter term began at the local School of Art, Lizzie began going to the women's classes twice a week. 'I am used to having Mr Rossetti as my teacher, of course,' she had told the principal, a snub-nosed young man named Mr Mitchell. 'But he has been commissioned to paint some murals in Oxford and so I thought I would come north for a while. Visit my kin. London was just so thin of company. Mr Ruskin, of course, has been busy about Mr Turner's legacy, else I would have stayed to work with him.'

'You know Mr Ruskin?' The question had been asked with awe.

'Oh, yes, indeed. Why, he has been so kind as to extend his patronage to me. Of course, now that my work is touring in America I no longer need it, but we have remained friends.'

'Miss Siddal, it shall be an honour to have you frequent our humble school. May I ask, have you met Mr Millais?'

'Frequently,' she answered. 'And Mr Holman Hunt too.'

'Is he as ... temperamental ... as they say?'

'Indeed, yes. We all call him the Maniac, you know.'

He had drawn his chair closer. 'Tell me more, Miss Siddal!'

The other girls were jealous of Mr Mitchell's attentions. They began to tease her, just like the other apprentice milliners used to do. They called her Carrots or Freckles or String-bean. And they made nasty comments about her clothes. Lizzie thought it was ridiculous to wear a crinoline while painting. One could scarcely reach the easel with all those hoops in the way. And she had no need of a corset to give her a waist measurement of only sixteen inches. Hers had been less than that for years.

In September, Mr Mitchell organised a trip to Manchester to see the Great Exhibition. Lizzie had dug out the clothes she had bought in Paris, and turned up in grand style. Mr Mitchell offered her his arm, and she swept on to the train in front of all those jealous cats.

In Manchester, though, a stranger accosted her as they strolled around the exhibition. He was a dapper young gentleman, with dark curls carefully combed through with sweet-scented macassar oil and a fluffy little moustache. Around his neck, he wore a flamboyant gilt cross hanging from a red ribbon.

'I say, aren't you Miss Siddal?' he asked.

Lizzie turned warily. 'Yes.'

'I recognised you from Mr Millais's *Ophelia*. And, of course, from so many of Mr Rossetti's paintings. You are indeed his favourite model.'

Lizzie looked around quickly, to make sure no-one was listening. But of course, they all were, wide-eyed.

'Charles Augustus Howell is my name. It's a pleasure to meet you … though, of course, I feel as if I know you, seeing your face depicted on so many canvases.'

She felt sick and dizzy. A few of the girls were whispering and laughing. A few others looked down their noses at her. 'Nothing but a common model,' she thought someone whispered. Hot and cold flashes all over her body.

She managed a stiff bow and murmured something. Mr Howell did not take the hint, but stood chatting a while longer, asking her if Gabriel was painting her in anything new. He did not mention her own art, or that she had sold a painting for thirty-five whole guineas. His tone seemed patronising. She noticed that he had a markedly receding chin.

Lizzie excused herself and stumbled away, leaving him staring after her. She felt faint. The blasted corset was cutting off all the air to her lungs. There was nowhere she could hide. She had to endure the long journey back to Sheffield with everyone staring at her, whispering about her. Mr Mitchell did not offer her his arm, or indeed speak to her.

That night Lizzie crept down to the kitchen, and ate all the food she could find. She did so hurriedly, surreptitiously, afraid that every creak of the old house was someone sneaking down the stairs to find her. She had barely swallowed one mouthful before her hand was cramming something else in.

She ate till she was ill, and then she ate more.

The next day there were great scenes of consternation at the discovery of the empty pantry.

'Maybe it was rats,' her uncle said.

'Mighty clean rats is all I'm going to say,' Aunt Sarah said.

Nobody seemed to suspect Lizzie. Yet she felt as if every move, every mouthful, was scrutinised even more closely than before. She became more secretive. Eating on the sly, purging any chance she could.

Days narrowing, leaves orange as her hair. And still no sign of Gabriel.

Of course she suspected he was trifling with some other girl. When a letter came from Emma saying all the boys in Oxford seemed to have gone mad over some new Stunner, Lizzie knew she had been right. She wrote a dozen letters to him, the ink smeared with her tears, tore them up, wrote him another, tore it up too. She walked the damp cobbled streets for hours in a trance, searching for food to cram into her mouth. Sometimes she picked through garbage. She sickened herself.

One day she fainted, getting out of bed. Her aunt wrote to her parents. Lydia came, and took her back to Matlock Gorge. Lizzie wrote to Gabriel, begging him to come and rescue her. He came, but was stiff and stern with her. He told her she must do everything the doctors said, else he would leave again.

Lizzie did not want him to leave her. She wanted to be well enough to lie smiling in his arms, as he wound her long hair about his fingers and called her his love, his dove, his darling. But it was as if she had been turned into some kind of clockwork automaton, programmed to purge.

Lizzie lay utterly motionless, feeling her stomach gurgle and heave. Slowly the light faded. She heard Gabriel stoke up the fire, and then sit back down in the chair. He sighed. For a while, he seemed to read but then there was only silence.

Lizzie wondered if it was safe.

She opened her eyes. The room was dim, lit only by a shaded lamp on a table and the glow of the fire. Gabriel's head was leaning back against the cushion. His long lashes rested on his cheek.

Lizzie began to ease herself out of the bed. She stood up. The world spun. She had to sit down and wait till the dizziness passed. Holding on to the furniture, she staggered over to the window. It was firmly shut against the dangerous night air. It took all her strength to open it. It creaked loudly, and she glanced over her shoulder. Gabriel did not move.

Bracing her bony hips against the windowsill, Lizzie leant outside. It was cold. Ivy grew up the wall, the glossy leaves fluttering in the wind.

It took only a moment for Lizzie to jam her fingers against the soft flesh at the back of her throat. She vomited so quickly it gushed over her hand. Most of it, though, fell down into the ivy below. She shook her hand clean and wiped her mouth.

'What are you doing?'

Lizzie jumped violently. She spun around. Gabriel was on his feet, his eyes fixed on her, blackly dilated.

'I … I felt so sick.'

'I saw you …' He made a thrusting gesture with his fingers towards his mouth.

A slow red burn of humiliation. 'No … I …'

'I saw you.' There was accusation in his voice.

'I had to get it out. It was making me sick.'

'What? The food? No, the food is to make you well and strong again.'

Lizzie pressed both her hands against her aching stomach. She did not know how to explain herself.

'So you were making yourself sick on purpose? All those times … you did it to yourself on purpose?'

'No, no. It's not like that.' But she could see by the expression on his face that Gabriel did not believe her. She could see him remembering the dozens and dozens of times that he had held her, wiped her mouth and comforted her. His face hardened. He caught up his coat and pulled it on.

'Gabriel, no … please …'

'It's over, Lizzie,' he told her. 'I can't do this anymore. I could not bear to hurt you when you were so sick … I thought you were dying … but now I see that it was all some crazy kind of pretence.'

Lizzie caught hold of the table to stop herself from falling.

Gabriel's look was contemptuous. 'I will not be taken in by your tricks anymore.'

Lizzie tried to speak, but tears suspended her voice.

He went swiftly across the room, pausing as he opened the door. 'Oh, and Lizzie, you know that girl you were so worried about? Well, it's true. I'm in love with her. I'm going now to tell her.'

Gabriel slammed the door shut behind him.

8

Poison Or the Dagger
Summer 1858

Janey sat at the table, a book spread before her, her head bent in concentration.

'Learn from this no' …'

'Not,' Miss Leigh said, emphasising the 't'.

'Not,' Janey repeated. 'Learn from this not to despise li'l things …'

'Little,' Miss Leigh said.

'Little,' Janey repeated. 'Learn, also, not to be … dis … dis …. discouraged by great labours …'

'You are doing so well. Keep going.'

'The greatest labour becomes easy, if divided into parts. Ye … *you* do *not* … jump over a mountain; *but* … step by step takes *you* … to the other side.'

'You, my sweet girl, are jumping mountains! Well done. Have you had enough? Shall we break for tea?'

'No,' Janey said carefully. 'I would prefer to keep goin' … *going* … please, Miss Leigh.'

'Certainly, my dear. Read the next paragraph.'

'Do *not* fear, therefore, to … attempt great things. Always remember that the whole o' … *of* … that great …' Janey pronounced the 't' with intense concentration, '… buildin' … *building* is only … one brick upon … another.' On she went, slowly gaining in fluidity, till the whole page was read.

'Oh well done, my dear! Let's ring for tea, and I shall read to you for a while, shall I?' Miss Leigh put out her hand and pulled the cord. A far distant tinkle could be heard.

Janey put down her schoolbook with a relieved sigh. Her neck was stiff, her shoulders tense, and her voice hoarse. There was so much to remember.

Rule 1: Avoid suppressing letters in pronunciation.

Rule 2: Avoid substituting the sound of one letter for another.

Rule 3: Avoid suppressing syllables in pronunciation, unless correct utterance requires it (how was a body meant to know?).

Rule 4: Avoid pronouncing *ow* like *er* (Miss Leigh had made a little rhyme for her to chant: 'Yellow, fellow, hollow, swallow, sorrow, tomorrow, narrow, shallow, billow, pillow.' After a while, it sounded like a love song, with all those oh, oh, ohs!)

Rule 5: Avoid the dropping of the 'g' sound.

Rule 6: Avoid an imperfect utterance of the sub-vocals and aspirates in a succession of similar sounds …

Janey still had not got the hang of that one.

Miss Leigh was very kind to her, though. They only did elocution twice a day, for half an hour at a time, and then she always rewarded Janey with something she loved to do. Playing the piano and singing rounds. Walking by the river and picking wildflowers. Reading more of *The Heir of Redclyffe*, which they were both enjoying hugely. It did Janey good just to hear Miss Leigh reading aloud, her voice was so sweet and pure. Janey could practise the sounds of the words silently, inside her, and each day it got a little easier to say them right.

It had been five months since Topsy had hired this pretty little cottage on the banks of the River Thames, just on the outskirts of Godstow. It was a low white house, with a small garden crowded with roses, foxgloves and larkspur. It looked out over the calm green waters of the millstream.

The road led over a little humped stone bridge towards the Thames. Beyond were an arched bridge and the Trout Inn, and then a lock where boats could be raised and lowered through control of the water level. Topsy found that fascinating. Every time he came to visit, he and Janey would walk down and watch the locksman work the machinery. A footpath then led through the meadows towards Godstow Abbey, an old ruin on a little island where the river forked.

Usually Topsy would come to visit Janey and Miss Leigh by boat, paddling down the Thames from Oxford. Janey thought he found the whole idea of it wildly romantic.

He was the perfect suitor. He would sit in the sitting-room, a tiny cup and saucer perched on his knee, making polite conversation and blushing each time Janey spoke to him with her carefully enunciated vowels. 'How do you do, Mr Morris? Is it not fine today, Mr Morris?'

Miss Leigh was a strict chaperone, but she allowed Topsy and Janey to walk alone together, as long as they never strayed from her sight. She walked behind them, leaning only slightly upon her stick, and pretended great interest in the play of light upon the river.

After that one kiss when Janey had said she would marry him, Topsy had barely touched her. A shy hand to help her over a damp spot. A low bow when he said goodbye. It was as if he wanted to pretend that she had always lived in Godstow with Miss Leigh, and that this was a conventional courtship. This was an easy pretence for Janey to make. She wished it were true.

Miss Leigh, her old parish school teacher, had been on the verge on being sent to the workhouse when Topsy had asked Janey if she knew anyone who could live with her awhile and teach her how to manage in polite society. He had rented them this cottage, hired them a skivvy, and opened accounts for them at all the best shops in Oxford. He had secured the services of a dancing master, a French teacher, a music teacher, and someone who could show her how to paint a competent watercolour. The teachers came and went all day, greased in the palm to be kind, and Janey – who had dreaded the lessons – found that she began to enjoy them. With

Miss Leigh's gentle encouragement, she learned how to walk with a book balanced on her head, how to curtsey in a country dance, when to remove one's hat and when to leave it on (the rules did not seem to make much sense), and – to Janey's great relief – what fork to use to eat oysters.

Violet the maid brought in the tea tray and set it down before Miss Leigh. She then stood back against the wall, watching with great interest, as Miss Leigh gently instructed Janey in the best manner of pouring and serving and eating and drinking. 'Never pour your tea into the saucer to cool it, Janey. A lady is always patient. Wait for it to be the perfect temperature for sipping. A napkin is only used to dab your mouth clean, Janey. Never use it to blow your nose or wipe your brow.'

Janey was practising holding her tea cup in the accepted manner – saucer in the palm of her left hand, her thumb holding it steady, her right hand lifting the cup to her mouth, a sip without noise, return the cup to the saucer without spilling a drop – when she unexpectedly heard the gate open.

She was so surprised she splashed a little tea into her saucer.

'Who could that be?' she asked, craning to see out the window. 'Topsy ... I mean, Mr Morris ... is still in France, ain't he?'

'I believe he is, my dear. Put down your cup, a lady does not slop tea everywhere. Please do not be so uncouth as to look out the window. Violet, go and stand ready to answer the door, there's a good girl. Straighten your apron. Janey, my dear, perhaps just a little attention to your hair?'

Violet opened the door, her face bright pink.

'It's a gen'leman!' she cried, then corrected herself conscientiously. 'A *gentleman*. To see Miss Burden.'

It was Gabriel.

Janey jumped to her feet, sending the tea tray crashing to the ground. Flushing hotly, she bent to clean up the mess.

'Miss Burden, my dear, no need to trouble yourself,' Miss Leigh said, her voice as calm as ever. 'Violet?'

As the skivvy dashed forward to pick up the broken china, Janey subsided back into her chair. She could not look at Gabriel.

'I do not believe I have had the pleasure of your acquaintance,' Miss Leigh said. 'Have you left your card with us previously, sir?'

Gabriel was taken aback. 'No ... I mean, I'm an old friend of Janey's ...'

'Indeed. How nice. And you are ...?'

'I'm Gabriel ... Dante Gabriel Rossetti.' He affected a gracious bow.

'Delighted,' Miss Leigh answered, cooler than ever. 'Will you join us for tea, Mr Rossetti? Violet, a fresh pot, please.'

Violet rushed out and Gabriel sat down. 'Well, thank you. I'm gasping for a cup of tea, actually. It's been a long day. Janey, I've been looking for you everywhere. Why didn't you leave word where you were going?'

Janey had no answer for him. It had been nine months since she had last seen him.

'I collect you must be a friend of Miss Burden's betrothed, Mr Morris,' Miss Leigh said. 'I am sure he would have given you Miss Burden's address if you had asked him.'

Gabriel looked tired and sallow. He leant forward, grabbing Janey's hands. 'I heard a rumour ... but surely it can't be true.'

Janey had a strange sensation, as if her blood was being released from her body by a series of mechanical locks. She took her hands back, twisting them in the fabric of her skirt. The silk crumpled immediately. She tried to smooth it out.

'It is indeed true, Mr Rossetti. Miss Burden and Mr Morris have been betrothed five months or more. They are to be married next spring. Ah, Violet, the tea! Excellent. Miss Burden, shall you pour?'

Mechanically Janey went through the process of pouring the tea, arranging the teaspoons, handing around the cups.

Miss Leigh kept up a gentle murmur. After a moment Gabriel responded politely, though his jaw was tight.

'Yes, I am one of the artists who were working on the murals at the debating hall. I ... I was called away unexpectedly and so my painting was not completed. I have come back ... to finish unfinished business.'

Janey's eyes flew to his face.

'An artist? Really?' Miss Leigh was both intrigued and pleasantly shocked.

Gabriel showed her his painters' box with its multitude of brushes and little squares of watercolour paints and rolled-up tubes of oils. 'I wanted to draw Janey … I mean, Miss Burden … that is one reason why I am here. Would you like me to show you?'

When Miss Leigh concurred in delight, he got out his sketching book and some charcoals and chalks, and began to draw swiftly, explaining what he was doing as he went along.

Each stroke of the charcoal on the paper was like a stroke of his finger upon her skin. Janey tried to keep her composure.

'And why did you leave your murals unfinished?' Miss Leigh asked.

'I … I had to go away. Up north. A … a friend was ill.'

'Oh, dear, I am sorry. I do hope he is feeling better now.'

Blood rushed up under Gabriel's fine skin. He looked at Janey.

'My friend was very ill. I … I thought … I thought she'd die. I could not … I could not just abandon her. As soon as I could … as soon as I could I told her ... that I must come back to Oxford. But then I heard of your betrothal, Janey.'

There was a long charged silence, then Miss Leigh said sweetly, 'May I offer you a scone?'

'No, thank you.' Gabriel laid down the charcoal, wiping his fingers on a rag. 'Janey, please, I need to talk to you.'

Another awkward silence, then Miss Leigh patted her pocket for her lorgnette, put it on the end of her nose, and glanced up at the clock. 'It must be time for our constitutional, don't you think, Miss Burden? Perhaps Mr Rossetti would care to join us? The river is so lovely at this time of day.'

Janey stood up. Miss Leigh led the way out of the sitting-room, the tap of her stick the only sound. Outside, the sky was golden as the sun disappeared behind the trees. In single file, they walked down the old brick path towards the road. Janey's dress brushed against the flowers on either side, releasing a rich perfume into the air.

'You haven't said a word, Janey,' Gabriel said in a low voice, drawing her back with one hand on her arm.

Janey realised this was true. Sometimes it seemed as if the more deeply she felt, the more padlocked her tongue.

'I ... I didn't expect to see you,' she said. 'You've surprised me.'

'So it seems,' he said bitterly.

'It's been nine months since I last saw you,' she pointed out.

He looked discomfited. 'I know. I'm sorry. But Lizzie was very sick ... the worst I've ever seen her. I could not leave her ... I scarcely had time to write and let my mother know where I was.'

'An' she's better now?'

He made a hopeless gesture with his hands. 'I don't know. I left her there.'

'You said ... you said you told her ... something. What?'

He looked at her. 'I told her I was in love with you.'

The words were like a blow to the chest. It drove all the air out of her lungs. This was what she had hoped for, all those long lonely months.

'Why ... now?' she said with difficulty. 'After all this time? Is it because you heard about ...' She could not say his name.

'About Topsy?' Gabriel spoke his name with scorn. 'The idea of you marrying him is absurd. He's a clown ...'

'He's not,' Janey said. 'He's a good man.'

'Surely you cannot want to marry him?'

'I do.' Even to her own ears, her tone lacked conviction.

He did not believe her. As they walked he argued with her. Janey felt a little spark of anger. Gabriel had not wanted her for himself. He only wanted her now she was someone else's. He was like a spoilt child who threw down one toy in order to grab another, and ended up breaking them both.

They had walked over the bridge and past the inn, Miss Leigh demurely keeping just out of earshot. The river shimmered like a brown satin ribbon. A swan floated past, followed by a train of fluffy grey cygnets. Miss Leigh stopped to gaze at them.

Gabriel halted in the shade of a great chestnut tree, its branches hanging with prickly burrs. From here, Miss Leigh could not see them. He drew her close, his hands sliding around her waist. He bent and kissed her. His mouth was warm and greedy.

'Does it mean nothing to you, what we did together ... back in Oxford?' He kissed her again. It was hard to turn her head away.

'I thought it meant nothing to you.' Her voice was very low.

'Of course it did! How could you think it didn't?'

He pressed her closer to him, one hand sliding down her rump.

She stepped away from him, hugging herself. 'I waited,' she said fiercely. 'I waited and waited. But I heard no word from you. Nor did I have any reason to think that I should. You were betrothed to that other girl ... and Ned told me that it's been years that you've kept her waiting too ... always promising and then breaking your promise ...'

Gabriel's olive skin flushed. 'I suppose I deserve that.'

'You do deserve it. And now ... now that I'm here an' found some kind of happiness ... it's now that you come, and tell me that you love me, an' you've broken it off with that poor sick girl.'

'You don't understand. I tried to do the right thing ... I intended to honour my promise ... but I couldn't forget you, and then ...' He broke off abruptly.

'So are you wanting me to break my promise to Topsy an' marry you instead?'

He hesitated just a moment too long.

Janey turned away, dashing away her tears with the back of her glove. She had imagined that Gabriel was to be her knight, come to rescue her. But it was Topsy who had stayed with her, Topsy who had asked her to marry him. Gabriel had left her without a word. She walked, her skirts swinging, to the bridge. Her hands clenched on the rail, she looked across to the grey ruins of the abbey on the island, half-hidden behind trees.

Gabriel came up beside her, eager and ready to speak, to entrance her like he always did with his silver tongue and his easy charm.

She held up one hand, forcing him to stop.

'Did you know the abbey is haunted?' Janey said.

'I ... no.'

'Topsy told me the story. There was once this king who fell in love with a beautiful girl. He kept her hidden in a tower in the middle o' a maze, for fear o' his jealous wife. The queen found out about the tower an' went there in secret. As she crept through the maze, she found the end o' a red thread that had unravelled from the girl's embroidery ...'

'Ah, yes, I know this tale. It's the story of Fair Rosamund, isn't it?'

Janey nodded. 'The queen picked up the end o' the red thread and followed it through the maze. Once inside, she offered the girl the choice o' poison or the dagger. Rosamund chose the poison. She drank it down an' died, and so the queen had her revenge. Poor Rosamund was buried here, at Godstow. Years later, a bishop came by. He said she was a moll. A harlot, you know.' She enunciated the word precisely. 'He had her bones dug up an' thrown outside, and now they say her ghost cannot rest.'

'But Janey ...' Gabriel began.

Janey struggled to explain what she was feeling. 'I don't want to be the moll, Gabriel. I want ... I want to be the queen.'

Gabriel misunderstood her. Drawing away, he said, 'I see. It's because Topsy is rich. I've been rushing around and calling in as much tin as I could, thinking to ask you to marry me. But you'd rather be a queen.' He mocked her words cruelly.

Blood rushed into Janey's face. He had meant to ask her to marry him? And he thought that she was only marrying Topsy for his money? It was not what she had meant at all. Clutching her hands together at her breast, she began to stammer something but he did not wait to listen.

As he strode away, Janey found her voice. 'Gabriel ...wait ... don't go!'

He ignored her.

'Please ... wait. Where are you going?'

'To the Devil!'

9

Pricked by the Needle
Spring 1859

Janey sewed her own wedding dress.

It was made of fine light wool, white as snow, and cut with the severe medieval lines that Topsy loved so much and which Janey knew suited her tall, slender figure well. She wore no jewellery, and carried nothing but a simple bouquet of violets that she had gathered herself that morning in the woods.

She wanted everything to be as simple and plain as possible.

Gabriel thought she was marrying Topsy for his money. Perhaps his other friends all thought so too; although Ned's face was bright with joy as she walked up the church aisle towards the altar. He at least was happy for his friend. He thought their story a true romance. Janey wished it was so.

The church was decorated as simply. A few knots of white ribbons, a few white roses. It was almost empty. Miss Leigh and Violet sat in the second row of the bride's side, wearing their best and beaming proudly. Janey's brother Will sat alone in the first pew, turning his hat around and around.

Janey's father walked beside her, dwarfing everyone else in the church. His arm beneath her hand was rigid as an iron bar, he was so nervous of doing something wrong. Bessie led the way, dressed more conventionally in a crinoline and heavy flounced skirt. She was pleased as punch with it, and walked with such a sway she threatened to show her lace-edged pantaloons.

The other side of the church was almost as bare. Apart from Ned, there was Charley Faulkner and a few other friends from the Oxford set. Topsy's family had not made the journey from Essex, and Gabriel had not come down from London. Janey told herself it was a blessing. She wondered if Topsy minded very much.

At least her mother was not there. That had been one of Janey's most pressing fears. She had gone to great lengths to make sure Annie would not turn up, drunk and shouting, ruining this day for her. No banns had been read. Topsy had paid for a special licence. And they were not married in Janey's parish church, but instead in St Michael at the North Gate, near Topsy's lodgings in George Street.

Seeing no sign of her mother, Janey was able to relax a little. She stood beside Topsy, who was looking pale and tense. He gave her a little smile and took her hand. She smiled back. *Everything will be fine*, she told herself.

One of Topsy's friends was officiating. He was nervous and stumbled through the service. When it came time to exchange vows, he said, 'William, will you take Mary to be your wife?'

A great shout of laughter came from Ned and Charley and the other young men. The minister turned crimson, muttered an oath, and said, 'I knew I'd get it wrong, with all your coaching! William, will you take *Jane* to be your wife?'

'I will,' Topsy said, scowling over his shoulder at his laughing friends.

Then it was Janey's turn. She said the words with a thick voice and a hard-beating heart. Somehow she had not thought it would happen. She did not know what she had expected. Gabriel turning up at the last minute, and galloping away with her over the pommel of his saddle. Topsy deciding it was all a great mistake and she must go back to the slums. The church being struck by lightning. Janey's feet beginning to run, despite herself.

But lightning did not strike, her feet stayed rooted to the stone, and soon it was done and she was Mrs William Morris. To the sound of church bells, she went out into the sharp spring sunshine, arm in arm with her new husband, keeping her chin high, just like a queen.

Topsy had organised a wedding breakfast at one of the better inns in town. After the dimness and austerity of the church, everyone seemed giddy with joy and relief. Champagne flowed. Lobster patties and roast pheasant were served. Will ate without seeming to pause for breath, and Miss Leigh got a little tiddly.

It was Janey's first true opportunity to show how much she herself had learned. She tended to her guests with as much grace and composure as she could muster, and made sure every glass was brimming.

As she brought her father a frothing tankard of beer, she saw Topsy and Ned standing in close conversation near the window. She moved towards them, meaning to ask if they would prefer beer too.

'How is he?' Topsy asked in a low voice.

Ned looked grave. 'He says he's never been better. But to tell you the truth, I think he's burning the candle at both ends. He never stops for a moment. He's out each night with Val, visiting every fleshpot in London …'

Topsy muttered something Janey could not catch.

'Well, you know Gabriello. He's going around with that Stunner he discovered in the pleasure garden,' Ned said.

Janey realised they were speaking of Gabriel. Blood rushed up her face.

'You know the one,' Ned continued in a low voice. 'Fanny Cox, she calls herself. A lovely looking girl. Simply masses of golden hair. He's painting her whenever he can get her, but has promised her to me for that painting I want to do of the witch Sidonie. She's perfect for it. So very seductive.'

'So it's all over … his betrothal?'

'I think so,' Ned said. 'He never speaks of her.'

Janey slipped away. *I made the right choice*, she told herself. *He would never have been faithful.*

Yet she felt bruised. So easily had Gabriel forgotten her.

It was very strange, that night, to go back to their hotel room and lie in the great bed in her nightgown, and feel Topsy's hand creep up her bare thigh. Janey shuddered, and then was sorry. She put her arms about him and kissed the hairy vee of his neckline, and did all she could to make it easier for him.

She needed spit.

Every Sunday, when Janey was a little girl, she had got up before dawn to search for flowers in the meadows and woods to sell. At Christmas time, she found holly and ivy and mistletoe. In springtime, primroses and violets. Poppies and cornflowers in summer, and snowdrops and wild clematis in early winter. She would stand on the street corner, dressed in her ragged dress and battered boots, holding out her little bunches tied with twine, crying piteously, 'Oh, please, kind lady, buy me flowers. Help a poor li'l girl?'

Janey remembered one day acutely. It had been winter, and snow had fallen overnight. Her boots had holes in them, and she had stuffed them with rags to try to keep the cold out. It had taken her almost an hour to reach the woods near Iffley, slosheting through deep snow the whole way. Her dress was damp and bedraggled, and her feet were like lumps of ice. But she was too glad to be worried about the cold. Janey loved the winter woods at dawn. Everything was so pure and clean. It felt as if she was alone in the world, with no-one to shriek at her or beat her. There was no sound but birdsong, and nothing to look at but winter-bare trees with rooks' nests hanging in their branches, their roots buried in snow.

Janey made her way to one of the secret glades she knew, far from the road or the railway track. Snowdrops pushed their green leaves and drooping pale bells out of the snow, and Janey gathered them quickly, glancing about her all the while in case someone should come. By now, the sun had risen and glittered through the icicles hanging from the tree branches. A fox ran past, leaving tiny pockmarks in the snow.

When Janey's basket was full, she turned to trudge back to Oxford. She wanted to be back in time for the morning service, in case the vicar's wife might like some flowers for the altar, or some parishioners a bunch to brighten their Sunday dinner table.

Her legs were leaden, but Janey pushed on. As she came over the hill, she saw the towers and spires of Oxford floating above the snow-dusted trees. It was beautiful enough to catch one's breath. But Janey knew that stinking rookeries were hidden in the shadows of those golden walls, never more than a few steps away.

Janey came to the old lychgate and stood within its arch. As ladies and gentlemen in their Sunday best hurried towards the church, she held out the bunches of drooping snowdrops imploringly, calling, 'Buy me flowers. Candlemas bells, the first sign o' spring! Please, sir, buy some fer the lady?'

One woman gazed at her in pity. 'Why, look at you! You're quite blue with cold. And so ragged and thin.'

'She just dresses that way to try to cozen you out of a few more coins,' said the gentleman with her. 'Really, it's a disgrace. The idle poor in this country should all be locked up in workhouses and taught the value of industry.'

For a moment Janey could not speak, a lump in her throat. The lady looked troubled. 'Here, let me buy your flowers. They're so pretty, they give me hope this interminable winter will soon be over. How much will you charge me?'

'A penny a bunch,' Janey answered huskily. 'Lor' bless ye.'

The lady paid Janey and took the bunch of snowdrops. As she walked away, arm-in-arm with the gentleman, he scolded her about encouraging social parasites. Janey stared after him. She knew what that word meant. Fleas, and lice, and bedbugs, and worms in the gut. She wondered if he had ever scratched his own skin raw.

One day, Janey had thought, *I'll have my own little house in a garden, with a mattress that's as soft as clouds and sheets as white as new snow. I'll have teacups that all match, and a silver spoon to stir the sugar. The house will be as clean as scrubbing can get it, and I'll have fresh flowers and books in every room, as many books as I can find. I'll wear a silk dress as blue as a summer sky.*

One day, I'll escape from here and I'll never ever come back.

The morning after her wedding night, Janey opened her eyes and looked around the room in which she lay. The linen was white and crisp, the counterpane rich red velvet. Flowers stood on every surface. The maid had just brought in a tray, set with fine china patterned with roses and a silver teapot. Everything was clean and ordered and sweet-smelling.

It was as if she had longed for this life so hard that she had somehow conjured it into being. Janey hardly dared breathe or blink in case it all dissolved away.

'Morning, Janey,' Topsy said and brought a cup of tea, setting it on the table beside her. He kissed her clumsily.

'Thank you,' she said, and on an impulse caught his big, square hand and brought it to her lips. 'Thank you so much.'

She knew she had made the wisest choice, the only choice.

And yet there was still so much sadness inside her.

Don't ask for too much, she told herself. *Keep your dreams small.*

Their honeymoon was a whirligig of cathedrals, churches, castles and cobbled laneways. It was as if Topsy wanted to show her everything that had ever inspired him. Janey was content to go with him, listening quietly as he poured out his heart to her. As she gazed up at the immense vaulted stone ceilings, raised so high and so long ago, she thought to herself that all this was built, brick by brick, stone by stone.

It made her think anything was possible.

In Bayeux, she and Topsy went to see Queen Mathilde's famous tapestry. It was not really a tapestry at all. It was the longest piece of embroidery in the world. Janey walked along its immense length, protected by sheets of glass, as Topsy told her the history it revealed. Betrayal and anger, banquets and battles.

She saw each careful stitch, and imagined the hands that wielded the needle. Had they been young and smooth, or old and gnarled? Had the seamstresses seen what they described in coloured thread – the sword thrust, the screaming horses, the tumbling severed head, the arrow through the eye? Had their fingers been pricked by the needle, smearing the thread with blood?

It made her long to make something as powerful. Janey had never thought that her skill with a needle was anything more than a useful pastime. Yet now she saw that, stitch by stitch, a woman's needle could bring the past alive. It could tell a story.

She longed to do the same.

10

Death-Watch
Spring 1860

Lizzie lay motionless.

Her eyes were fixed on the small square of glass above her. Clouds drifted across the blue. Sometimes the light darkened for a moment. She could feel the heavy pound of her pulse in her temples.

Her thoughts were untethered. Memories, dreams, lists of things she had not done, splinters of conversations both spoken and imagined, slivers of poems.

Dim phantoms of an unknown ill float through my tired brain ... unformed visions of my life pass by in ghostly train ...

For years, Lizzie had heard the faint insistent click of the deathwatch beetle in her rafters. She did not understand how she had lived so long. Her brother Charlie had wasted away so rapidly. Within months he had been gone. Yet her spirit lived on in this frail husk of a body, defying all the doctors and all the doomsayers. If she survived another dozen or so weeks, the local church would be tolling thirty-one strokes for her death knell. And anyone who heard would wonder, for a moment, who had died, then go on with their daily business.

It had been two years since Gabriel had abandoned her. Lizzie had thought she would die that very night. Yet it seemed one did not die of a broken heart. The doctors had enforced their cruel rest cure, then sent her back home to her parents. Lizzie could not, she thought, bear the humiliation.

Yet, in the end, what did it matter? The days passed, each as grey and empty as the day before. Her father died, and Lizzie was barely able to muster enough strength to help her mother drape the mirrors and stop the clocks.

Frozen like a thing of stone ...

Her body was barren, her poems unpublished, her art ridiculed, her lover unfaithful, her ring finger bare, her soul a desert of ice.

No-one knew what to do with her. Finally Lizzie agreed to go back to Hastings. She had been happy there, once.

Can God bring back the day when we two stood, beneath the clinging trees in that dark wood?

She thought of Gabriel a lot. Almost as often as she thought of food. Her hunger for one was like her hunger for the other. Gnawing away at her flesh. Apparently Gabriel had a new mistress now. A voluptuous beauty with hair like rippling wheat-fields and breasts like melons. Not that Emma had written so. Lizzie had read between the lines. She never answered Emma's letter and after a while her friend stopped writing.

The hills grow darker to my sight

And thoughts begin to swim.

A door opened somewhere. Footsteps, slow and heavy. Then a knock at her door. Lizzie did not turn her head. She just wished her landlady would stop bothering her. It was no use anymore. She did not need to jam her fingers down her throat to purge herself. Even the smell of any food was enough to start her retching helplessly.

The door opened. 'Miss Siddal?' Her landlady's voice was shrill and anxious. Lizzie guessed she did not want anyone dying under her roof, particularly when they were so far behind with the rent. 'You have a visitor.'

Lizzie took a slow painful breath, and managed to look towards the door. Even that small motion made the world spin. She pressed her hands flat against the bed, trying to steady her nausea.

Her name was whispered. She knew that voice. She had to wait for the dizziness to subside before she could see him. He was staring at her with black dilated eyes.

'Lizzie. Oh my God.'

She could only stare at him. Was he real?

O Heaven help my foolish heart

Which heeded not the passing time

That dragged my idol from its place

And shattered all its shrine.

Gabriel looked older. His forehead was higher, the lines about his mouth deeper, the flesh of his body softer. His eyes were bloodshot. He came and sat beside her, gingerly taking one of her hands. He spread her fingers, looking at the knots of bone beneath the papery skin. Her knuckles were red with callouses, the veins standing out like purple cords.

'What are you doing here?' she whispered.

Her words were so weak he had to bend his head to hear them. She smelt the sharp citrus of his hair oil, the warm musk of his skin. Her stomach heaved. She managed to roll away from him, bringing her knees up to the hollow of her chest as she retched into the bucket beside her bed. The paroxysm lasted a minute or so. Nothing came up. After it was over, she laid her head down on the pillow and closed her eyes.

'The landlady says you have barely touched a bite of food in days.'

She lifted her shoulders a fraction of an inch.

'Lizzie, if you don't eat … you're going to die.' His voice broke. She opened her eyes and looked at him. His face was contorted. 'Please, Lizzie …'

She lifted his hand, bringing it to her mouth to kiss. 'I can't.'

Impossible to explain. She did not understand herself.

Food was poison.

Yet she longed to devour it.

She had to be strong.

She could smell it. She could lick it.

But she could not taste it. She could not swallow it.

Each time she did, she was sick.

So she had to try not to tempt herself.

'Lizzie, let me give you just a little broth. It's as clear as spring water. Nothing that could harm you. Look, I will have a sip.' Gabriel lifted the invalid cup to his own mouth and drank a mouthful. 'Mmmm. So delicious. Here, now it's your turn.'

She stared at him. She must have swooned a while. The window was dark. A lamp had been lit, finding threads of grey in his dark curls. He lifted her up. His arm like an iron bar. 'Just a sip, Lizzie. Just one. Then I will let you rest.'

She swallowed a mouthful. So rich and greasy in her mouth. She gagged. He rubbed her back soothingly. 'There, there, it's all right. Take a deep breath. Lean on my arm.'

She did as she was told. No strength left to fight. Her stomach roiled like the ocean. Then up it came again.

He dampened a towel and washed her face and throat. The vomit had collected in the little cups behind her collar-bones. He had to dip the towel inside to clean it up. All the while, he talked to her in a low, reassuring murmur. 'Your landlady is very worried about you, did you know that? She's been at her wits' end. She wrote to your sister, who wrote to Mr Ruskin, who wrote to me. So I came down.'

Lizzie could remember the landlady begging her for a name, an address, anything. She had said Gabriel's name. Her landlady had thought she was praying to the holy angels. The thought made her smile.

She looked up into his dear face. 'I wanted to say goodbye.'

The movement was too much. Once again her stomach rebelled. Once again Gabriel washed her face. He gave her some water to drink. She refused it. He insisted. 'You need something in your stomach, Lizzie. It will hurt less if you have something to throw up.'

She shook her head.

'Please, Lizzie. I don't want you to die. This is all my fault. Please, just eat a little.'

She shook her head.

'If you'll just eat, you'll get better. Please, I promise you, if you can get strong enough to walk to the little church just down the lane, I'll marry you, I'll take you home, I'll look after you. Please, Lizzie, please. I mean it this time.'

She gazed in wonderment at the tears in his eyes. He buried his face in her arm, and she felt the wetness through the cambric of her nightgown. She stroked his hair and murmured something. After a while he sat up again, dashing his arm across his eyes. 'Just a little mouthful, Lizzie. What harm could that do?'

To please him, she sipped the soup. Once. Twice. Then she shook her head and pushed her cup away. She was tired. She wanted to sleep. With a trembling hand she reached for her laudanum.

Gabriel took it away.

She tried to snatch it back, but did not have the strength.

'Finish your soup, and you can have your medicine,' he told her.

Lizzie did not want to. If she drank all the soup, she would have to throw it up again, and she did not want to lose her laudanum too. It was the only thing that stopped the burning in her stomach. She began to weep.

Gabriel did not relent. He held the brown bottle out of her reach, bringing the spout of the cup close to her mouth. 'Two quick mouthfuls, that's all you need to do. Just drink it down, Lizzie, then you can rest.'

She drank resentfully. When the soup was all gone, he passed her the laudanum bottle. She measured out her drops and drank them down eagerly.

'Let's get you clean and tidy, and then you can sleep.' Gabriel washed her face and hands with lavender water, helped her into a fresh nightgown, and changed her sheets. He put the vomit-filled bucket outside her door so she did not need to smell it.

She was afraid to be without it.

'I will get it for you if you need it,' he said. 'I'll be right here for anything you need.'

She lay in her clean sheets, hands gripped together. It was her habit, every night, to run her fingers from the uneven flutter of the pulse in the hollow of her throat, over her protruding collar-bones, and then to tap down her ribs, pair by pair, as if playing some kind of macabre xylophone, counting all the way, until she reached the deep swoop to the skin of her belly. She was afraid that her belly would not be still and flat tonight. It would be swollen and sore. It would slosh if she laid her hands on it. She wanted to hurl it all away from her as hard as she could.

Yet Gabriel would leave her again if he saw her purge.

She laid her hands flat on her chest, feeling the awful bang and hesitation of her heart, and willed herself to endure.

Somehow, she slept.

So the days passed. Gabriel alternated between begging and threatening her. He ate and drank a little from every dish to prove it was not poisoned. He pretended the spoon was a train and her mouth the train tunnel, trying to make her smile so he could slide the food inside her. He brushed her hair and plaited it into a thin braid. He lifted her, as easily as if she was a doll made of china and cloth, and set her in a chair by the window. She could look out at the people passing by. He took away her laudanum until she submitted, and watched her every mouthful like a cat watching a bird pretending to be dead.

'Just a little more, sweetheart,' he'd say. 'Then, when you are strong enough, we'll get married. You'd like that, wouldn't you?'

She swallowed and gagged, then wept and begged him to leave her alone. He coaxed and bullied her, she swallowed some more, then hated herself for her weakness.

It was frightening and shameful. Lizzie felt as though her body was a battleground, between the dark demon of hunger and the avenging angel of her lover. She hated Gabriel too at times. Knocked hot soup over his hand, accused him. He tried to keep his temper, tried to be gentle and kind. She tried to find ways to flay him.

It was like she was reeling about in a world in which all laws of nature had been violently overthrown. There was no vertical, no horizontal, no heaven, no hell, no laws of gravity to stop her from simply drifting away.

Yet each day she somehow managed to swallow a little more.

Mid-May, Lizzie could bear it no longer. The very thought of food touching her lips sent her into a frenzy. She accused him of wanting to be rid of her so he could marry his mistress. She sneered over her name. 'Fanny Cox … oh that's subtle!' She wanted to know when Gabriel had first slept with Fanny, and then would not believe him when he said it was long after they had parted ways. She did not believe him when he said it was over. She threw her bowl of beef tea at him, and then her glass of water. It smashed on the wall. When he begged her to be calm, she flung herself on the bed, screaming and flailing her arms and beating at her own head with her hands. Someone was hissing evil things in her ear. Someone like the Devil himself.

Gabriel could not stand it. He went out, slamming the door behind him. He was gone for hours. Slowly Lizzie grew cold and afraid. When he at last came back, she crept into his arms and promised that she would try, she would eat, just, please, please, don't leave her.

'You must try,' he told her. 'If I lose you, I shall go mad.'

After that, Lizzie tried hard to eat. She forced herself to chew and swallow, she forced herself to breathe deep and stop the food gushing up again within her. She could not bear Gabriel to ever be far from her side. She was afraid the dark demon would slither back inside her again, choking her, killing her.

One day Lizzie was strong enough to lift herself while Gabriel arranged pillows behind her. Then she found the strength to rise from her bed and walk a few steps to the wash-basin, holding on to the furniture all the way. A few days later she managed to brush her own hair, though the effort exhausted her.

One day she was well enough to rise and dress herself and come down the stairs, eating in the dining-room with all the other lodgers. It was hard, every step of it and every bite of it. But she did it.

Afterwards Gabriel helped her out into the courtyard, where yellow dandelions were growing between the cracks in the pavement.

He took her hand. 'We can be married tomorrow, if you like. If you're well enough.'

A tremulous smile curved her lips. 'I'm well enough now. Thanks to you.'

He squeezed her hand, and they sat in silence, listening to the seagulls cry, feeling the sun warm on their limbs.

11

Mrs Jones
Summer 1860

'I really don't mind what day we have the wedding,' Georgie said.

Ned walked up and down their carpet, his hands deep in his pockets. 'But is it a good omen, or a bad omen?'

'A good omen,' she said at once. 'Four years to the day that we got engaged.'

'But it is also the day Beatrice died. Surely that's a bad omen?'

'Beatrice died heaven knows how long ago. Five hundred years ago!'

'Five hundred and seventy,' he corrected her.

'People die every day,' she said rather desperately. 'Hundreds of them. And if we don't take that date, it might be another month before we can get another.'

Ned shook his head. 'I don't think it's a good omen.'

'If we get married now, we can go to Paris and see Gabriel,' she said. 'Paris in June is meant to be lovely.'

The mention of Gabriel swayed him, as she knew it would. Ned pondered a long moment, then nodded solemnly. 'Very well then. June the ninth it is.'

Georgie flew up to embrace him, but grew shy as soon as her hands touched him and only squeezed his arms lightly.

As the day of the wedding came closer Ned became more tense and white. It troubled Georgie, these strange fits and starts that came over him. It was as if the nerves of his body and the strings of his soul were strung more tightly than anyone else, always just a tremor away from breaking.

The day before the wedding he went out walking for hours, and was caught in a sudden downpour. He came home late, wet through, and the next day he was feverish. Valiantly he went through with the service, pausing often to blow his nose.

I am Mrs Jones now, Georgie thought in a daze. She looked at him, standing beside her in his new suit, his hand trembling as he signed his name in the register. *Tonight he will make me his wife.*

Her stomach clenched. Georgie had no idea what that meant. Her mother had only wept and told her that she must submit to her husband's demands, no matter how much it hurt. Georgie could not imagine Ned hurting her. He was the gentlest man alive. But still she feared what lay ahead. She had heard rumours from some of the other girls in their congregation. Talk of deflowering, breaking and entering, blood.

After the wedding, Georgie and Ned caught a train to Chester. The plan was to spend the night there and attend service at the cathedral the next day, before heading to Paris to join Gabriel and Lizzie. Georgie was curious indeed to meet the red-headed beauty, whose face was so familiar to her from the many hundreds of drawings and paintings in Gabriel's studio.

She had imagined walking Chester's winding cobblestoned streets hand in hand with Ned, dining somewhere lit with candles, and returning to their hotel to lie in each other's arms, discovering together whatever it was husbands and wives do.

The reality was very different. Ned was hoarse and shivering by the time they reached their hotel, and Georgie spent the night doing her best to nurse him. The innkeeper's wife was displeased to be roused with requests for camphor and mustard compresses, and Georgie was too shy to ring for her again when Ned became quite delirious. He kept shouting out strange things, and Georgie could only try to soothe and comfort him, snatching a few minutes' sleep herself when she could.

His temperature soared so high, Georgie asked the innkeeper to send for a doctor the following day. Then she ran around the hotel room, packing away any signs of their wedding finery. She got out her sewing basket and sat by the fire, darning Ned's socks and hoping the doctor would not tease them about being an old married couple. The doctor was fat and fussy. He frowned over Ned, and asked a great many questions that Georgie found hard to answer. At last he pronounced gloomily that Mr Jones must on no account attempt the rigours of a journey to Paris, and would be best at home in his own bed.

Georgie gasped a little when the doctor told her how much she had to pay him, and counted out the coins with fingers that trembled. Then she sat down and wrote to Gabriel to tell him they would not be coming to Paris.

There's plenty of time for Paris, she told herself stoutly, but wept a few quiet tears that night, once again sitting up in the chair so Ned could sleep more comfortably in the narrow hotel bed.

The next few days were difficult. Ned was so sick, and Georgie felt very young and alone. She wished there was someone to help her. She had never been on her own before, and felt sure the innkeeper knew she was only nineteen and had no notion of how much to pay for their food and drink. Ned's purse was frighteningly thin. She bought only what she must, and wondered how she was to get her husband home to London when she had barely enough for the train fare.

'It's not much of a honeymoon for you,' Ned croaked.

'That's all right,' Georgie lied.

At last he was well enough to travel, well wrapped up against the rain that lashed the windows. It was a struggle getting to the station with all their bags, but there was not enough money for a hansom cab. Georgie did her best.

At last they made it safely to Russell Square. It was only a few rooms, with nothing but a few sticks of old furniture. Topsy had taken everything he owned when he had married Janey. There were no chairs to sit on. Georgie had to stand to drink her tea.

'I'm so sorry, Georgie,' Ned said, coughing into his handkerchief. 'It's not much of a home for you.'

'It's the only home I want.'

She was busy for a while, unpacking their clothes, putting them in neat piles on the floor because there was no wardrobe. Eventually there was nothing else to do but change shyly into her nightgown, her back to Ned who was already in bed, dressed in his night-shirt. The springs creaked loudly as she climbed in, and the mattress was hard and lumpy.

She blew out the candle, then lay still, her body stretched out flat, her arms by her side like a tin soldier's.

'I'm sorry I've been so sick,' Ned said.

She murmured something.

'And that we didn't make it to Paris.'

She nodded.

He put out one cold hand and touched her arm. She turned towards him, her stomach fluttering with nerves. Clumsily they kissed. His beard was scratchy. She turned her face away. Hesitantly he lifted the hem of her nightgown. Georgie shrank back, shy and flustered. She had no idea why he would want to touch her up there. After a while, she forced her knees to relax and let him steal his hand higher. It was hard not to squeak and flinch. They gave each other shy pecks on the cheek and neck. He slid her nightgown higher, bunching it under her armpits, and positioned himself above her. Georgie put her hands on his shoulders. Something hard pushed between her legs. She felt uneasy and a little frightened. Ned put down his hand. She gasped in surprise. It hurt. He tried to push it deeper. She could hardly breathe with his weight on top of her. She craned her neck sideways. He kissed her cheek and groaned, rocking back and forth. The bed springs squealed rustily. Georgie could feel him digging inside her. Then suddenly he stiffened. His hips jerked. Then he collapsed on her neck, panting.

She lay still. The secret place between her legs felt sore and bruised.

Ned rolled off her. 'Oh, my,' he said. He lay next to her, his breath coming unevenly. 'So that's why …'

After a while, he gave her a shy pat in the darkness. 'That was lovely,' he whispered.

'Yes,' she whispered back.

The next time did not hurt so much, though Georgie found it hard to have anyone touch her in such forbidden places.

As the days passed, she dared to slide her hands up under his nightshirt to touch the smooth bare skin of his back. Once, lying beneath him, she felt a kind of strange sensation pass through her, like a thrum along a wire.

Otherwise, she enjoyed being a wife. It was like playing with a big doll's house. Someone gave her a piano for a wedding present, and she was able to sing whatever songs she liked. Ned slowly recovered his health, and was able to draw and paint again. She read to him most days, keeping him company in the studio, and when he was busy, she practised drawing in her sketchbook. One day she asked their skivvy to stand and pose for a while so she could draw her. There was no-one to frown at her and tell her such pastimes were a waste of time.

They were very poor, but Georgie was used to that.

One afternoon in late June, Ned told Georgie that Topsy had invited them all over for supper. 'You'd like to go, wouldn't you? He's been on his honeymoon for so long.'

She smiled at him. 'Of course. When does he want us?'

'We could go tonight, if you liked.'

'That would be nice. I'd like to see her. His wife, I mean.'

A shadow passed over Ned's face. Most people would not have noticed. But Georgie had set herself to learn the language of her husband's expressions as others learned Latin.

'I believe she is very beautiful,' she said hesitantly.

Ned nodded. 'There's something about her. It's not beauty, exactly. That is easily admired and forgotten. Something about her is … haunting.'

Georgie's heart sank.

She dressed with more than usual care. But what was the use? Her clothes were cut for economy, not style. And only Ned had ever called her beautiful.

Topsy and Mrs Topsy – as Ned insisted on calling them – had settled into lodgings on Great Ormond Street, only ten minutes from Ned's rooms on Russell Square. Georgie and Ned were able to walk there, through the sunset streets.

Topsy bounced up to greet them with his usual exuberance, diving straight into a discussion about stained glass and flying buttresses and gothic arches. His wife, meanwhile, rose to her feet. Georgie had to lift her eyes as if she was about to greet a bishop.

Mrs Morris was extraordinarily tall – taller than many men – but slender and pliant as a willow stem. Her hair was black but without any gloss, and so thick and corrugated it could not be confined in smooth bands, but rose out from her face like a dark aureole.

Her skin was a smooth olive, and the bones of her face were both strong and yet somehow delicate, formed in a way that seemed utterly un-English. With that face and that hair, her eyes should have been black. Instead they were harebell-blue. Framed by heavy dark brows, they looked unearthly and full of sorrow.

Her most striking feature was her mouth. Full-lipped and red, it looked sulky in rest. Yet as Janey stepped forward and offered her hand to Georgie, she smiled shyly. Suddenly her whole face was transformed.

Then, in an instant, the light was gone. Her mouth fell again into its heavy sensuality.

Georgie wanted badly to see her smile again. She tried – through various attempts at winsomeness and jocularity – but failed. Janey's smiles were even more rare than her voice. Georgie had never met such a silent woman. She seemed to have no store of small talk, no understanding of the need to bat conversation back and forth like a shuttlecock. Mostly she listened, with an expression of intense concentration, turning her face from one speaker to another, her hands clasped tightly in her lap.

Georgie found herself wanting badly for Janey to look at her, to smile at her, to answer her in some way. She understood absolutely how Topsy had fallen so madly in love with her.

Georgie felt herself a poor dab of a thing against such wild beauty.

Yet, as they rose to leave, Janey came and took her hand and bent down to say, in a soft voice full of a country burr that she tried to hide, 'I am so pleased to meet you. I do hope we can be friends. Please do no' mind me. 'Tis all so new an' strange. All this, I mean.'

Her hand made a helpless gesture. Suddenly Georgie felt like she was much more than just one year older, and not the country mouse she had always imagined herself to be. She took Janey's hand and pressed it between her own. 'I would be so happy to be friends. My husband loves yours so much, I feel that I must love you too. Will you call on me? And may I call on you?'

'I would like that,' Janey said. Her lips suddenly curved and Georgie received the smile she had looked for all night. 'Thank you.'

Georgie went out into the smoggy summer night in a strange daze of happiness. In the hansom cab, Ned drew her close. 'I find her terrifying,' he confessed. 'She is such an Amazon.'

Georgie shook her head. 'She's very tall,' she admitted, 'but not an Amazon. I think she's the one who is afraid. You must be very kind to her, Ned.'

'I will then,' he answered, as if he was not the kindest of men.

Georgie rested her hand against her hot cheek. She wished with all her heart that she were lovely enough to haunt a man's imagination. Yet it was impossible to hate Janey. She did not have any of the arrogance of the beautiful, carrying herself as if hunched about some old wound. Georgie, who barely reached her shoulder, wanted to protect her and look after her, as if Janey were a shy child.

That night she dreamt of Janey. She saw her as a giantess, barefoot, standing on a tiny isle in the midst of a dark surging ocean. Her hair was black and billowing as thunderclouds. She held something small cradled in her hands. She bent her head over it, weeping.

Georgie wanted to know what she wept over.

But she could not see.

'What in heaven's name is the Wombat's Lair?' Georgie asked, hanging over Ned's shoulder as he read a note written in Gabriel's distinctive scrawl.

'A most dark and holy place,' Ned said solemnly. 'It is a sign of the high regard that you are held in by Gabriel that he proposes that you should be initiated into its mysteries.'

'Will Lizzie be there?'

'We can only hope.'

Georgie had never been to the zoo. She smelt it first – a whiff of something like a cow-byre multiplied by thousands – and then heard it – shrieks and bellows and strange wild jungle cries.

She squeezed Ned's arm in excitement. 'What was that?'

'A baboon,' he said.

'Really?'

He laughed. 'I don't know. Maybe.'

The zoo was crowded with people out to enjoy the summer sunshine. The women's skirts were all so huge it was hard to find a way between them. Many were vividly coloured in mauve, purple or magenta, the shocking new colour so popular that season. Georgie gazed in amazement. As always, she was wearing a simple home-made frock of some dark, cheap material that would wear well. Her only decoration was a white linen collar. She could not help indignantly calculating just how much each gown and beribboned bonnet must have cost, and how many of the needy poor it might have fed.

They wandered about happily, waiting for the others. Ned suddenly stiffened. 'Georgie, look!'

'What is it?' She turned, realising his eyes were dancing with mischief.

'Look what's in the enclosure.'

She looked, and fell at once into laughter. 'Camels!'

'I shall have to write and tell Mrs Sampson I have finally seen some camels,' Ned said solemnly. 'She will be pleased.'

Then they saw Gabriel, walking arm in arm with a tall slender woman with loosely pinned hair the colour of flames. He introduced her proudly as his wife, Lizzie. Her face was beautifully modelled, with a straight nose and broad cheekbones, and her skin was pale and dusted with tiny golden freckles. Her eyes were deeply hooded, and her agate-grey eyes wonderfully luminous.

Murmuring a polite greeting, Lizzie smiled and held out her hand to Georgie. It was delicate, long-fingered and cold.

'Look at us, all growned up and married,' Gabriel said. 'Come on, there are Bruno and Emma.'

Lizzie and Emma were evidently old friends, for they greeted each other with delight, kissing each other's cheeks and talking excitedly.

'To the Wombat Lair!' Gabriel shouted, raising high his walking stick.

'He just loves wombats,' Lizzie said in explanation to Georgie. 'He thinks they are the drollest creatures alive.'

'They make me miss Topsy,' Ned said sadly.

'Are he and Janey not coming?' Georgie asked in surprise. 'I thought we would see them here.'

'Topsy is too busy building his palace to associate with the likes of us,' Gabriel said over his shoulder.

The wombats were just as funny as Gabriel had promised. He calmly climbed the railing, and stuck his walking stick through to scratch the wombat's furry back. It made small grunts of pleasure, and waggled its furry behind back and forth.

The other great attraction was the giraffes. Georgie had never seen creatures like them. 'I wonder for what purpose God created them?' she asked.

'To amaze us,' Gabriel said. 'Or in case we need to reach anything really, really high. One would have been useful in the debating hall, wouldn't it, Ned? To hand us up sandwiches and soda bottles. Or we could have stuck a paintbrush in its mouth, and got it to help poor old Tops. I'm sure a giraffe would have done a better job of painting all those sunflowers.'

Georgie was caught between giggles and gasps at his rudeness. She noticed that Lizzie did not laugh, but watched him closely, almost suspiciously.

Yet if Gabriel went wandering off with one of the other men, Lizzie grew restless and unhappy. She looked out for him constantly, her fingers twisting the end of the ribbon that bound her narrow waist. When he came back, she seemed to relax, tucking her hand into the crook of his arm and smiling once more.

Afterwards, Georgie and Ned went back to Gabriel and Lizzie's rooms at Hampstead. Gabriel and Ned were deep in a conversation about the poet Dante, and so Georgie went up to the dark little bedroom with Lizzie to take off her bonnet. The sun was just setting over the Heath, a few low red rays striking in through the lattice window. It made Lizzie's hair gleam like a freshly polished copper kettle.

'Gabriel tells me that you have been taking art classes with Bruno?' Lizzie asked with warm interest. 'I've heard he's a brilliant teacher.'

'Yes,' Georgie replied eagerly. 'He's so kind and I'm learning so much.'

'Do you know that I paint too?' Lizzie asked. 'I'm working on a drawing now. Would you like to see it?'

'Oh, yes, please.' Georgie came forward with a rush, as Lizzie drew out a drawing from between some boards. It was crowded with figures, most with shadowy faces. A knight in dark armour knelt by the side of a young man, who appeared to be dead or fainting. A woman with a crown on her head had turned away her face in grief. She looked a lot like Lizzie. Georgie could see it was about something tragic.

'I call it the Woeful Victory,' Lizzie said.

'It's very good. So much feeling in it. And it looks like an old medieval woodcut. I just love that look. That's what I'm trying to learn to do.' Georgie hesitated, then confided shyly, 'I'd like to write and illustrate a collection of old fairytales. You know, the Sleeping Princess in the Wood, and Cinderella, and so on.'

'That's a fine ambition,' Lizzie cried. 'Perhaps we could work together. Like Gabriel did with Johnny Millais and the others with those Tennyson poems.'

'Oh, I'd like that,' Georgie said.

Lizzie smiled at her. 'Let's do it then! Why let the men have all the glory?'

Georgie went home in a joyful daze, her head filled with dreams of creating something beautiful herself.

12

Red House
Summer 1860

It was a house out of a fairytale.

Janey walked through the garden, marvelling at the steep-roofed building set amongst its apple trees as if it had always been there. Wild roses, sweetbriar and honeysuckle clambered over the trellises, and tall hollyhocks and lilies grew from a tumult of daisies. The air was full of the scent of lavender and rosemary, and birds sang in the flowering crabapple. It had rained that morning, but now the sun had come out and all the leaves shone as if they had been polished with lemon oil.

The house itself was made of red Kentish brick, with sharply pitched irregular roofs and gables of red tile, topped with tall chimneys. The arched front door was hidden within a deep porch, with white sashed windows in a tall gothic-pointed recess above. Jasmine climbed up one wall, filling the air with its heady fragrance.

'Come and see the well and the rest of the garden before we go inside,' Topsy said, pulling at her hand.

Smiling, Janey followed him around the side of the house to a small, enclosed garden basking in the late summer sunshine. Sitting in the corner of the two wings of the house was the quaintest well she had ever seen, topped with a conical roof like a witch's hat.

'Oh, Topsy, it's beautiful!' she exclaimed.

He beamed. 'I knew you'd like the well.'

'It's like something out of a story book.'

'That was the feeling I wanted.'

Nothing matched anything else. One wall had three round windows in a row, another wall had two traditionally shaped sash windows set above an open archway, and yet another a tall narrow window like a medieval arrow-slit, set in a gothic arch. Behind the well was a stair tower topped by a simple iron weathervane. Janey shaded her eyes with one hand, trying to make out the pattern.

'It says *W. M. 1859.*' Topsy sounded very pleased with himself.

As her husband led her through the garden, he pointed out what rooms were hidden behind the windows. Janey's head whirled with it all. A studio and dining room. A library and morning room. A kitchen, fitted out with a range and a pantry. A buttery. Three water closets! She could hardly take it all in.

Kitchen gardens had been laid out on the far side, with bees humming happily amongst the pea flowers and the lavender. Pear trees espaliered against the wall were already showing tiny green globes of fruit.

'You must've planted the garden while the house was still being built,' Janey exclaimed.

'Of course I did,' her husband answered, looking surprised. 'Nothing makes a house look so new as not having a garden.'

On the west face of the house was a long lawn where Topsy planned to play bowls, overlooked by a funny little window standing on a slim brick pillar. Topsy told her it was called an oriel window, then led her back round to the front door again.

'May my lady be pleased to enter her castle?' Topsy opened the door with a deep flourishing bow.

Janey clasped her hands together, stepping past him into a great entrance hall. Then she stood, gazing about her, almost overcome. Never could she have expected she would live in such a grand house.

The floor was tiled in deep red, the walls whitewashed. Ahead was a broad oak staircase, its posts carved like something out of a cathedral. A huge wooden cupboard was pushed against one wall, with a low seat below.

'Here's the dining room.' Topsy showed her to the right, into a long room with a red brick fireplace built with a dramatic medieval-shaped hood. Against one wall was a wooden plate dresser painted a vivid ox-blood red. 'I asked our architect to design that for you. See how high it is? He built it so you would never need to stoop to fetch the plates.'

Janey blinked away tears. 'It's beautiful,' she said again.

'I'm having two long tables made, so we can have feasts here like a medieval king and queen,' he told her.

As she was led from room to room, Topsy proudly showing her each unique feature, Janey thought that she had never seen a house like it. Everything was grand in size but utterly simple in design. There was none of the heavy ornamentation seen in most houses she had visited. Even the roof beams were left exposed in the stairwell.

'It feels like a church,' Janey said.

He cast her a quick look of approval. 'That's it! That's what we wanted. Houses for people can be just as beautiful as houses for God.'

'It's all I've ever wanted,' she said huskily. 'A home of my own.'

Topsy said eagerly, 'I know it's very bare and plain at the moment, but I have such plans. I thought we could paint murals on the walls. Ned and Gabriel will help me. And we'll make some tapestries for the bedrooms. Look. I thought this room could be the nursery.'

He led her into a small room, with a lovely view out over the garden. Janey smiled. Unconsciously her hands moved to press against the gentle swell of her belly. Topsy stood behind her, putting his arms about her and laying his big hands over hers.

'Are you pleased, Janey?'

She slid her hands out so she could lay them over his, pressing them more closely about her. 'Oh, yes,' she whispered.

*

Janey's new life was full of trials.

Meeting so many new people. Giving orders to servants. Worrying about household accounts when she had never been taught to reckon.

The greatest ordeal, though, would be seeing Gabriel again.

She knew it could not be avoided. Topsy loved and admired Gabriel as much as ever. His name was mentioned a dozen times a day. Now he was married too, and everyone was full of curiosity about his new bride.

One day in early autumn, Topsy told her they had been invited to a party at the house of Gabriel's mother and sisters. Janey nodded, though her chest tightened at once. It was some comfort to know that Ned and Georgie would be there. Janey felt that she and Georgie were growing to be friends, the first she had ever had.

'We'll not be able to stay long,' Topsy said. 'I'd like to catch the evening train back to Kent.'

She nodded again. Topsy knew that she did not like London. The red glare on the horizon, the black smoking chimneys, the stench of sweat and cinders and sewage, the clank and rattle of carriages and cabs, the shriek of trains and steamboats, the shrill insistent cries of the costermongers, the roar from the public houses on every corner, the shove and tumult of the footpaths, the desperate neigh of horses whipped beyond endurance, the beggars and prostitutes on every corner.

Janey could not bear it.

She only ever came up to London reluctantly. They needed to furnish their house, however, so she and Topsy had spent a few days looking through shops and warehouses. Nothing felt right to them. Their house – so medieval in spirit – needed dressing to match. Topsy was full of plans for creating what they wanted themselves. Janey had found a length of serge that had been dyed a soft, warm indigo-blue that she thought would make a lovely wall-hanging. Topsy had sketched a quick design of wild daisies on the back of his railway timetable, inspired by one of his favourite medieval manuscripts. She was eager to get home to start work on it, with nothing but birdsong in her ears and the fresh, sweet country air in her lungs.

But first she must endure the party in Albany Street.

She was introduced first to Mrs Rossetti, a grim-faced woman in black with a white cap with long streamers. Her son William was a taller, gaunter version of Gabriel, with a high receding hairline and a serious expression. The two sisters sat either side of their mother, backs straight, hands folded, heads bent. Christina was the more attractive of the two, with a long face and pointed chin.

Mrs Rossetti bowed her head and said, in the manner of one conferring a great honour, 'Good evening, Mrs Morris. Welcome.'

'Thank you, Mrs Rossetti. Please forgive me for not taking off my bonnet. My husband and I have a train to catch.' Janey spoke carefully, aware of the sound of every vowel and consonant.

'Of course. We are so pleased to have a chance to meet you both. Gabriel says your husband is a most talented poet. He has had a book of poems published, I believe?'

'He has.' Janey glanced at her husband who had gone red and was fidgeting with his watch chain. Topsy's poetry had not been well received. Janey knew this hurt him, though he had never said a word. He had not tried to compose a verse since, however, nor showed anyone his little book.

Christina had been gazing off into space, thinking of something else, but at the mention of poetry her attention quickened. She looked at Topsy with an intense and frowning gaze.

'I write poetry too,' she said, in a low musical voice.

He nodded at her. 'I know. I read your work in *The Germ*. Gabriel told me it was by you. It was very fine. That one called "Dream Land". How did it go? "Where sunless rivers weep, their waves into the deep, she sleeps a charmed sleep ..."'

'"Awake her not,"' he and Christina said together.

Christina's face glowed.

'Very fine,' Topsy said again.

Christina bent her head in acknowledgement. It was clear she was pleased.

'There's Ned and Mrs Ned,' Topsy said, pointing at the Joneses.

At the sight of Janey, Georgie jumped up and held out her hands in greeting. She was so small, Janey had to bend down to kiss her. It was like embracing a child. As always Georgie was dressed simply, with no other ornament but her wedding ring and a little string of cheap wooden beads. Her dark hair was drawn back tightly, without a single softening curl or plait, but her eyes were so luminous and her dark lashes so long she was saved from plainness. Janey thought she had never met anyone with so much goodness shining out of her face.

'Janey, this is Letitia Bell Scott.' Georgie gestured to the short, dumpy woman to whom she had been speaking. 'Her husband William is an artist who teaches at the government school of design in Newcastle-on-Tyne. Letitia, this is the new Mrs William Morris! Though Ned calls her Mrs Topsy, of course.'

'Goodness gracious,' Letitia said, looking Janey up and down. 'Aren't you tall. You make Georgie and I look quite diminutive.'

Janey smiled, but did not know how to respond. Letitia did not need an answer. She rattled on, 'And where are you from?'

'From Oxford,' Janey replied.

'No, no, I mean your family. What country do they come from?'

'England,' Janey said.

'I mean, originally.'

'They come from England,' Janey repeated.

Letitia gave a little snort of polite disbelief. 'Really? Where?'

'Both my parents were born in little villages in the Cotswolds, but moved to Oxford for work. I was born there.'

Letitia looked her up and down again, then said, 'And so what does your father do, Mrs Morris?'

'He's an ostler.'

As Letitia gazed at her in horrified amazement, Janey added, with just a glint of a smile, 'You know. A man that works in the stables of an inn.'

'Your father works in a stable?'

'He does.' A devilish imp prompted her to add, 'We lived there when I was a child.'

'In the stable?'

'Yes.'

Letitia seemed at a loss for words. Then she gathered up her skirts and withdrew a few steps, her nose pinched as if she was afraid Janey must still smell of horseshit.

'Don't forget our Lord was born in a stable,' Georgie said in a cold voice. She tucked her hand into Janey's arm, and said, 'Come, Janey, there are so many other people I wish to introduce you to. Excuse us, Letitia.' With a curt nod, she led Janey away.

'What an unpleasant woman,' she said, as soon as they were out of earshot. 'I'm so sorry.'

'Perhaps I should make up a new history for myself,' Janey said. 'I could pretend I was a princess of the Ottoman Empire, hiding from assassins …'

'Sent by your cruel uncle who wishes to seize your throne,' Georgie said with delight.

'Or perhaps, since I am so unfashionably tall, I can say I am descended from the giants of Zanzibar …'

Then Gabriel came in.

Janey could not draw enough air into her lungs. She turned away, fighting for composure, and saw Topsy glance at her. She could only hope her face did not betray her.

'Oh, Lizzie's not here! I did so want her to meet you,' Georgie cried.

Gabriel went to greet his mother, kissing her on both cheeks. 'I'm so sorry, Mama. Lizzie was not well enough to come.'

'I am sorry to hear that,' Mrs Rossetti said, in a tone of polite disbelief.

'She is most unwell,' Gabriel said. 'I should have stayed to care for her, but I wanted a chance to see Mr and Mrs Topsy.' He looked across the room, straight into Janey's eyes. There was something hard and mocking in his glance. Despite herself, colour flamed in Janey's cheeks. She gripped her hands together, looking down at the ground. Gabriel came to their sides, shaking Topsy's hand and clapping him on the shoulder. 'Congratulations! Don't things change? Who would have guessed we'd all be old married men so soon?'

Topsy responded in kind. Then it was Janey's turn. He shook her hand and said coolly, 'Well, married life seems to be suiting you, Mrs Topsy.'

She could not speak. One hand went instinctively to the curve of her belly, half-hidden by the swell of her gown. He saw the movement, and his face stiffened. 'I see. So that's why you are glowing. Congratulations to you both.'

'And to you too,' she managed to say.

Then Gabriel was greeting Ned and Georgie, and the awful first moment was over.

'And so tell me, how goes the Towers of Topsy?' Gabriel asked them, after all the exclamations and explanations were done with.

Topsy grinned. 'It's just as wonderful as I had hoped. Still rather bare. I say, you should all come down and stay with us. We've plenty of room.'

'Oh, we'd love to!' Georgie clapped her hands.

'Come down as soon as you can,' Topsy said. 'The sunflowers will be out.'

'Making your garden look just like your mural of jealous King Mark,' Gabriel said. There was some kind of sly dig in his words that Janey did not fully understand. She saw Topsy flinch a little, and look at her. Then she remembered that King Mark had been the cuckolded husband of Iseult, the queen Janey had modelled.

She slid her hand inside Topsy's arm. 'If we don't go soon, we'll miss our train.'

'Yes, we must go,' he answered in some relief. 'So sorry we didn't get to see Mrs Gabriel. Come down and see us soon!'

As they made their farewells, Janey thought how strange it was that the men all called the wives by their friends' first names. It was friendly and funny, but also somehow diminishing, as if they had no name or no existence outside their husbands.

Lizzie, she thought. *Her name is Lizzie.*

Janey had thought tonight would be the last of the great ordeals she had to face. But she still had not met the woman she could not help thinking of as her rival and her enemy.

13

Queen of Hearts
Autumn–Winter 1860

I have never been so happy, Lizzie told herself. Her thin hands worried at the knitted blanket that covered her, unravelling a loose thread. *Gabriel will be home soon. It's natural to feel a little low with such weather.*

Rain beat against the windows. The world was a watery blur beyond.

She looked about the room. They had rented a small furnished cottage near Hampstead Heath. The sitting room was overcrowded with dark mahogany furniture. Lace antimacassars on the backs of the over-stuffed chairs. A fly-spotted portrait of a young Queen Victoria on the wall.

Lizzie wished they could find a nicer place to live. It was disheartening being left alone all day while Gabriel went into the studio at Blackfriars to paint. She wanted a house with a garden and a studio attached, so that she could keep an eye on him.

She laid her hands on her stomach. It felt uneasy below her hands, as if her inner sea was troubled by storms. A bucket was close to hand, for almost anything could trigger a wave of nausea. She could not bear the slightest whiff of cooking, nor could she walk past the butcher's shop with its gutted rabbit carcasses hanging from hooks.

The doctor had told her that a child was growing in her belly, and that was the cause of her constant queasiness. Lizzie had been afraid that it was a return of her old madness, and she had seen the same fear in Gabriel's eyes. But the doctor assured her that it was normal to feel so ill. It was the baby drawing upon her strength and vitality. It will soon pass, he promised her. She just had to endure these first few months.

The doctor had called her Mrs Rossetti. It felt strange but wonderful to be addressed so. Sometimes Lizzie practised writing her new name. Elizabeth Eleanor Rossetti. It sounded so grand.

She did not feel like herself anymore at all. The girl she had been was gone. Now she was Mrs Rossetti, a mother to be. She could spend her days writing poetry and drawing and painting, if she had the strength. And at night, she slept pressed close to the warmth of Gabriel's body, her cold feet tucked between his.

Lizzie was almost sure her husband no longer saw any of those brazen models of his. Annie Miller was thought to have become the mistress of an aristocratic rake; and Gabriel had told her that Fanny Cox had married, which surprised her. Lizzie had thought Fanny a street-walker. Not that it mattered. Fanny was married and gone out of Gabriel's life. He was working on a painting of Lizzie as the Queen of Hearts; there was no shame in modelling for him when she was his wife.

Lizzie picked up her pencil again and made a few desultory marks on the page, but she could not concentrate. She glanced at the clock on the mantelpiece, then took up the little bottle that always sat beside her and measured out a few more drops. Bless that kind doctor, who had told Gabriel that laudanum was the best thing to counteract her morning sickness.

Soon the bittersweet liquid worked its usual magic, and Lizzie drifted away on a stream of disconnected thoughts. A bairn on the way. No red hair, she hoped. Or freckles. Gabriel's dark curls, Gabriel's beautiful voice. A little Gabriello to lift up chubby arms to her. Calling *Mamma, mamma.* She'd be a better mother by far than her own. She'd love that little mite with all her heart. Grazed knees, falling down stockings. She'd laugh and swoop him up in her arms and kiss him. Best mamma in the world.

She thought of her father. His face and hair and coat covered in fine silvery glitter after the day's work. His cough, as he bent over the grinding stone. He was dead now, gone to his grave thinking her a worthless whore. If only he had known Gabriel would marry her in the end. Would he have forgiven her?

She stood and went to the window, the blanket wrapped around her. She could see her face. Thin and white. Hollow-eyed. It made her think of that strange painting Gabriel had worked on when they were in Paris, on their honeymoon. He called it his bogey painting. A couple, walking in a gloomy wood in the gloaming, met their own doubles, exact in every respect. The man - who looked just like Gabriel - drew his sword but could not find the strength to wield it. The woman - who looked just like Lizzie - swooned. Their doppelgängers stared at them indifferently, hallowed with unearthly light.

Omen of death to come.

Lizzie dragged the curtains shut with a rattle, then rushed from lamp to lamp, lighting the wicks with fingers that quivered. She stoked up the fire and stood close to it, trying to warm herself.

Where was he? Why was he so late?

She had to stay calm. Lizzie knew her flash points. She tried to read. But the words swam. She clenched her fists, shut her eyes, and tried not to listen to the strident voice of suspicion within.

The gate squeaked, then clanged shut. Lizzie rearranged her skirts, tidied her hair, pretended to be engrossed in her book.

The door opened. Gabriel came in, streaming wet, taking off his hat and shaking back damp curls. He was carrying a pot from the local cookhouse. The fug of it filled the room.

'What a day! Look at me. I'm wet to the skin.'

'You're so late. Where've you been?'

'Trying to get home. All the buses were packed.'

He's lying, she thought but did not say.

Gabriel tossed his wet coat and hat on to a chair, and came to put the pot from the cookhouse in the ashes to warm. Then he sat down and unbuttoned his shoes, kicking them off and setting them to dry on the hearth. He pulled off his stockings and wrung them dry.

She set the table and Gabriel began to serve up the stew. Lizzie could not say that she was not hungry, or that the smell made her feel sick. It would only upset him. She sat down, pretending to be eager to eat.

As always, Gabriel watched her closely. She cut her meal into neat squares, and chewed each mouthful twenty-five times. Then she ate only twenty-five bites. It was the only way she could manage to eat without being overcome by panic. When she had eaten the right number of mouthfuls, she laid down her fork and pushed her plate as far away from her as she could. Then she concentrated all her will on keeping the food down.

Lizzie wanted to be well. She wanted to make Gabriel happy. She wanted this tiny being within her womb to grow as he or she should. That meant Lizzie had to eat, as much as she disliked it.

'Look, I can pluck an apple just by reaching my hand out the window!' Georgie caught hold of an apple, bringing it into the house in a little shower of leaves. She bit into it with triumph.

'It is the beautifulest place in the world,' Ned said.

'See how I've contrived a minstrels' gallery for us.' Topsy climbed up the rungs of a ladder that had been built on the side of a tall sideboard. 'What jolly parties we shall have!'

'Is Gabriel coming down?' Ned asked eagerly.

A shadow darkened Topsy's face. 'No. Mrs Gabriel is still unwell.'

'I wonder what is wrong with her?' Georgie said. 'Gabriel said the doctors are sure now it's not consumption.'

'She is very delicately made,' Ned said. 'She looks like a puff of wind would break her in two.'

Georgie picked an apple and threw it to Janey, laughing. 'I'm sure Lizzie would be well if she only came down here! Who could not be well down here in the country, with that sweet wind blowing and an apple a day to keep the doctor away?'

'It can't be good for her, living in London,' Ned said.

The two men wandered off to look at the ceiling of the studio. Georgie followed Janey into the garden.

'Look at those sunflowers! Don't they make the garden look cheerful?'

'Topsy loves sunflowers,' Janey said. 'He likes the way they all stand an' face the east.'

She showed Georgie the sunny little porch which Topsy called the Pilgrim's Rest, in honour of Chaucer's pilgrims to Canterbury who were thought to have passed nearby. It looked out onto the garden and the well with the red conical roof like a dunce's cap. Topsy had built rose-covered trellises to enclose the lawn, creating the feel of a medieval walled garden.

'Oh this is delightful!' Georgie cried. 'Let us sit out here and enjoy the sunshine.'

The two women fetched their sewing baskets and books, and made a little camp out in the porch with cushions and quilts. It became their habit to retire there each morning, sewing and talking and laughing, while the two men painted kings and queens and knights and damsels upon the drawing-room wall, all with the faces of their friends.

After lunch every day, the two women went out driving in the quaint little wagonette, sitting under a chintz canopy, stopping to pick blackberries, rosehips, haws and sloes. Janey knew a lot about what grew in the hedgerows and meadows.

As the sun slanted through the autumn-yellow leaves, the two young women took their laden baskets back to the kitchen, to turn the fruit into jams and jellies and tisanes and teas. Georgie found it interesting that Janey was not content to leave all the work of the house and garden in her servants' hands. She wanted to make her own bread, and grow her own vegetables, and spin her own wool, just as if she was a medieval lady and not a modern-day middle-class woman with staff. At first Georgie thought Janey just wanted to gratify Topsy, but she came to believe that Janey took fierce pleasure in keeping her house spotless and sweet smelling, and presiding over a table laden with the fruits of her own labours.

At night, Georgie played the piano for them and sang, or sometimes they played silly childish games like blind man's bluff. Friends came to visit them on the weekends, and sometimes the men wrestled together or pelted each other with windfall apples. One night they played hide-and-seek all through the house. Janey was the finder, and crept along the passages with her candle flame flickering in the draughts. When Ned leapt out at her, growling like a bear, she screamed and dropped her candle, as if expecting to encounter some kind of wild animal. It was all glorious fun, and Georgie hated the thought of having to return to London and their own cramped and damp-smelling lodgings.

One morning in late September, Georgie sat beside Janey in the Pilgrims' Rest, working away with her engraving tools on a little square of wood where she was attempting to cut out the shape of a wild rose. Georgie had been practising hard, and was growing more adept every day.

'There,' she said with a flourish, laying down her graver. 'What do you think?'

'Very pretty,' Janey said. 'You're clever with your fingers.'

'So are you,' Georgie replied, looking admiringly at the design of daisies flowering on the indigo-blue serge.

'I can embroider well enough if I am given the pattern, but I am not so good at inventing the design.' Janey smoothed her stitches with one finger. 'While Topsy comes up with a dozen new designs every hour, but doesn't have the patience to sit and sew it.'

'Be glad he sits and sews at all,' Georgie said. 'I've ever known a man to do so before.'

'He's not your usual man.'

Georgie looked at Janey quickly, for there was an odd note in her voice. But Janey's face was as serene as ever. Georgie wondered again at the strange marriage of these two young people: Topsy so short and rotund and boisterous, and his wife so tall and beautiful and silent. Perhaps it worked because they were so different. And both seemed content enough, if always busy about their own concerns.

Her hands were hurting from their work with the graver, so she packed her tools away and took up an edge of the serge to help embroider daisies. Then she saw, tucked away down in the bottom of Janey's work basket, a soft new garment, made for someone very small.

Her eyes flew up to Janey's face. She was smiling as she sewed, her thoughts far away. Georgie smiled too, a little wistfully. Already everything was changing.

Lizzie waited till Gabriel had gone out, then tiptoed into his studio.

It smelt of turpentine and oil paints, making her stomach clench. She put her hands on her belly. Round and hard. Sometimes she felt an inexplicable flutter deep within. Like something somersaulting inside her. She wondered if it was her baby, groping its way around the confines of her womb. She could hardly imagine it.

The studio was in as much disorder as ever. Paintings stacked against the walls, or propped up on easels. A table laden with drawings. Lizzie rifled through them. Hands, eyes, faces, hair. Lizzie did not think any were hers.

Lizzie turned to the canvases. Carefully she leaned them forward, scrutinising each one before moving on to the next. The edges of many were furred with dust. She tried not to leave any pale incriminating fingermarks.

The Queen of Hearts painting had not turned out well. Lizzie looked sick and green, her face dwarfed by the heavy masses of red hair. She stared at her own face for a long time. It was how she looked now, she had to admit.

At least she had persuaded Gabriel that they should move back to Blackfriars. She could lie in their bed, resting, and hear him moving about in the studio next door.

Lizzie had thought living at Blackfriars would ease the suspicion that gnawed at her. But it had not helped. Gabriel was often out, leaving her alone for hours. Sometimes he went to work at his friend Roddy's studio. Other times she heard quick feminine steps and giggles coming from the studio. Lizzie would go and stand outside, leaning to press her ear to the door, only to hurry away at the firm approaching tread of her husband's feet. He was working on some new commissions, she knew, but he was vague on the details.

Some canvases on easels were shrouded with paint-stained cloths. Lizzie lifted one away. Beneath was a sensuous painting of a woman with masses of golden hair, a white rose tucked behind one ear, marigolds behind her. Her jacket was unbuttoned to show the white frill of her chemise, and her plump lips were slightly puckered, as if offering them up to be kissed.

Fanny Cox. Though now she called herself Fanny Cornforth. It was not the last name of her husband. She had given herself a new name. As if hoping to start life afresh.

Lizzie wanted to tear the canvas down, put her heel through it, slash at it with a palette knife, tear it to shreds. Instead she carefully covered it up again, and went back to the bedroom, curling up and clutching a pillow, weeping into it till it was wet through.

She knew Gabriel had been lying to her.

When at last her husband came home, Lizzie accused him, in a voice shaking with tears, of sneaking out to see Fanny behind her back.

Gabriel stared at her. 'I haven't seen Fanny in months,' he said flatly.

'I saw the painting of her.'

'I did that a year or more ago,' he said. 'My old friend Boyce bought it from me, but I've borrowed it back since my dealer wants another just like it. I'm having trouble with it, though. I need to see Fanny to get her down right, but didn't want to upset you when you're in such a delicate condition.'

'Liar!' She sat up and flung the pillow at him. 'All you ever do is lie.'

Gabriel turned on his heel and strode away, but she stumbled after him, hurling accusations at him. It was their worst argument since they had got married.

The first crack in the ice.

*

Lizzie wrote swiftly, covering the page with her sprawling handwriting.

> My Dear Little Georgie,
> I hope you intend coming over with Ned tomorrow evening like a sweetmeat, it seems so long since I saw you dear. Janey will be here I hope to meet you.
> With a willow-pattern dish full of love to you and Ned
> Lizzie

She wanted Georgie there to help bolster her courage. Lizzie had not yet met Janey Morris, and she was very afraid that she would prove to be another rival for Gabriel's affections. There had been something odd in the way he had told Lizzie that the Morrises were coming to supper. His face had been flushed, and he had not met her eye. It might have been the heat from the stove. It might have been her imagination. But Lizzie could not help being suspicious.

She was greatly relieved when Topsy and his new wife arrived, bundled up to the eyebrows against the bitter November weather. Janey was tall as a man! Bushy black hair and eyebrows that practically met in the middle. And so angular and awkward. She barely said a word all supper, leaving the others to keep the conversation running along merrily. Lizzie relaxed. Gabriel liked confident, outspoken women with golden-red hair and easy manners. She did not need to fear this black-browed close-mouthed gypsy.

Georgie and Ned were full of the delights of Red House, urging Gabriel to come and join them in painting and decorating the bare walls and ceilings.

'We're painting the romance of Sir Degravaunt in the dining room,' Ned said.

'Which scenes?' Gabriel languidly swilled his wine. 'The one where he first sets eyes on the fair maiden Melidor and falls in love with her at first sight, *le coup de foudre*? Or the scene in which he does battle for her hand, not once, not twice, but thrice?'

'I've had to start at the end of the story,' Ned said. 'With the wedding. Because of the light, you know.'

'A wedding is not always the end of the story,' Gabriel said. 'Mrs Topsy, your glass is empty. Can I pour you some wine?'

Janey held out her goblet, and Gabriel put one hand over hers to hold it steady. When he let go, Janey slopped a little wine on the tablecloth and mopped it up hastily with her napkin, mumbling apologies. Lizzie remembered she was the daughter of a stable hand; one had to forgive her any clumsiness.

'What about the scene where Melidor's serving maid smuggled Sir Degravaunt into her room?' Gabriel asked. 'Will you paint that?'

'I was thinking more of the wedding procession. With minstrels and things, you know.' Ned sketched with his hands in the air. 'I'm drawing Topsy as King Arthur and Janey as Queen Guenevere. It'll be so romantic.'

Gabriel coughed violently into his napkin. 'Sorry. A little gristle in my throat. What about you, Topsy? What are you painting?'

'I'm pricking patterns into the damp plaster of the ceilings,' Topsy said. 'I'm putting stylised peacock feathers in the studio. To represent immortality.'

Gabriel turned to Janey. 'That's an old belief, Mrs Topsy. It's because they believed peacock flesh did not decay.'

'I thought it was because the peacocks regrow new feathers every spring,' Ned said. 'Making them a symbol of resurrection and eternal life.'

'I thought they were symbols of false pride and vanity,' Georgie said. 'You know, proud as a peacock.'

'So very appropriate for Topsy's studio,' Gabriel said at once. Then he held up both hands, laughing. 'I'm sorry. I couldn't resist.'

Topsy turned red, and drank down most of his glass of wine.

'You must come down and help too,' Georgie said, looking from Gabriel to Lizzie with wide blue-grey eyes that seemed impossibly innocent. 'You are both such wonderful artists. Think what you could create.'

'You could paint scenes of Dante and Beatrice,' Topsy said to Gabriel. 'A love that never wavers or dies, that endures even after death.' He looked at his wife, and put out a timid hand to touch her wrist. 'Wouldn't that be wonderful, Janey?'

She nodded, all her attention on crumbling her bread.

Topsy looked at Lizzie. 'We would love to have you both. Please, come down for Christmas. We'll recreate our famous party at Red Lion Square.'

'When you hurled the Christmas pudding at the poor housekeeper's head.' Georgie laughed at the memory.

Gabriel hesitated. He looked at Janey. 'If you have room ...'

'We have plenty of room,' she answered, not looking at him. 'It's a very large house.'

'Well ... perhaps we could. It's only ... I have so much work to do. I'm getting a great many new commissions now. It must have been my painting of Guenevere.'

Janey looked up. 'It must be lonely for Lizzie, with you working so hard. Perhaps she would like to come down and stay with us a while.' Her colour had risen. 'We'd be most glad to have you. You could keep me company while Topsy paints.'

'What an excellent idea,' Gabriel said at once. 'The fresh air will do you the world of good, Lizzie. I'll come down and join you all for Christmas.'

Lizzie looked from one to the other. She did not want to leave Gabriel alone in London, but it was hard to refuse without seeming rude.

'I'll come too,' Georgie said, clapping her hands. 'I'll look after you both, and bring you tea and toast. Oh do say you will, Lizzie! It will be such a lark.'

So, a week later, Lizzie found herself put on a train and sent to the country, leaving Gabriel behind to do who knew what.

14

Mistletoe
Winter 1860

The garden was dusted with snow like icing sugar.

Janey stood by the window, her shawl wrapped tight around her. Behind her, the drawing room was magically lit by firelight and candlelight, glimmering on the little fir tree that stood in the corner, hung with gilded stars and sugar canes. Outside, the sky was leaden, the bare trees black, the countryside ashen.

She could hear Lizzie and Georgie talking and laughing as they sketched by the fire, but she did not turn her head to listen. All her attention was on the gateway, standing open to the road.

Gabriel was coming.

Topsy had gone to pick him and Ned up from the train station. Soon Gabriel would be here, sleeping under her roof, eating at her table. Janey did not know if she could bear it.

She had thought she had subdued her feelings for Gabriel, like her father tamed wild colts to the bridle. Yet each time Janey saw him she felt a kick to the pit of her stomach. He only had to touch her hand, or look at her with those laughing eyes. Janey did not know how she had kept her countenance the night of the supper party at Blackfriars. Everything he had said had been laden with double meanings, designed to make her stomach twist with fearful longing. Both Topsy and Lizzie had been wary, watching the interplay between them. Janey had tried hard to show nothing, but within was a storm of feelings.

She heard the ring of hooves on the frosty road, then saw the horse pulling the wagon through the trees, steam blowing from its nostrils. Three men were huddled in the wagon, wrapped in coats and mufflers. They would all be chilled to the bone. Janey hurried to the kitchen, to ask for some hot mulled wine. By the time the men came down the driveway, blowing into their gloved hands and stamping their feet, she stood by the door, hands clasped tightly. A tray of goblets steamed on the table beside her.

Gabriel came in first. He carried a great bouquet of mistletoe in his hands. He came straight to her, held the mistletoe above her head, and bent to kiss her on the cheek. Janey flinched, then – trying to compose herself – turned her face to greet him. His lips brushed the corner of hers. Desire jerked in her abdomen. He felt the catch of her breath, and drew away. They gazed at each other with sombre surprise, then he bent his head and pressed his mouth to hers again. Janey could not help herself. She pressed close as she could, the old hunger quickening in her blood.

Then Janey heard footsteps. She pulled herself away, pressing her hand to her mouth.

She cast a quick hunted look around. Topsy was coming through the porch, Ned at his heels. Georgie was hurrying down the steps, Lizzie behind her. How much had they seen? Janey did not know.

Gabriel recovered first. He bounded up the stairs and held the mistletoe above the other women's heads, kissing them both with gusto. 'I love Christmas. Any more girls in the house?'

'Only the cook and the parlour maid.' Topsy took a goblet of wine, warming his hands on it. 'And I beg you not to accost them, Gabriel, else they'll be packing their bags and quitting, and you'll be cooking the Christmas goose yourself.'

'What's sauce for the goose is sauce for the gander,' Gabriel said, in husky tones that somehow made the old saying sound quite wicked.

Janey took a goblet of wine and drank deeply, trying to hide her betraying mouth. Ned had come in and was saying, in mock affront, 'Unhand my wife, I say!'

'Never!' Gabriel responded, holding the mistletoe above Georgie's head so he could again steal a kiss. 'I shall challenge you to a duel for the honour of her hand.'

'My hand is very much taken, I'm afraid,' Georgie responded, laughing.

'Ah, then, I shall simply have to make do with my own lovely wife.' Gabriel drew close to Lizzie, one hand holding the mistletoe above her head. He kissed her, but could not help glancing at Janey to see her expression. Janey stared down into the ruby depths of her goblet. Her cheeks were burning.

She followed the others upstairs, carrying the tray with hands that felt unnerved. Everyone was talking and laughing. Surely no-one had seen.

'How was your journey?' Georgie asked Gabriel, as they came into the drawing room. The men all stood before the fire, warming themselves, as Lizzie and Georgie sat once more, skirts spread out.

'Unutterably dreary and cold till we learned the true name of the Towers of Topsy. Did you know it was originally called Hogs' Hole? Isn't it perfect!' Gabriel slapped Topsy across the belly. 'Hogs' Hole!'

'I'm sorry,' Ned said to Topsy, trying to contain his own laughter. 'But you must admit it's funny ...'

Topsy looked resigned. 'It's not the name of our land,' he told Janey, 'but the cottages down the road. It's not an unusual name for a place where pigs were once set to graze.'

This pronouncement sent Gabriel and Ned off into fresh paroxysms of mirth.

'We should buy Topsy a new name plate for the house.' Gabriel drank down his goblet of mulled wine, and held it out for more. 'With a little engraving of pigs wallowing in mud.'

'Or a piglet painting sunflowers,' Ned suggested.

'A pig in a curly wig!' Gabriel leaned over and triumphantly clinked glasses with Ned, then scoffed down the wine.

'I should've known better than to tell them,' Topsy said.

Janey tried to smile. 'Never mind. If it hadn't been Hogs' Hole, it'd have been something else.'

Topsy shrugged. 'It seems I am to be the butt of all the jokes.'

'It cannot be helped,' Gabriel said solemnly. 'Given the size of your . . .'

Janey looked at him. He laughed, and raised his glass to her. 'Your wish is my command, my lady. I shall say no more.' He mimicked locking his lips and throwing the key away.

Lizzie was glancing from one face to the other. Her wine glass was already empty. Janey went and filled it up for her.

'I think we need more wine,' Topsy said. 'I'll just go down to the cellar.'

'A wine cellar!' Gabriel laughed. 'We are living it up. By all means, old chap. Bring up the best you have.'

Topsy disappeared, and came in some time later, beaming, a bottle of wine in each hand and two more tucked under his armpits.

Gabriel was in brilliant funning form all evening, taking every advantage to tease or discompose his host. Janey felt on edge, thinking he was taking it all too far. Topsy took it in good part, though. He was glad to have his friends here, admiring the house he had built.

As always, Georgie drank nothing but water, and Janey drank not much more. The baby was pressing heavily on her stomach, giving her heartburn. She noticed Lizzie only picked at her food too. Janey thought she might offer her some warm milk with honey before bedtime, to ease her nausea.

It had been strange, having Gabriel's wife living here, under her roof. Janey had thought she must hate Lizzie, but it was impossible. She was so delicate, so highly strung, like a swift that slept on the wing. Hate was too heavy for such a light-boned creature to carry.

Lizzie is Gabriel's wife, Janey kept telling herself. *And Topsy is your husband. You made your choice. It was the right choice.*

But every time Janey thought about that sinful stolen kiss, her muscles clenched with desire.

At dinner that night, Gabriel suddenly took it into his head to try his hand at limericks. He had been teasing Ned and Topsy about their beards, which were growing to rather magnificent proportions, and declaimed, 'There was an old man with a beard, who said it is just as I feared! Two owls and a hen, four larks and a wren, have all built their nests in my beard!' He then pretended to search for birds' nests in Topsy's riotous beard, parting the thick curls with his knife.

Topsy batted his hand away good naturedly.

'Isn't that Edward Lear?' Georgie cried. 'My sisters and I love his nonsense rhymes.'

'I was hoping you'd think it was mine,' Gabriel replied. 'Though I'm sure I can do better. Let me see. Georgie, Georgie, pudding and pie … no, that's been done. Help me, fellows. What rhymes with Georgie?'

'Clergy?' Ned suggested.

'But what kind of limerick has clergy in it? No, no. I know! Orgy!' Gabriel stood up, almost fell over, then steadied himself on Ned's shoulder. He raised high one hand. 'There is a young person named Georgie … who indulges each night in an orgy: soda-water and brandy … are always kept handy … to efface the effects of that orgy.'

He bowed, accepting their applause and laughter with bows all around. Georgie was laughing too, though her cheeks were rosy.

'What about Ned?' she cried. 'Make one up about Ned!'

'Pooh! Too easy!' Gabriel resumed his dramatic pose, though he swayed a little. 'There is a young artist named Jones … whose conduct no genius atones … his behaviour in life … is a pang to the wife … and a plague to the neighbours of Jones.'

'You could not have just made that up on the spot,' Georgie cried indignantly. 'You've done it at home and learned it off by heart.'

'No, no, I protest … done on the spot …'

'Then make up another one.' Georgie looked around and her glance alighted on her host. 'Do Topsy!'

Gabriel drank down his wine, then said swiftly and with scarcely a slur, 'There was a poor devil named Topsy … who feared he was suffering from dropsy … he shook like a jelly, but the doctor cried "Belly!" Then sad but relieved was poor Topsy.'

Shouts of laughter rang out from everyone. Even Janey smiled, though she pressed one hand to her mouth to hide it. Topsy ruefully took his belly in both hands and shook it. 'Too much good living,' he said.

'Marriage has made you soft,' Gabriel jeered.

Topsy stiffened, and shot Gabriel a look under his brows. Ned looked from one to the other, a little surprised.

Janey was troubled. A sharper edge seemed to have been whetted on to Gabriel's wit. She remembered how affectionate his teasing of Topsy had been when she had first met them, and how much her husband had adored Gabriel. She feared that was no longer the case. If so, Janey knew it was her fault.

'Do another one,' Georgie said. 'Do Lizzie.'

Gabriel sat back in his chair, regarding his wife with glinting eyes. He thought for a moment, then said slowly, enunciating his words carefully, 'There was a poor creature called Lizzie ... whose pictures are dear at a tizzy ... and of this great proof ... Is all that stand aloof ... from paying that sum unto Lizzie.'

Colour flamed into Lizzie's pale cheeks. She stood up abruptly. Janey frowned. A tizzy was a slang word for a sixpence. It seemed a cruel joke.

'Just teasing, Guggums,' Gabriel said swiftly.

'I ... I think it's time to go to bed. Gug, will you come?' Lizzie's voice was pleading.

He took a slow sip of his wine. 'Oh, I don't think so.' He flashed Topsy a grin. 'We still have that whole wine cellar to drain dry.'

Lizzie turned away blindly.

Janey stood up. 'Well, I think we'll leave you to it. Lizzie, let me heat you up some milk ...' She saw the flash of distaste on Lizzie's face, and said quickly, 'Or can I make you some chamomile tea? To help you sleep?'

'Thank you,' Lizzie said huskily.

Georgie laid down her napkin and stood up too, her luminous blue-grey eyes moving from one face to another. 'I'll retire now too.'

'What about Janey?' Topsy said, splashing more wine into his glass. 'You've made a rhyme for all of us ... what about my wife? Don't you have a limerick for her?'

Gabriel regarded Janey with dark brooding eyes. 'No. I don't think I do. She is above limericks, I feel.'

Lizzie went out of the room with faltering steps, and Janey hurried after her. Georgie followed close behind. 'Your husband is so quick, isn't he?' she said to Lizzie. 'Though I can't believe he said I like orgies!'

Lizzie tried to smile. 'He likes to tease.'

The next day, the men groaned and found it hard to get out of bed.

Outside, the snow fell heavily. Janey stood in the doorway, gazing across the pristine lawns, catching snowflakes on her tongue as if she was still a child. She could not explain her feelings. Joy and trepidation, fear and expectation, all twisted together within her.

The friends all settled down to work, despite the men's aching heads. Gabriel crouched over the doors to the settle, painting an angel with crimson wings. Ned and Topsy lay on their backs on the scaffolding, painting the ceiling. The women painted flowers and apple trees, and dresses of gorgeous design. Lizzie showed them how to lay their brushstrokes as carefully as embroidery stitches. With her red hair knotted at the base of her neck, her dress flowing loosely about her, she was as graceful as a nymph. While Georgie was a dancing, laughing child, taking pleasure in everything. Janey felt gigantic and gawkish beside them.

More wine was served with lunch, and the party was merry once again. Jokes and riddles flew back and forth, and Janey could not help being pleased with all the compliments showered on her for her cooking. Georgie begged her for her recipe. Lizzie ate more than a few mouthfuls. Topsy was aglow with happiness.

The afternoon was spent working on the murals in the drawing room, with the women painting alongside the men. The idea was to create the look of a tapestry unfurling across the wall. Topsy created a pattern of roses repeated on a blue background on the upper third of the wall, while Gabriel amused himself by painting a wombat curled up asleep under a chair.

Topsy was delighted with the result. 'We should start a company of Fine Art Workmen, to do this for other people's houses,' he declared. 'We could paint furniture and embroider wall-hangings.'

'What about wallpaper?' Gabriel said. 'Then we would only have to do the design once, print it and stick it up with glue. Much less work!'

'We could create beautiful stained-glass windows like they had in medieval days,' Ned said dreamily.

'Let's do it!' Topsy cried. 'We'll make a fortune.'

'And roll everywhere in yellow coaches,' Ned said.

The day was short; winter dusk closed in early. Topsy hurried to finish painting scrolls here and there on the lower third of the wall. 'I'll paint the motto there in the morning,' he said, laying down his brush at last, paint in his hair and beard, and smeared all over his shirt.

'What motto is that?' Gabriel asked.

'If I can,' Topsy replied proudly. 'From the Flemish painter, Jan van Eyck. Janey and I saw his work when we were in Bruges on our honeymoon. His portraits are so full of personality. I've never seen anything quite like them.'

Gabriel did not look pleased. Janey wanted to reassure him that Topsy did not mean to compare Gabriel to van Eyck unfavourably. *Topsy admires your work immensely too*, she wanted to say. *It's just that van Eyck's work is so alive, so real, so human. You see their feelings in their faces … and that is not your strength, I'm afraid …*

But, of course, she said nothing.

Janey was tired the next day, and found it hard to rise from her warm bed in the sharp winter dawn. Then she heard a bellow of rage. Tumbling from the bed, dragging on robe and slippers, she hurried down the hall. Topsy stood in the drawing room, dressed in his smock, his painting box dropped and broken on the floor. Stamping his feet, shaking his fists, he was cursing with great vigour and fluency.

'What's wrong?' she cried.

Topy's face was suffused with blood. He pointed to the mural. Janey stared. It took her a moment to realise someone had painted 'As I Can't' in every single scroll.

Her heart sank.

It had been Gabriel, of course.

'It was just a prank,' Gabriel said. 'You can paint over them again.'

But for once Topsy would not be mollified. Even when Gabriel and Ned together painted over the mocking words and replaced them with the motto he had chosen, Topsy remained stiff and angry.

So his two friends sent him to Coventry. Not a word would they say to him.

Gabriel would scribble a note that said 'Pass the salt, please' or 'Is there any more wine?' and lob it to Janey, who would then give the note to her husband. Topsy would fold his arms and glower and refuse to reply. So Janey would pass the salt or pour the wine, feeling that twist of anxiety in the pit of her stomach once more.

Lizzie shook her head at Gabriel, and told him to stop being so unkind. He took exception to this, and declared, 'Topsy needs to learn to take a joke.'

'Gabriel needs to learn to be more respectful,' Topsy growled under his breath.

'Topsy has to stop taking himself so seriously,' Gabriel said.

'Gabriel can go home if he doesn't like it here.'

'Is that any way for a host to speak to his honoured guest? Besides I like it here. I think I'll hibernate here all winter. All I need is a warm bed and a little honey.'

Topsy struggled to find a riposte. Gabriel gave a sardonic laugh and passed his glass to Janey to fill.

Janey begged Topsy to forgive Gabriel, and begged Gabriel to relent and speak to Topsy. Neither paid her any heed at all.

So things went on for the next day or two, till Topsy rose one morning and went to his wardrobe to get dressed. He pulled on his waistcoat but to his surprise and chagrin, could not do his buttons up. He swore loudly, and danced around in rage till his buttons all popped off.

'I've eaten too much!' he cried. 'Oh, Janey, I've got fat.'

Janey regarded him seriously for a moment, then rose and came to his side. She drew the waistcoat from his shoulders and showed him the inner lining. The seams had been taken in with large crooked stitches.

She was filled with trepidation. *You've gone too far this time, Gabriel*, she thought.

But Topsy began to laugh. Janey laughed too, in surprise and relief.

'Those fellows!' he cried. 'You've got to love them.'

Janey's daughter was born in the midst of January, just before dawn. She came quickly and easily, eager to be out in the world. Topsy had insisted on being present for the birth, and he took the bawling, red-faced mite into his arms with such tenderness it brought tears to Janey's eyes.

A fire cast its warm glow over the great bed with its carved posts and the indigo-blue wall-hangings. It gleamed on the brass jug of hot water, and danced in the diamond-paned windows. Janey lay back on her pillows, exhausted, as Topsy carefully washed and wrapped his daughter, then brought her to Janey's outstretched arms. As she lifted her daughter to her breast, Topsy held them both close.

This is enough, she told herself. *It is all you ever wanted. Be happy.*

Tears ran down her face as she felt her baby's sweet tug on her nipple. Topsy kissed them away.

15

The Best Part of Her
Spring–Winter 1861

Lizzie had not felt the baby kick for days.

She laid her hands on her hard round belly. Hot under her fingers, like a furnace. She lifted up her nightgown to examine the mound. Shape and size of a pumpkin. Marred with silvery stretch marks. Below, the thin sticks of her legs.

The mound was still. No strange rippling of her skin as the child inside turned over. No sudden shove or pull.

The doctors had told her not to distress herself. All she could do was wait and hope that all was well.

Lizzie could not rest. She struggled to a sitting position, trying not to wake Gabriel. Her feet were swollen and sore. It hurt to walk, but she shuffled slowly across to the empty cradle, set by the fireplace. She rocked it lightly with one toe.

When will you come, little one? We're waiting for you …

No tiny flutter of reaching fingers. No sharp prod of a foot.

Lizzie told herself she was being a fool. Perhaps the baby was just resting, readying itself for the struggle ahead. Maybe there was no room in there for wriggling about.

She went slowly through to the drawing room. She and Gabriel had decorated it with such gusto. Blue-and-white delft tiles around the fire-place. A fan of peacock feathers on the wall. A Spanish shawl flung over the sofa. Her watercolours, framed and hung like tiny glowing jewels.

It was beginning to lighten outside. Lizzie stood at the window and looked down at the river. Even this early in the day, it was busy with wherries and steamers. Smoke plumed grey against the dark buildings. The sky was a dirty yellow to the east. Slowly the colour deepened till it was red as a blister.

Lizzie bit her fingernails. Something was wrong. She knew it.

A sudden hot gush of liquid from between her legs. Her nightgown stained. Puddle spreading dark and bloody across the floor. 'Gabriel!' she screamed.

He came running, hair tousled, his legs bare beneath his nightshirt. He helped her back to bed, passing her a towel to staunch the flow.

'I'll fetch the doctor,' he cried, throwing on his clothes.

'Don't leave me!'

'I'll call Mrs Birrell. Don't worry, I won't be long.'

The blood continued to ooze out of her. Cramps bent her double. She could only whimper his name. Their landlady Mrs Birrell came and fussed about her, changing the sodden towel, bringing her a fresh one. 'Cup of tea, love?' she offered.

Lizzie shook her head. Both fists balled against her groin. Sharp pain. Sudden relief. Sharp pain again.

'Baby's coming, I warrant,' Mrs Birrell said.

Time passed. Lizzie's world narrowed to a pinpoint. Tossing on tidal waves. Struggling to catch a breath.

At last Gabriel returned, with the red-nosed doctor already rolling up his sleeves. He folded down the sheets to cover her hips, then gingerly lifted her stained nightgown, turning his head away so as to preserve Lizzie's modesty. He put his cold stethoscope against her hot painful stomach. It felt like he was branding her.

'I'm sorry,' he said at last. 'There is no heartbeat.'

'No … what? What do you mean?' Gabriel squeezed Lizzie's hand so hard it hurt.

'I'm afraid I can hear no heartbeat. It means the child may have died in the womb. We must get it out as fast as we can …'

Lizzie heard no more. She began to sob. Her belly convulsed. She tried to curl up against the pain. She heard the doctor say something to Gabriel, who then went out, shutting the door behind him. Lizzie called out to him in desperation. He did not return.

Suddenly the doctor held down her shoulders, pressing her back to the bed. Lizzie struggled to be free. Awful memories of feeding tubes. He pressed a handkerchief over her nose and mouth. Couldn't breathe. Sweet, pungent smell. Lizzie choked. Her arms and legs felt numb. Fingers tingling. Darkness closing in on her.

Is this death?

Agony between her legs. Sharp pincers tearing at her. Lizzie grunted like an animal. She swam to the surface. Lifted eyelids. The doctor bending over her, a hook in his bloody hand. She screamed.

Once again, the brutish sweet smell, the cloth against her mouth and nose. Choking. Floating. Glints of orange light between the slits of her eyelids. Flashes of images. The doctor, grunting. A sudden gush, a strange lightness in her body. Something small and bloody in his hands.

'My baby?' she tried to say. 'Where's my baby?'

'I'm sorry.' The doctor wrapped the bloody something in a cloth and dropped it in the basin.

Lizzie shook all over. Rattling bones. Ring of fire.

The doctor lifted her and gave her laudanum. She gulped it down, holding his hands with her own. The crescents of his fingernails were red. Blood engrained in the wrinkles about his knuckles.

'Try to sleep.' He turned away, wiping his torture instruments clean with a cloth.

Lizzie turned her head sideways, trying to see what lay in the basin.

'Was it … was it a girl or a boy?'

'Better not to think of it.'

'Please ... let me see ... what ...'

She lifted herself up on her elbows. All she could see was a tiny round head, hair dark and damp with blood.

He took the basin away.

'Tell me ...' Her voice rose to a scream.

He turned back at the door. 'Calm yourself. It was a little girl. There was nothing I could do.'

The door shut behind him. Lizzie drifted. An empty punt on relentless tides. Her body hollowed out. Dimly aware of Gabriel. Fingers clenched on her hand. Tears falling on her wrist. She squeezed shut her eyes. Oh God let it not be true. Let it not be true. Let it not be true.

But the best part of her was dead.

The door opened, and Gabriel looked out. He was haggard.

'How is she?' Georgie whispered.

He shrugged. 'Well enough in her body, considering what she went through. She is grieving most bitterly, though, as I'm sure you can imagine.'

'May we see her?'

He nodded. 'Please, come in. I know I do not have to ask you to be gentle with her.'

Georgie went through into the apartment, followed by Ned. Tense and white, he clenched his hat in both hands. Georgie smiled at him reassuringly, even as she pressed her own hands protectively over her swelling abdomen. Ned found any illness or death difficult. It brought back unhappy memories of his father's grief that had blighted his whole childhood. He was both overjoyed at the idea of becoming a father himself and terrified that his wife would be torn from him in the same way his mother had been.

Georgie thought that their baby may have been conceived in mid-January, at a time when she and Ned were down at Red House celebrating the christening of baby Jane Alice Morris, called Jenny to differentiate her from her mother. It had been a source of secret delight to Georgie, falling pregnant so close in time to Janey and Lizzie. She had imagined them all sitting together, dandling their babes on their laps, sharing the challenges and the joys.

Yet now Lizzie was cut out of that picture. Janey's joy, Georgie's anticipation, could not help but hurt her. Georgie had dressed in a loose dress, and wrapped a shawl about her, in the hope of concealing her changing shape. Yet she feared Lizzie's gaze would see straight past her poor camouflage to the secret she carried within her.

Gabriel showed them into the bedroom. It was untidy and smelt unpleasant. Georgie wondered if it was the lingering smell of the Thames outside, or something else.

Lizzie sat in a low chair by the fireplace, the cradle on the floor beside her. Her hands were folded in her lap, her eyes distant. She was humming a soft lullaby under her breath.

'Lizzie, my dear,' Ned began, his voice hoarse with emotion.

'Hush, Ned, you'll waken it!' Lizzie cried, looking up with something wild and desperate in her eyes.

Georgie could not speak. A hard lump in her throat.

'Lizzie, you know there is no baby there.' Gabriel put his hands on her shoulders. 'The baby died. You know that.'

'Oh, yes.' Lizzie looked back down at the empty cradle. 'I know.'

She did not speak again. Ned and Gabriel made desultory conversation over her head, repeating what the doctor had said and what arrangements had been made. Awkwardly Georgie knelt beside Lizzie, taking one thin cold hand in hers.

'I'm so sorry,' she managed to say.

'Yes,' Lizzie replied.

Her gaze returned to the empty cradle. She rocked it slightly with one foot.

'Can I make some tea?' Georgie asked in desperation.

'Mrs Birrell will bring us up some,' Gabriel said, escaping from the room with what seemed like relief.

Ned and Georgie were left alone with Lizzie, who softly began to hum, rocking the cradle back and forth. Their gazes met over her head. Ned lifted up his eyes in a gesture of exasperation. He thought she was being overly dramatic. But Georgie felt as shaken and fearful as she had when her own sister Carrie had died. There was something so eerie and unsettling about the frail young woman, rocking a cold cradle and singing a lullaby to nothingness.

A month or so later Emma Brown came to visit in a state of high distress. She and Bruno had offered to look after Lizzie for a while, to allow Gabriel to try to get some work done. Lizzie had walked out, though, finding her way back to Blackfriars on her own.

'She just up and left without a word,' Emma told Georgie indignantly. 'I can tell you, we feared the worst! Finding her bed empty like that.'

'Maybe it was hard for her ... seeing your little ones running around so happily,' Georgie ventured.

'Well, yes, maybe ... but she could have told us she was leaving ... Bruno spent an anxious hour or so searching for her.'

'I'm sure Lizzie didn't mean to cause you any trouble.'

'In a way it's a relief she's gone. She just sat, staring into space. It made us all most uncomfortable.'

Georgie leant forward to pat Emma's plump hands, clasping and unclasping themselves in her distress. 'You did your best,' she said soothingly.

'Yes, I did. And I feel sorry for her, I really do. But to run off like that ... without a word.' Emma bit her lip. 'It's frightening,' she whispered.

Georgie knew what she meant. 'Time heals all wounds,' she said, without conviction.

But Emma nodded and smiled, and rose to put on her hat. 'So I told her! But she did not seem to like me telling her so.'

A few weeks later, Georgie was glad to hear that Lizzie had gone down to stay with Janey at Red House. The fresh sweet-scented air and nourishing home-cooked food were just what she needed. Georgie wished that she could go down too. But she and Ned had just moved into new lodgings at 62 Great Russell Street, right opposite the British Museum. She had much to do putting her house in order, and preparing the nursery.

Besides, she and Ned had their own worries. One of his most generous patrons had died suddenly, and the trustees of his estate were demanding that Ned and Gabriel and Bruno all pay back the money he had advanced them against future paintings. It was quite a large sum, which Ned and Georgie simply did not have. Luckily for Ned, he was getting some commissions from the decorating firm that he and Topsy and Gabriel had started together with a few other friends. Gabriel, however, owed a huge amount. Six-hundred-and-eighty guineas. He could never pay back such a sum. His only hope was to convince the trustees to wait for the paintings he still had to paint. He had to work like a maniac to even hope to fulfil the commissions, plus he went back to teaching at the Men's Working Club in order to earn a little to live on.

Then Georgie heard that Lizzie had fled Red House too. Janey was with child once more, and the sight of her glowing happiness had simply been too much for Lizzie to bear. Georgie's heart ached for her. But there was nothing anyone could do. Lizzie had to find her own way through.

The summer passed and cooler days arrived, much to Georgie's relief. She was only small, and the child within seemed much too large and heavy. The ache in her lower back grew fiercer every day, and she found it hard to sit and work at her wood carving or to meet any of her sisters for tea.

She could not help being jittery about what was to come. Lizzie's grief was too raw and recent to forget. She knew Ned was apprehensive too. He joked that he was afraid they'd give birth to a little monster. Georgie knew he was trying to hide his very real fear.

The midwife reassured her. 'I'll be there for you,' she promised. 'Nothing will go wrong.'

One morning in early October, the ache in Georgie's back grew so fierce that she could only lie on her bed and clench her teeth together. Ned was painting in the little front room he fondly called his studio.

The discomfort moved through her in ever-increasing waves. Feeling a sudden surge of panic, she tried to get up. Her legs wobbled alarmingly. She could only manage to walk by hanging on to one piece of furniture after another.

It's too soon. It can't be time yet. I'm not ready!

Her only thought was to get to Ned. Another ripple of pain. Georgie called to Ned. She heard his footsteps rushing towards her. Pain sharp as a shard. She groaned out loud.

'Georgie? What's wrong? Is the baby coming? I'll go and get the midwife.' He caught up his coat and ran out the door, bare headed.

Georgie was left alone. She hung on to the table with all her strength. The pain was too much. She fell to her knees. The next few minutes were all a blur. Then her baby came out with a slither. He was blue. Georgie lifted him to her shoulder, patting him frantically. A moment later, a high, thin wail. Georgie collapsed with relief. She clutched the tiny thing close. He cried and cried. She tried to suckle him, sitting on the floor in the hallway, but did not know how. His hungry mouth slurped at the skin of her breast but could not latch on to the nipple.

Another sharp ripple of pain. Georgie tensed. What was happening? Another baby? Was she having twins? She had to lie the screaming baby down as her body bent and convulsed. Then something else slipped from her. Georgie bent to see, then recoiled in horror. Something red and fleshly and deformed had slithered out of her. Then a sliding pool of blood. Great gulps of sobs. Georgie looked around for help, but she was all alone. The baby was screaming, blue and naked on the floor. She picked him up and wrapped him tightly in her shawl and brought him once more to her breast. This time she succeeded in getting the nipple into his mouth. He sucked strongly. All Georgie felt was a giddy relief at the silence.

At last the door opened and Ned rushed in. Mrs Wheeler the midwife was beside him, a basket in her hand. Ned took one look at Georgie, her skirts smeared with blood, and fell to the floor in a dead faint. Mrs Wheeler dropped to the floor beside him and began to chafe his hands.

She drew a bottle of smelling salts out of her basket and waved it under his nose. At last Ned began to stir and moan.

'Do you think,' Georgie said, 'you could take a look at me?'

Georgie sat, tears sliding down her cheeks and dropping on to the downy head of the baby she suckled at her breast. She could hear the roar of laughter and conversation from the studio. It was hard to sit here alone, feeding her baby, so cut off from life.

Ned loved her, she knew. And he adored his baby son.

Yet no-one but Georgie could feed her baby.

By her side was a letter from John Ruskin, in which he cautioned her not to try to keep up with her woodcutting.

'I can't imagine anything prettier or more wifely than cutting one's husband's drawings on the woodblock: there is just the proper quantity of echo in it ... only never work hard at it. Keep your rooms tidy, and baby happy – and then after that as much woodwork as you've time and liking for.'

Except there was no time for it. Every second of the day was sucked up into keeping baby happy. Ned went about his usual daily business, drawing, sketching, scowling at canvases, going out with friends. Georgie scarcely had time to pin up her hair or change her petticoat.

Ned's laugh rang out from the other room.

Georgie's tears fell faster.

16

Lord, May I Come?
Winter 1862

A barrier of dark glass stood between Lizzie and the world.

She could hear what was said to her, if she concentrated hard. She tried to smile and pretend that their words had meaning. It was all play acting.

She found it almost impossible to meet anyone's eyes.

Eyes were the mirror of the soul, people said. She could not bear anyone to look into hers.

Everything was hard. She did not have the strength to brush her hair and pin it up. She just screwed it back and stuck a paintbrush through it. What did it matter anyway? She was ugly as sin. Lips cracked and sore. Wrists like sticks. No wonder Gabriel didn't want to paint her anymore.

Soft curves, round flushed cheeks, bare shoulders broad enough to carry a yoke. That's what he wanted now. Corn-gold hair, cherry-red lips, milkmaid skin.

Fanny Cornforth. What a name. What a pouting sluttish name. Lizzie said it over and over to herself, when Gabriel was sleeping. Fanny Cornforth. Fanny Cornforth. He painted her as a girl tying up mistletoe. Begging to be kissed. He painted her as Lucrezia Borgia. Beautiful as belladonna. He painted her as Fair Rosamund. The king's whore.

Did he think she did not know that his paintings were confessions?

Lizzie could not sleep. Lizzie could not eat. She lay in the crumpled sour-smelling bed all day, scarcely moving, unable to muster enough energy to drink the soup Mrs Birrell brought her. Sometimes, when Gabriel was out, she got up and went into the studio to spy on what he was painting. The effort cost her all her strength. When Gabriel came home, she'd be lying down again, red-eyed and weeping. Gabriel would sit beside her and brush the tangled hair away from her forehead, bending to press his lips to hers.

She wondered what other lips he had kissed while he had been gone.

He swore he had not betrayed her. But how could she believe him?

Who would be faithful to a woman like her? Sick and pale and ailing all the time, unable even to carry a child to term. He had wanted that child so badly. She had failed him. Like she had failed at everything.

Lizzie had wanted to give all the baby clothes she had made to Georgie, but Gabriel wouldn't let her. 'We'll have another baby,' he promised her, holding her tight. She smiled and nodded. But deep down she knew that any other baby would just die too. Her womb was poisoned. All that bitter-sweet poppy juice. She had not known. How could she have known?

But the scandal about the Opium Wars in China had caused everyone to talk about laudanum's evil influences. The newspapers said the Chinese emperor himself was addicted, and that was why he had ordered the terrible torture and murder of British diplomats and journalists. Then a newspaper had reported that little babies in England were dying of starvation after being kept so doped up with laudanum they never cried for milk. Lizzie had wept when she read this, and Gabriel had taken the newspaper away and forbidden her to read anymore. But Lizzie could not stop thinking about it. She felt sure that her black drops were why her baby had died. Which meant it was all her fault.

It was strange. She hated the black drops now, and yet she craved them horribly. She had to bribe Mrs Birrell's daughter to go and fill up her bottle, for Gabriel would not. She hid the laudanum in her pocket, so that she could take a quick surreptitious sip whenever he wasn't watching. She tried and tried to withstand the craving, but every single time she broke.

At night, when Gabriel made love to her, she lay silently, her face turned away. She tried to smile and pretend she enjoyed it, but she felt nothing at all. And when the doctor told her that she had conceived again, and that another child grew within the black corroded wasteland of her womb, she still felt nothing. Not hope. Not fear. Just a relentless bleakness.

For surely this baby would die too.

Lizzie heard the outer door open, and Gabriel's heavy steps coming towards her. Sighing, she sat up and pushed back her hair. He came and sat on the bed beside her.

'How are you feeling, Gug?'

If only she could be sure the tenderness in his voice was not feigned. She leant into his arms, sniffing his collar for any trace of perfume. He smelt only of fresh air, and rain, and his own familiar lemony scent.

'Did you eat anything?' he asked.

She nodded. 'A little. Mrs Birrell brought me up some tea and toast.'

'Do you want to go out to dinner? Algernon would like to see you.' Gabriel spoke hopefully. He knew that Lizzie loved young Algernon Swinburne. His gaunt face, wicked eyes and cloud of red hair reminded her of her brother Charlie, and he never failed to make her laugh.

'All right. If you like.'

'It'd do you good.'

Lizzie nodded and got up. A whirl of dizziness washed over her. She stood motionless for a moment till it passed. Then she rubbed a wet towel against her face till it tingled, pinned her hair up as best she could, and dressed herself. She looked at herself in the mirror. Pale face. Sunken eyes. Bloodless lips.

Only that month Gabriel had painted her as Princess Sabra, kneeling and kissing the bloodied hands of Saint George. The knight had just slaughtered the dragon to save her. Sabra's face was white as a ghost, her eyes deeply shadowed. All her vitality seemed drained into her hair, scarlet and writhing down her back. Saint George gazed over her head at the dead body of the dragon outside. He looked as if he was about to pull his hands away from her feverish lips. He looked as if he longed to be free.

Lizzie could not bear to think about what lay ahead. Another dead baby, rotting in her womb? Gabriel could not pretend to love her anymore after that. What would happen? Where could she go?

'Shall we go to La Sablonnière?' Gabriel put his head in the door.

She nodded. 'Just a minute.'

He withdrew. Hurriedly Lizzie took out her bottle of laudanum, gulping a mouthful. She could not go out ... she could not face all those teeming crowds ... she could not pretend to smile and laugh and eat ... without it.

She refused to think of the little worm of a child within her. She refused to think of the promise she had made Gabriel. What was the use? This child would die like the last. Perhaps she too would die. She had prepared for death for so long it felt familiar and comfortable to her now. Did you not see your loved ones again in death? She would hold her little daughter, she would hug her dearest brother, she would reach up to kiss her father's rough cheek, glinting with silver dust. All mistakes would be forgiven.

'Cab's here!' Gabriel called.

She drank another measure, then hid the bottle again.

Algy was waiting inside the hansom cab. He was so glad to see her. Yet Lizzie was so drowsy she could scarcely string a sentence together.

Gabriel was worried. 'Are you well enough for dinner? Shall we turn back?'

Lizzie roused herself enough to say, 'No, no, I'm fine. Algy, how does the poetry go?'

Algernon was a finely drawn, restless young poet with beautiful hands and an instinct for self-destruction. He drank too much, daringly smoked opium like a Chinaman, begged strangers to flagellate him when he was drunk, and wrote the most exquisite poems. He only came up to Lizzie's shoulder, but when he was in the room no-one looked at anyone else. Gabriel should have despised him, but was tender and solicitous, as if Algernon was a guttering candle that the slightest breath would blow out. When Lizzie was with him, she felt like the girl she used to be. Bold, laughing, filled with dreams of glory. And she knew that Gabriel loved the girl she was then, rather than the poor husk of a thing she was now. So she drew on all her reserves of strength to banter and laugh as Algernon declaimed his poetry to them, in the darkness of the hansom cab as it clopped slowly through the icy winter streets.

He had written a hymn to Prosperine. Phrases pierced her through.

I am weary of days and hours ... Blown buds of barren flowers ... Desires and dreams and powers ... And everything but sleep ...

It awoke in Lizzie all her old longing to write poetry and paint art to make all who saw it weep. It had the same effect on Gabriel. He imagined painting Proserpine at the moment she realised she could not return to the world of life. He spouted his own poetry back to Algernon, and Lizzie joined in. The three of them quoted back and forth at one another, in the close darkness of the cab, improvising to the slow spondee rhythm of the horse's hooves. Lizzie felt something quicken within her for the first time in months. Perhaps it was not too late. Perhaps she could truly make something worthwhile of the ruin of her life. Her baby had died; she had another one growing within her. Her art had failed; she could make new art. She had driven Gabriel from her with her sickness and despair; could she not draw him back to her with the crimson thread of her love?

That dinner was the merriest they had shared for a while. Lizzie had to rest her head on her bent hand, and occasionally she felt a wave of dizziness rock her. But she laughed and pecked at her food and drank some wine, and saw some of the heavy despondency lift from Gabriel. In the cab on the way home, she nestled into his arm and imagined that tonight, perhaps, she might embrace him with real joy.

'I'll just see you safely home,' Gabriel said, 'and go on.'

Lizzie stiffened; drew herself away. 'Go on where?'

'I'm teaching tonight. At the Men's Working Club.'

All the old suspicions rushed back on her. Lizzie said waspishly, 'So you say.'

He sighed in exasperation. 'Lizzie, you know I have to work. We're in so much debt. All those doctors' bills.'

It was an unkind thing to say. Tears rushed to her eyes. 'I'm sorry I cost you so much money.'

'I didn't mean it like that, Lizzie. You know I didn't. It's just … you know. Bills, bills, bills.' His laugh sounded artificial.

'It would have been better if you'd never married me.'

'No, Guggums, don't say that. I'm sorry, I shouldn't have mentioned the doctors' bills. It's just … it's just so cruel I have to pay them … when … you know.' His voice was choked with emotion, but Lizzie had no strength to give to him.

'Are you going to see her?' Her voice was flat with despair.

'Who?' Gabriel's voice sounded strange. Sharp and guilty.

'That Fanny girl.'

He sighed. 'No, Lizzie. I'm not going to see Fanny. I've told you, she's married now. I'm going to teach.'

'I know you've been seeing her. I've seen all the drawings, the paintings.'

'People want paintings of her, Lizzie. They sell. And we need the money.'

'And paintings of me don't sell?' Her voice thin and high.

'Not nearly as well,' he answered, losing his temper at last. 'And I can't just keep painting the same thing over and over, Lizzie. I need new models, new subjects. I need to find new patrons. Why can't you understand?'

'Oh I understand all too well.' Her temper rose to match his. 'I'm too old and sick and ugly … and … and … barren.' She forced the last word out.

'Lizzie …'

'Don't! Just don't! I don't want to hear it.' She pressed her hands over her ears, rocking back and forth. 'Oh I hate you! I hate you. Why did I waste my life loving you? When I think of all the years, all the promises, all the lies.'

The cab had drawn up in front of their building. She wrenched open the door and tried to jump out, only to stumble and fall to her knees on the cobblestones. Ice cracked under her weight, sharp against the heels of her hands. She managed to get to her feet, trying to keep herself steady by holding on to the cab door.

The horse's body steamed in the icy air, wreathing it in an unearthly halo. The driver was just a black shape against the blur of the gaslight, hunched over the reins. Gabriel climbed down and paid, ignoring her. She could not see his face in the darkness. Lizzie fled across the street and inside the door. She stumbled again going up the stairs. Her head was swimming. Too much wine on an empty stomach. She held on to the wall and climbed up to their door. She could not get in. She had to wait for Gabriel who had their key. Lizzie pressed her head against the wall, giving in to her sobs. She heard Gabriel's slow reluctant footsteps behind her. He said her name again.

'Just go,' she said. 'Go on. Go and have your fun. But don't even think of coming home again.'

Gabriel unlocked the door for her. 'I'm going to work.' Each word enunciated slowly and clearly.

Lizzie went inside the apartment and slammed the door behind her. He did not follow her or try to call her name again. She felt an acute and unreasonable disappointment. Remorse overwhelmed her. She flung open the door again, and ran to the balustrade. Leaning over, she cried, 'Stay with me, Gug, stay with me!'

His echoing footsteps did not falter. She heard the front door slam shut.

Lurching through the apartment, Lizzie knocked over a brass urn and banged her knee on the edge of the table. She undressed, pulling her long white nightgown over her head and unpinning her hair so it fell in heavy copper waves about her. She found one of her hidden bottles and recklessly drank half the bottle. She wanted to sleep tonight. Deeply, dreamlessly. Oh, please, dreamlessly.

Lizzie crawled into bed and drew a sheaf of papers towards her. She had been struggling with a poem for some time. Now the words poured from her.

Life and night are falling from me,
Death and day are opening on me,
Wherever my footsteps come and go,
Life is a stony way of woe.
Lord, have I long to go?
Hallow hearts are ever near me,
Soulless eyes have ceased to cheer me:
Lord may I come to thee?
Life and youth and summer weather
To my heart no joy can gather.
Lord, lift me from life's stony way!
Loved eyes long closed in death watch for me:
Holy death is waiting for me –
Lord, may I come to-day?

Her hand was weak. The words were mere scratches of ink. Tears fell on the page and made the words smear. But she wrote on, though she could scarcely see what to write. *Gabriel, why aren't you here? Don't you know I need you?*

He's gone to her. The thought was sharp as a stiletto blade. Lizzie lifted the little bottle of laudanum and drank the rest down.

I'll make it all better ... tomorrow ... just let me sleep now ... free of pain ...

She folded the poem with clumsy fingers and slipped it back inside her sketchbook. Then she lay down her head. Thoughts ground past in their old deep groove.

Slowly Lizzie let herself fall.

17

Her Ghost Is Unquiet
Winter–Autumn 1862

Such a cold, bitter morning.

Georgie sat in the hansom cab. Tears ran unchecked down her face.

Could it be true? Could Lizzie really be dead?

Georgie caught back a sob. The cab drew up in Blackfriars. Fog drifted about the iron railings. The dismal call of foghorns. She clambered down and shook the straw from her skirts, before paying the driver and beginning the climb up to Gabriel's apartment.

Bruno opened the door. 'Hello, Georgie.' He allowed her to step through to the hallway and shut the door behind her. All was gloomy and dark, for the lamps had not been lit. 'A sad day.'

'So it's true?'

'Oh yes. She died early this morning. The doctors worked on her all night, pumping her stomach, trying to revive her. It was no use.'

Georgie pressed her hand over her mouth. 'Gabriel?' she managed to ask.

Bruno shook his head. 'He's in a bad way.'

Georgie scrubbed at her eyes.

'You'll want to see her. She's through here.'

As Bruno led her down past the drawing room, Georgie saw a glimpse of the glowing hearth, the fan of peacock feathers on the wall, the blue-and-white china of which Lizzie had been so proud. Then she saw Gabriel, sunk to his knees before one of his most beautiful drawings of his wife, his head bent down into his hands.

Georgie looked away, her throat closing over. She followed Bruno into the cold bedroom, where no fire was lit.

Lizzie lay in bed, her hands crossed over each other on top of a neatly folded counterpane. Her eyes were shut, her red-gold hair tumbling down on either side. If it were not for the pallor of her skin and the bruised colour of her eyelids, Georgie would have thought her sleeping. But her chest did not move, her eyes did not twitch, her fingernails were blue.

Georgie caught hold of a chair to steady herself.

'There will have to be an inquest,' Bruno said. 'We can only hope that they see what a terrible accident this is.'

Georgie nodded. When a young woman of only thirty-two years of age dies unexpectedly, questions must be asked.

'If they could just have seen him,' Bruno said in such a low voice she only just caught the words. 'On his knees, clutching her to him, begging her to come back to him. They could never suspect ...'

Georgie lifted her eyes to his face in wonder. It had never occurred to her that Gabriel would fall under suspicion. All her fear had been that Lizzie would be accused of killing herself whilst of unsound mind. If so, she would be buried in unconsecrated ground. The stigma of suicide would have been a heavy cross to bear. But the idea of murder ...

Georgie's knees weakened and she had to sit down for a moment. She could not look at the still white figure on the bed. A cloth had been flung over the mirror at Lizzie's dressing table. The clock on the mantelpiece had been stopped, its hands set at a little after seven o'clock. Lizzie's dress lay where she had discarded it, her gloves flung down on a chair like limp white hands.

Georgie could hardly believe that Lizzie would never wear them again. She got up blindly, and stumbled from the room.

*

Georgie had to get out her mourning dress, which she had last worn when Carrie had died. She could hardly bear the cold touch of the bombazine upon her skin, its faint smell of damp.

A hearse was drawn up in the square, drawn by four black horses with feathers nodding from their brow straps. The coachman wore a tall silk hat. So too did the two mutes, standing by the front door, swathed in heavy shawls, holding tall staves elaborately wrapped and bound in black with a white riband. Their faces were set in expressions of deep melancholy.

Georgie clutched Ned's arm, as much to support him as to comfort herself, as they climbed the stairs.

The drawing room was lit only by candles, the many drawings and paintings of Lizzie all turned to face the wall. White lilies stood in vases on the mantelpiece and table. Their scent did not conceal the faint smell of putrefaction in the air.

Lizzie lay in the satin-lined casket, her hands folded upon her breast, her golden-red hair loose and flowing. Gabriel must have gone even further into debt, Georgie thought, to have paid for such a fine coffin. It seemed wrong, when the living were in need of such help.

Gabriel stood by the coffin, dressed in black. His brother and sisters were by his side, Mrs Rossetti seated in a chair nearby. They all looked haggard. Georgie knew they would have shared in his vigil these past six days. A long time to sit by the corpse. Bruno said that Gabriel had refused to believe Lizzie was truly dead. He kept hoping she would wake and open her eyes and look at him.

On the far side of the room stood another small group, many of them with red hair and freckles, which she guessed must be Lizzie's family. Her mother was stone-faced, her sisters weeping into their handkerchiefs. Two young men stood by, looking uncomfortable in their stiff collars. One was moon faced and childlike, and kept asking, 'Why is Lizzie sleeping? Why doesn't she wake up?'

Ned and Georgie shook hands with Gabriel and his brother, and muttered a few inadequate words. Gabriel nodded and thanked them quietly.

Then they had to pass on, to look upon Lizzie in her coffin. Ned could not look; he clutched so hard at Georgie's hand she was afraid he might break her fingers. Then he saw Topsy and Bruno by the window and went to them, his face working with emotion.

Georgie joined Janey and Emma nearby, kissing their cheeks.

'Isn't it sad?' Georgie had to dab at her eyes again.

'I can't believe it's true. Poor Gabriel.' Janey clenched her hands together, white-knuckled.

'He's not holding up at all well.' Emma lowered her voice. 'He says he sees her every night, standing at the foot of his bed, staring at him.'

Georgie felt a cold prickle run down her. 'You mean ...?'

'Yes. Her ghost is unquiet.'

'Her ghost? Her ghost is haunting him?' Janey's face was blanched of all colour.

'The poor thing died before her time,' Emma said. 'And so she walks.'

'Surely not,' Georgie said. 'It must be just a nightmare. Not surprising, really. Once she is safely buried in the ground, Gabriel will find things easier.'

The undertaker had bent to whisper something in his ear. Georgie saw the men were standing ready to close the casket and carry it down to the hearse.

Gabriel bent his head, all his weight borne down on his two hands which clenched the back of his mother's chair. Then he straightened and drew a notebook out of his coat pocket.

'My poems ... I wrote them for you, Lizzie ... they must go with you.' He stepped forward and laid the notebook beside her cheek, cradled in her bright hair.

'Gabriello, no!' Bruno protested.

William Rossetti held up his hand. 'Let him do as he wishes.'

Gabriel bent and kissed Lizzie's cold cheek. The lid of the casket was hammered shut, and the undertaker's men hoisted it high and carried it down to where the mutes stood waiting, ready to begin the long walk to Highgate Cemetery.

Gabriel stood alone, his head bowed. Unable to bear it, Georgie went to him and pressed his arm between both of her small hands.

He said, more to himself than to her, 'I cannot believe it. I cannot believe she is dead.'

No winter had seemed so long.

First Ned was sick, then baby Phil. Georgie hurried from one to the other, falling exhausted into bed every night.

John Ruskin came to their rescue. He wanted to take Ned to France and Italy, to see great art and great cathedrals. Georgie was torn in two. On the one hand, she had never been outside England, and could not bear the thought of Ned being away from her for so many months. On the other hand, Phil was so small and frail. She hated the thought of leaving him behind.

'Just leave him with Mama,' her sister Alice advised. 'It'd do her good to have something new to fuss over.'

'Are you sure?' Georgie looked down at the little dark head nestled in the crook of her arm. 'I'm afraid he'll fret for me.'

'He's only a shrimp; he won't even know you're gone.'

So, with a heart full of mingled excitement and misgivings, Georgie had left her baby boy with her parents in early May and crossed the Channel with John Ruskin and her husband, headed towards France.

Paris was a troubling city. On the one hand, it was so beautiful. Napoleon III had built grand avenues lined with chestnut trees that were bursting into bloom in the spring sunshine. The Seine ran like a golden satin ribbon under arched bridges, past great palaces and cathedrals with soaring spires. At dusk, the *allumeurs* made their rounds, carrying long poles hung with a little lantern, to light the tall black gas-lamps. Soon the boulevards along the river were illuminated with strings of light, and the Arc de Triomphe was crowned with fire.

Yet behind the parks and palaces was a vast maze of dirty medieval streets infested with beggars and rag pickers, who swarmed out at dawn to rummage through the piles of garbage dumped outside every house. The Seine stank. The night was made awful by the clatter of wagons arriving at the marketplace at Les Halles, and each dawn Georgie was woken by the raucous calls of the street vendors.

Mr Ruskin took them to the Louvre, which had once been the royal palace of the French kings but had been turned into a museum during the French Revolution. The Emperor, Napoleon III, had spent millions of francs restoring the museum and stocking it with new treasures from all over the world.

Walking the vast echoing halls, with their marble floors and gilded cornices, their ceilings painted with frescoes, their walls hung with huge paintings of kings and queens and popes, heathen gods and goddesses, satyrs and bare-breasted nymphs, Georgie felt herself very drab and insignificant in her plain blue dress, sturdy boots on her feet, much-darned cotton gloves on her hands, and a plain straw bonnet on her head. Everywhere she looked was something to put her to the blush.

Silently she followed Ned and Mr Ruskin through hall after hall, overwhelmed by the grandeur and magnificence she saw on every side, the vanity and pride and lust, the ambitions and passions and appetites displayed with such wantonness.

A little spurt of anger kindled in her breast.

No wonder, she thought, the French rose up and dragged down their kings.

The next day, she did not go with them back to the Louvre. Her feet ached, and she had seen enough. Mr Ruskin smiled and said, 'Of course, you'll want to go shopping. I know you women.' Georgie did not know how to explain to him that the unnecessary expenditure of money on frivolities was not something she enjoyed. She walked in the park, fed bread to the pigeons, then sat in the shade writing in her diary.

As she walked down the Rue de Rivoli to their hotel, she saw a gypsy girl kneeling on the ground, tattered skirts spread out about her, hair hidden beneath a knotted scarf. Her nails were dirty and broken, her bare feet blackened with filth, her face bruised. She held out two hands in a begging gesture. On the rug beside her was a thin kitten, mewling in hunger.

Georgie gave the girl all her money.

She knew it was foolish. She knew Mr Ruskin would reprimand her if he knew. She did not care.

A few weeks later they came down the pass into Italy.

'I say!' Ned pointed to a young woman with bare feet and masses of heavy dark hair, a basket of oranges on her head. 'Look at that girl there. Doesn't she look like a spoiled study of Mrs Topsy?'

Georgie knew just what he meant. As striking as the Italian girl was, she could not hold a candle to Janey. As always, Georgie tried not to mind. She knew caring about one's looks was vanity. Far better to care about one's soul.

As the sun set, the woods turned into a fairyland with millions of dancing fireflies. Georgie let herself be entranced. Had Ned not chosen her, out of all the women in the world? Was it not her arms he crept into, when at last they were alone in their bed? Were they not alive, when poor Lizzie was dead?

The next few weeks were a blur of faces. Real and painted. Georgie knew how lucky she was, yet still she yearned for her baby. Looking at countless fat-cheeked cherubs, Georgie began to think about having another. Perhaps a little girl. Ned would love a baby daughter.

Ruskin refused to go to Venice. Too many unhappy memories of his wife, Georgie supposed. Yet both Ned and Georgie badly wanted to go. It was hard to stand against Ruskin's will when they were so beholden to him. Somehow Ned found the courage to insist.

Georgie would never forget her first sight of Venice. Pale domes and towers rose out of a golden mist, casting long trembling reflections into the waters of the lagoon. Everywhere she looked was beauty and decay, as if the city was slowly rotting from its water-drenched foundations. The smell of the canals was so powerful that the women carried silver vinaigrette boxes or pomanders made of clove-studded oranges, to lift to their noses at need. Yet each turn of the cobblestoned alleys showed another cathedral or palace, built to glorify. Bare-footed tousle-haired children ran and played in squares where soldiers strutted in their gaudy Austrian uniforms. Women in simple peasant dress leaned out from windows to hang out ragged washing above canals where women in red satin gowns were poled along in black gondolas with high curved prows shaped like dragon heads.

Georgie did not know whether to be fascinated or scandalised. It was such bliss, though, to be alone with Ned at last, that she forgave the city its pomp and splendour, and saw only its fortitude and grace.

It was no hardship to spend all day looking at paintings when it was just her and Ned. He did not lecture her, or talk to her as if she was a child. One day she saw a little jewel of a painting tucked away in the corner of a dark church, and said, 'Look at this, Ned. Isn't it a nice little thing? It looks like that one you showed me yesterday by that painter called …' She hesitated, then said tentatively, '… Bonnie-face?'

Ned came to see, then caught her hand and squeezed it. 'It is indeed a Bonifacio. You're developing a good eye, Georgie.'

She glowed with pleasure. If it had not been for her longing to see her baby boy, she would have been perfectly happy.

Ned, however, was making himself ill again. Ruskin had told him sternly he was not to waste time painting all those myths and fairytales he loved so much, but to do nothing but copy the great works of the masters. It made Ned unhappy. He wanted to please his patron, but he found it so hard to spend each day copying the work of others when his brain was teeming with visions he wanted to bring to life on canvas.

On their last day in Venice, Ned and Georgie were exploring the shadowy nave of a great church when they heard the deep sombre tones of a *basso profundo*. Georgie at once had to follow the sound, having never heard anything so deep, so sad. A red-draped coffin was being carried down the aisle, preceded by children in long smocks carrying candles and singing an eerie high accompaniment. Chills ran over her body.

The coffin was followed by mourners, all dressed in black, the women veiled, heads bent in grief. Georgie put her hand in the crook of Ned's elbow, wanting to hold him back, but he pulled against her grasp and followed the funeral procession out of the darkness of the church and into the sunlit square. Georgie had to follow. They watched as the coffin was loaded into a black gondola, with winged gilded angels and a red cross above the catafalque. More gondolas were lined up behind for the mourners, the gondoliers all dressed in black with red sashes.

The coffin was lowered into the gondola and rowed away to the island of the dead, accompanied by the strange, melancholy song of the gondoliers.

Ned stood, chest heaving, tears running down his thin face. Georgie could do nothing but press his arm between her two small hands and wish that his mother had not died, his father had not been so broken by grief, and that Lizzie still lived.

'I'm glad to be home,' Ned said, as they stepped over the pile of letters and handbills inside their front door.

'So am I!'

Their rooms smelt stuffy, so Georgie laid her little boy down on the rug and went around, flinging up the windows and letting the soft summer air flood in. Across the park the great pillars of the British Museum glowed golden in the evening sunshine. Horses clopped past, carriage wheels clattered, and birds twittered in the plane trees. A muffin man passed down the street, tinkling his bell and calling out, 'Muffins. Hot muffins.'

Georgie stood for a moment, listening in quiet pleasure. Their apartment was small and sparsely furnished, and nothing like the grand hotels in which they had stayed with John Ruskin. But it was home.

She turned, and saw that Phil had crawled down the hall and was peeping in the doorway at her. Georgie flew across the room and caught him up, pressing kisses all over his beaming cheeks. 'Oh, you clever boy, are you crawling now? I can see there'll be no peace for me now.'

She carried him down the hall to the studio, and found Ned sitting, reading letters. His face was pale and distressed.

'I've heard from Topsy. Poor Gabriel's moved away from Blackfriars. He says the place is haunted now. He's looking for somewhere else to stay. Topsy says he is working like mad. So many debts …'

'And funerals are so expensive,' Georgie said. She remembered how crippling the costs had been for her father, with so many little coffins to bury in the earth.

Ned nodded. 'Topsy says the International Exhibition was a great success, and the Firm has dozens of new orders. That should help.'

'Any work for you?' Money was a constant worry for them too.

Ned nodded. His hand reached out and found a pencil and a scrap of paper. 'Mmmm-hmmm. A client is building a grand house in Surrey and wants to commission some tiles for his fireplaces. He wants a fairytale theme. I am thinking of Sleeping Beauty …' He began to sketch.

Georgie tiptoed away. He did not even notice she was gone.

Over the next few days Ned was in the studio from first light till long after the gaslights had been ignited. One night, after laying Phil down in his cot, she went down the hall in her nightgown to try to entice Ned to bed.

He sat at his table, painting away.

'What are you doing?' Georgie put her arms about him.

He was working on a design inspired by the Sleeping Beauty fairytale. A girl in a white nightgown lay on a bed, swirls of roses behind her. A peacock spread its gaudy tail on the far wall. The girl's golden-red hair rippled out across the pillow. On his knees beside her was a knight with long dark curls, bending to kiss her.

Beneath the drawing were pasted words in a flowing scroll, written in Topsy's elegant scrawl. 'Of a certain prince who delivered a King's daughter from a sleep of a hundred years, wherein she and all hers had been cast by enchantment'.

The next sketch showed the knight and the awakened maiden, hurrying through the castle on their way to their wedding. The knight looked like a young Gabriel, while the glowing-haired princess was the image of Lizzie before she grew so sick and sad. Georgie's eyes dampened. She kissed Ned's cheek. He put his hands up to cover hers.

'If only she was sleeping,' he whispered. 'If only she could be awakened with a kiss.'

Part III

Beauty & Misfortune
1864–1871

Two things had tremendous power over him – beauty and misfortune – and far would he go to serve either.
Lady Georgiana Burne-Jones
Memorials of Edward Burne-Jones, Volume I

1

Scarlet Fever
Autumn 1864

Afterwards, Georgie would marvel that she had felt no presentiment. Surely such grief, such pain, should throw back a shadow to warn you?

If only she had foreseen what was to come. If only she had taken more care.

It had been such a lovely summer. Ned and Georgie had taken their little boy to the seaside, in company with Topsy and Janey and their two little girls, Jenny and Mary, who everyone called May. Charley Faulkner came along too, and his mother and sisters, Lucy and Kate. Charley had known Ned and Topsy at Oxford and was one of the founding members of the Firm, while Lucy and Kate painted many of the tiles the Firm produced, including the beautiful Sleeping Beauty tiles that Ned had designed.

The three families had taken lodgings at Littlehampton on the Sussex coast, and the days had been spent playing with the children on the brown-sugar sands and paddling in the water. Lucy and Kate had even tried swimming from one of the bathing machines drawn down to the water's edge. Georgie was with child once more, and so spent most of her time sitting in the shade of a striped parasol, sewing little white garments and thinking of names. Janey kept her company, reading out loud the latest instalment in Elizabeth Gaskell's serial *Wives and Daughters* and darning May's stockings, which were always getting torn.

'Wouldn't it be lovely if I had another boy?' Georgie said. 'Then we'd have two of each to play with each other.'

'They will all have such fun when you and Ned move down to Red House,' Janey said, biting short her thread. 'I am looking forward to it, Georgie. Topsy is finding the travel back and forth to London every day rather taxing, as you can imagine. He will get so much work done without all those hours on the train every day.'

'He's probably hoping he can drive Ned along a little faster,' Georgie said. 'I know he gets a little exasperated that Ned works so slowly, but indeed it's worth it, Janey. You should see his cartoons for the "Good Women" hangings. They are just exquisite.'

'I love that painting he did of *Green Summer*,' Janey replied, laying each stitch neatly. 'It just seems to sum up everything I love about Red House. The outlook onto forests and meadows, the wildflowers in the grass, friends ...'

'Family,' Georgie added, smiling to think of her sisters who had modelled for Ned's painting, along with Janey and herself. They had been quite reluctant to discard their crinolines to wear the loose medieval gowns that Ned had insisted upon. The effect, however, had been lovely.

Georgie laid one hand on the roundness of her belly. The child within was lively, kicking vigorously at all hours. Georgie felt sure it was another boy, and joked that it would grow up to be either a morris dancer or a football player. 'It will be wonderful to have more room,' she went on. 'Our rooms at Great Russell Street are really too small for another baby, and now Phil is racing around everywhere ... well, he needs a garden.'

'Plenty of garden at Red House.' Janey laid down her darning to smile at her friend.

The plan to build another wing at Red House had been suggested by Topsy, and he had asked his architect to draw up plans, allowing for separate entrances so that the two families could keep some privacy whilst still living side by side. Georgie was thrilled at the idea. She had never hoped to live in such a grand and beautiful place.

'If only we could make room for Gabriel,' she went on, thinking aloud. 'I'm sure it would do him good, to get him away from London and all those sad memories.'

Janey bent her head over her darning again. 'By all accounts, Gabriel is managing to keep himself amused.'

'Do you mean that woman . . . the one he's installed as his housekeeper? Is it true she's really his mistress?'

'I have no idea. It wouldn't surprise me.'

Georgie said hesitantly, 'Ned says Gabriel's hard at work, painting all sorts of beautiful things. Of course, he's still in such debt . . . and that new house of his must be costing a pretty penny.'

Janey bit off the end of her thread with a decided snap. Georgie looked down at the water's edge, where Ned was building sandcastles with Phil.

'We haven't seen much of him since the funeral,' Georgie said wistfully. 'Though, of course, he's still in mourning and can't attend supper parties. Have ... have you seen him?'

'No.' Janey stood up. 'Come, it's almost teatime. Let's round up those children.'

Topsy had spent the day in London, looking after the business of the Firm, but he got back down to Littlehampton in time for supper. Every evening the three men played whist together and – lacking a man – had set up an artist's lay dummy to play the fourth hand. It was Topsy's dummy and so the very best of its kind, with a papier-mâché face moulded into human-like features, a stuffed leather body with anatomically correct musculature, and flexible, jointed limbs. So in demand was this dummy that one or other of the men were always hiring hansoms to ferry it from one studio to another, much to the alarm of the cab drivers.

Ned and Charley had spent the afternoon devising a trick to play on Topsy. Somehow they had contrived to ensure the dummy had a splendid hand, so that it seemed Topsy must win gloriously, only to always somehow trump him. Georgie heard the roar of rage from her bedroom, and then – inevitably – the great explosion of laughter. She smiled to herself.

The next day was hotter than ever, with the sun blazing down from a brazen sky. Everyone lingered on the beach, for it was their last day in Littlehampton and all would be returning to London the following morning. Georgie fanned herself with her book, and wished she had the energy to go and cool her swollen feet in the water, skirts discreetly raised. But she just did not feel capable of labouring over the broad stretch of burning sand. She could not concentrate on her book, either. The words seem to dance on the page. Her temples throbbed, and she thought longingly of her cool white bed in the lodging house on the hill.

Their landlady had not been feeling well that day however. A sore throat, a sick head. She had asked them to let her rest a while. So Georgie sat quietly, watching the children play, till the sun had set and the long summer twilight was fading.

That night, Phil's forehead was hot, and the little boy was restless and unhappy. A red burn spread down his cheeks and neck. Georgie drew him on to her lap, and he sat astride her legs, his scarlet cheek resting on the hard mound of her belly. 'The sun has been so hot. It's just a touch of heatstroke,' she told Ned.

Phil had an unsettled night, and Georgie was glad that they were catching the train back to London that day. He had had enough sun, she thought. Phil grizzled the whole way. Georgie felt she could hardly bear it, but Ned was busy sketching new designs in his notebook and she did not like to interrupt him.

Topsy and Janey had invited them to Red House for the weekend, so they left Phil in the care of his nurse and went down to Kent, spending the day pacing out the dimensions of the planned extension and discussing where to put the water closets. But then a telegram arrived. Phil was much worse.

Georgie sent word to call the doctor, and she and Ned caught the next train back to London. When they reached their rooms at 62 Great Russell Street, it was to find the doctor's gig drawn up outside, a boy holding the horse's reins. They hurried upstairs. They found the doctor waiting for them, looking severe.

'Scarlet fever,' he said.

Georgie's heart shrank. Scarlet fever. They said it killed more children than any other disease.

Phil was lying in his cot, dressed in nothing but his white gown. The sunburn on his face and chest spread down his limbs, to places that the sun had never touched. His tongue was red as if he had been sucking a lollipop. Georgie hung over him, weeping, kissing his fevered cheeks. She could not believe that she had left him so blithely. Ned was frightened, but she had no time to soothe his nervous fears. Their son might be dying. When Ned grew too distressed, she snapped at him and banished him from the sickroom. It was like having another child instead of a husband, she thought angrily.

The next few days passed like an awful dream. With the curtains drawn, night had no more meaning than day. Georgie slept when she could, her head resting on a pillow beside her little boy, one hand on his fever-restless body, the other cradling her swollen womb.

Things seemed strange. Georgie heard trains rattling towards them. She tried to shield Phil. Ghost train rushing past. Sucking away the air. How her throat hurt. Like she had swallowed razors. She woke up to find that Phil was gone. She ran through the house, looking for him. Door after door opened into unfamiliar rooms. People she had never seen before turned to stare at her. Laughing at her distress. Georgie realised she was barefoot. In her nightgown. She ran on, desperate, scrabbling at door handles, unable to find her son. Now the rooms were empty. Abandoned. Windows stood open, doors creaked on their hinges, dust and leaves swirled in ever quickening eddies, changed into great black birds stabbing at her with their sharp beaks. She screamed and tried to protect herself. Blood ran down her face. The birds whirled about her, pecking at her, flapping their awful wings, screeching.

She woke. She was so hot. She was lying in her own bed, but the room seemed strange, unfamiliar. The lamp was hidden behind a red shade. It made everything bloody.

'Ssssh ...' Ned leant forward from the darkness. 'Lie still.'

'Phil! Where's Phil?'

'He's sleeping.'

'I have to see him. Where is he?'

'He's asleep. No, Georgie! The doctor says you must stay in bed.'

Georgie tried to get up. The room spun. Her knees buckled. 'What … what's wrong with me?'

'You have scarlet fever too. The doctor says you must be kept quiet.'

Georgie became aware that her head was strangely light and cold. She put up her hands. Bound in damp rags. She pulled them off. Her scalp was bristled. Her hair. Where was her hair? She turned clumsily, and looked at herself in the mirror. Her head had been shaved. Bald as a baby bird. Her face livid and spotted. Her lips swollen and inflamed.

Georgie sank back to her bed, and buried her face in the pillow. She felt so bare, so vulnerable, so ugly. Ned lifted her legs and tucked them back under the coverlet. Her swollen belly a crucible of white-hot iron.

'But … Phil …' Georgie tried once more to rise. Her body failed her.

'I've sent for your mother. She'll be here soon.'

'No … no …'

Prayers on your knees, the smell of camphor, clocks stopped, dead children white as marble. Georgie refused. She pushed away with all her strength.

Life became one long black screaming nightmare.

The baby came too soon. Georgie tried to feed him. No milk. He was so hungry. Screamed all the time. Face purple as a plum. Little arms and legs clutching desperately at life. The doctor put leeches behind her ears, painted her throat with nitrate of silver. Her mother wept and prayed and shrieked. Ned sick and silent, wanting to clutch at her hand.

The fever came in shining rattling sheets, a hail of steel nails.

Such dreadful dreams. A graveyard full of dead silent children, beckoning her to join them. A boat made of paper tossed on a sea of lava. Spiders crawling over her, stinging her, wrapping her in icy silk, suffocating her.

His thin mottled body lying so still. Great dark staring eyes. Lips blue.

Nothing to be done.

Georgie wept till she was wrung out of all tears.

Later she heard how Ned had not slept for days, keeping vigil by her bedside, and how John Ruskin had had the street strewn with straw so the rattle of the carriage wheels would not hurt her ears. She did not care.

Her baby boy had lived just three weeks. Ned named him Christopher. The little thing had borne such a heavy burden in his short life. He was buried in Brampton Cemetery. Not beside Carrie. He had a tiny grave all of his own.

Georgie would not sleep in the room in which he had died. It was terrible to her. They had to move somewhere else, she told Ned. She could not stay here.

All her thoughts were of Red House.

Apples would be blushing on the gnarled and mossy branches, the hedges would be full of red rosehips and crimson haws, and the seed heads of traveller's joy would be foaming in the verges. She and Phil could collect the silver coins of honesty and play at shops, and together they'd walk in the meadows and gather blackberries to make jam.

But there was to be no new wing at Red House. Ned had not worked in weeks and weeks. Bills piling up. Commissions unfinished. And, as always, Topsy's plans were grandiloquent. Ned simply did not have the money.

Topsy cried, he said, when he heard the news. He had been sick too and unable to help Ned through his trial.

It seemed like the end of all the happy times.

*

Georgie could not bear her husband's grief. It was a yoke of stone. She freed her fingers from his, she turned away from him in bed. She held her living son so tightly he struggled to be free, but would not let her husband creep close for comfort.

Winter darkened the skies, and it seemed impossible spring would ever come again.

2

The Dolorous Gard
Winter–Autumn 1865

Misfortunes never come singly, Janey thought.

First Topsy had come down with rheumatic fever and for a while, had been little better than a cripple.

Then her father died. She had not thought it would sadden her so.

Afterwards Bessie wrote, pleading to be given a home. *I don't want to go back to Ma's.*

Janey could understand that. But she dreaded the thought of having her sister live with her. She knew Topsy would hate it. And surely the servants would snigger to see Bessie with her rough red hands and her working-class ways.

She remembered two little girls, huddled on a dirt floor, their dresses little more than rags and patches, eating together from the same old tin bowl. Soup made from old dripping and blackened crusts of bread begged from the baker's wife. Their hair matted, their faces grimy. Janey told Bessie a story of two sisters who made friends with a bear. 'An' they were never cold or hungry again,' she had whispered.

Janey could not fail to help her sister, when she had so much.

So Bessie came to stay, with one small carpet-bag holding all she owned. She was overawed by the big house and so grateful and deferential to Topsy, she almost drove him mad. His temper was worse than ever that winter, exacerbated by his ill health and worries over money.

Janey had never learnt to laugh at her husband's rages. When he began to shout and stamp, every muscle in her body tensed like steel fibres stretched beyond their strength. Her jaw would be rigid. She could not speak. She simply could not understand how Ned and the others could tease him to breaking point, then roar with laughter as he smashed plates and threw puddings and wrenched his spectacles in two. In Littlehampton, she had lain in her bed, fists clenched, listening to him fume at the trick Ned and Charley had played upon him, wishing they would not provoke him so.

One day, at breakfast, Topsy looked up from his mail with a pleased smile.

'Gabriello's invited us for dinner. At his new house in Chelsea.'

Janey's heart gave a single hard painful thump. She laid down her knife.

'I suppose his mourning period must be over. How long has it been?'

'Two years and two months,' Janey answered, then brought her cup hastily to her mouth, afraid of a betraying flush.

She had not seen Gabriel since the day of Lizzie's funeral. He had become a recluse, Topsy said, unable to bear seeing anyone who reminded him of his dead wife. Janey could understand how awful it was for Gabriel to come to Red House, to see her two little girls laughing and playing in the garden, when his own daughter had never even had chance to draw a single breath. It must be hard for him to see her and Topsy, living together in this grand house, working together as he and Lizzie had once done, while he had been left alone, in debt, wracked with remorse. Each richly decorated wall of the house, every green corner of the garden, was filled with memories of games and pranks and stories, in the midst of which Lizzie's slim figure danced, laughing.

Janey could understand why he would not come. But it hurt her, nonetheless.

'Do you wish to go?' Topsy asked, looking over the top of his spectacles.

Still she did not speak, her hand clenched on her butter knife.

'I know London is awful in April, but we can't miss seeing Gabriel.' His bearded face was eager.

'We can go, if you'd like to,' Janey said at last. She hesitated, then said in a low voice, 'May we take Bessie? I think she's finding things rather slow here.'

Topsy sighed. 'I suppose so. I will write and ask Gabriel if he can lay another place.'

Janey made herself a new dress for the occasion, having found a length of silk with the iridescent blue-black sheen of a raven's plumage. She cut it simply, with long full sleeves, and wore it with a doubled string of yellow beads. Knowing how much Gabriel loved wild roses, she cut herself a little bouquet and pinned it at her waist.

They caught a train to London, and then hired a hansom cab to take them to Chelsea. Topsy very kindly ordered the cab driver to take them the long way, past Buckingham Palace and the Green Park Arch, with its huge statue on top of the Duke of Wellington astride his horse. Bessie hung out the cab window, her eyes rounded with amazement.

'Do ye think we'll see the Queen?' she asked.

Topsy snorted. 'No-one's seen the Queen since her poor dear Albert died. I heard someone even put up a notice on the railings of the palace, saying, "These premises to be let or sold in consequence of the late occupant's declining business."'

'I wonder they dared,' Bessie said.

'They'll dare a lot more if she continues in this way,' he answered robustly.

Janey did not enter the conversation. Her thoughts were all centred on Gabriel. She wondered if he still grieved for Lizzie, and if it was true that he had a mistress installed in his house. She wondered whether he would be pleased to see her.

Their hansom cab drew up, and Topsy jumped to the ground, turning to hand out the ladies. Bessie clambered out eagerly, but Janey sat, smoothing her gloves over her wrists, stricken with sudden shyness.

'Janey?' Topsy asked.

She took a deep breath, and climbed down into the street.

Lights shone from a tall handsome brick house, with a white ornate turret built above the portico, set with rows of three-sided bay windows. High iron railings enclosed the front courtyard, with a tall filigree gate. The house looked out towards the Thames, cloth of silver under the moonlight.

'Gabriello must be doing well for himself,' Topsy said. 'Bruno tells me he's been working like a madman, poor fellow.'

With her hand tucked in Topsy's elbow, Janey climbed the stairs. Gabriel stood, a drink in his hand, in the crowded front hall. More people milled about in the two front rooms. Janey saw Ned and Georgie, William Rossetti, Arthur Hughes and his beautiful wife, Tryphena, and Algernon Swinburne, gesticulating wildly, his red hair standing on end.

Topsy tapped Gabriel on the shoulder. He turned and flung open his arms. 'Topsy, my dear fellow! Look at you. Fatter than ever. Mrs Topsy feeds you too well.'

'I thought we were coming for a dinner party.' Topsy shook Gabriel's hand warmly. 'But it looks like you've invited half of London.'

'Well, once you invite one you've got to invite a dozen, don't you find? Come in, you'll see plenty of people you know.'

Gabriel was speaking to Topsy, but his eyes were on Janey. She gazed back at him. The years had not been kind to him. His curls were thinning, and his body thickening. His eyes were shadowed, and his brow furrowed. Yet none of that mattered to Janey. She wanted to take his dear tired face between her hands and kiss away the marks of grief and pain.

He bowed to her gravely, and took her cold hand in both of his big, warm ones. 'Are you well, Janey?'

'Very well, thank you,' she answered, with a crooked smile.

'I'm glad you could come. Topsy told me you're in mourning for your father. I am sorry. No matter how much our parents bother us when they're alive, it's always hard to lose them.'

Tears stung her eyes at his understanding. She nodded, and he drew her hand through his arm.

'Come and let me show you the house. It's not Hogs' Hole, but it has its charms.' He led her away down the hall, Bessie and Topsy having to fall in behind them. 'It used to be called Queen's House, but no queen ever lived here, I'm afraid. Unless you wish to move in, Janey?' He smiled at her.

They passed through an archway, with two ingenious little seats tucked in either side, and then into a broad hallway that ran at right angles across the house. A staircase stood at either end. One was traditionally built, the other a grand spiral with a balustrade made of beautifully forged iron.

Topsy exclaimed at once with pleasure, and went to examine its workmanship. As Gabriel showed him the carved brackets, Janey looked upwards to see the circular shape of the staircase as it looped up. She got a glimpse of a woman's face, framed by heavy waves of guinea-gold hair. There was a squeak of dismay, and the woman sprang back, her silky embroidered robe flaring over the edge of the step. Footsteps pounded away.

Janey looked at Gabriel. He grinned at her. 'Some people have mice in their ceilings. I have elephants.'

She did not know how to answer.

'Very useful for washing windows, you know,' he said, and led her back down the hall and into the wild disorder of his studio. Costumes were draped over lay-figures, and brushes were stuck in jars filled with thick grey sludge. A half-empty cup of cold coffee held down a stack of drawings, and a fine blue-and-white china bowl was being used as an ashtray. Hundreds of paintings were stacked against the walls or hung on every available surface. Many of them showed Lizzie's red-golden hair and heavy-lidded eyes. Janey felt a wrench of grief at the sight of them. She looked at Gabriel. He was staring at them with so much pain and sorrow in his face, she wanted to put her arms about him and hold him close as if he were a child. He took a deep breath, braced his shoulders and turned back to her.

'It is time for me to paint something new.' Gabriel took her hand. 'Will you come and sit for me, Janey? Please?'

'I don't know … I shouldn't …' Her eyes sought her husband. He was standing in the doorway, frowning at them. Janey realised that she was standing very close to Gabriel, her hand clasped in his. She stepped back, drawing her hand free. 'I do not come up to London very often, I'm afraid.'

'But you must! Come up with Topsy on the train, and spend the day here, in the studio, then he can come and have supper and then take you home.' He turned to Topsy. 'What do you say, Tops? Will you let your wife be painted by me? It's a shame to keep all that beauty mouldering away in the country.'

Janey's cheeks were hot, and her breath was coming short. She realised her hands were plucking at her necklace, and clasped them together to still them. Her attention was caught by a small watercolour leaning against the wall. She bent down to look at it more closely.

It showed a man seated in an alcove between two women. The one on the right was clearly modelled on Lizzie, with her bright golden-red hair loose on her shoulders. Dressed in green, she played a lute. The man – who looked like an idealised portrait of Gabriel – listened with rapt attention.

On his left sat a sad-looking woman in blue who looked just like Janey, with a cloud of dark hair and lowered brows. She clutched at the man's hand, as if trying to reclaim his attention. At her foot was a glass full of wine. The other two had drained their glasses dry.

Janey sucked in a sharp breath.

Gabriel turned the painting to the wall. 'Just a little something I did for George Price Boyle. He's meant to have picked it up by now.'

Janey tried to keep her voice steady. 'What … what do you call it?'

'*The Merciless Lady*.'

Their eyes met for a long charged moment. Then Janey looked away, heat scorching her skin. She brushed past Bessie and joined the crowd in the drawing room.

What did the little painting mean? Did Gabriel think himself caught between two loves? Janey's pulse quickened at the thought, till she felt quite dizzy and frightened. She accepted a glass of wine, nodded and smiled as everyone around her talked and laughed, and kept stealing glances at Gabriel. Every single time his gaze met hers.

Who was the Merciless Lady?

Was it Lizzie?

Or was it her?

'Don't smile,' Gabriel said.

'Why not?' Janey asked, smiling.

'It's not the happiness in you I want to catch. It's the sadness.'

Janey nodded. She looked away from him, clenching her hands together. Always he saw too much.

It seemed to Janey that happiness was a gift she had not been given. Everything seemed to weigh on her more heavily than it did on others. Each evening, as she kissed her daughters goodnight, she feared she might not see them again. As if death's sickle might cut their delicate thread while she slept.

It was a hot afternoon in July, and Gabriel had set up a marquee in his garden for her to pose in. Bessie had come with her, to act as her chaperone. A photographer had been hired to make studies of her, so Janey stood or sat or reclined as Gabriel instructed, dressed in her dark blue dress, her hair pinned loosely.

It was easier to pose for the camera than for Gabriel. The staring glass eye was dead. It did not look inside her soul. It did not see the sorrow twisted deep with her weft.

Gabriel gently changed the angle of her jaw. She looked down, not wanting him to know how badly she wanted him to kiss her.

Why could the heart not choose whom to love?

If Janey could, she would love her husband. She would feel a little thrill in the pit of her stomach every time he touched her. She would hang on his every word, and be proud of his cleverness. She would smile at his rage, and tease him into laughter. She would go to bed each night eagerly, and press her skin against his, and shiver with longing as his hand crept between her legs.

But she did not love him. She did not want him. She could not bear him.

Why was the heart so contrary?

Janey told her husband that she was tired. That she was not well. That her head ached. She did her best to pretend nothing was wrong, but it was a poor performance.

At night she dreamed of Gabriel. Her dreams made her twist and squirm in her bed, unable to find a way to ease the constant ache of desire. She walked for miles along the roads, besmirching her skirts. She scrubbed the table till it was white, while the servants watched with resentful eyes. She sewed till her fingertips were sore.

Topsy was working long hours, coming home so tired he hardly noticed her. They sat together by the fire each night, Janey sewing silently, Topsy scribbling poems, sketching designs for wallpapers and fabrics, or frowning over bills and letters. The clock mocked the passing moments. Eventually Janey would fold away her embroidery, and say goodnight. When her husband came to bed, she would pretend to be asleep. When at last his breathing relaxed into snores, she would rise and tiptoe out, lighting a candle, leaning over her sleeping daughters to make sure they still breathed, standing at the dark window and staring at the reflection of her face.

Such beauty, Gabriel had whispered, holding her face in his hands the one time he had lain with her. Such beauty.

The garden at Red House was a riot of clematis and delphiniums and wild roses. Janey worked in it every day, her skirts hitched up through her belt. Jenny and May helped her, toddling about with little buckets and spades, and pulling up daisies along with the weeds. Janey made them chains of pink clover flowers to hang about their necks, and told them that foxglove bells were worn as hats by fairies. Topsy sat in the Pilgrim's Rest, pipe clenched between his teeth, sketching the rose trellis for a wallpaper design.

Be happy, Janey told herself. *Do not think about him.*

Yet when Gabriel wrote to ask her to come again, to sit for some pencil sketches, Janey went the very next day. She sat in silence beside her husband in the train all the way to London, twisting her handkerchief in her fingers till it tore.

Gabriel did not lie with her. Gabriel did not kiss her. He barely touched her at all.

Yet his drawings were small miracles of tenderness and yearning.

When Topsy saw them that afternoon, his mouth set grimly. He looked from Gabriel to Janey suspiciously. Gabriel made a joke. Janey was the Queen of Beauty, he said, impossible to draw badly. Topsy did not smile.

Janey sat in silence beside him all the way home.

That Sunday, Topsy took his palette and his brushes, and went to work on the great settle in the front hall. He had been intermittently painting a scene from Malory's Joyous Gard for months, with the help of his friends. He had painted a golden sky, tall slender apple trees, flower-scattered grass. On one door, a man in a medieval hood, looking much like Topsy himself, played a lute to a woman in a red gown who sat leaning towards him, listening. This woman had been drawn with Janey's strong jaw and dark rumpled waves of hair. Two other women, partly completed, stood on either side, framing the seated couple. Janey thought that Topsy may have modelled them on Lucy and Kate Faulkner, who had often visited Red House with their brother.

The second panel was almost completed. A man, modelled by Ned, fed a small fruit to his lover, modelled by Georgie. Another woman reached up one hand to break a branch from an apple tree. Two more figures were rising to dance. Janey knew that Topsy had intended them to be Gabriel and Lizzie, but he had felt unable to finish the painting of their faces after her death.

Janey knew the story of the Joyous Gard well. It had been a great castle once named the Dolorous Gard, for it had been inhabited by a cruel lord. King Arthur had told Sir Lancelot that he might have the castle if he could free it from its wicked owner. So the young Sir Lancelot set out to do battle with the monster that guarded it and broke the sinister enchantment upon the land. He turned the castle into a place of great beauty, where art and music flourished. It was renamed the Joyous Gard, and King Arthur and Queen Guenevere visited him there. Later, when his tragic love for his king's wife had been exposed, Sir Lancelot rescued Queen Guenevere from being burned alive and fled with her back to his castle. King Arthur besieged the castle, the lovers were forced to part, and the castle was ruined. It was once again named the Dolorous Gard, a place of treachery and grief.

Gabriel had told Janey the story, long ago in Oxford, as he had painted her as the queen and himself as the faithless friend.

Suddenly Janey heard a great din. She ran into the hall. Topsy was hammering the hilt of his palette knife into his painting of Janey's face. 'I can't do it, I can't do it, I can't do it,' he cried.

Janey stood and stared at him. He glared at her in angry accusation. She shrank back. He hurled his palette and knife across the hall and went out, slamming the front door behind him.

Janey stood before the settle. The painting of her face was damaged beyond repair. Janey reached up and covered it with her hand, the splintered wood rough beneath her fingers. Her chest was rising and falling quickly. Her eyes burned.

The palette had broken, leaving a mess of paint on the floor. Wet brushes lay tumbled everywhere, the knife flung clear across the wall. Janey bent to clear up the mess. Her finger slipped into the wet black paint.

Janey rose and carefully drew ripples of dark hair above the sketched face of the dancing woman. The woman who should have been Lizzie.

In the early autumn, Topsy told her that they had to leave Red House.

'The Firm is not making enough money,' he said brusquely, 'and my income from my father's investments has halved this year.'

Janey stared at him.

'I can't go on like this. Hours of travel every day, worrying over the bills, having no time for anything.' He looked at her directly for the first time. 'Wondering what you are doing all day while I am gone.'

'Where shall we go? What will happen to the house?' She could scarcely manage to whisper the words.

'We have to sell the house.' He made no effort to soften the blow. 'I am looking for somewhere in town, somewhere where we can live above the workshops.'

She was dumb with misery.

Part of her realised that it was Topsy's own grief at the loss of the house that made him so curt. He loved it as much as her; it was the house of his dreams. Yet once he had decided to sell, he poured all his energies into making it happen. It was Janey who could not recover from the blow.

3

A Pearl Beyond Price
Summer 1866

'What do you think it'll be?' Ned asked Phil one morning, as Georgie struggled to her feet, one fist pressed into the curve of her back.

Phil put his head to one side. 'It'll be either a girl or a boy,' he pronounced, after due deliberation.

Ned shouted with laughter, then agreed he thought Phil might be right.

Georgie laid both hands on the hard swell of her stomach. It would be a girl, she knew it. She had had a most vivid dream nine months ago. She had imagined herself swimming in a deep green pool of water, ripples of light passing over her naked body. A slim silver fish swam below her. Its fins brushed against her belly. Georgie had swum to the surface, and rolled over on to her back. Her belly was swelling round and pale and luminous, as if she had the moon within her womb. She cradled it with both arms, and her skin parted and unfurled like the petals of a wild rose, revealing a tiny child curled within the secret golden heart. The child had been a girl, and Georgie had woken knowing both that she was once again with child, and that this time she would have the daughter she had always longed for.

The months after baby Christopher's death had been the darkest and most melancholy Georgie had ever known. She had not been able to bear to stay at their rooms at Great Russell Street. So they had moved to the first house they could find, in Kensington Square. The building faced north, and was cold and draughty. The narrow garden smelt of cat urine. The rooms were small and gloomy, and Ned complained that the light was too poor for painting. Georgie had wanted to find a house with a big, sunny garden, and apple trees, but Ned had wanted to stay close to Kensington. His old friend, Val Prinsep, lived only a short stroll away. His family – who had made their fortune in India – had created a lively artistic salon at their home, Little Holland House. Ned had taken to going there often, leaving Georgie at home with Phil.

With his big blue eyes and dark curls, five-year-old Phil looked as if he would have the sweetest of tempers. He was a little autocrat, however, who loved ordering around the young maid-of-all-work. He would climb up on a chair in the kitchen, point a wooden spoon at the cupboard, and say, 'Jam and bread. Now.' He hated being put to bed, particularly now the evenings were light for so long, and would struggle and scream and fight till Georgie was exhausted. Ned was no use; he did not have an autocratic bone in his body, and simply looked surprised when Georgie begged him to intervene.

Once Georgie lost all patience and threatened her little boy with a spanking. He stared at her defiantly, his full lower lip quivering, saying, 'How cruel of you.'

She could not bear to strike him, and so he stayed up till all hours, playing on the carpet with his trains and his wooden blocks, till at last weariness overcame and his eyes fluttered closed, his head pillowed on his plump arms. Georgie carried him up to bed, tucking him in beside her so she could soothe him back to sleep if he woke.

As the days grew longer, Georgie's stomach swelled till she could no longer disguise her shape with shawls. She was filled with apprehension, unable to forget the last terrible birth and its tragic aftermath. She comforted herself by remembering the dream she had had, of a baby girl curled in the centre of a rose. Surely it meant that this child would live?

If Georgie was fearful, Ned was petrified. He hovered over her, trying to make her rest, begging her to stay home, away from the contagion of the streets.

Yet he did not feel any need to stay home himself. He went to Little Holland House most days, and often stayed late, smoking and drinking and talking. Sometimes he did not get home till the wee hours of the morning, coming in with his boots in his hand but knocking over the umbrella stand on the way.

Georgie could not believe her own husband was proving the ills of alcohol.

She would lie awake for hours, listening to cats squall out in the garden, arguing with Ned silently in her mind. Yet when he came in, she shut her eyes and pretended to be asleep, unable to bear the idea of quarrelling with him.

She had no-one to talk to. Her mother and youngest sister, Edith, were in Bewdley, looking after her ailing father. Alice and her husband, John Kipling, were in India, nursing a baby boy they had called Rudyard. Agnes was engaged to an ambitious young painter called Edward Poynter, and Louie had betrothed herself to an up-and-coming politician named Alfred Baldwin. Ned had been most cast down at their engagements, hating the idea of the little girls he had known being old enough to marry and have children. He had written a letter to Louie, which said: '*I am unchangeable in my love for you, don't doubt it: nothing will ever divide us – no chance nor circumstance will bring that about – but a little gloomy sulkiness is excusable in me. I only had two wenches and they are both gone …*'

He meant it to be a joke, but Georgie could tell her husband was truly unhappy. It was one of the strange crimps in his nature. He wanted to immobilise any moment of happiness, like a mayfly caught in golden amber. Yet the bright-winged insect always struggled to escape, to fly, to live out its short ecstatic life before it fell, spent, to the water. Ned could not catch them, and so it grieved him to see those swift, ephemeral moments pass by and be lost.

In May, the collapse of a London bank caused widespread panic. The papers reported a run on the city banks as people tried to get their money out. Other banks began to fall. Georgie lay awake, worrying about money. Ned had no head for business at all. He had once bought Georgie a watch, studded with bright peridots, with the last eight pounds they possessed. He owed a staggering amount to the Firm because he kept borrowing from it. And Georgie had once found an uncashed cheque shoved in one of his coat pockets. When she asked him why he had not cashed it, Ned had admitted that he did not have a cheque account and had no idea how to open one. Georgie had to ask Topsy to help him, and then she had taken over the keeping of the accounts and the paying of the servants, giving Ned a few pounds a week as pocket money. It was the only way, she had discovered, to be sure their affairs were in order.

If only Ned was not so slow with his paintings!

Gabriel came to visit them, the first time he had come to their home in more than two years. He admired their new pomegranate wallpaper, and their black Sussex rush-bottom chairs, all bought on credit from the Firm, and then suggested that Ned hire a studio assistant, to help hurry him along. Which was all well and good, except that Ned said there was not enough room for the two of them in his small cramped studio and spent even more time at Val Prinsep's. Which meant that Georgie had to order tea for a stranger, and worry about the salary of another member of staff.

Meanwhile, her whole body swelled. Even her face was as round and hot as a dumpling. She had trouble sleeping, and so asked Ned to move to another room so she did not have to listen to his snoring. Phil began to wake with nightmares, and each day was a struggle to try to manage his temper.

Since her scarlet fever, everything had seemed so difficult. She looked back at the Georgie she had been before and it was like a different girl, a different life.

Or perhaps it was not the scarlet fever that had so changed her, but Lizzie's death. It seemed like the end of their golden youth, their heedless innocence.

Her daughter came quickly and easily into the world on June 3rd, a pale little creature with the biggest bluest eyes Georgie had ever seen. Ned and Georgie decided to call her Margaret, for she was a pearl beyond price.

Lying quietly, looking about her, she sucked her thumb. Ned very gently freed her tiny hand from the swaddling bands. She closed it firmly about his finger.

He was utterly enchanted.

Georgie's world narrowed down to a pinprick.

Between feeding the baby, soaking the nappies, bathing and dressing her little boy, kneading bread, shelling peas, peeling potatoes, paying the butcher, totting up her account book, and sewing on buttons, she barely had time to sleep.

Less than a week after Margaret's birth, Georgie unwrapped the newspaper the fish had been delivered in, and found an article declaring that a member of parliament called John Stuart Mill had presented a petition to the House of Commons proposing women be permitted to vote. The long scroll had contained so many names that two women had been needed to carry it. The women had been so afraid someone would seize their petition and tear it to bits, they had hidden it under the stall of an apple seller till Mr Mill was there to take charge of it.

More than one and a half thousand people had signed it. Georgie marvelled at the thought of it. She looked down at her tiny daughter, nestled in her arms, and wondered what life would hold in store for her.

Elizabeth Garrett, one of the women who had carried the petition, had trained secretly to be a doctor. Her friend Emily Davies had founded a college for women.

Perhaps, one day, Georgie thought, her daughter would have all the things that she had been denied. A proper education, the right to work, the right to vote. The idea excited and unsettled her. She read everything she could find about the petition, and wished that she had had a chance to sign it.

Georgie's head was filled with new ideas, but she had no-one to talk to. Ned was hardly ever home. He spent most of his days at the Prinseps, and went out on the town with his bachelor friends in the evenings. He would come home, humming some vulgar music hall song, reeking of beer and pipe smoke. In the mornings, he would groan and cover his eyes with one hand, and only manage a few dabs of paint.

Georgie tried to talk to him, but he only got defensive and clammed up.

'Just try to finish a painting!' she would admonish him. 'Else we'll need to move somewhere cheaper.'

'I cannot paint any faster,' he cried. 'Do you want me to just slap paint on the canvases like those damned French fellows?'

Another time he said, 'When did you turn into such a nag?'

Crying alone in her bedroom, Georgie knew he was right. She had turned into a nag. But he was a father now. He had responsibilities.

One day, her sister Agnes came for tea. Always the prettiest of the family, Agnes was turned out in fine style in one of the new crinolettes, which only employed hoops at the back. It made sitting rather difficult, so Agnes was perched sideways on her chair, her silken skirts bunched up behind her.

'So where is Ned?' she asked, after properly admiring baby Margaret – now called Margot for short – in her cradle.

Georgie shrugged. 'He's gone to Little Holland House again. It's Sunday, and they have an open house that day.'

Agnes looked at her questioningly. 'Where?'

'Little Holland House. Where the Prinseps live.'

Understanding dawned on her sister's face. 'Ah yes, of course. The patrons of Mr Watts. Isn't Mrs Prinsep one of the celebrated Pattle sisters?'

Georgie nodded.

Agnes sipped her tea. 'Are they not famous for their beauty?'

'Oh, yes, and for their wit and talent too,' Georgie replied rather bitterly.

'Do you not wish to go too?' Agnes asked. 'To Little Holland House, I mean. I believe that the crème de la crème of London society is to be found there.'

Georgie shrugged and looked uncomfortable. 'They wouldn't welcome the children ... Phil is just at that rambunctious age, you know.'

'Leave them at home,' Agnes suggested, selecting a thin cucumber sandwich from the selection on the plate. 'Your skivvy Sukey wouldn't mind watching them, would she?'

'Oh, no, I can't,' Georgie said. When Agnes looked surprised, she tried to explain. 'Sukey is little more than a child herself. Something might happen ...'

'Georgie, what happened to Christopher was not your fault,' Agnes said gently. 'We of all people know just how easily a baby can die.'

Georgie found herself choking up, and had to dab at her eyes with her napkin.

'It'll do you good to go. Fresh faces and all that. If you like, I can come and mind the children for a couple of hours. Little Holland House is only a block away. A message would reach you in a trice.'

Georgie imagined an afternoon away from the house and the children, enjoying Ned's company, talking of books and art and politics, eating food someone else had cooked.

She smiled at her sister gratefully. 'Thank you, Agnes. I'd like that.'

'You might want to get a new dress,' Agnes said. 'And do something with your hair, for goodness sake.'

4

The Three Graces
Autumn 1866

The following Sunday, Georgie put on her bonnet and walked with Ned through the bright fallen leaves to Little Holland House. It had once been the dower house for the noble Holland family, and was a gracious old building with tall chimneys and steep tiled gables set in the midst of a huge old garden.

Women in delicate white frocks and big hats stood under the elm trees, croquet mallets in their hands. Georgie at once felt herself at a disadvantage. She had not liked to tell Agnes, but there was no money for her to buy a new dress or a more fashionable hat. She had to make do with what she had.

Georgie knew she must look a dowd.

Men sat nearby, some smoking cigars, others playing cards at a little white table. A long table was set up under the tree, set with blue-and-white china and silver cutlery, and white wine in green glass carafes. Bowls were heaped with the biggest, reddest strawberries Georgie had ever seen. A large platter of saffron-hued rice was topped with sizzling lamb. A stout man with the weathered skin of someone who had seen a few Indian summers was carving roast chicken with strangely crimson skin, and the air was filled with an exotic spicy smell that Georgie had never before encountered.

Georgie clutched Ned's arm self-consciously, as he was greeted warmly on all sides. Mrs Dalrymple – the youngest of the sisters – came and took his hand and kissed his cheek, before giving Georgie a vague smile. Her soft white dress blew in the breeze, giving a faint impression of her long lithe limbs beneath. Silver bangles tinkled on her wrists.

'Ned, my dear, so lovely to see you again. So you have brought your wife ...' she hesitated, obviously not remembering Georgie's name. 'You are welcome, of course. Do, please, come and sit. Can I offer you a glass of wine?'

'No, thank you,' Georgie replied, more curtly than she had intended.

Mrs Dalrymple lifted both finely plucked eyebrows. 'Some tea then? Coffee?'

When Georgie named her choice, she snapped her fingers at one of the black-clad men-servants nearby. 'Mitchell, some tea, if you please.'

'If it's not too much bother,' Georgie said apologetically.

'It's no bother,' Mrs Dalrymple said in a bored tone. 'Ned, will you come and meet Mrs Cassavetti? She is looking to commission some paintings, and I am sure she will adore you.' She tucked her hands into the crook of his elbow, smiling up at him as she led him away.

Georgie sat down, smoothing her skirts.

'Mrs Dalrymple does love a handsome young artist,' a laughing voice said, close to Georgie's ear. 'I always expect her to fall to her knees and offer to feed them fresh grapes.'

Georgie's vision had been obscured by a mist of tears. She blinked them away, and turned to see a handsome young woman smiling satirically at her. She was dressed in a severely cut coat and skirt, with her dark hair parted in the middle and smoothed back to a low chignon.

'You must be Mrs Jones. I'm Rosalind Howard.' She held out her hand to Georgie. Her handshake was swift and firm, like a boy's. 'I'm very pleased to meet you. Is this your first visit to Pattledom?' She laughed at Georgie's expression of surprise, saying, 'That's what I call it. The Kingdom of the Pattle sisters. Where Art and Beauty is worshipped, and Convention and Morality scorned. I can see you too scorn convention, refusing to let yourself be trapped within a corset and crinoline. Good on you! And you do not drink alcohol either? I can see we shall be friends.' She lifted her teacup in an ironical salute.

Rosalind had a lively tongue and a quick mind, and she amused Georgie by giving her a potted history of all the other guests. 'That man in the black skull-cap and the beard of a prophet is Mr Watts, the painter. Sara likes to say he came to visit for three days and stayed for thirty years.

Georgie laughed.

Rosalind grinned boyishly, and pointed to a young man with black curls and scowling brows. 'That handsome young Greek god is Luke Ionides. He and his family live at No. 1 Holland Park, and are famous for their fancy dress parties. One night the American painter James Whistler confounded everyone by turning up dressed as a chimney-sweep, so convincingly old Mr Ionides almost had the footmen throw him out. I have seen your husband there many times, but not you. Do you not care for fancy dress parties?'

'No.' Georgie made a helpless gesture at her frock. 'And I have little ones ...'

'Oh, but you must never let children stand in the way of romance,' Rosalind said, laughing. 'I hope to have a dozen children, but I won't let that stop me from attending a party!'

The stout man with the dark skin was serving lunch. The food made Georgie's mouth burn. She could not eat a mouthful of it. Rosalind ate heartily though, talking all the while.

'You must know Robert Browning, of course. No? That's him over there with the fringe of a beard and the ink-stained fingers. I will introduce you later if you like.'

'Thank you,' Georgie stammered, a little overwhelmed. 'I love his poems.'

'You like to read? Have you read *Adam Bede* by George Eliot? Did you know it was really written by a woman? Miss Evans is not here today, but

I shall introduce you next time if you like. Though you must not mind that she is living in sin. Would you mind that?'

The question was shot at her, taking Georgie aback. She said slowly, 'I do not know. I suppose it depends on the circumstances.'

'Very true. It is a delicate situation, of course. Her lover Mr Lewes is married already, but his wife fell in love with his best friend. They cannot divorce, Mr Lewes being accused of being complicit in his wife's adultery, but Mr Lewes and Miss Evans act in every way as man and wife. They are not accepted in society, of course, but here in Pattledom such petty-minded rules are not enforced.'

Georgie was shocked, though she tried hard not to show it. She had never heard of a man and woman who lived happily together in sin. She wondered uneasily what kind of bad influence these people must be having on Ned. She wished she had not come.

Rosalind put one hand on hers. 'I'm sorry, I did not mean to scandalise you. Mr Lewes and Miss Evans are truly good people, I promise you that. If they could marry, they would. It is the fault of this society we live in, where appearances and conventions mean more than the truth in people's hearts.'

Georgie nodded slowly. Her new friend was right, she knew. And when Georgie had married Ned, she had wanted to live in his world and put aside all the intolerant teachings of her mother and her church.

She looked down the table, to where Ned had sat down next to a high-nosed, olive-skinned older woman with a mass of loosely fastened dark red hair, which owed more than a little – Georgie thought – to the henna plant.

'That is Mrs Cassavetti,' Rosalind said in a low voice. 'She is the sister of Alexander Ionides, the Greek consul. There are hordes of them here in London, very closely knit, very proud, and very, very rich. We call them the Greek colony. It would be a feather in your husband's cap, if he could secure the Greeks as his patron.

Mrs Cassavetti had her hand on Ned's arm. She lifted her other arm and pointed up the hill towards the house. Ned gazed where he pointed. His face changed. He looked thunderstruck.

Georgie looked to see what had so caught his attention.

Three slender young women were walking down the green slope, laughing. All three were clad in soft blowing muslins, and their mass of dark curling hair was so loosely bound that long tendrils floated about their faces. All shared a classical profile, and large dark eyes fringed by thick eyelashes. Two were olive-skinned and brown-haired. The one in the middle, however, had pale skin and lustrous dark-red hair, and the muslin dress seemed to cling to the sinuous lines of her body.

Georgie licked her dry lips. 'Who ... who is she?'

Rosalind turned to look. 'Ah, the Three Graces. Part of the Greek colony. The one with the lighter brown hair is Aglaia Coronio. She's Mr Ionides's daughter and the sister of the Greek god I pointed out to you before. The tall dark one is her cousin, Marie Spartali. I'm surprised you don't know her. She's been taking painting lessons with Ford Madox Brown for a couple of years now and is said to have some real talent.'

She paused, shot a quick look at Georgie's face, then said lightly, 'The one with the marvellous hair is Madame Zambaco. I've never met her before. She made a shocking mesalliance a few years ago. Eloped from her father's death-bed with his doctor. I've heard he was a brute to her, so she fled in the dead of night with her two little ones and not much more than the clothes she stood up in. Luckily for her, her parents had tied up her fortune so the wicked doctor couldn't get his claws into it. I've heard she's worth eighty thousand pounds, which is not to be sneezed at.'

While Rosalind was talking, Madame Zambaco and her cousins had reached the table where they were met with cries of delight and welcome. She was smiling at Ned, offering him her hand. He stood up to take it. Her riotously curling hair was the colour of polished mahogany. It must reach her waist if released from its combs.

'Excuse me,' Georgie said, and got up clumsily. She made her way to Ned's side.

'But, of course, I would love to paint you,' he was saying. 'If your mother is truly so kind as to commission me. Surely you must come and visit me, and see my work first? To be sure you like it?'

'I'd love to,' Madame Zambaco said. 'I am free tomorrow, if that would suit you.'

'Yes, indeed, of course. Any time.'

'Ned,' Georgie said.

He turned at the sound of her voice. 'Oh. Georgie. There you are. This is Madame Zambaco. Her mother wishes me to paint her. I said I would be honoured, of course. Madame Zambaco, this ... this is my wife.'

Did Georgie imagine the hesitation in his voice, his reluctance to introduce her?

She smiled politely, offered her hand, spoke all that was expected of her in a colourless voice.

To her chagrin, she barely came up to Madame Zambaco's shoulder.

'A pleasure to meet you, Mrs Jones.' Her voice was sweet, melodious, with an exotic hint of a foreign accent. 'Please, you must call me Maria. I have no desire to be known by my husband's name. If I had my way, I'd be in court tomorrow and declaring before the judges my husband's life-threatening cruelty. But they have no interest in that. Only adultery matters to them, and of that I have no proof, only endless suspicions.'

Georgie felt herself moved to pity despite herself. Maria Zambaco's voice was so full of pain and melancholy.

'But ... please, forgive me ... I do not mean to burden you with my problems. What a bore I have become! Ned ... may I call you Ned? I shall see you tomorrow.' With a brilliant smile, and what Georgie considered a most familiar press of Ned's hand between both of her own, Maria Zambaco moved gracefully away.

Ned stared after her.

*

Ned would not betray me, Georgie told herself. *He loves me.*

Maria Zambaco came to the studio at least two times a week, so that Ned could make pencil studies of her face. He was planning to paint her as Psyche, the woman whose beauty made Venus jealous. Topsy had spent much of the last year composing an epic poem about Cupid and Psyche, and Ned planned to illustrate it.

Sometimes, Georgie stood outside the studio door, straining her ears to listen to what was happening inside. She heard nothing but a soft murmur of voices, and the occasional laugh. Often, she heard nothing but silence.

Miserable, she crept back down to the sitting room. To her sewing and her account book and her children. Ned seemed different. Restless, impatient, quick to find fault with her. She began to feature in his quickly-tossed-off caricatures as a short fat dumpling, her arms always filled with the baby.

He finished the painting of Maria Zambaco, but said it was not good enough and began at once on another. In the second painting, Psyche lay asleep, her robe slipping from her shoulder and exposing one small, perfect breast. Georgie wondered if Maria had posed that way for Ned, shamelessly sliding the silk down her skin, her head flung back.

Society women did not pose nude, she reassured herself. Madame Zambaco would have just posed for the face, and perhaps those beautiful white hands. Ned would have used a common model to paint the body. Though those sinuous lines and luminous white skin looked like Madame Zambaco.

Then Maria began coming every day. Ned said he was giving her lessons.

'Lessons in what?' Georgie asked.

'She wants to learn to paint,' he answered curtly.

Georgie remembered her own dreams of creating art. She thought of her early sketches and watercolours, her wood-carving tools, untouched now for years, her piano sitting mute and unused in a corner of the drawing room, her feeble attempts to write poetry. Her eyes burned, her throat constricted.

'She has true talent,' Ned said. 'It's a shame to let such a gift go to waste.'

Does she not have children too? Georgie wanted to ask. *Who darns their stockings? Who teaches them their letters? Who makes sure there is fresh bread for their tea?*

But she only turned away and mechanically tidied up Phil's crayons and drawings. She knew the answer. With a fortune of eighty thousand pounds, Maria would not even have to button up her son's boots for him.

Six weeks after Margot's first birthday, Georgie received word that their landlord had sold their house and they needed to move. Georgie's heart leapt. If she could just persuade Ned to leave London. If they could move to the country, away from the Prinseps and their Pattledom, away from the pot houses and music halls, away from Maria Zambaco. A house with a garden, a house with a bright and airy studio so he did not need to go and paint in Val Prinsep's all the time. Georgie began to try to persuade him.

Ned flatly refused.

Their arguments grew ever more bitter.

In the end they compromised and moved to a new house in North End Lane, Fulham. It had plenty of room for a gallery to show off Ned's paintings, and a garden still sweet with late-blooming roses and lavender. There was a big room with north-facing windows that Ned could paint in. It was only twenty minutes to Kensington in a hansom cab, but at least Ned could not walk over to Little Holland House whenever he wanted, and it was another half an hour or so to Gloucester Gardens, where Maria lived with her mother.

Georgie could only hope it was far enough away.

5

Seizing Joy
Winter–Spring 1868

Janey had always hated London.

She hated the spindly, soot-black trees. She hated the smoke and the fog and the sleet. She hated always feeling sick.

Topsy had moved his family into a tall, thin house at 26 Queen Square. It had three steps up to the front door, and an iron railing that looked down to the grimy windows of the basements, exactly like all the other houses on either side. It had no garden. Only a yard with workshops that rang all day with the clang of iron and the whirr of the weavers' looms and the scraping of the carpenter's adze. The air was always tainted with smoke from the kiln.

There was no peace to be had. Topsy was there all day, stamping about, shouting orders at the workmen. Their apartment above the shop had been turned into a display area, so that customers traipsed through all day to see the dining room hung with his sumptuous red Indian wallpaper, the blue-and-white scrolled foliage and fruit pattern he called Queen Anne, and the daisy design in the bedroom.

Topsy was hard at work on the proofs for his new book of poetry, and left long curls of paper everywhere, scribbled all over with his quick impatient scrawl. His epic poem, 'The Life and Death of Jason', had been met with such applause Topsy was encouraged to proceed with the rest of his *Earthly Paradise*. The girls were always getting into trouble for drawing on his proofs, or cutting them up to make paper dolls, so Janey did her best to keep his work in order and out of the children's way. It did not do much good. Topsy's temper was shorter than ever, and the girls always underfoot, getting in his way.

One afternoon May set about burying her favourite doll – named Lady Audley because of her golden hair – in a flowerpot in the courtyard. Amused, all the workmen stopped to watch her. Topsy saw them idling, and came out to shout at them to get back to work. When he saw the mess that May had made, he erupted into rage. It was like he was possessed. Janey could do nothing but shield the weeping little girl in her arms, and try not to shrink back as her husband shouted at them both.

Afterwards, she tucked May up in bed and lay beside her. The nursery was hung with Topsy's first-ever wallpaper design, called 'Trellis', inspired by the rose garden at Red House. Wild roses clambered on green thorny stems over wooden squares, with blue birds and damsel flies hovering in the midst. May did not like the birds. They stared at her, she said. Janey petted and soothed her till she was asleep, then lay staring at the repeating pattern till it seemed the birds moved and the insects whirred their wings.

It was like a cage enclosing her.

In early March, Ned and Georgie held a housewarming party at their new house, which was called The Grange. Ned had decorated his studio with orange trees in pots, and Georgie hung coloured paper lanterns along the terrace.

Georgie showed Janey and Topsy about the house, then took them into the studio where most of the men had congregated, drinking wine and looking over Ned's paintings. The Maniac was there, for the first time in years; and Algy Swinburne, and Bruno, and Roddy Stanhope, and William Bell Scott, as well as Ned and Topsy and Gabriel. Janey could not help but notice that a new model featured in many of Ned's drawings and paintings, a young woman with a slender lithe figure and masses of dark-red hair. Everyone was exclaiming over the new boldness and sensuality of Ned's style, and the beauty of his model, whom he had painted with her robe slipping from her shoulder, revealing one small breast.

'She is a Stunner, no mistake,' Roddy said, unable to tear his eyes from the canvas. 'Did she really pose nude for you? You old dog.'

Georgie turned and slipped away, her face downturned and unhappy. Janey hesitated, not knowing whether to follow her or to stay to greet the others. Gabriel decided for her. He had been scowling and looking saturnine, but his face lit up at the sight of her and he held out his hand. It seemed natural to walk over, and put her hand in his, and smile at him. Topsy scowled. Janey released her fingers from Gabriel's, but did not move from his side.

All the men crowded around Topsy, slapping him on his back, congratulating him on the success of his poetry, crowing over his reviews. He grinned, admitting that he was pleased with what he called 'the puffs'. Janey and Gabriel stood quietly at the back of the crowd, not quite looking at each other.

'Are you well, Janey?' Gabriel asked in a low voice.

Janey hesitated. She had not been well. Ever since moving to Queen Square, she had suffered headaches and sore throats and a sick feeling in the pit of her stomach. Her back ached all the time, and all the chores she had once done easily were now exhausting, as if she were seventy-eight instead of only twenty-eight. Janey blamed London in general, and the dust and smoke and noise of the workshops in particular, but she did not like to complain.

'I'll be glad when the winter is over,' she said instead.

Gabriel nodded. 'It seems like spring will never come, doesn't it?'

He was standing where the light was most dim, but had one hand raised to shield his eyes from the light of the oil lamps.

'What's wrong?' she asked, keeping her voice low.

'I . . . I should not have come . . . but I feel so lonely sometimes. As if life is going on without me.'

‘I thought you had plenty of company,’ she answered, a faint edge to her voice.

Colour rushed up under his olive skin. He put his hand on her wrist, clasping it warmly. ‘You, of all people, should not believe all the rumours you hear.’

Janey met his eyes, a question in hers.

He opened his mouth to say more, but Topsy bounced over, looking ruffled and bearish, his waistcoat straining at the buttons. Gabriel dropped his hand. Topsy put his arm around Janey. It was all she could do not to shake it off. She stood, stiff and stoical, as the two men talked about Topsy’s poems and Topsy’s new triumphs with the Firm and Topsy’s new wallpaper designs, selling like hot cakes. After a while, Gabriel excused himself and went out. Janey waited till Topsy was once again drawn into the general conversation of the other men, and then she slipped away too.

She found Gabriel in the shadowy garden, sitting on a bench under a tree, smoking. Though the air was crisp and cold, the sky was bright with stars. The red glowing tip of his cigar was the only colour, like a winking firefly.

He moved over, making room for her on the seat. Janey sat down beside him, burying her cold hands in the velvet of her mantle. She was very aware of the closeness of his body to hers. She wondered how to ask him what she wanted to know.

‘You think my housekeeper Fanny is my mistress,’ Gabriel said, after a long moment of tense expectant silence. ‘She was, I do not deny it.’ He looked down at the cigar in his hands, then gently tapped away the ash. When he sucked on the end, it illuminated his face for a moment, dark and frowning.

‘When you told me you were going to marry Topsy, I told you I was going to go to the Devil. Well, Fanny was that Devil.’ He glanced at her angrily. ‘Don’t look at me like that. What was I meant to do? You didn’t want me …’

Janey looked away, her lips pressed together to stop them from trembling.

After a while, Gabriel went on. 'And then I married Lizzie. You think I didn't really love her, but I did. I loved her with all my heart. It was just … she was so sick … all the time … and there was a kind of madness in it. I don't know how to explain it. Perhaps it was the laudanum … perhaps she was just too finely wrought a creature to live in this world. I don't know. What I do know is …' His voice dropped till Janey had to lean forward to hear it. 'I have a lot with which to reproach myself.'

'You were unfaithful to her?' Janey asked softly, afraid of breaking the spell of confidences that the starlit night seemed to be casting.

He nodded, and smoked for a while in silence, the fiery tip flaring and fading, sweet-scented smoke billowing around them.

'I wish I hadn't,' he burst out after a while. 'If only I had stayed with her that night … if only I hadn't gone to see Fan …'

'You can't blame yourself,' Janey said. 'It was an accident …'

'I can and do blame myself,' he answered sharply. 'And now I am paying the price.'

'What do you mean?'

He smoked the cigar down to its last ember, then flicked the butt away into the undergrowth. The night seemed much colder and darker without its tiny fire.

Janey shifted a little closer to Gabriel, repeating her question.

He looked away from her. 'I … it's hard to say, Janey. Please don't tell anyone.'

'Of course I won't,' she said.

'I … I'm having trouble … I cannot … I cannot make love anymore.' His voice was tortured.

Janey pressed her hand over her mouth. It was not what she had been expecting at all. 'But … why? What's wrong?' she managed to say at last.

He made a violent gesture with his hands. 'I shouldn't be talking like this to you. What am I thinking?'

'Rubbish,' she answered angrily. 'I grew up in a stable yard. You know I'm not one of those gently reared young ladies who faints away at the sight of a piano leg. Tell me what's wrong, Gabriel.'

'I'm impotent,' Gabriel told her bluntly, almost as if he wished to shock her. 'One of my testicles is swollen up like a pig's bladder.'

Janey was shocked, but not for the reasons he thought. She took his hand and pressed it between her own. 'Does it hurt?' she asked fearfully.

'Only when I make love,' he admitted. 'That's why … you know.'

That was why he thought he was being punished for his infidelity, Janey realised. 'What does the doctor say?' she asked.

Gabriel shrugged. 'He says it's most probably a side effect of the mumps I had a few years ago.'

'Can anything be done?'

'It can be lanced … but the idea of a quack hacking away at my manly parts with a knife …' He shuddered.

'But wouldn't it be worth the risk?'

He looked at her sombrely. 'Do you not think I should pay for what I did?'

'No,' Janey replied hotly. 'Lizzie would never want you to torment yourself so. You know she wouldn't.'

'Then why does she haunt me?' he demanded. 'I see her in my dreams, staring at me with accusing eyes … I see her in her coffin, all her hair spread out about her like cloth of gold… and then she sits up and calls for me, and her eyes are weeping worms and beetles …'

Janey stared at him in horror.

'I cannot sleep … I wake up with such a start, my heart pounding a hundred miles an hour … I swear I feel her sometimes, touching me with her cold fingers. And she tries to reach me all the time, knocking on windows, rapping at the table … she does not rest quietly, Janey, I'm telling you!'

All the hairs on Janey's arms were standing up, and sweat had broken out in the small of her back. She remembered being a little girl, and hearing weeping in the night. Her father had told her it was the ghost of a young woman who had drowned herself in the old moat when her lover had been killed fighting for King Charles the First. Janey had often felt the ghost's cold breath on the nape of her neck, and the brush of wet icy fingers along her face. She had always been afraid, creeping down the alleyway at night, in case the ghost should catch her.

Gabriel kept on talking, words tumbling out incoherently. 'I cannot paint anymore ... there's a mist over my eyes all the time ... like her ghost floats before me ... and the light stabs my eyes ... even candlelight ... and the flames in gas-lamps ... dancing and flickering ... the world whirls about me ... it's how she must have felt before she died, Janey ... sometimes my head feels as if it's about to burst ... I cannot sleep ... I cannot go out ... she wants me to join her, Janey ... in darkness and death ... she wants to make sure I love nobody else ... and nothing else ... I cannot paint ... I cannot write ...'

Janey put her arms about him and rocked him as if he was a weeping child.

'If only I could help her rest,' he went on. 'If only I could be free ...'

'It's all right,' she crooned.

He wrenched himself out of her arms, staring into her face, grasping her hands so tightly he hurt her. 'And I'm being left behind. Ned is painting works of such genius ... such power ... and Topsy ... Topsy! He's famous now for his poems ... while mine ... mine are buried with Lizzie!'

'You are a great painter and a great poet,' she told him. 'Try not to lose faith. It takes time to recover from such a hard blow as Lizzie's death dealt you. But it's been six years now. You must forgive yourself and move on.'

'How can I forgive myself when she haunts me so?' he whispered. 'If I could just know that she was able to rest ...'

Again they sat in silence. From the house came the sound of music and laughter, but here in the garden all was quiet. Gabriel was searching her face with eyes dark with misery.

'Janey, are you happy?' he asked. 'In your marriage, I mean.'

She shook her head. 'It was a mistake. I should never have married him.'

'Yet you did.'

'Yes. And you married Lizzie.'

'What a mess we made of things.'

She felt an overwhelming sadness. *If only . . .*

But then Janey thought of her daughters, laughing and playing hide-and-seek with her and bringing their dollies for her to kiss goodnight.

'I must get back.' Janey tried to stand up but Gabriel gripped her hand tighter.

'Janey, I want to paint you . . . but I am afraid.'

She knew why, but she wanted to hear him say it. 'Afraid of what?'

He hesitated, then said, 'Afraid of making a worse mess. Afraid of upsetting Topsy. Oh, afraid of everything.'

It was not what she had wanted to hear. But it was a beginning.

'You can't be afraid anymore, Gabriel. It's time for you to start living again.'

'Then you'll let me paint you? You aren't worried what people will think?'

'They will always think badly of me anyway, Gabriel. You know. The whiff of the stable. Besides, I have no desire to be a fine lady. I'd rather be painted by you.'

She gently freed her hand and stood up. 'I'll come this week if you like. Write and tell me what day suits.'

'Any day,' he answered. 'You know that . . . Janey dear.'

Gabriel painted Janey as the sorrowful Pia de' Tolomei, from the fifth canto of Dante's 'Purgatorio'. Imprisoned by her jealous husband in a castle in the marshes of Tuscany, Pia sat, playing with her wedding ring, old love letters scattered beside her. Ivy enshrouded the wall, and ravens flew past, wings shadowing the sky.

For the first week, while Gabriel did preparatory drawings and studies, Topsy and Janey came to stay in Chelsea. Topsy went to work each day, leaving her sister Bessie to act as chaperone. It was impossible to talk, with Bessie sitting there. He spent hours drawing her hands alone, entwining her fingers in a frenzy of unhappiness. Janey sat quietly, letting her thoughts maunder away, imagining another life she might have lived.

In the evenings, Gabriel entertained guests for dinner and, once, took Topsy and Janey to a séance in the hope of proving to them that Lizzie's ghost still walked. To her horror, Janey saw a faint pale light hovering behind Gabriel and was sure it was his dead wife's spirit. She pressed her hands together and said silently, *Please, Lizzie, don't punish him anymore. Whatever he did to hurt you, he has suffered enough. Please let him go.*

But no-one else saw anything. Topsy made much mock of the whole affair.

Janey could not bear the look on Gabriel's face. She gathered together her courage and said quietly, 'I saw her, Gabriel. Or at least I saw a light . . .'

'Which must, of course, mean you saw a ghost,' Topsy jeered.

Janey flushed.

'What fools you've made of yourselves, believing in such tripe,' Topsy went on. 'That fraud of a medium simply tricks you with smoke and mirrors. I've heard they create those raps and knocks by cracking their knuckles and toe joints. A child wouldn't be taken in by such damn tomfoolery.'

Perhaps it was then that Janey decided. She could not bear cruelty in any form. She had hated it when Gabriel was unkind to her husband. Now that Topsy was the one being unkind, she hated it even more. It was unworthy of him, she felt, when he had everything that Gabriel had ever wanted.

That night Janey lay in bed, listening to Topsy snore, and nerving herself to seduce one of his best friends. It was not that she felt any guilt at the prospect of being unfaithful to her husband. In the world of her childhood, sex was something that was grabbed when wanted, like bread when you were hungry or a blanket when you were cold. Janey had given her body to her husband for almost ten years, in gratitude to him from rescuing her from the rookeries and giving her a home and family of her own. She felt she had paid her dues.

So it was not the fear of sin that held her back. It was the fear of the hurt she knew lay ahead. Janey knew how hard she would fall. She knew the damage she would cause. She knew the price she must pay.

Two weeks later, as she and Bessie settled back into the cracked leather seats of their hansom cab, Janey leant forward and took her sister's hand. 'Will you do something for me?'

'What?'

'Would you spend the day at the British Museum?'

Bessie did not misunderstand her. 'Are you crazy?'

Janey gave a crooked little smile, and nodded.

Bessie sighed. 'What if Mr Topsy finds out?'

'He won't. Besides, it's worth the risk.'

'You always were head over heels for that Mr Rossetti.'

'Yes,' Janey agreed.

She dropped Bessie at the British Museum, then went on towards Chelsea alone. It was a crisp, bright morning. Daffodils swayed under the bare trees in Hyde Park. The Serpentine gleamed. Domes and spires and gables and chimneypots were wreathed in a golden mist, but the sky above was the colour of harebells.

For the first time, London looked beautiful to Janey's eyes.

As soon as Gabriel opened the door to her, he noticed the absence of her sister.

She smiled at him, took his hand and led him through the house. Not to the drawing room, hung with Lizzie's paintings of her own sad face. Not to the studio, hung with Gabriel's. Not to the bedroom, where he had kept company with Fanny. She went out to the garden, wild and overgrown and tangled with honeysuckle.

Gabriel flinched at the bright sunshine. Laughing, Janey covered his eyes with her two hands. She was so tall she did not need to reach up.

'Do you trust me?' she whispered, guiding his faltering steps forward, her body pressed close behind his.

'Yes ...' he whispered. 'But ...'

'No buts!'

She guided him through the long grass, her silk skirts rustling against her legs, then through the hanging branches of the old mulberry tree. Within its green canopy, the light was dim and cool.

He turned within the circle of her arms. 'Janey, we mustn't ...'

She pressed her mouth against his.

The shock of it went right through his body. For a moment he was stiff and unyielding in her arms. She kissed him again, touching her tongue to the closed seam of his lips. He groaned and held her away from him.

'Janey ... you're married ... what about Topsy?'

'I don't care,' she said fiercely. 'But if you don't want me I will go.'

'Janey, Janey, are you mad? Of course I want you ... but I don't know if I can ...'

'There are many different ways of loving,' Janey whispered. 'We do not have to do anything that will hurt you. Just let me know if I cause you any pain.'

'Janey ... oh God ... it's not that ... it's ...' He wanted to say Lizzie's name but she would not let him, she stopped his mouth with hers, and kissed him with all of her longing and passion and pent-up desire.

Once more, Gabriel tried to stop her. 'Janey, we can't.'

'Yes, we can. We have to seize joy whenever we can. Don't you see?'

His own ardent need overtook him. Her dress crumpled to the ground with the sound of paper catching fire. His clothes followed. She touched him tenderly. He groaned. Urgent hands ran over her body. Feverishly Janey drew him closer, hands stroking down his smooth bare skin, breathing in the wonderful scent of him, already feeling the tightly locked vault inside her springing open, the white roar of the bursting dam.

Mouths against mouths, skin against skin, fingers working frantically.

Janey cried aloud in jubilation.

6

The Letter
Summer 1868

Georgie found the letter in the bottom of Ned's coat pocket.

It was her habit to turn his pockets out before she brushed his coat and hung it up. She had found half-sovereigns that way before, and uncashed cheques, and unposted letters.

She did not mean to snoop.

Yet as she uncrumpled the note to see what it was, phrases leapt out at her.

My darling … my skin hungers for yours …

Georgie did not recognise the handwriting. But it was signed with a flamboyant M.

She sat down, crushing the note in her hand. She felt lightheaded, giddy. Her heart was thumping fast and loud, so that she was aware of its echoes in her chest.

'Georgie?' Her sister Alice called. 'It's time for the boys to go.'

She hardly registered the words.

Alice put her head in the door. 'Georgie?'

She tried to rouse herself, tried to paste a smile on her lips and find the strength to rise, but it was as if the strings that connected her mind to her body had been severed.

Alice waddled towards her. She was large with child, and had come from India to stay at The Grange so Georgie could help with the birth. 'What's wrong?' she asked. When Georgie did not answer, she bent to take the note from her sister's slack hand. That galvanised Georgie into sudden explosive movement. She leapt up, her fingers clenched on the note. She shoved it into her sleeve. 'Nothing. Nothing's wrong. The boys? Did you say the boys are ready to go? I'm coming.'

She hurried out of the bedroom and led the way downstairs. High-pitched screams resonated through the front hallway, and Georgie's heart sank.

Her youngest sister, Edie, stood in the front hallway, dressed in a dark serviceable travelling gown, a bound trunk at her feet. With little Margot on one hip, she was bending over Alice's son Rudyard, who lay on his stomach, yelling and flailing his arms and legs. He was dressed in a short frock over starched petticoats and front-buttoning drawers. His face was red and tear-stained, and he only stopped screaming to take the occasional breath.

Phil stood with his legs set apart, his hands on his hips, a mulish expression on his face. A toy train was shoved in his back pocket.

'Phil, what did you say?' Georgie cried.

'Nothing. I just told him he was a baby. And he is. Wearing skirts like a girl.'

'He's not yet three years old,' Alice cried in exasperation, hurrying down the stairs. 'We'll breech him at Christmas time, when he has his birthday.'

'You weren't breeched till you were three either,' Georgie added.

'And he's a baby 'cos he cried when I took my train away from him. It's my train.' Phil's lower lip was stuck out, and his cheeks were hot with outrage.

'You were very generous for letting him play with it,' Georgie said, 'and I am sure Ruddy is grateful. It's time to go on the real train now. You know how much you were looking forward to that. Why don't you let Ruddy play with your toy train just a little longer? Just to make sure you don't miss your real train?'

Rudyard had stopped crying for a moment, lifting his head to stare at Phil.

'No.' Phil crossed his arms.

Rudyard began to weep again.

Georgie looked out the door. The hansom cab was waiting outside the front gate, the cab driver smoking his pipe, one hand on the horse's reins. The horse wore blinkers, and stood with its head drooping, one leg relaxed. If Edie did not leave now, they would miss their train to Bewdley, where Georgie's parents were waiting to welcome them.

'Please, Phil,' Georgie coaxed.

'No. It's mine.'

'Then I shall give him your other train – your favourite train – for him to keep,' Georgie said, losing patience. She began to walk towards the parlour, where Phil's train collection was kept in a box on the shelf.

'No! No!' Phil shouted and hurled the train at Ruddy, hitting him on the head. The little boy began to scream, and Alice rushed to comfort him. She tried to pick him up, but he was too heavy for her. Edie put down Margot so she could lift Ruddy into his mother's arms, then picked up the little wooden train and pressed it into the boy's hands. The tears cleared away miraculously, and Ruddy began to spin the wheels with his finger. Georgie, meanwhile, had taken two trains out of the box and given them to her son, saying, 'You'll need to take care not to lose them, Phil. These are your very best trains that Uncle Topsy gave you.'

He clutched them close, and she took his hot hand, leading him back out into the front hallway. Alice and Edie were whispering together, and turned to look at her as she came towards them. Georgie's steps slowed.

'Alice says you found a letter. Is it from ... you know who?' Edie said. She had never been known for her tact.

Georgie went crimson. 'No. It's nothing. Come on, you need to go else you'll miss your train.'

'You need to talk to Ned,' Alice said. 'You can't keep pretending nothing is wrong, Georgie.'

She felt as if someone was tightening a vice about her chest. Alice had been here only a week. Was it so obvious that things were amiss? Georgie thought she had kept up a creditable front.

'Not in front of the children,' she said, then looked about her. 'Where's Margot?'

Her sisters looked around them, surprise on their faces. Georgie let go of Phil's hand and ran out the front door.

Margot was sitting on the back of the horse, held in place by the cab driver. Her short legs stuck out either side, and she was beaming.

'Eh, but she's a bold lass,' he told Georgie, his pipe clenched in the corner of his mouth. 'Ran right out an' tried to pat me old Bess. Lucky she weren't trodden on.'

'Thank you.' Georgie lifted her daughter down. For some reason, she was trembling, close to tears, close to fury.

Her sisters had followed her on to the street. 'Driver, if you could get the trunk,' Alice commanded. As he went into the house to get the boys' luggage, Edie said, 'I'm so sorry, Georgie. I only put her down for a moment.'

Georgie nodded. Edie kissed her and then kissed Margot, who had her arms reached out, struggling to get back to the horse. 'I'm sorry about Ned,' she whispered. 'I'm sure it's nothing. It'll blow over.'

Georgie could not speak. Edie lifted the little boys into the hansom cab. Georgie managed to reach out and ruffle Phil's curls, and whisper a goodbye. It was the first time he had ever gone away from home.

'Be good!' Alice told her son, whose lip had begun to tremble again. 'You'll have such a lovely time with Grandmama and Grandpapa. Goodbye!'

As the carriage door closed and the horse began to clop away down the street, Ruddy suddenly realised that his mother was not going with him. He began to hurl himself against the window, screaming at the top of his voice. Edie tried desperately to calm him, and Alice followed alongside, waving and blowing kisses and trying not to cry herself.

Georgie stood silently, her squirming daughter in her arms. She felt utterly exhausted. At last the hansom cab had turned the corner, and was out of sight and sound. She went back inside and put Margot down on the ground, holding on tight to her leading-strings. When Alice had followed her in and shut the door behind her, Georgie said abruptly, 'I must put this little one down for her nap. You look all done-in. Why don't you have a rest too? I will see you at tea.'

She lifted Margot up and took her to the nursery, and rang for some milk to be warmed. She lay on the bed, Margot beside her, and counted her toes and sang 'This Little Pig' and 'I Had A Little Nut Tree'. Every now and again she had to wipe away her tears. When at last Margot was asleep, she lay quietly, wondering what she was to do.

Georgie had tried hard these past few months to regain her husband's regard. She had nursed him through another winter of coughs and colds and sore throats and feverish misery. She had hosted a housewarming party with all his oldest and dearest friends. She had cut her hair in a new and more flattering style, with soft curls on her forehead. She had made herself a soft white muslin dress, with a blue riband to define her waist, and another of yellow silk, hoping she looked like a dancing daffodil. She had tried hard to take an interest in Ned's work, even though it seemed all he could paint was the sinuous white form and fiery hair of Maria Zambaco.

It doesn't mean that he loves her, she told herself. *It's just a passing fancy, one of his short-lived obsessions. He'll soon tire of her.*

But Ned still slept in another room, and she did not know how to invite him to return to her bed. The very thought embarrassed her.

After a long while, she rose and put the letter back in Ned's pocket, where she had found it. She did not say anything to him.

Georgie had always found it most difficult to speak when she felt the most deeply.

*

For Margot's second birthday, Georgie planned to host a special feast with all their best friends.

Topsy and Janey and their two little girls would be there, and Gabriel and his sister Christina. Johnny and Effie Millais were coming with their multitudes of children, and Arthur and Tryphena Hughes with theirs. Roddy Stanhope and his wife and daughter were invited, and two new friends, the potter William De Morgan and his sixteen-year-old sister, Mary, who could be counted on to entertain all the children with her storytelling.

Georgie was in the kitchen, an apron tied over an old dress, her hair dragged back into a knob at the back of her head, when the front doorbell rang unexpectedly.

Wiping her hands, Georgie hurried to answer it, wondering who it could be. Any supplies or models for Ned always went in the side entrance, and Georgie was not expecting her guests for another few hours.

Charles Howell stood on the front step, a woman wearing a veiled hat behind him. Georgie stared at them blankly. She knew Mr Howell, of course. He was a good friend of Gabriel and Ned's, and was present at every party. He seemed to make his living by finding patrons for artists, or sourcing old china or tapestries, or acting as a go-between between the money-lenders and the temporarily indigent. He wore a heavy scarlet-and-gold cross hanging from a broad red ribbon, saying it was an old family order from his noble Portuguese mother. He claimed he had supported his mothers and sisters by diving for treasure in sunken galleons, and it was rumoured that he had had to flee Portugal after being caught cheating at cards.

Georgie did not like him at all, thinking he was a bad influence on Ned. So she said coolly, 'Mr Howell, what a surprise. I'm afraid Ned is not here. I'm expecting him home any moment, though.'

'It is not Ned I've come to see, but you, Mrs Jones,' he answered with an easy smile, striding in over the doorstep.

Georgie automatically moved back. 'You wish to see me? Is something wrong?'

'Not at all. At least ... there is someone I wish you to meet.' He indicated the woman behind him, who had silently followed him into the hall. She wore an elegant morning dress of dark red silk, banded with black velvet, with a matching hat worn tilted over one eye. A black dotted veil had been lowered to conceal her face.

Georgie was surprised, but far too well-mannered to do anything but show her unexpected guests into the drawing room. She took off her apron, laid it on a table, and tried to smooth back her hair, which the heat of the kitchen had frizzled. 'May I offer you tea?' she asked automatically, then looked up in surprise as Mr Howell stepped into the hall and shut the door behind him.

The woman laid back her veil. It was Maria Zambaco.

'You will think me very forward in coming to see you in this way, but I must talk to you,' she said.

Georgie stared at her in amazement.

'Ned and I are in love. It is wrong of you to hold on to him like this. You must let him go.'

Blood was roaring in Georgie's ears. 'He ... he's my husband,' she managed to say.

'Do you think I don't know that? He says he cannot leave you, that it would break your heart. You must tell him that you do not want him anymore, that he is free to be with me.'

Georgie had to sit down. Maria was pacing the carpet, words pouring out of her. Terrible hurtful words.

'There's no need for you to divorce him. My husband refuses to sunder our marriage anyway. We would not stay here. I know that would be unkind. We'd go to the Continent, to Italy, or Greece. He wants to see Mount Olympus and the home of the gods. You'd do well enough here, with your dear sweet children and your flower-arranging. It's not as if you'd suffer without him in your bed. He tells me you haven't an ounce of passion anywhere in your body. It's cruel to tie him to your apron strings.'

On and on Maria went, pacing the floor like a caged tigress, gesturing wildly with her hands. Georgie tried to defend herself, but all her words were trite and easily torn to shreds by Maria. 'A grand passion should not be confined by stupid convention! It's petty of you … small-minded … selfish.'

'Selfish!' Georgie gasped.

'Yes, selfish. For you don't love him and yet you want to keep him all to yourself.'

Georgie could not help the hot tears that spilled down her face. She loved Ned with all her heart. She had loved him from the moment she had first met him, wearing a pinafore with her hair in a long plait. She had nursed him when he was sick, darned his socks, emptied his chamber-pot, comforted him when he was overcome with blue devils. She had borne his children, and put aside her own cherished dreams to support his.

The door swung open. Ned stood in the doorway. He looked from Georgie to Maria, and the colour drained from his face. Charles Howell was just behind him, his face alight with malice. Georgie wondered wearily just how much Charles had heard.

'Tell her!' Maria cried. 'Tell her that it's me you love.'

Ned stumbled into the room. 'Maria … what are you doing here?' he managed to say.

'Telling her! Telling her the truth. It's time that she knew.'

Ned could not look at Georgie. He said her name in a broken voice. 'I'm so sorry … I didn't want you to find out this way.'

'So it's true?' she whispered. Stupid words. She knew it was true.

'He fell in love with me the moment he saw me,' Maria said. 'He practically tore the clothes from my body the first time I came to his studio. You were only a few rooms away, playing peek-a-boo with your sweet little baby.'

'Maria, don't be so cruel.' Ned put out one hand, clinging to the mantelpiece for support.

'How could you?' Georgie said. 'Oh, Ned, how could you?'

'Love cannot be denied,' Maria said magnificently.

Georgie stood up. She had to stiffen her knees to stop her legs from shaking. 'What of the children? You mean to abandon them? What will we do? How will we live?'

'I … I'd support you, of course.'

'How? The scandal will be terrible. You'll never sell another painting.'

Ned was ashen.

'We'll live a life of art!' Maria cried. 'What do we need of patrons and galleries? We'll live on a Greek island and swim in the wine-dark sea every day and make love on the sand and paint what we like.'

Georgie fixed her eyes on Ned's face. In a low, husky voice, she said, 'You know it'll ruin our little girl. She'll never be free of the scandal. Her life will be blighted.'

Ned was swaying where he stood. Georgie's heart was stricken with sudden pity. 'Oh, Ned, darling,' she whispered. 'You can't do this. You can't.'

'No …' Ned's voice was faint. His knees buckled under him. He pitched forward, striking his head hard against the marble fireplace, then crumpled to the floor.

Georgie ran to him, falling to her knees beside him. There was blood running down his face. She drew out her handkerchief and pressed it to his temple. 'Look what you've done!' she cried. 'Get out! Both of you. Don't you dare come back.'

Maria hesitated, obviously wanting to go to Ned. Georgie leapt to her feet and rushed at her, beside herself with fury. 'Get out! Get out!'

Maria retreated into the hallway, Charles Howell putting up both hands to fend Georgie off. Sukey, the little maid-of-all-work, raced up the passageway, a rolling-pin in her hand. Alice came to the foot of the stairs, Margot on her hip. 'What is it? What's happening? Who are these people?'

'And so we gracefully beat a retreat,' Charles said, taking Maria's arm and leading her away.

'It's not over!' Maria called back over her shoulder.

'Yes, it is!' Georgie slammed the door shut, then stood against it. Sobs shook her.

'What's happened? Who were those people?' Alice demanded.

Georgie took a deep breath, trying to compose herself. 'Sukey, I need water. Smelling salts. Brandy.'

‘Brandy?’ Alice was shocked.

‘Ned has fainted. Please, can you help me lift him?’

The skivvy took hold of Ned’s armpits and dragged him up on to the sofa. ‘Nice goings on,’ she remarked, then went back to the kitchen. Georgie knelt beside her husband, dabbing at the cut on his temple. He began to stir, groaning in pain.

‘Who was she?’ Alice asked. ‘That woman? Was she …’ Her voice trailed away.

Georgie bent and kissed Ned’s cheek. ‘Nobody. She’s nobody.’

7

Gossip
Winter 1868

Janey sat up, reaching for her dress.

'I must get ready. Topsy will be here soon.'

Gabriel lifted away the great mass of her hair so he could kiss her naked back. 'I wish you did not need to go.'

'So do I.' She was silent for a moment, shivering under the trail of kisses that Gabriel emblazoned up her spine. He slid one hand round to cup her breast. Her breath caught. 'Gabriel, you mustn't.'

'But I have not seen you in so long. And I do not know when we can meet again.' He kissed the long slope of her shoulder blade, then gently turned her so he could kiss the little dip between her collarbones. Janey sighed in longing.

'I'll be quick,' Gabriel said, laying her down in the tumbled sheets. 'And the weather outside is foul. Topsy will be held up.'

'Unless he sets out early ... Hoping to catch us ...'

Gabriel lifted his head. 'You think he suspects?'

'I don't know ... he saw me burning one of your letters ... I made up some excuse ...'

Gabriel played with her hair, pulling one of her curls straight then watching it rebound into its tight ringlet. 'What would he do? If he found out?'

'I don't know …' Janey's throat tightened at the very thought. She looked at Gabriel beseechingly. 'We cannot risk him finding out. You mustn't make him suspicious, or tell anyone. Promise me.'

Gabriel's lips tightened. He sat up, thrusting a pillow behind his back. 'It just makes me so angry … seeing the way he speaks to you …'

'You know he doesn't mean it.' Janey rolled over on to her stomach, smiling up at Gabriel. 'Are we going to spend our last few minutes together talking about my husband? I thought you had other plans …' As she spoke, she slid both hands up his thighs, then cradled him gently, kissing where her fingers stroked. He groaned, writhing his hand through her hair. 'Oh, Janey. Oh, God.'

She loved the power she had over him. The way she could coax him from a fit of the sullens to passion in moments. She loved the feel of his skin against hers, the very smell of him. Her own body was quick to reignite. As Gabriel slid his hands down her hips, lifting her up to straddle him, Janey was ready and eager for him. They rocked together, each crying aloud, each working to bring the other to climax. Janey felt again that dizzy rush through her, blinding and deafening her, losing her to herself.

'I love you so much,' he whispered, as she collapsed into the bed beside him. He pressed his body into the curve of hers. 'I feel so afraid … something bad is going to happen, Janey. I know it.'

She laid her finger over his mouth. 'Nothing bad will happen,' she whispered, even though she felt the same disquiet within her. 'You are feeling so much better …'

Gabriel had submitted to the surgeon's knife and had his swollen testicle successfully lanced, much to his relief. The doctor had prescribed a soporific for him, and told him to stop drinking too much whisky, advice which Gabriel ignored. The doctor had also recommended Gabriel exercise, and so every night he went out walking along the Thames, crossing Old Battersea Bridge to walk in the park beyond. He was sleeping better and seemed calmer. Janey liked to think it was because of her.

She slid out of bed and began to dress. He lay, watching her.

'I wish you would let me make you that bracelet. It irks me that Topsy has given you all you own.'

Janey's hands stilled. 'You know I would love it. The design is so beautiful. But how could I explain it to Topsy?'

'You could hide it.'

'But what if he found it?' Janey cried.

The bracelet Gabriel had designed was a lovely thing of interlinked rosettes, engraved with the two dates of their coming together: *September 1857 – April 14 1868*. Janey would have loved to wear it. But it was too dangerous. Topsy was already hurt and suspicious. Janey was frightened of what he might do if he discovered the affair. She lay awake at night, fearing the divorce courts, the girls taken away from her, all her friends shunning her.

'We have to be careful,' she said again, pressing her hands against her hectic cheeks in an attempt to cool them. 'Please, Gabriel.' She hunted around for her hairpins.

He was surly, his arms crossed over his chest. 'I don't know how you can bear it,' he burst out. 'Does he touch you, Janey? Does he sleep with you?'

Janey hesitated. She did not want to admit that she sometimes let Topsy lie with her, to abate his suspicions and ease his hurt feelings. She turned away, looking in the mirror as she pinned up her hair. 'No,' she lied. 'He knows that part of our marriage is over.'

In November, Janey and Bessie and Topsy went to dinner at the new house William Bell Scott and his wife, Letitia, had taken in Cheyne Walk, just down the road from Gabriel's home. Janey did not wish to go. She remembered all too vividly the way Letitia had drawn away from her when she had discovered Janey had been brought up in a stable yard.

And Janey hated her husband and her lover to be in the same room. Topsy was wary and on guard, and Gabriel found it hard to hide his jealous possessiveness. Janey could do nothing, but pretend unconcern and hope that nothing triggered one of Topsy's rages.

'I feel I should warn you the Scotts have an interesting domestic arrangement,' Topsy told her in the hansom cab.

'In what way?' Janey asked politely, staring out the window at the fog-bound streets.

'Scott fell in love with one of his pupils. But he did not want the scandal of a divorce. It would have wrecked his career, you know. So he and Letitia came to an arrangement. He spends the winters in London with his wife, and the summers in Scotland with his ... well, with Miss Boyd. She is the Laird of Penkill Castle, the most delightful old sixteenth-century place, with turrets and towers and whatnot. I'm sure Gabriel must have told you about it. He spent most of October staying there.'

Topsy said the last few sentences with his eyes fixed on Janey's face. But she was far too interested in what he was saying to start and blush guiltily, as Topsy had perhaps thought she would.

'And Mrs Scott does not mind?' she asked.

'Apparently not. I've heard that she sometimes goes and stays at Penkill Castle too, and Miss Boyd comes up to London and stays with them.'

'I wonder if they all share a bedroom,' Bessie said with a giggle. 'They'd want a big bed.'

Topsy looked pained. He found Bessie's vulgarity difficult to bear.

'Will she be there tonight?' Janey asked quickly. 'Miss Boyd, I mean. I should like to meet a lady laird.'

'I don't think so,' Topsy replied. 'Though you'd think she'd want to escape the Scottish winter.'

'Perhaps she doesn't want to endure a London winter,' Janey replied, with an edge to her voice.

Topsy began a long-winded explanation for why they could not afford to go to Italy for winter, like the Howards, but Janey did not listen. Her mind had gone wandering away, imagining a life in which she could safely love Gabriel without tearing her family apart. If only, she thought, they had a castle in the country …

William Bell Scott was rather stout, and had a mop of hair that did not sit quite right on his high domed forehead. Letitia was just as Janey remembered – short, dumpy, mousy, with a supercilious air. The other guests were interesting, however, including an architect who Topsy could talk to about old buildings – one of his favourite topics – a lady novelist, and some literary critics and journalists, including Mr Lewes who, Janey remembered, also lived in an interesting domestic arrangement with Marian Evans, the author who published under the name George Eliot. Miss Evans was not present, however, and Janey recollected that she never went out in society for fear of being snubbed or even openly abused. If Janey's affair with Gabriel was discovered, she too would be ostracised and shunned. Gabriel and Topsy, however, would still be welcomed just as Mr Lewes was.

It is not fair, Janey fumed silently. How she hated the humbug of the world they lived in.

Gabriel was standing by the fireplace, his coat tails lifted so he could warm his behind. His face kindled at the sight of her. Janey nodded politely and murmured a greeting, then went to sit with Bessie on the far side of the drawing room. She was certain she saw the Scotts exchange a significant glance, and took care not to look Gabriel's way.

There was much back-slapping and congratulations of Topsy, whose first volume of *The Earthly Paradise* was already into its fourth printing, only seven months after first publication. Janey had heard it so many times she could have recited it herself. She sat quietly, her hands folded, her thoughts far away.

When it was time to go for dinner, Gabriel automatically came to offer Janey his hand. She let him assist her to her feet, but said in a low voice, 'I believe Mr Scott is my partner tonight.'

Letitia tittered and said, far too loudly, 'Dear me, but Gabriel is fond of dear Mrs Topsy, isn't he?'

Gabriel dropped her arm at once and turned to Bessie, sitting nearby. Janey was all too aware of Topsy's frowning gaze upon them. She smiled at Mr Scott and took his arm, making polite conversation as he led her to the dining room. Topsy took down Letitia, but he made no attempt to converse with her, his eyes moving from Gabriel's face to Janey's and back again.

'I say, Janey,' Gabriel said as soon as they were seated, turning to face her. 'I was telling Scott about how much trouble I've been having with my eyesight and he suggested I try my hand at poetry again. I was a poet before I was a painter, you know, but I've not written a word since … well, you know. What do you think? Topsy and Algy have both had such success with their grinds … perhaps the time is right for me to look out all my old ravelled rags of verse.'

'I think that's a fine idea,' she said softly.

Gabriel would have liked to have kept on talking to her, but she gave him a reproving glance and turned to politely address the architect on her other side. She did her best to keep Gabriel at arm's length, but he seemed impervious to hints and seemingly unaware of the interested and somewhat scandalised looks of the others around the table.

Janey wanted no gossip.

But she feared it was already too late.

It rained nearly every day for the next two weeks, with Janey finding it difficult to keep her daughters busy and amused. They squabbled constantly, and she found the smell of damp in the drawing room gave her an intense headache that was not relieved by lying down.

As soon as the rain blew over, she took the girls out marching around their square in mackintoshes and galoshes, trying to keep their umbrellas from blowing inside out. But the rain would begin again, cold and relentless with nasty spits of ice in it, and she would have to hurry the girls back inside, damp and chilled through. At the sound of their boots in the hallway, Topsy would shout out for some peace and quiet. He was now deeply immersed in the translation of some old Norse myths, having met an Icelandic scholar who shared his passionate interest. Janey hoped that was the only reason he was so surly and preoccupied. She feared, though, that he too had heard the gossip and suspected her. The thought frightened her.

She did not know what to do. On the one hand, she longed for Gabriel and kept trying to think of ways she could go to him without arising any more suspicions. On the other, she dreaded a blow-up with Topsy, and the possible consequences.

Gabriel was working on a new painting of her as Pandora, created by the gods to be the most beautiful of temptresses. Janey resumed her sittings at Tudor House, Topsy staying with her to preserve the niceties. It was strange and awkward to sit and eat her dinner in the company of the two men she knew the most intimately in the world, knowing that Topsy was watching every flicker of expression on their faces. It was too exhausting, so Janey said that she was too unwell to sit anymore and went home, to her daughters and her dusting and her sewing.

On 18th December, Gabriel wrote to her in high agitation, begging her to come and see him. Janey made up some excuse and went to him, though she could not sit still in the hansom cab, constantly checking the road behind to make sure she was not being followed. She was grateful for the lashing rain, which made it easy for her to conceal her face with a veiled hat and her umbrella, as she hurried up the steps to the front door.

Gabriel had obviously been watching for her, as he opened the door before she had time to knock. Janey expected him to kiss her, and lead her to the bedroom, but instead he grasped hold of her arms tightly. His face was pale, his eyes shadowed, his hands shaking.

'Janey, I need to talk to you.' He hustled her towards the studio, talking all the while. 'Charles Howell has made the most extraordinary suggestion. I don't know what to think of it. You know I've been writing again … and thinking of putting together a collection of poems …'

He opened the door and Janey went in. It gave her a deep secret pleasure to see that the studio walls were now dominated by chalk drawings and watercolours of her face. The pictures of Lizzie had all been put away, and all his other golden-haired beauties as well.

Gabriel began to pace around the studio. 'I've been hunting about, trying to find copies of some of my old poems … but I buried them, Janey, I buried them all with Lizzie. All my best poems. I've been tearing out my hair trying to rewrite them, but it's no use, it's been too long. Janey, Janey … Howell suggests I have the coffin dug up … to get my manuscript back.'

Janey sank down into a chair. 'What?'

'People are dug up all the time, you know, to move them to a different grave, or to make sure they haven't been poisoned.' Gabriel came to a halt before her, his face beseeching.

'Janey, what do you think? Will people condemn me? I mean her no disrespect … but, Janey, my poems!'

She could only stare at him in horror.

8

Love Enough
Winter 1869

Georgie was woken very early one morning, by the shrill ring of the doorbell.

It took her a while to wake up, and find her slippers and robe, and stumble down to the front hall. The doorbell rang insistently the whole time.

She opened the door to a wintry dawn streaked with red claw marks.

The poet Robert Browning stood on her doorstep, wrapped in a heavy cloak. Next to him – slump-shouldered, soaked to the skin, shivering with cold – was Ned.

'There was an unfortunate incident,' Mr Browning said. 'Madame Zambaco almost drowned. In the canal behind my house.'

Georgie stared at him blankly, then looked at her husband.

'I'm so sorry,' he muttered.

'But ... what happened?'

Mr Browning did not look at Ned. His voice was bland. 'Perhaps she slipped. Though the police found an empty bottle of laudanum.'

'The police?'

'Yes. There was ... some disturbance to the peace.'

Ned's clothes dripped onto the doorstep. Pond weed tangled in his hair.

'I am sorry,' Mr Browning said. 'If it is any consolation, the police will not be pressing charges.'

'Thank you,' Georgie said. 'May I offer you some tea?'

For the first time she understood why manners had been invented.

'No, thank you. I do not wish to keep my horses standing in this weather.' He hesitated, then took her hand and squeezed it. 'I am so very sorry.'

Georgie drew her husband inside and closed the door behind him. She could feel the tremors racking his body. His lips were blue, and he could not catch his breath. She ran to the linen cupboard and found a blanket to wrap him in, then hustled him to the kitchen, stoking up the fire, putting the kettle on to boil, dragging the hipbath out of the cupboard. She drew off his sodden shoes and socks, and rubbed his ice-white feet with a towel.

She could not look at him.

'Oh, Georgie,' he whispered. 'It was so awful.'

Focusing on her task, she asked curtly, 'What happened?'

'I had gone to visit Luke ... when I came out, she was waiting for me. Georgie, you know I'd promised not to see her again ... you know I'd tried to break things off ... but she wouldn't let me, Georgie, she wouldn't let me!'

It was a cry from the heart, like a bewildered child's.

'Is she your master, then, as well as your mistress?' Georgie said coldly.

'You don't understand,' he whispered. 'It is like she has cast a spell on me.' He shuddered violently. 'A curse, more like.'

Georgie stared at him. She imagined Maria, stepping out from the shadows, her pale face stricken. Perhaps she flung herself into his arms, weeping. Perhaps she fell to her knees before him. Perhaps she laughed, and slid her cold hand inside his clothes.

She turned away, busying herself putting pots of water on to boil for the bath.

'Georgie, I swear. I did not arrange to see her ...'

'So how did you end up taking a midnight swim with her in the canal behind Mr Browning's house?'

Ned could not meet her gaze. Huddling the blanket around him, he began to tell her in short bursts of words, stopping often to cough. Georgie listened quietly. She imagined the dark deserted street, the woman with her beseeching voice, the fog swirling around them, blurring the gaslights on the street so they seemed to float, dandelion puffs with no stems for support.

He had walked her home. Georgie thought it was just like him. Too chivalrous for his own good. But Maria had not wanted to go inside. She had begged him to walk on with her, just a little way.

'Are you not cold?' Ned had asked.

She nodded. 'Yes. But I cannot bear to go in yet. I cannot bear to say goodbye.'

Georgie imagined the woman pressed close to him, trembling. The sweet voice, begging him not to leave her. The clutch of her fingers, the press of cold clinging lips.

And so they had walked on. Footsteps echoing. Across the railway bridge, the lines gleaming below them. Down the steps to the canal. Along the narrow path. A faint smell of decay, water sucking against invisible bricks.

'Where are we going?' Ned had whispered.

Maria had led him onto a small bridge that hung over the canal. Below was a wide dark pool, where two canals met. Willows hung weeping tendrils. The distant yellow fuzz of a gaslight. Otherwise, all was dark. All was quiet. Frost hanging from their mouths.

'Why have we come here?' Ned asked. Georgie imagined the faintest edge of alarm to his voice.

'I wanted to say goodbye,' Maria said.

Ned had fallen silent. Steam hung above the hipbath like fog must have hung above that dark wintry pool.

'What did you say?' Georgie whispered.

'I said yes.' Ned's voice was tired.

'Yes?'

'Yes. It had to be goodbye. Forever, I said.'

Georgie loosened a breath. After a long silence, in which Ned rested his head on the back of the chair and closed his eyes, Georgie asked, 'So what happened then?'

'She tried to kill herself.'

Georgie sucked in a sharp breath.

'She had laudanum. Two bottles of it. One for her and one for me. She tried to make me drink it with her. I would not. Oh, Georgie! She was mad with grief. She drank both the bottles, Georgie, one after another. And then she threw herself into the canal.'

Georgie pressed the back of her hand to her mouth, staring at Ned in horror.

She imagined the swirling apart of the fog, the surging up of the bitter-cold water. Maria's skirts billowing out. Water rushing past her face. A gasp of fire.

Of course Ned had jumped in after her. Of course he had. He could do nothing else. He'd have struggled to drag her ashore. Maria would have been screaming and fighting. Lights kindling in all the houses around. Dogs barking, geese honking. No wonder the police had come running, truncheons drawn.

Ned and Maria wrestling together on the muddy shore. Clothes wet and clinging. Breaths like plumes of smoke.

'Oh, how awful, how awful,' Georgie whispered. 'And Mr Browning? He saw . . . he heard it all?'

'And Maria's cousin, Luke. He came running up too. He must've followed us . . . I thought I heard footsteps in the fog.'

'All of London will hear the tale then,' she said.

Ned covered his face with his hands.

Georgie rolled up her sleeve, then bent and tested the temperature of the bath with her elbow. Then she carefully measured in a few drops of camphor oil. 'You'd best get in. Else you'll catch your death of cold.'

Ned nodded, and struggled out of his clothes. He was thin and white, his chest sunken. Georgie felt nothing, seeing his nakedness. She helped him into the bath, then moved around mechanically, hanging the blanket by the fire to dry, wringing out his wet trousers. She was moving as if in a dream, hardly able to comprehend what Ned had told her. It was like something out of a melodramatic novel. Not the sort of thing real people did. Every now and again she would shiver, and have to swallow hard. Flashes of angry words lit up her brain, but then darkness and dullness descended again.

When Ned was clean and warm, she dressed him in his pyjamas like he was a child, and put him to bed.

'I'm sorry,' he said, the words he had been repeating again and again like some kind of incantation.

She put a hot-water bottle at his back, numbly, automatically, looking after her husband as she had done so many times before.

Then Ned said, as if wanting to hurt her, 'You're so strong, so capable. You must understand ... she's not like that ... she's so sensitive ... so easily hurt ... oh, God, what if she tries to kill herself again! I should not have left her.'

'Her family will care for her.'

'But the scandal! What if they shun her? What if they turn her out?'

'She has money enough to put herself up in the most expensive hotel in London. Stop fretting over stupid things. Go to sleep.'

He closed his eyes and seemed to sleep, his breathing a little easier. Georgie locked herself away, to cry in private.

The day jerked forward in steel cogs and ratchets. Georgie could not lie in bed, curled around her pain. The children had to be fed, the bread had to be set to rise, she had to wash Ned's clothes. The smell of them sickened her.

Mid-afternoon, Topsy came. He put his arms about her and she laid her head on his shoulder and cried. It was such a comfort to have him there. At last she drew away and groped for a handkerchief, only to have him mop her face with his own, as if she were a child.

'You heard the news then?' she asked dully. 'I suppose it's all over London.'

He nodded, looking uncomfortable. 'Afraid so, old chap.'

Tears welled up again. 'I'm sorry. It's just … so … so …'

She did not know the word she wanted. Hurtful. Humiliating. Cruel.

'I know how you feel,' he said, patting her shoulder gently. She thought of the rumours about Janey and Gabriel, and blushed in chagrin and apologised again.

'How is he?' Topsy asked.

'Not well in mind or body. I don't know what to do.'

'He should leave London for a while, till it all blows over.'

Georgie thought about Johnny and Effie Millais. That scandal had never blown over. Even though they had moved back to London, things were not easy for such a scandal-smirched woman. The Queen refused to receive her, and without the Queen's approval, polite society was closed to her. Effie's life centred on her children and her husband, and those few friends who refused to bow and scrape to convention.

'May I see him?' Topsy asked.

Georgie nodded and took him upstairs to where Ned lay in his bed, the curtains drawn. He was wheezing painfully.

Georgie did not go in. She did not want to see him or talk to him.

After a long time, Topsy came downstairs, looking troubled. 'I think he needs to get away from her for a while.'

Georgie felt the tears well up again. She knew Topsy meant that her husband was still ensnared by his lover.

'I've told him that we'll go away together,' Topsy said, taking Georgie's hand and squeezing it. 'He's in no state to travel alone. He's always wanted to go to Rome. We'll go there. It'll be a distraction to him, and maybe he'll be inspired and get some work done.'

Topsy knew that it had been months since Ned had finished any work, and that Georgie spent her evenings frowning over their debts.

She tried to smile. Topsy was their truest friend, she thought, and the kindest and most generous soul she had ever known. It broke her heart that Janey could hurt him so.

'Thank you,' she said, showing him to the door. 'I'll pack a bag for him.'

Although it was only four o'clock in the afternoon, it was growing dark outside. Rain lashed against the windows. Georgie lit the oil-lamps and stirred up the fire, then went to draw the curtains.

A woman in a dark hooded cloak was standing out on the pavement, staring up at the house. Georgie's heart thumped unpleasantly hard. She crept out on to the landing where no lights had been kindled, and peered out.

It was Maria Zambaco, of course. Her face as white as bone. Wet hair snaking.

Maria stumbled to the front door and began to bang on it with her hands. 'Ned!' she called. 'Let me in! Please!'

Georgie ran down to the front door and bolted it shut. The door was shaking with the force of Maria's blows. 'Let me in, let me in!'

She then knelt and lifted the letter-flap with her fingers, putting her mouth to the gap and screaming Ned's name.

Georgie ran to the drawing-room and checked all the windows were locked and the curtains drawn. The skivvy had come out of the kitchen, a rolling-pin clenched in her hand. 'Shall I call for the police, ma'am?' she asked in a shaking voice.

'No, no. Run up to the nursery, will you, Sadie? Make sure the children are safe and then lock yourself in with them. Sing them some nursery rhymes so they cannot hear her.'

'No nursery rhyme will drown out that racket,' Sadie said sourly, but did as she had been asked.

Georgie went, slowly and painfully, into Ned's room.

He was standing at the window, staring down at Maria who was now clinging to the iron railings, calling up to the house in a piteous, broken voice.

'She'll be so cold,' he whispered. 'She should not be out in this weather.'

'No,' Georgie answered. 'She should go home. Home to her children.'

'Could we not ask her in? Let her get warm?'

'I don't want her in my house,' Georgie said.

He looked at her wonderingly. 'But … Georgie … how can you be so unkind? She's hurting … she's sick …'

'I don't want her in my house,' she repeated. 'Ned, can you not see how unkind you are being to me? You are my husband, the father of my children …'

'I never wanted all this to happen. But she's right … love cannot be denied.'

Georgie laughed. It startled her as much as it startled him.

She went rapidly out of the room, trying to control her unseemly mirth, trying to find a place where she could be still and quiet and try to make sense of what she was feeling. She wanted to smash something, she wanted to make Ned look at her and see her pain and know what he had done.

Outside the rain was lashing the windows, the wind was rattling the frames. It was bitterly cold.

Once again the knocking came. Georgie ran to the front door and stood before it, barring it from Ned, who had come running down the stairs.

'When did you get so heartless?' Ned whispered.

'When you broke my heart,' she answered.

His shoulders slumped. 'I never meant to.'

Georgie did not speak. She listened with all her strength. She heard heartbroken sobbing, and a soft scrabbling sound at the base of the door. At last it died away. She went to the window, and saw the hunched figure stumble away into the darkness. Georgie went to her own room, and lay on her bed, huddled under the counterpane. Her eyes were dry and hot. She did not know how to go on living. It was as if her soul had been scooped out, and only the empty husk remained.

She heard Margot calling, 'Mama! Mama! Where are you?'

Georgie sat up, pressed her cold hands to her hot cheeks, and called, 'In here, littley!'

Then Margot's arms were about her neck and her soft lips were pressed against her face, and Georgie knew that, somehow, she had to find the strength to go on.

Topsy and Ned only made it as far as Dover.

Then Ned was so overcome, Topsy had to bring him home again.

Rosalind Howard and her husband came to see Georgie, bringing her some money in case she needed it. Their thoughtfulness cut her to the heart. Georgie lied and said that Ned was not there. She knew he wanted to see no-one.

As she showed her guests out, Georgie saw that Ned's coat and hat were hanging in the hallway as usual, and that her friends would know she had lied to them. This troubled her almost more than anything. She sat down and wrote Rosalind a letter: '*Forgive my reserve, but I am greatly obliged to show it in times of trouble or I should break down ... I am now able to tell you that he is home again, having been too weak to face the journey ...*'

Ned was laid low for many weeks. Georgie nursed him stoically.

When he was out of danger, Georgie took the children and went to Oxford. She stayed for a month, spending her days reading and writing and walking in the park, thinking.

The laws of England said that a woman could only divorce a man if she could prove that he had not only been unfaithful to her, but that he had also committed incest or rape or sodomy or bestiality, or that he had deserted her for more than two years without due cause, or that his cruelty to her had endangered her life.

Georgie had been reading the writings of Lady Caroline Norton, who had some years earlier written an impassioned letter to Queen Victoria begging her to address what she called 'the grotesque anomaly' that married women in England were considered to have no legal existence of their own in a country ruled by a female sovereign. A woman's property was her husband's property. She could not make a will. She could not claim her own earnings. She could not leave her husband's house without his permission. She could not sign a lease, or borrow money from a bank. She could not vote.

A woman's children were not her own. Legally, they belonged to the husband. If Georgie divorced Ned, she could lose all access to the children she adored. Once Georgie would have thought it impossible that Ned would ever do such a thing to her. Now she felt she did not know what he might do.

She could throw him out. But the prospect of being a deserted wife was not a pleasant one. And Georgie was desperately worried about money. They were deep in debt now, and the financial manager of the Firm had warned them that any more scandal would ruin all of their prospects. Georgie had no means of supporting herself. She had not been trained for anything. If Ned left her, she would be left alone with two small children and no way to feed them. She remembered the beggar women she had seen as a child, barefoot and ragged on the streets of Birmingham, babies on their hips, cupped hands held out.

It was the bleakest time of her life. She had never felt so lonely, or so afraid of the future.

And Georgie longed for her husband with all her heart. She wanted to press herself against his tall slender form, her head nestled against his heart, his arms about her.

In the end, she went home. What other choice did she have?

You're a heroine, Rosalind wrote to her.

Georgie wrote back: *Indeed my dear I am no heroine at all and I know where I come short as well as anyone else does – I have simply acted all along from very simple little reasons which God and my husband know better than anyone – I don't know what God thinks of them.*

Dearest Rosalind, be hard on no-one in this matter and exalt no-one. May we all come through it at last. I know one thing and that there is love enough between Edward and me to last out a long life if it is given us . . .

9

Willow-wood
Autumn 1869–Winter 1870

Janey stood at the window, looking out at the street. Autumn leaves lay sodden on the cobblestones, occasionally rising and skirling as the wind rose. The rain had blown over, but mist drifted through the bare branches of the plane trees and obscured the iron railings.

Behind her, Jenny and May were playing bears with Topsy on the carpet. On all fours, he growled and pretended to chase them, then rolled them over, tickling their tummies. The girls were screaming with laughter. The room was bright with lamplight, and behind the guard flames danced.

In Highgate Cemetery, the gravediggers would be straining to lift the slab of marble from Lizzie's grave. The ground would be wet. The men's trousers muddied to their knees. Their breath smoking white. A small bonfire the only contrivance of colour. Smoke and mist together, smelling of autumn. Digging deep, earth rising high. The sudden clink as shovels hit the coffin. Squelch as someone jumps down into the grave. Heaving the coffin up. Mufflers over mouths. The awful job of levering up the lid. Gagging. Flame-light and shadows sorrowing at the bones and tatters within.

Mr Howell would be standing by in his frockcoat and blood-red slash of ribbon, his top hat in his hand, his eyes lowered. He would be enjoying the drama of the moment. The doctor and the lawyer, standing back, disliking this task. Perhaps the lawyer would have his watch in his hand, thinking of his tea. He was there at the order of the cemetery, in case this exhumation was some elaborate trick to regain a secret will. The doctor would be uneasy, shifting from foot to foot, rubbing his gloved hands together. It was his job to disinfect the manuscript.

Seven years it had been lying in Lizzie's coffin, nestled between her cheek and her hair. Seven years of rotting away, food for maggots and worms.

Janey did not know how Gabriel could do it.

She was one of only six people who knew what was happening. His own mother did not know, even though the gravesite belonged to her. His brother and sisters did not know. His best friends did not know.

Janey wished she did not know either.

She thought of the poem he had written, the night that Charles Howell had first suggested digging up Lizzie's coffin. Called 'Willow-wood', it was an interlinked sequence of four sonnets, and his first poem in almost seven years. Janey knew it off by heart. Phrases ran through her mind:

> O ye, all ye that walk in Willow-wood,
> That walk with hollow faces burning white;
> What fathom-depth of soul-struck widowhood,
> What long, what longer hours, one lifelong night ...
> And her face fell back drowned, and was as grey
> as its grey eyes; and if it ever may
> meet mine again I know not ...

Janey shuddered.

Gabriel should not disturb Lizzie's grave.

If her ghost had been unquiet for seven years already, how restless would she be now?

Surely she would haunt Gabriel into his very grave?

*

It was the longest, coldest winter Janey could ever remember.

She felt ill all the time. Her back ached, and the muscles in her legs and feet would twitch and cramp constantly, making it hard to sleep. Food tasted strange to her, and often she felt nauseous. Her womanly cramps never seemed to ease, no matter the time of month, and she was always so tired. No-one could tell her what was wrong with her.

Janey blamed London. Which meant she blamed her husband.

She and Gabriel had not seen each other since Lizzie's grave had been opened and the tattered book of poems recovered. There was too much gossip, too much speculation. Despite all Gabriel's efforts to keep the exhumation secret, the news had leaked out.

London was full of strange rumours. Lizzie's body had not rotted away. Her face was still as perfect as the day she was buried. Her hair had kept growing long after death, so the coffin was overflowing with fiery golden coils. People said that her ghost was seen at Highgate Cemetery, drifting through the stone crosses and angels, her hair dragging behind her.

In January, Janey went to see Gabriel, unable to bear it any longer.

The Thames was grey and sludged with ice along the banks. Boys wrapped up to their eyes in mufflers poked about in the rubbish on the mudflats, looking for something to sell. A lone robin sat on a brittle branch, feathers ruffled up. The hems of Janey's skirts were dirtied with smutty snow by the time she had walked from the curb of the street to Gabriel's front door. She pulled her gloved hand out of her muff, and knocked on the door. After a long pause, she knocked again and then again.

The door was opened slowly. Gabriel peered out. His eyes were deeply shadowed. He smiled when he saw her, though, and drew her inside, looking quickly up and down the street to make sure no-one was watching.

'You have not written, asking me to sit for you,' she said.

'I cannot draw … or paint … my eyes … and look … my hands.' He held them before her, and she saw they were trembling.

'Oh, Gabriel. What is it? What's wrong?'

'Who knows? Not I. The doctor says to stop drinking so much whisky, and to go to bed before midnight, and not to work. But you know I cannot do that.'

'But if you cannot draw?'

'I've been working on the poems.'

She caught her breath. 'So the manuscript? It was intact?'

He did not answer her at first, leading her into the studio where at least it was warm. The room was dirtier and more crowded than ever, however, and Janey wished he would set her loose with a good stiff broom and her dusters. The edges of the canvases were furred with dust; she was sure it could not be good for him.

Gabriel shovelled some more coal into the little pot-bellied stove, then drew her down to sit beside him, holding both her hands. His face was dark with tension. 'It was just dreadful, Janey. The thing stank, though the doctor assured me it was not dangerous. But I could scarcely turn the pages without my stomach heaving. And no matter how much I washed, I could smell it for hours afterwards, on my hands and in my hair.'

Janey's stomach lurched in sympathy.

'There were wormholes through the whole thing, destroying some of my best lines. And other pages had been stuck together and could not be eased apart. But I could see enough to reconstruct most of the poems, bit by bit.'

When the grim task was done, he had burnt the original, unable to tolerate having it in the house. Janey could understand why.

Gabriel hesitated. 'Janey, I'd like to dedicate it to you . . . so many of the new poems were written for you.'

She was aghast. 'Oh, Gabriel, no. You can't! Think of the scandal.'

'I have,' he said sombrely. 'Oh Janey, I cannot tell you how much I wish things were different. If only I had married you when I first met you.'

Janey found such words hard to bear. When she thought of her anguish when Gabriel had left her to go to Lizzie, and the long despair that had followed, it was hard to forgive him for the games he had played with her heart.

Yet she had married Topsy. Gabriel had come to her, he had tried to stop her, but she had not trusted him not to hurt her again. And so now they were trapped in this unbearable triangle, each forged to the other.

She laid her head on his chest, listening to the quick uneven tumult of his heart, his arms about her. There they stayed, not moving, not speaking, hardly breathing, till the room was dim about them. Then reluctantly Janey sat up, drawing herself out of his arms.

'I need to get home,' she said. 'Look, darkness is falling already.'

He rose too, putting out one hand to steady himself. He was haggard, his eyes red-rimmed. 'Janey, will you forgive me if I don't escort you home? I am so unwell ...'

She paused mid-step, torn between laughter and astonishment. Janey had always chafed against Gabriel's insistence that she must always be accompanied, either by himself or her husband. When she thought how she had roamed the rookeries of Oxford at all hours as a child, begging for scraps, fighting for any tossed penny, it seemed ludicrous to be concerned about a staid cab drive along the gas-lit streets of Chelsea.

Yet it was so unlike him. Gabriel was nothing if not chivalrous.

She put out her hand and pressed his. 'I'll be fine. Look after yourself, Gabriel. Do as the doctor orders. I hope to see you soon.'

'I'm worried about the poems,' he confessed, walking her to the door. 'So much of you is in them, Janey. What if someone guesses?'

Janey could not comfort him. This was her fear too. She waited on the doorstep as he went out to hail her a cab, then went down the steps into the cold winter night, her hands huddled into her muff. She glanced back at him, trying to smile, then allowed the cab driver to hand her up into the carriage.

She could not have explained what she felt. A kind of shadow on her soul, a sense that the ground was quaking under her feet.

The next day Gabriel wrote to her, '*The sight of you going down the dark steps to the cab all alone has plagued me ever since – you looked so lonely.*'

That was how Janey felt. She lived in a house buzzing with people – clients, customers, servants, carpenters, weavers, embroiders, her own sister, her own children, her own husband.

Yet she was lonely.

Gabriel wrote to her again a few days later, the letter as always being delivered clandestinely by Charles Howell.

'*Dear Janey, I expect this has come into my head because I feel so badly the want of speaking to you. No-one else seems alive to me now, and places that are empty of you are empty of all life. But more than all that for me, dear Janey, is the fact that you exist, that I can yet look forward to seeing you and speaking to you again … You are the noblest and dearest thing that the world has had to show me …*'

Janey wept and hid the letter carefully. She could not bear to burn it.

In early February, another note came, begging her to come. The handwriting was sprawled and shaky, the words urgent.

Janey had to go to him, but it was a risk. With Topsy working from home, he knew when she left and when she returned, and would never fail to ask where she was going. She could not lie and say she was going to see a friend. Topsy knew all her friends, and would quiz them about their meeting. So she made up some lie about matching embroidery silks, and took her sewing basket with her.

Gabriel looked sicker than she had ever seen him look before. His olive skin was sallow, his eyes sunk into their sockets, and his hands trembled noticeably. He was also drunk, even though it was early in the afternoon.

As soon as Janey stepped in over the threshold, he clutched at her. 'Janey, I heard my daughter. She was here.'

Chills ran over her.

'What? But …' She could not say it.

His daughter had never drawn a breath.

'I heard her, Janey. She was in the hallway, crying. I ran to the door and opened it, but nobody was there. I know it was my little girl, Janey. She would have been nine this year.'

Janey knew Gabriel had a fixation with the number nine, just as his hero Dante Alighieri had. In his final painting of Lizzie as *Beata Beatrix*, Gabriel had shown the sundial casting its shadow over the number nine, to mark the time he had last seen his wife alive.

She tried to reason with him. 'Perhaps it was one of your wild beasts, Gabriel. The wombat, or one of the armadillos.'

He shook his head, his eyes desolate. 'No, Janey. It was my daughter. Crying for me.' He began to weep. 'It was her ghost, calling for me. Wanting me.'

10

Beauty Like Hers Is Genius
Spring–Autumn 1870

Ned was commissioned to paint a series of four female figures to represent the four seasons.

He painted Georgie as Winter, draped in grey with a black hood and wimple like a nun, a book in one hand, the other held out above a small, smoky fire. Behind her a curtain, and beyond the bare branches of desolate winter trees.

Ned painted Maria as Summer, lithe and beautiful, naked beneath her transparent gown, surrounded by roses and apples, forget-me-nots clustered below.

Georgie found it hard to bear.

In early 1870, he told Georgie he needed almond blossom. Armfuls of it. Georgie asked Rosalind Howard for help. Rather to her amazement she had discovered that Rosalind was an aristocrat, born into one noble family and married into another. Her husband, George, was the heir to the Earl of Carlisle, and they had a country estate that was the closest thing to a fairy-tale castle that Georgie had ever seen. Rosalind sent her a box of the fragile pink-and-white blossom, the first sign of spring.

Ned painted as if in a fever, or a fit of madness. He painted Maria as Phyllis from Ovid's tales of metamorphosis. Phyllis had been transformed into an almond tree by the gods after killing herself for love. When her faithless lover Demophoön came to find her, he embraced the tree in desperate sorrow, and the tree miraculously burst into bloom.

In Edward's painting, Phyllis herself was reborn, struggling free of the tree's imprisoning wood, reaching for the fleeing figure of Demophoön. Her fiery red hair rippled across the almond blossoms, and her arms held the fleeing man as captive as the tree that still confined her body. On her face was a look of such longing. On his face, guilt and fear and horror. He was stark-naked, his bare legs entangled with the writhing green ribbons of the tree's fluid sap.

It was an extraordinary painting. The best thing Ned had ever done, and the most shocking. Georgie had never seen an unclothed man on a canvas before. Usually an artist concealed the sexual organs with draperies or leaves or a well-placed hand. Ned made no such attempt. His Demophoön was utterly naked and utterly vulnerable.

In April, Ned sent it and another four paintings to the Old Watercolour Society summer exhibition. Maria Zambaco's distinctive Grecian profile and huge, melancholy eyes were captured in every single one.

A quote from Ovid was inscribed in the catalogue notes for *Phyllis and Demophoön*, which, when translated, said: 'Tell me what I have done, except love unwisely.'

It was the twisting of a knife in the wound for Georgie. She hated the thought of all London seeing her husband's obsession with another woman.

Two weeks after the exhibition's opening, the President of the Old Watercolour Society wrote to Ned saying that they had received an anonymous letter complaining that *Phyllis and Demophoön* was lewd. They asked him to cover Demophoön's genitalia with coloured chalk. Ned refused. He was then asked to remove the painting from the exhibition. Ned did so, then – when the exhibition was over – resigned from the society, swearing he would never show his work again.

The scandal spread fast. Everyone was talking about Ned Jones and his voluptuous mistress and his lascivious paintings and his poor humiliated wife. Georgie took the children and fled London, going to stay near Marian Evans and George Lewes in Whitby.

She did not know how she was going to survive the shame.

The sun kept rising, the world kept spinning.

Georgie returned home, determined to find a way to make a life for herself. She took up French lessons and joined a choir. She began to play the piano again, and taught her children their letters and numbers. She read as many books as she could find.

Topsy dropped around to see her regularly, bringing her a bunch of bluebells or the latest novel. They talked of poetry and politics and their children, and never alluded to their spouses at all. He was such a square, solid lump of comfort.

One day, Topsy shyly presented her with a sheaf of poems. His eyes would not meet hers, and his cheeks were flushed. 'I wrote them for you, old chap,' he said, and bolted.

Georgie sat down and read her way through, and soon her own cheeks were flushed and her body warm.

They were love poems.

On the back of one of the poems, he had written: 'We two are in the same box and need conceal nothing.'

Georgie was agitated beyond reason. On the one hand, the poems were such a balm to her bruised heart. She had felt so unloved and so unlovely. And Georgie had always admired Topsy, who she thought had the noble look of a medieval king about him. It was true that he was short and sturdy compared to Ned, but then he was strong and robust and down to earth as well, while Ned was always sickly and in need of support. At times Georgie felt she was more a mother to him than a wife, always running up and down stairs with hot water bottles and camphor oil to rub his thin chest, always reassuring him and being the stalwart one. With Topsy, she could weep a little and be sure of a strong arm about her and a handkerchief with which to blow her nose. And Georgie was only little herself. She had to stand up on her toes to kiss Ned's cheek, while Topsy's shoulder was at just the right height for her. Sometimes she longed for Topsy to put his arm about her, and pat her back, and promise to fix whatever was amiss, just for the sheer relief of it.

Yet it was wrong. So wrong. He was her husband's best friend. She was married, he was married, for better or for worse.

It'd serve Ned right, an evil voice whispered inside her. What's sauce for the goose should be sauce for the gander. And why not? Her bed was cold and lonely, Topsy's bed was cold and lonely. Why should they not take a little warmth and company for themselves?

She wrote Topsy a note, and called out to a boy to take it for her before she could change her mind. Then she sent the children to her sister's for the rest of the day. Ned would be gone all afternoon, she knew, meeting Maria somewhere.

Topsy came straightaway. His hair was combed, his coat was neat, he carried a bunch of snowdrops. Hope and consolation, they meant in the language of flowers.

Georgie stepped into his arms and raised her face for his kiss. It was strange, to kiss a man other than her husband. He smelt and tasted different. His beard was much rougher, his hands bigger and clumsier. She felt a flare of desire within her, and drew away, the back of her hand pressed to her mouth.

Topsy said her name. There was such longing in his voice.

Georgie shook her head, 'I can't, I can't.'

'There's no sin, if there's love.' His voice was desperate.

'I still love him, I still love him, oh God save me, I still love him.' She dropped on to the couch, rubbing at her lips with the back of her hand. 'And you still love her, Topsy. You know you do.'

'No. I tried ... I wanted to make her happy ... I wanted to save her ... But I always knew she was not for me. And I have come to admire you so much, Georgie. Your strength. Your courage. Your goodness.'

'Admiration is not love.'

'I spoke badly. My feelings for you ... my very deep regard ...'

Georgie gazed up at him. 'Oh, Topsy, please don't. You know we can't do this. No matter how much pain we are in. I can't bear the thought of losing your friendship ... you are like ... like a brother to me ...'

He turned away. She could tell she had hurt him. Tremulously, Georgie said, 'Please forgive me.'

'There is nothing to forgive,' Topsy said, not looking at her, and went away.

The year crept past. Georgie had never known such a hard year. It seemed the whole world was at war.

In July, it was her thirtieth birthday. A few letters from her sisters, a cake she cooked herself, colourful cards scribbled by the children. A month later it was Ned's turn. Thirty-eight years old. He was trembly and sick all day. Four-year-old Margot wept because there was no money to buy him a present. Georgie did her best, but the world seemed a dark and unforgiving place.

The next day Topsy came to visit her. He had made her an illuminated book of poems, handwritten and hand-illustrated. Every page was a miracle of beauty. Tiny paintings of lovers and angels and lonely maidens, poems of love and longing, all entwined and wreathed with roses and forget-me-nots and daisies. Many long hours had gone into its making.

'For your birthday,' he said brusquely. 'Sorry it's late.'

She looked through it, speechless. Phrases leapt out at her. *Strong are thine arms O love, and strong, Thine heart to live and love and long, But thou art wed to grief and wrong: Live then and long, though hope is dead!*

'Is all hope dead?' he asked, very low.

Georgie rose and went to him, and kissed his bearded cheek.

'I cannot love you that way,' she said. 'Will you be content with what love I can give you? I promise that it's deep and true ... even if it's not the kind of love you want.'

'Any kind of love is good,' he said huskily, and squeezed her hand in his.

*

Janey knew she could not deceive her husband anymore.

Topsy was such a good man. It would have been easier if he had been unkind. But all he had ever wanted to do was make her happy.

She waited till Christmas was over and the New Year begun, not wishing to mar the festive season with anger. A dozen times a day she went to speak to him, then her courage failed her and she would turn away, the words unspoken.

Then Topsy began to talk about travelling to Iceland. He had been learning Old Norse and translating and rewriting some of the tales for *The Earthly Paradise*. She went to him one evening, when the children were tucked up in bed, and said, 'You should go. To Iceland, I mean.'

He laid down his pen and looked at her. 'Should I?' he asked mildly.

She nodded. 'You have always wanted to go. And you will do a better job of the new poem if you go.'

'What will you do when I am gone?'

'We could find a house in the country. Spend the summer there. We've all been so sick. It would do us such good.'

'You mean, you and the girls?'

Her heart quailed within her. She nodded.

Now is the time to tell him, she thought. *Tell him now.*

But she could not.

A long charged silence. Topsy did not look at her, but down at the paper on which he was writing.

'A house in the country would be expensive,' he said at last. 'Perhaps we should ask someone to share the cost with us.'

She was dismayed. 'But ... who?'

Topsy still did not look at her. 'I'm sure Gabriel would be glad of a summer holiday.'

Her breath caught. She stared at him in disbelief.

'I will write to him and suggest it.' Topsy drew a piece of paper towards him and began to write.

'You ... you know?' she faltered.

He hesitated, his pen spreading a blotch of ink on the paper, then laid his pen down and turned to her, taking both her hands.

'I cannot make you love me, Janey. I know that. It seems to me that no-one has the right to force someone else to love them, or say that they do, out of fear, or because they are beholden … it seems to cheapen the idea of love somehow. And I don't want to think of you coming to me because you think you have to … because we are married. It is your heart, your body. You've a right to do with them as you wish.'

She was startled by his words, and then moved and somehow thrilled. It was as if he had had a vision of the world as it should be, where men and women were both free to determine their own fates.

'I've been thinking that love comes in many guises,' he went on, talking as much to himself as to her. 'I had thought that love was like it was in the old poems, a knight laying his arms at the feet of a fair maiden and swearing to be ever faithful to her.'

Janey thought of Topsy and the armour he had designed, and the paintings of courtly love he had tried to paint, and smiled, returning the squeeze of his hand. 'That's one kind of love,' she managed to say. 'But there are others.'

'Yes. So I think. So I want to try to be happy with whatever love you can give me and I can give you, and not go around hurting each other and being unkind. Can we do that?'

'We can try,' she said tremulously.

'It'll be hard, I think,' he went on. 'There have been times when I just wanted to give Gabriel a punch in the nose. But I know you loved him first. And, really, why would you choose me when you could have him?'

She blushed and did not know how to answer him.

'Can you try not to let the whole world know?' he asked, not looking at her. 'A man does have his pride.'

Janey found herself able to move again. She stepped forward and bent, putting her arms about his neck and kissing him on his bearded cheek.

'Thank you,' she whispered.

Kelmscott Manor was an old grey stone house upon the Thames, surrounded by gardens and meadows and steep-roofed barns. Topsy had found it in an estate agent's catalogue, and both he and Janey had fallen in love with it at first sight.

Built in the late 1500s, the old part of the house had a low-ceilinged hall with stone-flagged floors and a vast fireplace, furnished with heavy oak chairs and table. The kitchen was dark and medieval-looking too, with a deep inglenook fireplace and deep-set window seats.

A small room to the right was full of light and air, however, with a wonderful stone fireplace decorated by a shield suspended by carved swags of apples and leaves. *I'll paint this white*, Janey thought. *As white and pure as snow. It'll be my room, where I can read and sew and be at peace.*

She smiled at the thought of it. There was so little peace and quiet at Queen Square, with every room papered over with Topsy's heavy intricate designs, and the constant banging and clanging and shouting of the workmen.

Upstairs were two bedrooms, separated by the stairwell. One of these rooms led into another long room, lit with big windows on three sides with views out onto the garden and the dovecote. *Gabriel can use this as his studio*, Janey thought happily but did not say.

A steep ladder led up into quaint garrets tucked into the strong timbers of the roof. Janey felt sure the girls would love to sleep up there, their little beds tucked under sloping rafters that almost touched the floor.

At the end of the garden was a stone outhouse topped with a steep slate roof, concealing a three-seater privy. An ancient mulberry tree was propped up on sticks in a garden protected by yew hedges and foaming with flowers.

'So shall we take it?' Topsy asked.

'Oh, yes, please,' Janey exclaimed, clasping his arm with both hands.

He smiled and put one of his big, square, calloused hands over hers.

It is strange, Janey thought, *how comfortable we are with each other now.*

Yet she saw that Topsy was hiding his hurt deep within, and she was sorry for it, even in the midst of her delight.

*

In early July, Janey and the two girls moved into the house, Topsy making sure they were settled before heading back to London to prepare for his trek to Iceland. Janey had hired a governess for the girls, for she was determined they would receive the education that she had been denied.

Topsy wrote to Janey: '*How beautiful the place looked last Monday: I grudged going away so; but I am very happy to think of you all happy there, and the children and you getting well.*' He ended the letter, '*Please, dear Janey, be well and happy.*'

Indeed, she was blessed to be married to such a man.

Ten days later, Gabriel arrived, bringing a few servants to help run the house, the trap filled with tightly wrapped canvases and boxes of paints and brushes and pencils. Janey showed him around the walled garden proudly, the girls running and skipping about them, and then they walked along the placid green stream, overhung with willows. When the girls were busy skipping pebbles across the water, Gabriel and Janey stole a kiss behind a tree.

'We shall have to be careful,' she whispered, resting lightly in his arms.

'I have never wanted to be less careful in my life,' he answered, and kissed her again.

It was an enchanted summer. Gabriel painted in the long, airy studio during the day, while Janey busied herself putting the house in order or reading in the garden. The two girls sat in the white panelled room and worked with their governess in the mornings, chewing the ends of their pens and staring out the window at the sunlit garden, listening to the blackbirds carolling and feasting among the gooseberries. At last they were released from their lessons, and able to run out to the farm to see the doe-eyed cows in their byres and the workers bringing in the hay, building a great golden tower in the yard. Jenny and May loved to climb up to the high gabled roof of the barn, and sit astride the ridge and gaze out across their kingdom. The sisters became so agile they would chase each other across the roofs and gables, tiled with overlapping grey slates as orderly and beautiful as fish scales. One day May found herself stuck, and Janey had to call the farmhands to find their longest ladders and help her down.

Gabriel had brought the whole set of Waverley novels down with him, and the girls devoured them greedily, managing to finish one a day. At night, they read Shakespeare aloud to each other, the girls acting out their favourite scenes.

One evening, after exploring a long way down the stream, the girls rode home on the hay wagon, lying under a sky the colour of marigolds. As the sun set, a great murmuration of starlings wheeled over the vast sky.

Winged too with wind it is, and winnowings of birds, Gabriel wrote. *As if the last day's hour in rings of strenuous flight must die …*

His book of poetry had been received well, with glowing reviews written by Topsy and Algy Swinburne helping the first print run of a thousand copies sell out within the month. He was determined to put together another volume, and kept a notebook and pencil in his pocket at all times, in case inspiration should strike.

Janey found her health and strength returning, and was able to walk miles through the countryside with Gabriel, admiring the wildflowers twining in the hedgerows and the thatched farm buildings dozing in the sun. Only a field away was the Thames, lazily wending its way through golden and bronze fields. They walked along its shores, talking or in companionable silence, taking care not to touch each other where anyone else could see.

Sometimes they lay in the punt on the stream, concealed by willow leaves, kissing and whispering.

Sometimes, they made love in the furrows of the rye fields, with no sound but the rustling wind and their exultant cries.

Gabriel wrote poems on scraps of paper, and drew dozens of sketches of Janey. He painted her with the winding river and the old gabled house in the background, willow boughs in her hands.

Beauty like hers is genius, he wrote.

It could not last. The summer must come to an end, her husband must return from his adventures, she and Gabriel must go back to their own lives.

He wrote her one last poem, called 'Severed Selves':

Two glances which together would rejoice
In love, now lost like stars beyond dark trees;
Two hands apart whose touch alone gives ease,
Two bosoms which, heart-shrined with mutual flame,
Would, meeting in one clasp, be made the same;
Two souls, the shores wave-mocked of sundering seas ...

11

Proserpina
Summer–Autumn 1872

All year Janey dreamed of returning to Kelmscott Manor.

The thought of it sustained her through another malicious London winter, racked with illness and longing.

One day in early June, Topsy came into the drawing room where she lay on her couch, working on an embroidered wall-hanging for the Firm. He was in a state, flushed and panting from having run up the stairs.

'Janey, I've just heard from William Rossetti … such dreadful news … Gabriel has gone mad.'

Janey slid the needle through the cloth and laid it down. 'What has he done now? Bought another wombat?'

'It's not a joke, Janey. He's completely unhinged. He thinks there's some kind of conspiracy against him, that spies surround him and plot to kill him.'

Janey could only stare at her husband as he paced around the room.

'His brother William has spent the past few days with him, trying to calm him. But he's out of control.'

Janey stood up, her embroidery falling unheeded to the floor. 'I need to go to him.'

'I don't think that's wise. They're calling the doctors.'

'He'll want me. I need to be there.' Feverishly, she began to hunt around for her hat.

'They don't want you there.'

'What? Who?'

'William Rossetti and William Bell Scott. They've asked specifically that I keep you away until the doctors have seen him.'

Janey sat down limply, staring at him. 'But . . . why?'

He did not answer.

Colour began to burn up her cheeks. 'They blame me? They think . . .' Looking away from him, she said faintly, 'They know?'

'I hope not,' Topsy said. 'But it seems so.'

Janey felt sick. She imagined the gossip, the sideways looks, the snubs. 'But he'll want me . . . he'll need me.'

Topsy sat down beside her, taking one of her hands. 'Janey. They're talking of putting him in an asylum.'

'An asylum? You mean . . . a madhouse?' When Topsy nodded, she said incredulously, 'Is he truly that mad?'

'I don't know. I hope not.'

'I know he'd been troubled by that review in the paper . . . and all the scandal that followed. He'd not been sleeping well, he said.'

'William says he is taking this new drug . . . it's called chloral . . . it's meant to help him sleep. But William thinks it is making things worse. That, and the whisky.'

Janey frowned. Gabriel had mentioned the chloral to her. It was the only way he could get any rest, he said.

Gabriel had been wild and strange these past few months.

It had all begun after their summer at Kelmscott Manor. An unknown critic had written a review of Gabriel's book of poems, calling it the 'Fleshly School of Poetry'. At first Gabriel had laughed it off, and made jokes. Then it turned out it was some old enemy called Robert Buchanan who had written the review under a pseudonym. Gabriel had been furious, and spent hours writing up a response. He'd paced about, reading it aloud to Janey and begging for her opinion. Janey had been sure he should not respond. She had always believed that old saying that silence was golden. It was like trying to bridle a runaway horse, however. Gabriel was determined to have his say.

His response was published before Christmas. Gabriel called it 'The Stealthy School of Criticism'. Everyone had thought it was very clever and funny, and they'd clinked their glasses and cheered him.

Then, in May, Mr Buchanan republished his review as a pamphlet printed on flesh-coloured paper. All the papers began to publish extracts from the pamphlet, and write articles quoting it, adding their own voices and opinions. Gabriel began to think it was a conspiracy, to destroy his reputation and drag him down.

Flushed and excited, Gabriel had read out bits from the newspapers to her. '"But honest plainness of speech is not the characteristic of the Fleshly School ..." See, everyone's calling us the Fleshly School now. It's stuck! I knew it would. "It is their sickly self-consciousness, their emasculated delight in brooding over and toying with matters which healthy, manly men put out of their thoughts ..." Emasculated! It is as if he knows about my swollen testicle, and is mocking me.'

'Surely not,' Janey had murmured. 'How could they know?'

'Someone's spying on me ... leaking it all to the press.'

She had stared at him in troubled amazement. 'But who? And why?'

The newspaper shook in his hands. 'Just listen! I'll prove it to you.' He read out loud: '"It is, in short, their utter unmanliness which is at once so disgusting ..." Unmanliness! Again. And, oh! Listen to this! "With Mr Rossetti the shutters seem to be always closed, the blinds down, there are candles for sunshine, and the atmosphere is of a close heavy kind that reminds one alternately of the sick-room and the conservatory." You cannot tell me that the writer has not been spying on me!'

'Well, you do keep all the curtains drawn,' Janey said. 'Anyone walking past can see that.'

'My eyes! My eyes! The light hurts my eyes!'

'I know, I know,' Janey had said soothingly.

Gabriel came over and caught her hands in his so tightly, she winced. 'Janey, you don't understand. I think Buchanan is hinting at our affair. And in the most awful of ways.'

Janey stared at him, her throat tight.

Gabriel gave her the pamphlet to read, pointing with a trembling finger at a few paragraphs. Janey read silently: 'I cannot forbear expressing my wonder, by the way, at the kind of women whom it seems the unhappy lot of these gentlemen to encounter. I have lived as long in the world as they have, but never yet come across persons of the other sex who conduct themselves in the manner described. Females who bite, scratch, scream, bubble, munch, sweat, writhe, twist, wriggle, foam, and in a general way slaver over their lovers, must surely possess some extraordinary qualities to counteract their otherwise most offensive mode of conducting themselves.'

Janey felt sick. Carefully she laid the paper down. 'We cannot see each other for a while. Not till the gossip has died down.'

In her head, words were shrieking about like frightened bats. What if her daughters overheard someone talking? What if a gutter journalist named her? She would be ruined, Topsy would be ruined.

'No!' Gabriel caught her hands. 'Janey, you can't mean it. Please! You are the one good thing … the only thing keeping me from going mad … Don't abandon me … don't leave me alone …'

Janey had pressed his hands close to her cheek, unable to speak. Eventually, though, she had to rise and go home and listen to her daughters' lessons and pretend that all was well. And she had been staunch in refusing to see Gabriel for a while, even though she had longed for him.

She had hoped the rumours and gossip would die down.

But now this.

Surely Gabriel could not really be mad? It was just his vehement Italian nature, his propensity for hyperbole, his love of drama. These cold-blooded Englishmen disliked such violence, such fervency. They did not understand him.

'It's not true,' she said. 'They're just jealous of his genius ... they want to tear him down ... he'll show them.'

Topsy kicked her embroidery again and went out, slamming the door behind him.

Janey was restless and unhappy the next few days. She wrote to Gabriel several times but tore up the letters and flung them on the fire. She read all the newspapers, her heart bruised by the innuendo.

A few days later, Mr Scott called at the house and asked to see Janey. Topsy was at work, and Janey busy playing tea parties with the girls. She hesitated, then nodded that he should be admitted. Asking the girls to go up to the nursery, she settled herself on the couch and picked up her embroidery.

Mr Scott was a florid-faced man with a rather noticeable hairpiece covering the bald dome of his head and a waistcoat straining at the buttons. Every line of his face and body spoke of his dislike and disapproval of her.

'Mrs Morris, I apologise for disturbing you. I ... have a rather unpleasant duty to discharge.'

'Yes?' she asked coolly.

'Are you aware that Gabriel has been ... suffering some delusions?'

'So my husband informed me.' Janey carefully set another stitch.

'We took him to Roehampton last Thursday, hoping that the country air and the quiet would help. It was a terrible journey. Gabriel kept ... hearing things ... bells. He kept banging on the roof of the cab with his stick. We tried to keep him quiet, but to no avail. Then, the next day, he ... there is no easy way to describe this. He saw some gypsies carrying a banner. It was Whitsun, you see. He thought they were setting up a gibbet. To hang him. He attacked them.'

Janey closed her eyes for a moment.

'We had to drag him back into the house. The gypsies ... we were lucky not to have started a riot.'

He waited a moment, as if expecting Janey to make some comment. She did not look at him, but down at her embroidery. Her hands were shaking. She closed one upon the other.

'That night … that night Gabriel heard voices whispering to him. He says they said insupportable things to him.'

Janey braced herself.

In a harsh voice, Mr Scott went on. 'Gabriel could not bear it. He drank a whole bottle of laudanum.'

She gasped. 'What? No!'

He leant forward, as if pleased to have provoked a response. 'Yes, he did. A whole bottle. No-one realised, though. Poor William was so relieved that his brother was sleeping at last that he did not try to rouse him. It was not till it was after four that William thought to check on him. He called the doctor, then went to collect his mother and sister so they could be there at the end.'

Janey could not move even a finger, or snatch even the faintest breath. Her eyes were fixed on Mr Scott's.

After a long moment, he went on, speaking in a voice of cold politeness. 'You will be glad to hear, Mrs Morris, that the doctor found the laudanum bottle and knew what to do. He administered black coffee and ammonia till at last Gabriel was awakened.'

Janey sucked in a breath. She felt so sick and giddy she had to put a hand on the arm of the sofa to steady herself.

'Is he … is he …' She could not manage the words, and so she closed her mouth and said nothing.

'He is weak down all one side of his body,' Mr Scott said. 'And very wild and unhappy in his thoughts. He shall need to be watched carefully. His mother thinks he should be committed to the care of an asylum. And poor William is at his wits' end trying to deal with his affairs. Apparently they are in some disorder.'

Let me watch him! Janey wanted to sob. *Let me care for him!*

She did not speak.

'We think it best to take him far away from London. For some reason, he is asking for you. He will not agree to go away until he has seen you. I am here to request you to be most circumspect in your approach to him. Any … hint of strong emotion … could be enough to tip him over the edge again.'

'So I … I can come and see him?'

'Tomorrow, if that suits.'

Janey picked up her embroidery again, set a stitch so large and wild it would need to be unpicked. 'Of course,' she said colourlessly. 'Shall I come early afternoon?'

Mr Scott stood up. 'That would suit admirably.'

Janey would not allow herself to break down until she knew he was gone. Then she sank to the floor, utterly undone. To think of Gabriel, the most brilliant of men, attacking cab drivers and gypsies, drinking laudanum. Laudanum! The drug that had killed Lizzie. What had the voices in the night said, to drive him to try to take his own life?

Murderer? Adulterer? Cuckolder?

Fool, failure, flop?

The next day Topsy took her to see Gabriel.

He was lying on the couch, pale and haggard. His hands shook.

The room was full of people. His brother William. Bruno. Mr Scott, damn his holier-than-thou air. Gabriel's studio assistant, Mr Dunn. Doctors.

They all stared at Janey as she came in. She shrank back, but then steeled her spine. She must give them no cause for gossip.

Gabriel's face lit up at the sight of her. It was one of the things she had always loved most about him. But Janey dared not show her own joy at the sight of him.

She sat down. 'So sorry to hear you've been unwell,' she heard herself say.

'I wanted you, Janey. Why didn't you come?'

She bent her head. 'I knew you were in good hands.'

'Good hands! Oh, yes, the very best. But I wanted yours.'

She wanted to tell him that they had forbidden her to come. That she had longed to be with him, looking after him, shielding him from all that hurt him. But it was impossible.

She heard herself say, as one would to a bare acquaintance: 'I do hope you are feeling better soon.'

Afterwards, she poured out her heart to him in a letter, incoherently trying to explain herself and begging his pardon. She had no answer. She wrote again and again, but never heard a word.

Janey suspected her letters were not being delivered. She had confirmation of this, two months later, when Gabriel's doctor wrote to her, very coldly, and said that Mr Rossetti had insisted on writing to her and would not be calm till he knew she had received his letter. 'I must insist that you send your response to me so that I may be sure it does no harm.'

As Janey wrote, she had to wipe away the tears that fell thick and fast. Yet her strongest emotion was anger. Because she was a woman … because she was an ostler's daughter … because she was married to another … because she had dared to flout their stupid rules … rules they were free to flout as it pleased them because they were men … because she was a woman who wanted … because …

Gabriel had written in his letter: *You are the one necessary person to me …*

Janey wrote as coolly and carefully as she could, so her letter would be delivered. But at the end she said, with all of her heart: *As you are to me.*

It was late September before Gabriel came to Kelmscott. The elms were flaming with autumn colour, and the willows were yellow. He came with a young man called George Hake, the son of one of his doctors. It took Janey only a few moments to understand that young Mr Hake was there to act as spy.

She and Gabriel could do no more than clasp hands, exchange greetings. Jenny and May were jumping about enthusiastically, showing Gabriel their new treasures – a blown robin's egg, shiny brown conkers, the fragile skeleton of a leaf.

Gabriel looked tired, but he smiled and seemed glad to be there. It smote Janey's heart to see how he needed a stick to walk. She made him as comfortable as she could, though he did not want tea but asked her to bring him the whisky decanter. With Mr Hake listening to every word, they made polite conversation.

The young man went out of the room for a moment, and at once Janey went to Gabriel and sank to her knees beside him and kissed the back of his hand. 'I am so sorry. I wrote, I truly did, and I tried to see you. They would not let me.'

A strange look contorted his face. 'It is hard to know who to trust. They are all in a conspiracy, you know. They seek to drag me down.'

She sat back on her heels. 'You can trust me, Gabriel.'

'If only . . .' he murmured. 'If only . . .'

She did not know what he meant and she could not ask. Mr Hake's quick footsteps coming along the hall. She had to rise and return to her seat, and pretend to be sewing, with her questions choking in her throat.

Gabriel drank a lot at dinner, and then settled down to play draughts with George Hake. He kept the decanter of whisky at his elbow.

All Janey wanted was to hold him in her arms, and be sure that all was well again. But there was no chance to be together. George Hake did not leave them alone for a moment. Eventually Janey went to bed, hoping Gabriel would come to her. She could hear the two men talking, laughing, playing cards. She rose often and went to listen at the door. Eventually she fell asleep, despite herself.

Gabriel woke her much later, banging at her door, calling out to her. He was drunk. She flew to let him in, trying to keep him quiet. He staggered in, almost knocking her over. He stumbled towards the bed, his hands heavy and clumsy on her body. His breath reeked of whisky and tobacco.

'Oh, Janey, it's been torture without you. I've been able to think of nothing else.'

She tried to embrace him, to comfort him, but he was in a state of agitation, afraid George was listening at the door or that someone was crouching beneath the window. The call of a hunting owl alarmed him. She reassured him and drew him down to lie with her, but just the touch of her hands was enough to arouse him and within moments, he had spent himself in her palm.

Afterwards, he slept heavily. She could not wake him. Janey was frantic with the fear that someone would find him in her bed. She had to heave him, drunk and half insensible, back to his own room, every stumble and slurred protest excruciatingly loud in the darkness of the night.

Then, aroused but unsatisfied, she tiptoed back to her own bed, shaking in terror at the thought of being caught.

He slept till well after noon the next day, disappointing the girls who kept asking why he slept so long. When at last he rose he was bleary-eyed and morose. He insisted on reading all the papers, looking for any mention of himself, or the Fleshly School. He thought his mail had been steamed open. Janey could not reassure him. She had seen George slip a few letters into his pocket before bringing them the morning post. She wondered bitterly if they were from the other women in Gabriel's life, his models, his so-called housekeeper.

It was catching, she told herself. Gabriel's fears, his suspicions, his manias. If she was not careful, she would be driven mad herself.

Every day there was some little sign of oddity. Gabriel opened doors abruptly, sure that someone was listening outside. He wanted all the curtains closed and the windows shut, even on a lovely day. He heard footsteps when there was no-one there, and alarm bells ringing in the middle of the night. The rooks in the elm trees perturbed him, with their constant wheeling and cawing. He thought the local villagers stared at him and muttered about him behind their hands. Janey had to admit they found Gabriel a strange sight, with his olive skin and intense stare, his flowered waistcoats and soft hats and nonchalantly knotted silk scarves. But then they stared at her too, and at the two lovely long-limbed girls in their loose medieval smocks and wooden beads.

George spoke of wishing to be published one day. Gabriel said most seriously, 'Then you should not be here with me. Any connection with my name is sure to arouse a swarm of malignity.'

The weeks before Gabriel had come had been calm and sweet and peaceful. Janey and the girls had read, and paddled about in the punt, and made bread together, and picked flowers for the house. Topsy had come down on the weekends, and delighted the girls by clipping the yew hedge into the fanciful shape of a dragon, which he christened 'Fafnir'. The mulberry tree had been heavy with fruit, and the girls' mouths had been stained red all day.

Gabriel changed all that. It was like thunder muttered about him and lightning struck from his heels.

Topsy came down once or twice, but he found Gabriel's habits difficult to bear. Topsy wanted to be up early in the dawn, fishing in the river, tramping over the fields, collecting birds' eggs with the girls.

One day William Rossetti came down to stay the weekend, while Topsy was there. He listened to Topsy talk excitedly about the Norse myths he was translating, then remarked in his colourless way, 'I am sure I cannot understand why anyone could be interested in a man who had a dragon for a brother.'

Topsy, goaded beyond endurance, retorted, 'I'd much rather have a dragon for a brother than a bloody fool.'

Janey was worn out trying to keep the peace between them all.

As the days slowly narrowed, and the fields grew stubbled and brown, Gabriel began painting Janey as Proserpina. The old myth had always intrigued him. The beautiful young woman abducted and raped by the God of the Underworld. The desperate search for Proserpina by her mother, the goddess of the earth. The winter of her despair that covered the land, making all dark and barren.

Meanwhile, in the Underworld, Proserpina eats six pomegranate seeds, and so is condemned to spend half of every year in the land of the dead.

Ever since, the world rejoices with her rebirth in the spring and grieves again for her imprisonment as winter closes in.

Gabriel painted Janey with the broken pomegranate in her hand, a gleam of light on the wall behind her, smoke and shadows about her. It became like a madness for him. He did not want her to go back to London. Janey realised that, for Gabriel, her husband was her captor, her abductor, the ruler of the Underworld.

He painted her as Proserpina again and again, and wrote a sonnet that ended:

'Woe me for thee, unhappy Proserpine.'

12

Heartbroken
Winter 1872

Georgie could not believe that Maria Zambaco was gone.

All sorts of rumours were whispered. Madame Zambaco had had a nervous breakdown and been put in an asylum. She was sick and thought likely to die. She had run off with another lover.

Ned was so heartbroken, Georgie suspected the latter.

He spent days locked in his bedroom, his arm over his eyes, the curtains drawn, the lights turned down. He did not touch his pencils or paintbrushes.

Once again, Georgie had piles of bills to pay and no money to pay them with. She wrote polite letters to all who owed them money and even politer letters to all whom they owed. She wrote to Topsy too, begging him to excuse Ned for not delivering the work for which he had already been paid. Topsy would understand, she knew.

Georgie had been afraid that her rejection of Topsy would harm a friendship that had grown very precious to her, but the opposite had proved true. They had grown even closer, and talked together of many things, as well as of love.

'How can you bear it?' she had asked him once, knowing Janey was down at Kelmscott Manor with Gabriel.

'I am trying to keep the world from narrowing on me, and to look at things bigly and kindly,' he had answered with a sad smile.

Georgie had been trying to do the same, but it was hard.

She went out into the cold damp afternoon to post the letters herself, not wanting to pay even the small coin a messenger boy would cost. The wind was full of wet black leaves that slapped her face. By the time she got home, her hair was bedraggled, the hem of her skirts were muddied, and one foot was wet because there was a hole in the sole of her boot. She unpinned her old bonnet and saw her face in the glimmer of the mirror. She looked thin and tired and beaten down, and her nose was red.

Georgie dried herself, then went wearily to her husband's studio. She had to see what paintings of Ned's were close to finishing, so that she could try to sell them and raise some funds. Christmas was close, and Georgie wanted to be able to create something beautiful and magical for the children.

She unlocked the door and stepped inside, her cold fingers fumbling to light the lamp. At last light flickered up, and she lifted the lamp high, beginning to look over the canvases that were stacked everywhere on the walls and trestles.

The light fell upon a large canvas set up on a platform.

A princess lying asleep on a bier, her maids slumped around her, roses and thorns bending close. Her dress was white and diaphanous, clinging to her long lithe limbs. Her hair was tossed half over her face, as if she had been writhing in her sleep. Her posture was sensuous, even provocative, the gossamer of her gown not concealing the jut of her breasts.

The sleeping princess was, of course, Maria Zambaco.

The lamp in Georgie's hand shook. She put it down abruptly, and then slowly slid down to the ground herself. Holding her knees tightly, she hunched around the pain.

Georgie's most treasured memory was of the day she had first met Ned, and heard the story of Briar Rose for the first time, in Tennyson's poem. She knew by heart the closing lines, and murmured them to herself, many times, with secret joy:

And o'er the hills, and far away
Beyond their utmost purple rim,
Beyond the night across the day,
Thro' all the world she follow'd him.

Almost as precious to her was the memory of the day when Ned had first drawn her, as the Sleeping Princess, and created out of her ordinary face something of such exquisite loveliness.

In the darkest times, Georgie had held on to these two faint shining memories as something talismanic, proof that deep down Ned truly loved her.

She pressed her hands into her face, shuddering with tears. For so long she had been strong, doing her best for the children, keeping up appearances to the world, waiting for the day Ned would remember her and return to her.

Yet he had done nothing but flaunt his love for that woman to the world, immortalising her in paint as he had never tried to do for Georgie, the one who truly loved him, the one who had been faithful and staunch.

She would never, ever forgive him.

Part IV

The Brightest of Bright Things
1881–1890

'Margaret came from school – the brightest of bright things is that damsel, half a head taller than her mother, and I sit and chuckle at the sight of her, and nudge my neighbour: also I praise her to her face that she may be used to flattery and be sick of it, and not astonished or touched when it is used by others – that is my way with her.'

Extract from a letter from Sir Edward Burne-Jones to Charles Eliot Norton
Quoted by Lady Georgiana Burne-Jones
Memorials of Edward Burne-Jones, Volume II

1

Shadow of Death
Spring-Summer 1881

She had always been afraid of dying.

Ever since she was a little girl, Margot had thought to herself: *One day I won't be here anymore. One day I'll be gone forever. Snuffed out like a candle flame, nothing left but smoke.*

Is this what death felt like? Light ebbing away, her limbs slowly turning to stone?

She could feel his eyes on her, intent on the curve of her lips, the fall of her lashes, the slope of her shoulder. She imagined his fingers, conjuring her face like magic on the paper.

'Ned! Can't you see the light has gone? It's freezing in here.' Margot's mother came in with a whirl of cold wind.

Margot opened her eyes. The room was filled with twilight, making everything strange and spooky. That wooden lay-figure could be a grinning skeleton, that drop cloth a wraith from the grave.

'I wanted to get as much down as I could.' Her father stood behind his easel, dressed in his paint-stained smock, his fingers smeared with colour.

Mammy shut the door with a bang. 'Margot must be so cold. And in that thin dress too! Do you want her to catch her death?'

'I'm sorry.' Papa sat by Margot, picking up her hand and rubbing it between his own. 'You should have said something.'

'You always say: sit still as a mouse and don't move even a whisker.'

'You could have given me just a little squeak, to let me know how cold and stiff you were.'

'I've brought you some tea.' Mammy thumped the tray on the table, and poured out some tea. Margot raised herself up on one elbow and took the cup, wrapping her fingers around it. Its warmth was very welcome.

'Your father. He'd paint all night if he could. Why didn't you light the lamp?'

Papa replied mildly, 'If I had realised how dark it was, I would've.' He stood at the easel, frowning over the work he had done that day.

Margot sat up, putting her teacup on the floor. 'May I see, Papa?' She jumped up and went to his side. Mammy came to stand with her, putting her arm about her. Together they gazed at the drawing.

Margot asleep, her face turned on a soft violet-coloured pillow, her cheek faintly flushed. The delicate suggestion of petals behind her.

'The sleeping princess?' her mother asked.

'You know I've wanted to do something big with the story for a while.'

'And Margot is to be your princess this time.' Her mother's voice was flat.

'Always.'

Margot had been hardly listening. 'Oh, Papa, couldn't you have made me a little more …' She made a sweeping gesture with one hand. It was the fashion just then for women to be voluptuous, and Margot feared she would be stick-thin forever.

'She's growing up so fast,' Papa said, a melancholy note in his voice.

'She is,' Mammy said briskly. 'But you can't hold back time.'

It was true Margot was growing up.

In June, she had her fifteenth birthday. Jenny and May Morris came over for afternoon tea. They played croquet in the garden, and giggled over the new Gilbert and Sullivan opera *Patience*, inspired by Papa and Uncle Topsy and Uncle Gabriel. It starred long-haired artists in velvet coats, drifting about the stage and declaiming their poetry to rapturous damsels in loose dresses, just like Margot and her friends always had to wear.

Two weeks later, Margot was up early. It was a bright summer day, but the air was already tainted with smog. She dressed quickly, for she was to travel down to Oxford with her father. The university was giving him an honorary degree. He had never graduated, having decided to throw it all in and become an artist. Pretending not to care, Papa said it was a good chance to go down and see Phil, who was in his first year there. Margot wore her new dress of white lawn and a rice-straw hat she had trimmed with tiny pink roses. It looked much better without all her hair hanging down and so she pinned it up, her heart beating fast at her temerity.

'So it doesn't get all blown about on the train,' she told her father. 'Don't look so sad! I promise I'll let it down again tomorrow, when it's just us at home.'

Papa sighed, and looked hunched and melancholy. Margot slowly put up her hands and unpinned her hair, letting it fall down her back again.

Her father hated trains, and it was a sign of how much he wanted to go to Oxford that he had consented to travel in one. As they waited on the station, Papa fidgeted with his watch chain, and Margot knew he was wishing he were back in his painting smock, in the peace and silence of his studio.

A long hooting, a gush of steam, then the train came snorting into the station like a one-eyed black dragon, billowing clouds of smoke and spitting fiery sparks. Margot held on to her bonnet. Tendrils of hair whipped about her face. Her father's beard was blown sideways.

'For every train they build, I shall paint another angel,' her father declared.

'The world can never have enough angels,' Margot smiled.

She did not like trains either. They were so strong, so dangerous. She hated tunnels the most. Darkness dropping like a sack. She could only sit, holding her breath and counting, till at last the train burst back out into sunshine.

The graduation ceremony was at the Sheldonian Theatre, set in its own square and surrounded by immense stone busts of bearded men with strange staring eyes. Papa had to wear a scarlet gown with wide crimson sleeves that were, he said, just like a flamingo's wings. He looked tall and gaunt and old amongst all the young well-fed graduates, his beard already turning silver. It touched Margot's heart to see how uncomfortable he was.

They managed to find Phil in the crowd. A slim youth with a sensitive face and floppy dark hair, he had the same luminous blue-grey eyes as Margot and their mother. He gave her a quick slap on the back in greeting, and endured his father's gentle questioning about his poor grades with gritted teeth.

'I do not much care whether you are at the top or the bottom of your class,' Papa said, 'as long as you find something that you love to do, and do it with all of your heart, and to the very best of your ability. That is all that matters.'

'Yes, Papa,' Phil replied dutifully, but rolled an agonised eye at Margot as soon as his father turned away. 'I wish he wouldn't jaw at me so,' he whispered, as they went to find their places.

'You know he means well,' she whispered back. 'And that he's right!'

'That makes it worse,' Phil grumbled.

The award ceremony dragged on. Phil yawned ostentatiously. Margot elbowed him to be quiet. It was hot, and she was uncomfortably aware of a prickling of moisture along her hairline. She coiled her hair up and stuck in a few pins, just to get the weight of it off the back of her neck. Papa did not need to know.

Towards the end of the ceremony, a tall young man went to the lectern. He had curly fair hair, combed back from a high broad forehead, a straight nose, and a small moustache that he kept trying to make lie flat. His eyes were striking, being so pale a grey as to seem translucent.

It seemed the young man had won a prize for his poetry, and was to read it out to the crowd. Phil groaned, and Margot elbowed him again.

'Midway between the vintage and the spring, the apple-flower and apple-gathering …' the poem began. Margot listened intently. She loved poetry, and the young man's verse was full of marching rhythms and simple rhymes. 'Yet still they fought, while through the ridge of spears, flashed in their eyes and sounded in their ears …' he declaimed in a rolling Scottish brogue. 'Death, and about their feet and through their breath, Death, and above their heads the shadow of death …'

Margot must have made some small involuntary movement, because his eyes found hers. His voice faltered. For a moment, they stared at each other. Then he looked away, cleared his voice, and continued, '… While the swift continuous arrow flight, hailed on their armour and to left and right …'

'Look how red you are,' Phil whispered. He fanned her with his programme. 'Is it the heat or Mr Mackail's handsome countenance?'

'What's his name?' she whispered back.

'Jack Mackail. He's the prize hog of the year. Won just about everything. They say he's the most brilliant undergraduate in years. And he bowls like a demon.'

Margot sat back, her eyes still fixed on Jack Mackail's face. He looked her way again, and she was sure she saw colour creeping up his lean cheek. He lost his place, and had to look down at his pages. When he spoke again, his voice was not quite so sure of itself. '… What evil chance the coming days bring; what shape of terror; and the air grew chill …'

When he had finished, Margot clapped enthusiastically. He looked at her again, smiled, then smoothed down his moustache self-consciously. Afterwards, he came and greeted Phil, and asked him how he was getting on.

Phil stammered an eager response, then hastened to introduce Jack to his father. Margot waited quietly, listening as he and Papa talked books and art. To her relief, Jack liked Keats and Browning and Tennyson. Papa would never have forgiven him if he did not. Then Jack turned to Margot and put out his hand to shake. She put her hand in his. She could feel the warmth and strength of his fingers even through her gloves. Hot colour surged up her cheeks.

'Do you like poetry too?'

'I love it,' she dared to answer. 'Congratulations on winning the poetry prize.'

'Did you like my poem?' His gaze was intent on her face.

'I did. It ... it was very fine.'

'It was unadulterated rot,' he said. 'When I think of who won the Newdigate in the past ... John Ruskin ... Edward Arnold ... Oscar Wilde ... well, I can't believe they gave it to me.'

'You deserved it. It was wonderful.'

He smiled in gratitude. 'I must go. But perhaps ...'

She waited, her heart beating uncomfortably hard.

'Perhaps I shall see you again? Do you live in Oxford?'

'No. In Fulham. London.' In the back of beyond, she thought. No-one ever came to Fulham unless they had to.

'Perhaps I might see you there,' he said gravely, and at last released her hand. Margot tucked it inside her other, her palm tingling. He bowed and walked away, then turned and looked back at her.

Margot could not help smiling. He smiled back, lifted one hand, then disappeared into the crowd.

'He seems like a nice enough chap.' Papa looked after him. 'Said he'd like to come and see my studio.'

Margot bit her lip to hide her smile.

The summer passed slowly.

Papa fretted over his painting. He wanted almond blossoms, and it was too late in the season to find them anywhere. 'But you've painted them before,' Mammy said. 'Why can't you go and look at your last painting of Phyllis and Demophoön?'

Her voice was cold. Margot was surprised. Mammy was usually very patient when Papa began to fret. But then again, Margot remembered, there had been some scandal over that painting. It had a nude man in it, and the Old Water-Colour Society had refused to hang it. Papa had resigned, and never exhibited with them again. Indeed, he had exhibited nowhere for the next seven years. Perhaps Mammy was being so unsympathetic because she feared the same would happen again.

'You know I cannot do that,' Papa replied in a suppressed voice. 'I need real almond blossoms.'

'Then you must wait till next spring,' Mammy said, closing the conversation.

Papa was so unhappy he made himself ill. Mammy nursed him stoically, as she always did.

Margot was restless in a way she did not understand. She wanted to walk for miles, or climb a mountain, or dance all night.

One Sunday, Jack Mackail came for tea. As always, the house was full of visitors. Some came to see Papa's studio, others came nervously clutching their portfolios in the hope of impressing him. He never refused anyone for fear, he said, of turning away an angel unawares. That day, the Dutch painter Mr Tadema and his wife, Laura, and two daughters were among the guests. Margot knew she was meant to entertain the daughters, but her shyness defeated her. She sat silently, her teacup balanced on her lap, sneaking peeks at Jack but unable to find a word to say to him.

'Have you always wished to be an artist, Mr Jones?' Mrs Tadema asked. A tall thin redhead, she was a painter of some note herself.

Papa hated being asked such questions. 'I did not know what an artist was. I can tell you I was always drawing. I had no mother – she died when I was just six days old – and my papa never stopped grieving for her. Without a sister or a brother, always alone, I was never unhappy because I was always drawing.'

Mammy deftly turned the conversation back to the work of Mr and Mrs Tadema. Margot did not pay much attention until Mr Tadema said that he had recently been invited to go and see a mummy before it was ground down into paint.

'A mummy?' Margot asked. 'A real live Egyptian mummy?'

'It's not alive,' one of his daughters said loftily. 'It's been dead for centuries.'

Margot tried not to shudder.

'But it's really a mummy?' Jack asked, drawing closer.

'Yes, indeed,' Mr Tadema said.

'But why is it to be ground down? Into paint, you said?' Jack was puzzled.

'Well, yes. It's the key ingredient in Mummy Brown.'

Now Papa's attention had been caught. 'You mean, the paint? Mummy Brown paint?' As his guest nodded, Papa shrank back. His face was filled with horror. 'Are you telling me that my favourite shade of brown is made from ground corpses?'

Mr Tadema began to look troubled. 'Well. Yes.'

Papa got up and went at once to his studio at the end of the garden. When he came back, he carried a bent half-squeezed tube of Mummy Brown oil paint. 'We must bury the poor thing,' he said.

Margot at once jumped up. She was used to the funerals of small things. Birds. Hedgehogs. Frogs. 'I will get the spade.'

A solemn procession formed. The two Tadema girls were inappropriately amused. Jack, to his credit, was grave. A hole was dug. The paint tube was buried. Papa recited a poem by Christina Rossetti, Uncle Gabriel's melancholic and reclusive sister: 'When I am dead, my dearest, sing no sad songs for me. Plant thou no roses at my head nor shady cypress tree ...'

Margot dug up a daisy root and it was ceremoniously planted above the Mummy Brown, with a little cross made of sticks.

'When I came here to tea, I was not expecting to attend the funeral of a mummy,' Jack said in Margot's ear.

'Do not mock. My father takes the death of small things very seriously.'

'I did not think an Egyptian mummy was such a small thing.'

'It is now,' Margot said sadly.

'It is indeed. An ignominious end for one who might once have been a Pharaoh.'

Margot looked up at him in amazement. He had spoken her very thought. He was smiling at her, and she felt her colour rise. She ducked her head and moved away. They did not speak again that afternoon, though every time she looked at him it seemed as if he was looking at her. When it came time to leave, he took her hand. 'Thank you, Miss Jones, for a most ... *interesting* afternoon. What will happen next time I come?'

She raised her eyes to his. 'Why, anything might happen.'

He smiled. 'I hope so.'

That night, when she snuffed out her candle before going to bed, her mind was full of him.

She hardly thought of death at all.

2

Prick
Winter 1881

Margot could not speak of Jack to her parents.

They still thought her a child. If her father thought Jack had any interest in her, he would ban him from the house forever. Yet she longed to talk him over with someone, to confess these strange new feelings that fevered her blood.

At last, in early November, Margot went to London with her father, telling him she was going to meet May Morris for tea. Papa was silent in the hansom cab, his eyes fixed on the view outside the window. Margot knew he did not see the sandwich-board men, shouting out their advertisements, or the women with sacks tied over their clean white aprons plodding home from the market, carrying heavy baskets on their head. Cabs and carriages jostled for space on the road, their iron wheels clattering on the cobblestones, and a policeman was blowing his whistle.

Papa saw or heard none of it. He was within some other enchanted landscape, and dreaming of the strokes of paint that would bring it to glowing life.

Margot dropped her father at Little Campden House – the studio was in its garden – then went on to Kensington Gardens, where she poured out her heart to May as they walked the paths beside the lake, which gleamed under the pale cloud-spun sky. Little boys were trundling guys in wheelbarrows and begging for pennies, accompanied by excited girls with scarves wrapped crosswise over their bodies. It was Guy Fawkes Night, Margot remembered.

'I don't see what the trouble is,' May said. 'Of course, you're only fifteen but I remember Mammy saying that your mother was not much older when she became engaged to your father. And my mother was only seventeen when she met Papa and Uncle Gabriel.'

'My father would never allow me to get engaged! You know what he's like. He wants me to stay a little girl forever.'

'Well, yes … but you can't, can you?'

Margot sighed. 'He won't let me put my hair up.'

'Then cut it all off.'

'Oh, but I couldn't! Papa …'

'Stop being such a milksop,' May said sternly. 'Just because Uncle Ned loves the Middle Ages doesn't mean he has to act like a medieval father. It's the modern day, for heaven's sake. Cut your hair, or put it up if you like, and tell your papa that you plan to come into town every week to attend a lecture, or something. Then let this Jack of yours know …'

'But how am I supposed to do that?'

May was exasperated. 'Write him a note and ask him to join you. Or find out what he likes and just turn up there, pretending it's a coincidence.'

Margot stared at her friend in consternation. 'Is that what you do?'

A faint colour tinged May's skin. 'Well, no, of course not, because I never make a cake of myself over some stupid fellow. I've better things to do. Like go to lectures myself.' She gave Margot a quick, stiff-armed hug. 'Got to go! Good luck with it.'

Margot had been a fool to think May might understand. May had never been overcome with shyness in her whole life. She said just what she thought, without ever considering other people's feelings, or the rules of polite society. Margot thought it must be the result of having a radical as a father.

Her stomach was cramping, and she felt sick with anxiety. Slowly Margot walked back through the park, her boots crunching on the frosted grass. The trees were all black with soot, their bare branches rattling in the wind. The gilded weathervane on top of Kensington Palace gleamed brightly against the leaden sky, lit up by the last vivid streaks of light.

Margot was cold. Her mother had told her to put on her red flannel petticoats before she left the house, but Margot could not bear the thought of being seen in London in such fusty old-fashioned wear. She had worn only her usual white linen petticoats under her pale dress, and now she regretted her decision. The wind blew up her skirt, biting at her skin through her thin combinations. She looked at the other girls her age, in cuirass bodices and velveteen half-bustles, feathered hats held aloft by high coils of hair, hands tucked inside fur muffs. She must look such a child beside them, her hair hanging down her back, her dress cut plain as a Puritan's. Her mother disapproved of corsets mightily, being a dress reformer. She would never understand that Margot just wanted to be like the other girls.

The cramps worsened. Margot stopped, bending over, pressing one hand to her side. She noticed a stain on the lap of her dress. Red as a poppy. She stared at it uncomprehendingly. Had she cut herself? She did not remember being caught by anything sharp, and her dress was not torn. Then she felt something wet trickle down the inside of her leg.

Terror gripped her. Margot did not know what to do. Was she bleeding internally? Margot had heard about girls coughing blood into handkerchiefs before they died. Perhaps this was some peculiar manifestation of the dreaded consumption. Perhaps she had pierced herself somehow, touching herself in the dark of the night. Shame flamed through her.

Margot needed to find a water-closet. The Queen had built a public lavatory in Kensington Gardens to commemorate her husband's death, but Margot could not go there. She had a horror of such places.

She began to hurry to her father's studio.

The streets were filled with people, laughing and pushing, dressed in costume, their faces smeared with soot. Some hoisted chairs between them, or pushed barrows, filled with effigies made of old clothes stuffed with straw. Men carried flaming torches, their smoke trailing in the wind. Children threw down firecrackers. The bang and starburst of their explosions made Margot flinch. The air stank of gunpowder. A bonfire had been built in the churchyard. Black figures danced around it, throwing on old rubbish and broken chairs. An effigy was tied to a pole at the top of the bonfire, fiery sparks hissing about him. His lopsided face was drawn with a wide grin that seemed to leer at her through the darkness. The children pranced about, carrying smoking sticks and chanting:

> Pray remember
> The Fifth of November
> Gunpowder Treason and Plot
> For I know of no reason
> Why Gunpowder Treason
> Should ever be forgot.
> Holla, boys! Holla, boys! Huzza!

Margot knew she should have been safe at home. Her mother would be anxiously watching for her. But she could not bear the thought of stepping into the firelit street where anyone might see the bloom of blood on her skirt, or sitting in a hansom cab, feeling her life fluid soak into the seat beneath her. All she could think of was reaching the safety of her father's arms.

A dark street. Creeping fingers of fog.

Margot stole down the pavement, listening for any footfall behind her. The last smears of sunset were gone, though she could see a flare of orange above the wall.

The gleam of light through high Gothic windows. Black twigs silhouetted.

She opened the gate and slipped inside. The garden was winter-bare, brittle with frost. Her steps made no sound on the path, deadened by the carpet of fallen rotting leaves.

The studio was a Gothic-style folly built in the garden of a seventeenth-century manor house that had once housed the servants of a German princess. Its most remarkable feature was the huge arched windows all along the southern wall that allowed light to flood inside during the day. Margot's heart had lifted at the sight of those windows glowing golden through the dusk. Her father had not yet left for the day. He must be painting by lamplight.

She let herself in the door and climbed the shadowy stairs to the upper floor. Papa was using one of two studios, set side by side on the southern side of the house. On the other side of the corridor were dressing rooms for the models, a water-closet, and a little kitchen where water could be boiled for tea. Margot rushed to the water-closet, cleaning herself up as best she could with the sheets of soft paper kept there. The seat of her combinations was badly stained, and her petticoats too, back and front. Margot was so afraid she found it hard to catch her breath. She washed herself, and tried to blot away the stains. Her hands were shaking and she feared her father would leave without knowing she was here. She could not hide in here all night. So she took a deep breath, gathered up her damp, discoloured skirts and went back along the corridor and into her father's studio.

So many canvases were stacked against the wall, they made a little antechamber just inside the door, hiding the rest of the studio from her sight. Margot could only see their colour-daubed linen sides, which together made up two short walls of smeared colour, like paintings seen through tear-filled eyes.

Mid-step, Margot halted.

'Why do you torment me so?' her father was saying in tones of anguish. 'You know I cannot run away with you.'

'Oh yes, I know,' a woman's voice said mockingly. 'The faithful little wife, the beloved little daughter.'

'I cannot ruin their lives.'

'And so you choose to ruin mine?'

'Maria, you know I don't want to hurt you. But it's been so long ... so much has happened ... can't this be enough for us?'

'An hour here, an hour there, always afraid we shall be caught? No, it's not enough for me. I want more, Ned. I want all of you.'

Margot crept forward, and peeped about the edge of the canvases.

A naked woman stood in the centre of the room. Her mahogany-red hair tumbled down her pale, slender form. Her arms were stretched out as if to embrace someone. Her breasts were small, the nipples hard and pebbled.

Margot's father was standing in front of a tall canvas, a paintbrush in one hand, a wooden palette in the other. His smock was daubed with paint of all colours, and his grey hair was rumpled. On the canvas was the painted shape of the naked woman, her body rising from the cleft of an almond tree, a froth of delicate blossoms lightly sketched in above her head and around her body. In her arms, the woman was clutching the naked form of a young man, turned away from her as if trying to wrest himself free. The man was only lightly sketched too, with chalk, but every line of his body spoke of frenzied emotion.

Margot recognised the story her father was painting. Phyllis, daughter of the King of Thrace, had fallen in love with Demophoön, son of Theseus. He had to leave her but promised he would return. When he failed to keep his promise, Phyllis hanged herself. The gods transformed her into an almond tree. When at last he did return, and realised the cost of his faithlessness, Demophoön was overcome with remorse and embraced the tree, which burst into bloom. Her father called the painting *The Tree of Forgiveness.*

She recognised the woman too. Her melancholy face and great dark eyes looked out from dozens of her father's paintings. Her name was Madame Zambaco. She and her cousins had once been the toast of London, called the Three Graces.

Margot had never seen her in the flesh before.

Nor had she ever seen anyone naked. She could not imagine standing like that, posed so suggestively, her hair flung back, every secret of her body exposed to another's gaze. She knew, of course, about life painting. Her father must have seen many nudes before. But somehow Margot had never expected to see it herself. Her throat was dry, her heart pounding, and the snarled feeling in the pit of her stomach had returned, worse than ever.

'Do you not find me beautiful anymore?'

'You know that I do.'

'I'm not a fresh-faced girl any longer.'

'You are the most beautiful woman I have ever seen.'

'More beautiful even than your sweet little wife? What about that daughter of yours? She must be almost a woman now.'

Her father put down his paintbrush and turned away.

'I'm sorry,' Madame Zambaco cried. 'I do not know why I keep picking away at the scab. It's just that I love you so, and want to be with you.' She went across the room to him, and wound her arms about his neck, and pressed her lithe naked body against his, kissing him on the mouth.

Papa kissed her back. Madame Zambaco put her hand to the fork of his trousers. He groaned.

Margot jerked back. Pain pierced her finger. Her hand had been resting on the linen-bound edge of a painting. A flax splinter had driven into her skin, sharp as a thorn. She could not dig it all out. Then she heard her father grunt. It sounded like he was in pain. Margot looked to see what was happening, and could not look away.

Madame Zambaco was sitting in the cradle of her father's legs. His mouth was on her bare breast. Her head was flung back, her dark-red hair swaying. She cried out. Margot realised they were gasps of pleasure, realised what her father and that woman were doing.

Margot jerked away. Somehow she managed to open the door and stumble out. She ran through the garden, branches catching her pale skirt and tearing it. The streets outside were filled with people, laughing and singing. Their soot-streaked faces seemed to jeer at her. She pushed her way through, choking with tears. At last she reached the high street, and hailed a cab. As the horse clopped along, Margot tried to calm herself. She could not catch her breath.

At last she got home. Her mother was white with worry. Margot fell into her arms. 'Oh, Mammy, I'm dying,' she wept, spreading out her stained skirt.

Her mother drew her close. 'You're not dying, my darling. It's just the curse. It means you are becoming a woman.'

'I don't want to, I don't want to.'

Her mother tucked her up in bed with a hot-water bottle. 'I'm so sorry,' Mammy whispered. 'I should have told you. Prepared you. I thought there was time ... but you are growing up so fast.'

Margot turned her face away. Her mother kissed her gently, and tiptoed out. Firelight gleamed on the frost-starred windows. Her counterpane was stuffed with goose feathers, her room smelt of roses. Margot was warm and safe at last.

She shut her eyes. She wanted to stay like this forever.

3

The Coffin in the Attic
Winter 1881

Outside the air was thick with mist, so that the world seemed mantled and asleep. The fire in her room had sunk low. Margot kept her head tucked down under her coverlet, making for herself a little warm shelter where no-one could see her face.

Margot was thinking of the very first Christmas she could remember. She had been six and her brother Phil had been eleven. Her cousins Rudyard and Ambrose and the two Morris girls had come for tea. They had played together in the snow all afternoon. When dusk had fallen, they had been called in, their hands stinging, their faces bright with the cold, stamping the snow from their boots. The big hall was dark, lit only by firelight and the little candles glinting on the Christmas tree. The mothers had taken off their coats and hung them up, and the children sat on the hearth before the fire, toasting chestnuts in a big pan. Aunty Janey was lying on a sofa, looking thin and pale and sad. Mammy and her sister Agnes sat nearby, making chains from golden paper to hang on the tree. The men were drinking hot punch and smoking cigars, blowing the smoke out through the cracked-open window. Papa came to play a magic-lantern show for them, and Margot was utterly thrilled to see a brightly coloured story unfolding for them in mid-air.

Then all the candles were doused, and the guard set before the fire, making the room as dark as a cave. Papa poured brandy into a big bowl, and flung handfuls of raisins in, then he lit a long wooden taper and set it to the liquid in the bowl. With a great whoosh, an eerie blue light sprang up. Margot cried out in fear, and her brother shushed her.

Then the men all gathered around, and tried to snatch raisins out of the burning bowl and throw them into their mouths to extinguish the dancing flames. Their faces were all lit up from below with blue fire. As they laughed and grimaced with pain and threw the blue-burning raisins into their mouths, their fingertips blazed blue too, and their cheeks glowed for a moment like corpse-lanterns. They looked like demons. Margot was frightened and began to cry. Her father turned to her and held out his arms. But the strange blue light still played over his hollow cheeks and shadowed eyes. For the first time ever, Margot did not run to him, but shrank back and fled to her mother, burying her face in her skirts.

Margot's bedroom door creaked open. She lay still, her eyes shut, pretending to be asleep.

'How are you feeling, little one?' her father whispered.

She did not answer. Papa bent and put his hand on her brow, smoothing back her hair. She did not respond. After a moment, he crept out again.

Margot did not know how she was ever going to be able to forgive her father. Grief surged up in her again, leaving her throat thick and her eyes burning.

She had not wanted to get out of bed for days now. The doctor had come, and told Mammy that she was suffering from green sickness. He had prescribed a brisk walk every morning, a diet high in meat, and a pint of dark beer each evening. But Margot did not have the strength to get out of bed, she would not eat the flesh of animals, and her mother never permitted her to drink alcohol, and so the doctor's advice was of no use to them.

Green sickness sounded somehow poetical and out of the ordinary, like she had been touched by fairies. Margot imagined her skin slowly being tinted green as her blood turned to sap, her hair writhing like tendrils of a vine, pale flowers blossoming from her pores. Would her father paint her as a dryad, entrapped within a tree?

Looking back on her childhood, she understood so much she had never realised before. Why her parents often seemed so sad. Why Mammy never went on holidays with Papa. Why she had been so cross about Papa wanting almond blossoms out of season.

Margot remembered her father writing to her from Paris the Easter before she had turned twelve: '*We saw a punch-theatre in the Champs Elysees – we paid a penny and went into a ring of people and sat on chairs and saw such a funny play and laughed till we screamed – and wanted your Mammy and you with us to laugh too. I think we shall come back, or is it so nice for you two women without us that you don't want us yet? Tell that dear Mammy that her hard-earned money flies so fast – I don't know how – by the end of the day our pockets are quite emptied ... I think next year I must bring you, and your Mammy must come – tell her she must make up her mind to travel and see bright things, else she'll forget what the world looks like ...*'

It made Margot feel a little better thinking about all the funny letters and drawings her father had made for her. Once he had drawn her a picture of her walking along hand in hand with an angel, and told her it was her guardian angel. She had a box full of his sketches – countless drawings of ducks, wombats, pigs, elephants, chubby babies and fat women in strong winds. She got her box out and looked through them again, smiling a little. But then she remembered how he had groaned as Madame Zambaco put her hand between his legs. Her stomach lurched. She pushed away all the drawings, not caring how they crumpled, and lay down again. She shut her eyes.

The door opened softly again. Margot heard her father's footstep, then felt a warm weight settle in the crook of her legs. Papa had brought in her cat. A lump in her throat. How she wished he would not be so thoughtful. It would be so much easier to hate him if he were not kind.

The hours drifted past. Her cat purred and kneaded her leg with the tips of his claws.

Margot tried to think of happy things.

On her thirteenth birthday, her father had given her thirteen silver bangles, drawing them out one by one from where he'd hidden them in his bed. One in a fold of the counterpane, one under the pillow, one hidden by his side, one tucked inside his slipper, one inside the pocket of his dressing-gown. Margot had been delighted with just one bangle, and was amazed to see more and more pretty tinkling things conjured from everywhere. How her father had laughed at her face of astonishment.

She remembered her first days at school, when she had cried because her mother always made her dress in such plain unfashionable gowns and bonnets. Her father had put his arm about her and drawn her close, saying solemnly, 'There will always be people telling you how you shall think and act and dress, my little, and what you are to say and how you are to live, down to the tiniest trifle, meaning that you are to think and act and dress as they do; and some sort of penalty you must pay all your life for differing from them. But you must never bow to their tyranny. You must be brave, my bright blue girl, and stand up to them.'

And so, for a while at least, Margot had thought herself most gallant, going to school every day in a shabby grey dress and a bonnet like a Quaker. She did her best not to long for a Dolly Varden dress and flower-trimmed hat like all the other girls wore.

At least the Morris girls had been at school with her, although they were a few years ahead. Jenny and May had never worn a corset or had cherry-red ribbons in their hair either. And Margot had to admit the three girls could not have played so many wild games or climbed so many trees if they had been dressed the way little girls were meant to be dressed.

When Margot was eight years old, Phil and Jenny had been thirteen and May a year younger. The four of them had formed a Secret Society. Phil had blacked all their faces and they had all sworn an oath to the Leader, who was, of course, Phil. He had given them all offices. Jenny was the Captain, May was the Secretary, and Margot the Standard Bearer. They made up a secret alphabet, and Phil wrote his orders out in invisible ink, which could only be read after the paper was held over a candle flame. The girls had to march up and down and carry out their Leader's orders.

Later in the day Phil had decided to dissolve the meeting and Jenny had said, forgetting her place, 'Go to it, old fellow.'

Phil had been most displeased. The next day, he stripped Jenny of her office and downgraded her to the rank of Standard Bearer. She had to suffer fifteen lashes from a whip made of a stick and six lengths of string, and then Phil locked her in the coal cellar for fifteen minutes.

May went to the cellar door and whispered, 'Shall we lock the leader out and mutiny?'

But Jenny stayed loyal and reported her sister to the Leader. Phil only laughed, though, and said he had told Captain May to say those words to try to tempt her. Jenny had been most upset with both Phil and May. But then Phil rewarded her for her trustworthiness by restoring her to the role of Captain (though he insisted on adding a footnote that the title of Captain must never be confounded with that of Leader).

The next time the Morris girls came to visit, the four children had hoisted the ladder to the attic and climbed up. It was a vast and gloomy space, filled with iron-bound trunks, wooden crates, unwanted furniture covered with dust sheets, a box of Christmas decorations, hobby-horses on sticks, and dirty dolls with broken faces.

Margot had found a long wooden box shaped just like a coffin, which frightened her.

'It's the coffin of Uncle Gabriel's dead wife,' Phil whispered. 'She died a long time ago and was buried in the graveyard, but then he had her dug up to get his poems. And she's haunted Uncle Gabriel ever since.'

Margot stared at the box in horror.

Phil lowered his voice even more. 'They say that when they dug her up, she hadn't rotted away and lay there looking just like she was asleep instead of dead, and her hair had grown and grown till it wrapped her up like a mummy, and so Uncle Gabriel couldn't bear to bury her again, and so they brought her coffin here and hid it in the attic, but she cannot rest, and so whenever you lie in bed and hear the floorboards creaking above your head it's her walking up and down, up and down, dragging her hair behind her and trying to find a way to get out. One day she'll find a crack or mouse-hole, and then she'll creep downstairs and look for you so she can suck out all your blood . . .'

'Rubbish!' May said stoutly, and put her arm around Margot who was weeping with terror. 'Don't listen to a word he says, Margot, he's just trying to scare you.'

Phil went red with rage. 'Insubordination!' he cried. 'I'll lock you both up in the attic for punishment. And I'll leave you there all night.'

'No, you won't,' May cried. 'Because I resign from the Society right now. And so does Margot!'

'You can't resign!'

'I can and I do,' she replied. 'Father says we have the right of free will and so I'm exercising it. So is Margot and so is Jenny.'

She marched back to the trapdoor, her arm around Margot, and took her down to the kitchens for hot milk and apples roasted in the fire. Jenny followed, after mouthing a silent apology to Phil. After a while he came down too, very red and very cross, but May said to him firmly, 'You're meant to look after your sister, not make her cry. She's only a littley, you know.'

'Too little to explore attics,' Phil said sneeringly, but took the poker out of May's hand and showed her how to hold it so the apple did not burn. The Secret Society was ended, however, and two years later Jenny got sick and their childhood games were over forever.

Margot had never forgotten the coffin in the attic. She terrified herself many a cold, windy night by imagining the white-clad ghost in the attic, trying to get out. Sometimes she dreamt of it. The lid slowly creaking back. The figure within sitting up. Sometimes just bones and hair. Sometimes a ghoulish face and staring eyes. Hands reaching for her. Margot would scream with all her strength, but make no sound. She'd wake, heart thudding, sure someone stood over her in the darkness.

After that, Phil loved to scare her with spooky tales of headless horsemen and demon dogs, cold hands that clutched your shoulder at night, ghost ships that sailed over the marshes, spinning wheels that turned with no hand or foot to guide them. Sometimes he would wait in the shadows at the top of the stairs, just so he could jump out and terrify her with clawed hands and sepulchral groans.

Margot had been afraid of ghosts ever since, and scared of all dead things too. She wept if she ever found a limp mouse in the pantry, or a nestling fallen to the ground, and she and her father would bury their carcasses in the garden, chanting poetry over the tiny graves. She always hated the museum with its cloth-wrapped mummies, and bones and butterflies in glass cases. Soon it seemed as if life itself frightened her. She did not like to go too far from home, or meet too many strangers.

She thought again of Maria Zambaco, and the way she had stood flaunting her nakedness in the bright lamplight. She looked like a woman who was afraid of nothing. Margot wished she had never seen her, or heard her father's groan. She wished that she could turn back the clock and go back to being a child again, safe in her father's arms.

But it was impossible. Margot could not undo the past. She could not stop time.

Burrowing deeper into her bed, Margot wished she could just disappear.

4

Stricken
Spring 1882

'Mother! Where are you?'

At the sound of her daughter's voice, Janey gave a little guilty start and hastily tucked away Gabriel's letters.

'What is it, May? Is it Jenny? Is she all right?'

'Yes, she's fine,' May said impatiently. 'I just wanted to show you my design for Father's book. Look. I've done a tree with crimson flowers on it, and the title on the scroll, and then acanthus leaves all around. I thought I'd do it on an indigo background, like your daisy hangings, only in silk, not serge.'

'It's beautiful. Your father will love it.' Janey examined the sketch May had thrust under her nose.

'I want to start work on it this afternoon. Shall we go and sit in the garden? The sun is shining for the first time in forever, and I think we should take advantage. I have lectures all week so it might be my only chance.'

'As long as you wrap up warmly, I don't want you taking cold. Where is Jenny? You didn't leave her alone, did you?'

'Mother, she's fine. I've only left her for a moment. She's writing a story.'

Janey hurried out the door and down the corridor. 'May, you must be more careful. You know you can't leave her alone for a second.'

May gave an exasperated sigh. 'It was only for a moment.'

'Even a moment is dangerous.'

'Jenny hates everyone hanging over her and watching her all the time.'

'It can't be helped. Please, May. I must be able to trust you.'

Janey rushed down the stairs and into the drawing room. Jenny sat at a little writing desk between the windows. She looked up as Janey rushed in, and her expression darkened.

'Nothing's wrong, Mother,' she said. 'As you can see, I am quite fine.'

'That's good … I'm glad … you know I worry.' Janey was a little out of breath.

'I wish you wouldn't.'

'I can't help it.'

Jenny gave an exaggerated sigh, and turned back to her writing. May had followed her mother in, and now stood watching, her drawing crushed in her hands.

'It's a lovely day,' Janey said. 'May thought we might sit out in the garden.'

'I'm quite comfortable here.' Jenny did not look up from her page.

'Oh. Very well.' Janey sat down at a nearby chair and took up her embroidery.

'There's no need for you to stay inside. Go and sit in the garden if you want to.' Jenny's hand was clenched on her pen.

'No. There's no need. I'll stay here.' Janey set a careful stitch.

Jenny threw down her pen. 'Oh, all right then. Let's go and sit in the garden. What does it matter anyway?' Her pen left a large blotch of ink on her paper, obscuring the words she had been writing. Jumping up, she ran from the room. Janey quickly gathered up her sewing and made to follow.

'She feels like she's a prisoner,' May said, picking up her embroidery hoop and basket of silks.

'What choice do I have?' Janey said wearily. 'She'd feel more like a prisoner if she was committed to an asylum, wouldn't she?'

*

Janey had feared, at one point, that she would lose everything because of her love for Gabriel.

Topsy had separated from her, renting her a small house at Turnham Green while he stayed at Queen Square, only coming on weekends to see the girls. He had thrown Gabriel out of Kelmscott Manor, taken control of the Firm, and resigned from his father's old company. It was as if he had made some decision about what he was prepared to put up with. Janey feared he meant to divorce her. It would be the ruin not only of her, but of her daughters too.

Janey was still seeing Gabriel whenever she could, but he would not give up the chloral for her. His need for it was greater than his need for her. He had showed her the rows of empty chloral bottles that he had drunk, and she had thought he must be making grim fun of her. Worst of all, he washed it down with whisky, gulping down a glassful as soon as he rose from bed in the morning.

Janey hated a drunkard. Her mother had been one and her father too. She could not bear the smell that rose from his skin, or the blast of his breath when he coughed, or the way his words slurred. She begged him to stop.

He would not.

And Janey knew that he was still supporting his mistress in town. She suffered agonies of jealousy, and would not believe Gabriel when he said, 'I love only you.'

He painted her as the goddess Astarte. Six foot tall, her arms and shoulders bare, her dark hair loose and heavy on either side of her thin face, her red lips swollen as if with rough kisses. One golden belt encircled her hips, and another was bound just under her breasts. Her strong hands toyed with each, as if she was about to untie them and step forth naked. Gabriel wrote a poem to accompany the painting. 'Her twofold girdle clasps the infinite boon of bliss ...'

Then Gabriel painted her fourteen-year-old daughter May as the angels standing behind her, faces upturned to the sky in ecstasy, carrying torches whose swirling smoke created the shape of a heart.

It was powerful, challenging and exceedingly erotic. Gabriel sold the painting for over two thousand pounds, the most he had ever been paid. Janey felt uncomfortable. It was impossible, she felt, for any man to gaze at that painting and not feel a frisson. She remembered stories of Gabriel's clients hanging his paintings in private rooms, for private viewings with other gentlemen. She imagined such gentlemen, gazing at her and her daughter, perhaps sliding a hand inside their trouser pocket.

So Janey had broken with Gabriel.

Gabriel did not believe her. He thought she had been listening to lies about him.

'You cannot leave me, Janey,' he had said, clasping both her hands. 'Not now that we have finally found each other. Please don't leave me.'

She had tried to tear herself away.

He had caught her. 'Tell me you do not love me, and I'll let you go.'

But it was not true. Janey loved him with all her heart. She could only shake her head and say, 'I'm sorry, I'm sorry.'

Gabriel thought she would come back to him, once he was well again. But he had only got sicker.

Then, like lightning out of a blue sky, everything had changed.

And Janey knew she could never go to Gabriel again.

Jenny had always been a bright, curious child.

She had her nose in a book all the time, and loved to write stories. For a while, she had edited a homemade magazine called *The Scribbler* which contained a range of writings from her and May, and the Jones children, and their cousin Rudyard, and other literary-minded friends. She studied so hard her teachers talked about her trying for a university degree at the new women's college that had recently opened in Cambridge. Janey was filled with wonderment at her clever daughter. To think that Janey's mother could not write her name, and yet Janey's daughter would go to university.

Then, one bright summer's day, Topsy and Janey and the two girls had gone for a picnic by the river. Jenny was fifteen, and May a year younger. They had hired a boat and rowed about on the Thames, throwing bread to the swans and fishing with hand-held lines. The sun had dazzled on the water, so that Janey had to hold up a parasol to shelter her eyes. Jenny knelt on the wooden seat, leaning forward to see what May was dragging up from the depths. Suddenly Jenny lost her balance and fell forward, striking her head on the gunwale. She toppled into the water and sank at once, her limbs flailing the water into brown foam.

Topsy tried to reach her, almost tipping them all into the river. Janey and May held him steady, crying out to Jenny. When her head did not break the water, Topsy dragged off his coat and plunged into the river. For a long awful moment both were gone. Then Topsy's head broke free. Jenny lay, limp and unconscious, in his arms. He managed to swim to shore, and dragged Jenny on to the bank. Wielding one oar each, Janey and May struggled to bring the boat about.

When Janey reached her daughter's side, she thought at first that Jenny was dead. Her face was colourless, her eyelids bruised with shadows. Topsy turned her on to her side, and water gushed from her mouth. Somehow they managed to get her home, water dripping from her sodden dress and boots, and found a doctor. He thought she had fainted, perhaps from studying too hard, and recommended rest.

A few days later, Janey and Topsy and the two girls were eating dinner when one of Jenny's arms suddenly stiffened, knocking over her glass. Her body twisted and jerked, then she fell, slamming her head into the sideboard. Her body shuddered and shook most strangely. Janey and Topsy tried to hold her still, but she thrashed under their hands like a fresh-caught eel. One hand caught Janey a glancing blow across the jaw. One foot juddered spasmodically.

Gradually the tremors subsided. Jenny lay still, her eyes twitching under their lids, one finger jerking. Janey's heart was racing, her breath coming as unevenly as if she had just run upstairs. Topsy was ashen. May stood nearby, her hands at her mouth, her eyes dark with shock.

'What is it, what's wrong?' Janey cried.

Topsy crooned his daughter's name, brushing the heavy hair away from her face. She looked dazed and vacant, and did not respond. He helped her sit up. She gazed about her, bewildered, then put up one hand to touch the back of her head. It was a few minutes before she seemed able to talk, or understand what had happened.

Janey helped her daughter to bed, tucked her in with a hot-water bottle, gave her water to drink, a lavender-scented handkerchief to hold. Janey hardly knew what she was doing. She felt strange and disconnected, as if her limbs would not quite work properly.

Topsy had gone out to fetch the doctor. After he examined Jenny, he took Topsy aside. Janey waited in a fever of anxiety outside the study door. When at last the doctor left, looking very sombre, Janey went in hesitantly.

Topsy was weeping.

'She has epilepsy,' he said roughly. 'The doctor says we need to send her to an asylum.'

Janey's knees weakened. She sank into a chair. 'No. No.'

'She'll never have a normal life. She won't be able to marry or have children. She can't go to university. The doctor says the seizures cannot be predicted or controlled. He's given me the name of an asylum in Kensington ...'

'No!' Janey struck her hands against the chair arms. 'No, I won't have it.'

Topsy scrubbed his hands through his hair. 'You want to keep her at home?'

'Yes. Of course. We must.'

He dashed his hand across his eyes. 'Are you sure? I must say I cannot bear the thought ...'

'Jenny will stay at home,' she said, trying to steady her voice.

Topsy gazed at her in gratitude. 'Thanks, old chap,' he said huskily. The highest compliment he could give.

That night Janey could not sleep, tortured by the fear that she had somehow brought this terrible affliction upon Jenny. It was the first of many sleepless nights.

The seizures came without warning. Once Jenny fell down the stairs and ended up with a badly bruised face and a twisted knee. Another time she stumbled while carrying a tray loaded with a steaming teapot and teacups. She burned her hand and arm badly and broke all the china. Only a few days later she fell heavily while standing on a chair to reach a book on a high shelf. Running to her, lifting her up from the ground, Janey hurt her back. She paid no attention at all to her own pain, only cradled her jerking daughter in her arms and tried to wipe away the blood pouring from a cut on her forehead.

Janey could never rest. Any sudden noise or cry brought her running. Sometimes it was another fit. Sometimes it was just children at play in the street, or a servant dropping a hearth-brush. Either way, Janey would startle like a hunted animal, her pulse accelerating.

The doctor prescribed bromide for Jenny, a type of sedative. It made her slow and stupid. She no longer read much, or wrote very many stories, or climbed trees, or practised dance steps with her sister. She sat, staring into space, her hands limp. Until the next fit came upon her, and she fell again, convulsing, as if stricken with lightning.

Janey would let no-one else care for her daughter.

It was her punishment.

The afternoon wore away, Janey and May keeping themselves busy with their embroidery and Jenny staring sullenly into space. She had grown podgy and round-shouldered since her diagnosis, and her eyes had a vacant look. She paid no attention to May's chatter about her studies at the South Kensington School of Art, and did not laugh when her sister called the Queen Mrs Brown. Janey was sorry she had made her anxiety too obvious, and tried to coax Jenny out of her sulks.

'I can have the lap desk brought out for you if you like,' Janey said.

Jenny shrugged. 'What's the point?'

'If you'd like to finish what you were writing.'

Jenny made no response.

'Were you working on a new story? I'd love to read it.'

'I'm not a child, Mother. You do not need to pretend interest in what I do.'

Janey was hurt. 'I'm not pretending. Please show me.'

Jenny jerked one shoulder. 'It's not worth showing.'

'I'm sure that's not true.'

Jenny got up so abruptly her chair fell over backwards. Janey was on her feet at once, ready to rush to her side.

'Just leave me alone,' Jenny said in a voice of suppressed tears. She ran into the house.

Janey bent and picked up her fallen embroidery, making sure the fine linen was not stained by grass. She began to follow her daughter into the house. 'Mother, just leave her be,' May said. 'You'll hear soon enough if she has a fit.'

Janey did not answer. She went quietly up the stairs and stood for a while outside Jenny's door. She could hear her daughter sobbing. She went down the hall and into her own room, sitting on her bed. A feeling of suffocation. Head pounding. Back aching. She took out her letters and poems from Gabriel, and lay back on the bed, undoing the ribbon and unfolding them one by one, reading all her favourite lines.

I have just kissed your handwriting, the most welcome thing in the world that I could have seen today …

… my deep regard for you – a feeling far deeper (though I know you never believed me) than I have entertained towards any other living creature at any time of my life. Would that circumstances had given me the power to prove this, for proved it wd. have been …

I really feel, seeing you so little, as if I must seem neglectful and careless of all you have to endure. But I hope you believe that it is never absent from my thoughts for a moment and that I never cease to long to be near you and doing whatever might be to distract and amuse you. To be with you and wait on you and read to you is absolutely the only happiness I can find or conceive in this world, dearest Janey ...

Janey lifted the letters to her lips and kissed his handwriting, as he had once kissed hers.

She remembered Gabriel as she had first seen him, handsome and laughing and telling her she was a rare beauty and that he must paint her. And then she remembered how she had last seen him, hobbling on a stick, his eyes pouched and sunken, his hands palsied.

It was cruel.

His last portrait of her had been another Proserpina. The eighth time he had drawn her as the goddess of spring trapped in the Underworld. In this last version, however, he painted her with Lizzie's auburn hair. It was as if he could not remember who was who.

It hurt so much.

If only things could have been different.

Janey lay on her soft four-poster bed, hung with richly embroidered cloths. There was a thick Oriental carpet on the floor, and a beautiful old gilded jug and bowl on her washstand. On the wall was one of Gabriel's most beautiful drawings of her. The curtains were open, showing a view of the garden and the vivid flowers of the tulip tree.

Janey would have given it all up if she could once again be a barefoot girl selling violets on the streets of Oxford, with her life before her and the chance to put her arms about Gabriel and never let him go. Looking back at her life, it seemed one long chain of mistakes and misunderstandings.

Yet here she was, a rich man's wife, in a house any sensible woman would envy.

She and Topsy had moved to this Georgian brick mansion after Jenny's diagnosis. They had needed room for servants to help with Jenny's care, and privacy where Jenny could be kept away from the stares and sniggers of the world. Epilepsy was considered a social shame by most people. Akin to idiocy, lunacy, catalepsy. If Jenny's condition was known, May might never be able to marry. They had to keep it secret.

The house had wonderful views over the river to Hammersmith Bridge, a coach-house where Topsy had set up his spinning-wheels and looms, a big garden and orchard, a glasshouse. It had once belonged to George MacDonald, who had written his beautiful fairytales *At the Back of the North Wind* and *The Princess and the Goblin* whilst living there. Topsy liked to think some of his fantastical imagination would rub off on him. The house had been called The Retreat, but Topsy thought it sounded too much like an asylum and changed its name to Kelmscott House, to link it with the other house that lay on the Thames one hundred and twenty miles away.

Topsy was busier than ever with work. There had been an arsenic scare, which culminated in Queen Victoria stripping all the wallpaper out of Buckingham Palace after a guest had complained of headaches and nightmares from sleeping in a room with green walls. The public had, of course, followed suit and sales of Morris & Co wallpaper had plummeted. It infuriated Topsy, who stormed about tearing at his hair and offering to eat a pound of the stuff to prove it wasn't poisonous. The Firm had to issue statements declaring they had already switched to arsenic-free dyes and paints, only to find that many of their products did, indeed, still contain arsenic.

Janey could not help wondering if Topsy's wallpapers were the cause of her own aches and pains and illnesses.

She never said a word, though.

That too was her punishment.

Janey became aware of feet pounding on the stairs, her name being shouted.

It was like being touched with a live wire. She was on her feet, the letters thrust under her pillow, her feet running towards the floor. 'Jenny!' she cried. 'What has happened? Is she hurt?'

Topsy was hurtling up the stairs before her, a telegram in his hand. His grey curly mop was wild, his face wet with tears.

She had only ever seen him weep once before.

'Oh God,' Janey whispered. 'What has happened?'

'He's dead,' Topsy wept. 'Oh, Janey, he's dead.'

Janey did not need to ask who.

The world tilted. She sank to her knees, her skirts ballooning about her. She stared without seeing before her.

Gabriel was dead.

5

Love-in-a-Mist
Spring–Autumn 1882

'It is like seeing a colossus come crashing down,' Ned said sadly.

'It's left a hole in the world that will not be filled in a hurry,' Topsy said.

The two men were sitting in the garden at the Grange, drinking tea. Georgie sat with them, her darning in her lap. It was a bright, brisk day, with daffodils tossing their yellow heads and a chaffinch chirping in the budding apple boughs. Georgie wore a warm woollen jacket over her dress, but was bareheaded. Ned was in his usual loose smock, daubed with paint, while Topsy was dressed like a sailor in a rough serge coat and loose trousers. His hands were woad-blue from his latest experiment in dyeing wool and silk.

'I went a few times to visit him, but it was just unbearable,' Ned said. 'It was like he was a ghost already.'

'Such a waste,' Topsy said. He went to say something else, then thought better of it, closing his mouth firmly over the words. Georgie knew that he felt a great deal of bitterness over Gabriel's betrayal of him, and a kind of grief over the tarnishing of his idol. He stood up. 'I had better get back to work. Thanks for tea, old chap.'

'Good to see you, Tops,' Ned said, standing up. His thoughts were already turning back to his painting.

'I'll walk you out,' Georgie said.

She went with Topsy to the garden gate, then asked him quietly, her hand on the latch, 'How is Jenny?'

'Worse. Much worse.' Topsy kicked at the damp ground with the heel of his boot. 'She's having seizures nearly every day now. When you see it … well, you can understand why they used to think epileptics were possessed by demons.'

'I'm so sorry. Is there nothing they can do?'

'No. I'd do anything … anything …' He stopped himself again, his face screwing up with the effort. 'It's all my damned fault, Georgie. She got it from me. How can I forgive myself?'

Georgie was surprised. 'But you don't have epilepsy, Topsy. Do you?'

'My mother had it … and I … damn it, sometimes I lose all control … I don't know where the hell I am or what I am saying …'

'You mustn't blame yourself,' Georgie said, giving his arm a squeeze.

He sighed. 'Who else am I to blame?'

God, Georgie thought but did not say.

'And what of Margot? Is she any better?'

Georgie thought of her beautiful, delicate daughter, who felt everything so intensely. 'I'm hoping she'll start feeling better now that spring is here. It was such a long, dark, hard winter, wasn't it?' She heard the melancholy in her voice, and tried to smile.

Topsy nodded. 'Indeed, I feel it's been an evil year. So much war, so much death. It's not just Gabriel. The troubles in Ireland … the Tsar being assassinated and the American President too … and even some crazy damned fool shooting at the Queen … because she did not like his poetry. It's madness!'

'Perhaps this year will be better.'

'I feel as if I must do something.'

Georgie smiled at him. 'You do so much. It'd be impossible for you to do any more.'

Topsy made one of his characteristic restless movements, broad hands gesticulating. 'I mean about the world. I want to leave the world a better place than it was when I came into it.'

'You already have,' she said firmly. 'Your poetry ... your beautiful designs ... your wonderful speeches on the importance of the arts.'

'That's all very good,' Topsy said, 'but who the hell ever listens to me?'

'I do,' Georgie said.

He flushed and shuffled his feet a little. 'Oh, yes, but you don't count, old chap.'

She gave his arm one last pat. 'Go on, off you go. I will see you soon.'

Georgie shut the gate behind him, and then went up to her daughter's bedroom. Margot lay curled around her cat, reading. There was a tottering pile of books next to her bed. Georgie recognised Margot's childhood favourites. *Black Beauty. The Princess and the Goblin. The Water Babies. Alice in Wonderland.* Georgie smiled a little. She had always thought Gabriel had been the model for the Mad Hatter, with his purple velvet coat with dormice peeking out of his pockets and wombats sleeping in pie dishes on his dining-room table.

Then her smile faded. It was impossible to think of Gabriel without grief.

Georgie steeled her nerve, then dragged back the curtains and flung open the window. The cold spring wind rushed inside, rustling the book's pages.

'Oh, Mammy, please don't,' Margot said.

'It's a beautiful day. I want you up and dressed and out in the sunshine.'

Margot heaved a huge sigh. 'Oh, do I have to?'

Georgie sat down on the end of her bed and took one of her thin, nervous hands. 'Jenny has been very sick.'

Margot was still at once, her eyes fixed on her mother's face.

'The fits come upon her any time of day or night. She cannot be left alone anymore. She can't have a bath without someone watching her, or go out to tea with friends.'

'That's so awful.'

'Her whole future is blighted, Margot. And there's nothing anyone can do.' Georgie stood up and went to her daughter's wardrobe, pulling out a warm blue dress and some thick stockings. 'Which is why you are going to get up and walk in the fresh air and give me some help in the house. I don't know why you've been so sad, Margot. I'm sorry for it, you know I am. I'm not, however, going to stand by and watch you wallow in misery when there's no need for it. You have your whole life lying before you, filled with every possibility of happiness. So get dressed and come downstairs. And whenever you feel a fit of the blues coming on, you just think of Jenny and be grateful that it's not you.'

As Georgie went out, she heard Margot slowly moving about her bedroom and felt a rush of relief. She had been so afraid that her daughter would sink into the slough of despond as her mother had done, never to recover.

Not while I have breath in my body, she vowed and went downstairs to start gathering daffodils.

In late summer, the whole family moved down to Rottingdean where they had bought a little house by the sea. Georgie loved it down there. She had no need to fear the notorious Madame Zambaco lurking in the bushes.

Georgie knew that Maria Zambaco had returned from Paris. Topsy had told her, in his usual brusque way. He had become close friends with Maria's cousin Aglaia Coronio, who had been one-third of the famous Three Graces. Georgie knew that Ned had never truly recovered from his affair with Madame Zambaco. Her beautiful, melancholy face had continued to appear in his paintings. She was Nimue, the cruel enchantress who beguiled and enchanted Merlin, snakes writhing through her dark-red hair. She was Venus, standing at the edge of a pool, draped in transparent gauze, haloed. She was an angel, playing a flageolet.

Yet it was the painting of *The Tree of Forgiveness* that had proved to Georgie that Maria Zambaco's claws were still deep in Ned's flesh.

It seemed that all she had to do was smile and beckon, and Ned would go to her. It still hurt, even after all these years.

In Rottingdean, though, Ned was all hers. They walked on the Downs together, she read to him whilst he painted as she had done when they were first married, and at night they played a game of draughts. Phil and Margot lay on the grass under the apple trees, Phil drawing and Margot reading. Huge black-and-golden bees buzzed in the sweetbriar roses. Swifts darted in and out of the eaves.

Soon after they arrived, a tinker came and played the fiddle on the green. Ned loved music, and went out to listen. Georgie and Margot watched from the window, as the tinker's daughter – a grubby little mite of about four – began to dance. Her face was solemn, her steps careful and precise, and she held up her ragged skirt with both small hands, showing filthy bare feet. Most people hurried past, throwing the occasional penny into the tinker's hat, but Ned watched to the very end. The little girl finished and curtseyed to him. Ned raised his hat to her, then poured all the pennies in his pocket into her eagerly outstretched hands. Her thin face was transfigured with joy. Then Ned nodded to the tinker and wished him good day.

Georgie heard Margot give a deep sigh, and put her arm about her.

'Truly, your father is a good man,' she whispered.

Margot nodded, and laid her head against her mother's arm.

That night, sitting by the fire, Ned began a new project. He carefully drew a circle in the middle of a new notebook and sketched lightly within it. When he was satisfied with his design, he carefully tinted it with a thin brush dipped in his palette of watercolours.

'What are you drawing, Papa?' Margot asked. It was the first time she had addressed her father directly in a long time.

'I want to paint the beautiful old names of flowers.' Ned showed her the page. He had painted an angel with red wings, caught in a swirling blue cloud. The angel's arms were raised high as if trying to protect his head.

There was not a single flower in the little painting.

'But where is the flower?' Margot asked.

'I don't want to paint the flowers themselves,' Ned said. 'Any poor fool could do that. No, I want to wring their secret from them. I want the names and the picture to be one soul together, indissoluble, as if they could not exist apart.'

'What flower is that, then?' Margot asked, leaning over in interest.

'Can't you guess?' Ned asked.

'Love-in-a-mist?'

Ned crowed with delight. 'You're right!'

Margot was pleased. 'What flower shall you do next?'

'What would you like me to do?'

'Rose? Daisy? Buttercup?' Phil suggested, and Ned frowned.

'That sounds like you're calling the cows home at night. No, no. I need flower names that seem to have some kind of hidden meaning to them. A story, or a fairytale. Something mysterious and magical.'

'Like Traveller's Joy,' Margot suggested. 'Or Adder's Tongue.'

'Yes!' Ned drew a scrap of paper towards him and scribbled down the names.

'Meadowsweet?' she suggested.

Ned was already sketching designs.

Georgie looked at the two heads bent over the page, names of flowers flying back and forth, and smiled.

Ned had a new studio built at the Grange that Christmas, at the end of the garden.

Georgie was sure he had wanted it so that Madame Zambaco could visit him there without any risk of being seen from the house. It had its own separate entrance so that models and tradesmen need not go through the house, and – Georgie had heard – Maria Zambaco had leased a house on the same street, only a block away.

To get to the studio, Ned had to walk through the garden, which had a copse of trees like an old forest and then a meadow of wild flowers. He was too sick that winter to use it much, but when spring came he had a skylight installed and a pot-bellied stove to keep the room warm. He began to go to the studio every day, enjoying the walk through the bluebell wood and the wild meadow. Many of the paintings he had been working on were carried down to the studio, and Georgie took the chance to give the long room in the house a thorough spring-clean.

One day, in late summer, a parcel of paints was mistakenly delivered to the house. It was a beautiful day, so Georgie untied her apron and took the parcel down to the studio herself. The walk was an enchanting one, through beds of hollyhocks and foxgloves, with plums and cherries beginning to swell on the trees.

She slowed as she approached the studio, not wanting to disturb Ned at his work. Not hearing any sounds, she knocked lightly, then went inside.

Ned lay asleep on his couch, one hand tucked under his bearded cheek. He looked so peaceful there, Georgie carefully covered him up with a rug, then bent and kissed his brow.

Light poured in through the windows, illuminating the paintings hung on the walls or propped up on trestles. She saw a large painting of a prince in armour standing at the edge of a rose-briar wood, other knights lying entangled in the thorns, caught in an enchanted sleep. There was a giant wheel of fortune, with naked men bound to it, turned by the hand of a terrible goddess. And there were dozens of gouache studies for paintings of Perseus and Andromeda, her white naked body glowing out of the darkness. Georgie turned away from those, and only then saw the tall narrow canvas set on the trestle at the far end of the room.

It was a painting of King Cophetua and the beggar-maid. Georgie recognised it at once, from the poem by Alfred Tennyson. The king – dark-skinned and black-haired – sat in his ornate armour, his helmet on his knee, looking up at the young woman, who sat above him dressed in grey rags that left her arms and feet bare.

The beggar-girl gazed straight out of the painting, meeting Georgie's eyes. It was like gazing into a mirror. She had Georgie's chestnut-brown hair, her clear blue-grey eyes. In one hand, she clutched a bouquet of red anemones. Georgie gazed at them in amazement. She knew that, in the symbolic language of flowers, anemones meant forsaken love. They were the first flowers to open in spring, and the first to die. They were said to have sprung from the blood of Adonis, the god of beauty and desire. She wondered what it meant, that Ned had painted her this way.

He had painted her only once since that dreadful depiction of her as chilly Winter. Again Georgie had been shown with a book in her hand, a blue pansy used as a bookmark. Her dark hair was dragged down over her temples, her jaw set, her expression thin-lipped and severe. Georgie had hated it. Even Phil had been moved to protest, saying, 'Really, Papa, must you make Mammy look so cross?' Ned had put the portrait away, its face to the wall, and not tried to paint her again.

This picture of the king and the beggar-maid was quite different. The look on her face was grave but composed, and seemed to show a certain pluck as she faced her future as the new queen. The beggar-maid was not beautiful, just as Georgie was not beautiful. It seemed as if it was her goodness, her simplicity, her steadfast courage, that had so enraptured the king.

Something new and warm swelled in her chest. Georgie put the parcel on the table and tiptoed out, wondering what it all meant.

'But what do you mean?' Ned gazed at Topsy in horror. 'You're standing on boxes on street corners? Shouting at people?'

'Mmmm-hmmm.' Topsy piled his plate high with bacon and eggs. 'And wearing sandwich boards too, old chap. Anything to get the word across.'

'But . . . your poetry . . . your designs . . .'

'No bloody time for all that now.'

Ned was distressed. 'Any old fellow can spout speeches, Topsy. But not one man in a thousand can do what you do.'

'Well, the thing is most people aren't so good at giving speeches, especially me. I can't figure why poetry is so easy and a speech so hard, when one rhymes and the other doesn't. Which is why I need your help.' Topsy turned to Georgie.

'Mine?'

'Well, yes. I'm working on a speech and I thought ... if I could read it to you ... you could make suggestions for me ... and maybe tell me if it's got anything of worth in it.'

As he spoke, Georgie felt herself begin to blush. Topsy had once brought the novel he was writing for her to read, with exactly the same request. She had had to gently tell him to put it away. It had laid out the strange geometry of love between her and Topsy and Ned far too clearly for her liking.

But Topsy was rushing on heedlessly. 'The speech is in Oxford, to talk about the importance of art, and it's too good an opportunity to pass up talking about other things too. But I want to do a good job.'

'How about you talk and I make notes on things that occur to me, and then we can go over it together?' Georgie suggested, rising to go and fetch pen and paper. Ned sighed and went to work on one of his cartoons for a stained glass window, while Margot quietly cleared the table so they could all work there together.

Topsy picked up his sheaf of scribbled pages and began to read aloud.

'You may well think I am not here to criticise any special school of art or artists, or to plead for any special style, or to give you any instructions, however general, as to the practice of the arts. Rather I want to take counsel with you as to what hindrances may lie in the way towards making art what it should be, a help and solace to the daily life of all men,' he said.

Georgie gazed at him, the ink on the nib of her pen drying. Topsy talked on, frank and brusque and passionate as ever, occasionally stopping to tear at his mop of grey curls as he tried to express what he meant.

'Without beating about the bush, let us consider what the real state of art is,' he said. 'I must ask you to extend the word art beyond those matters which are consciously works of art, to take in not only painting and sculpture, and architecture, but the shapes and colours of all household goods, nay, even the arrangement of the fields for tillage and pasture, the management of towns and of our highways of all kinds; in a word, to extend it to the aspect of the externals of our life.'

Ned had stopped in his sketching to gaze at his old friend. Margot sat with her book laid down in her lap.

'For I must ask you to believe that every one of the things that goes to make up the surroundings among which we live must be either beautiful or ugly, either elevating or degrading to us, either a torment and burden to the maker of it to make, or a pleasure and a solace to him.' Topsy stopped, cleared his voice, brought the papers close to his eyes, then far away, squinting as if trying to read his own handwriting.

'What kind of an account shall we be able to give to those who come after us of our dealings with the earth, which our forefathers handed down to us still beautiful, in spite of all the thousands of years of strife and carelessness and selfishness?'

As he spoke, Georgie felt a fierce flame leap up in her, a desire to create beauty and save the world.

'Art is man's expression of joy in his labour,' Topsy said, and then, as he reached the end of his speech, 'One man with an idea in his head is in danger of being considered a madman; two men with the same idea in common may be foolish, but can hardly be mad; ten men sharing an idea begin to act, a hundred draw attention as fanatics, a thousand and society begins to tremble, a hundred thousand and there is war abroad, and the cause has victories tangible and real; and why only a hundred thousand? You and I who agree together, it is we who have to answer that question!'

Georgie clapped her hands. 'Oh, Tops, it's wonderful!'

'Too long,' Ned grumbled. 'And too much about the proletariat.'

Topsy gazed at him, wounded.

'Well, that's interesting, because I think there was not enough about the proletariat so it means Topsy must have got it just right,' Georgie said. This was an old joke, inspired by what Gabriel had always said whenever anyone criticised his work. Both Ned and Topsy laughed and the slight was forgotten.

But there was a fissure between the two men that had never been there before, and it troubled her. Ned was unhappy. He could not bear that Topsy was turning his back on his art and entering politics.

He tried to explain his feelings to Georgie. 'A man should do what he was put on this earth to do. Topsy is a poet and an artist and a maker of beautiful things. His work enriches all of our lives. A man like that shouldn't be marching about wearing political slogans on sandwich boards, and standing on boxes ranting like a madman. It demeans him, and his work.'

'He feels passionately that there is so much wrong with this world,' Georgie protested. 'Children begging barefoot in the snow, and poor old folk forced to labour in workhouses, and rich men getting richer and filling their houses with ugly useless things that were made in factories by people so poor they cannot rest for even a moment, in fear of losing their jobs. It's like slavery! He wants to jolt the world awake, make them see the evil that lives right under their noses.'

'A man's art should say all that he wants to say,' Ned argued. 'Art is what will change the world, not shouting at people.'

'But Topsy wants to change the world now. He cannot bear to have to wait, and just hope that things will change. He's trying to force change.'

'But people don't like to be shouted at,' Ned objected. 'Isn't it better to create something that fills a man's life with beauty, and makes him long to do better? You know I am always on the side of rebellion, and witchcraft, and all unlucky causes anywhere, Georgie. I want to change the world too. But I want to do it with my art, not by marching in streets and arguing with people.'

Ned pointed at his painting of *King Cophetua and the Beggar-Maid*. 'Don't you see? The king has everything a man could want, a crown and jewels and a kingdom. But then he sees the beggar-maid ... who has nothing ... and he realises then that all he has is worthless without love. That is what I want the world to know.'

Georgie had to turn away, unable to speak.

Whenever she thought she had armoured her heart, Ned pierced all her defences and made her love him more fiercely than ever before.

6

Standing Stones
Summer 1884

Margot sat curled up on the window-seat, pretending to be reading. Her parents were arguing in hushed tones at the far end of the room, and she wanted to know what they were saying.

'Don't be so absurd, Ned,' Mama said. 'She is only going to Scotland, not to the wilds of Africa, and her brother will be with her. Margot will be perfectly fine.'

'I have such a terrible feeling of foreboding,' Papa said, hunched in his chair by the fire. 'Something bad is going to happen, I know.'

'Sssh,' Mamma said. 'Don't put any ideas into her head. This will be a good thing for her. She's eighteen years old now and should be having fun with people her own age.'

'Why must my beloveds always grow up and go away?' Papa asked miserably.

'You have to let her go, Ned,' Mama said. 'You have to let her grow up.'

Margot did not know how she felt about the trip to Scotland. All sorts of anxieties assailed her. What if Sally and Lily Norton did not like her anymore? It had been quite a few years since they had last met. And they were American. She imagined them brash, loud, assertive. Their father she remembered dimly as a stern-faced man with a bristly white moustache and a shining pink dome of a head. He was a great champion of Pre-Raphaelite art, her father had said. He had taken a number of paintings to America after their first exhibition in Russell Square, and had continued to buy and promote their art in the United States.

In the end, Margot found she had nothing to fear. Mr Norton was kindly and avuncular, and his daughters Sally and Lily were cheerful, kind-hearted girls who exclaimed over Margot's dainty figure and big blue eyes, while their brother Eliot was clearly quite smitten with her. He and Phil and the girls talked so enthusiastically about books and art and nature that, after a while, Margot dared to join in, a little at least.

By mid-June, they were in Arran, in the western islands of Scotland. Just twenty miles long and ten miles wide, it was a small island with tall peaked mountains wreathed with mist to the north and gentler rounded hills and meadows to the south. The party was staying in a hotel at Brodick, looking out across the bay to an old sandstone castle. Behind it was a sweep of dark forest leading to the foot of Goat Fell, a dramatic bare mountain with an almost perfect triangular point.

Margot was hurrying down the steps to supper, pulling on her gloves as she went, when she collided with a young man who was bounding up the steps.

'Oh, I'm so sorry,' she gasped.

'I do beg your pardon,' a deep voice with a lilting Scottish brogue said. She recognised the voice and looked up, startled, as the young man exclaimed, 'I say, it's Miss Jones!'

'Mr Mackail,' she said, blushing fiery-red.

'So have you been burying any more mummies?' Jack Mackail asked.

Her confusion increased. 'You must have thought us very odd.'

'I thought you were all utterly charming. I've never been to a Pharoah's funeral before.'

'Well, it was new for me too. Normally Papa and I just bury mice and birds. Most of them caught by my cat, I'm afraid. No matter how I scold him, I cannot seem to teach him to be kind.' She shook her head sadly, then looked up at him in wonder. 'Whatever are you doing here? I was not expecting ...'

'Weeeell, ye ken this is my part o' the world,' Jack said, laughing, his brogue exaggeratedly broad. 'No, really. I was born on Bute, only a hop, skip and a jump away. I'm on my summer break. What are you doing here?'

'Travelling with friends,' she answered.

Just then, Phil and Eliot came rushing down the stairs behind her. They paused when they saw Margot. She said, hot and flustered, 'Phil, do you remember Mr Mackail?'

'Of course I do,' Phil said eagerly, and came down the steps to shake his hand. 'How are you, Mackail? This is my friend, Eliot Norton.'

The three young men fell at once into eager conversation about fishing and cricket and mountain climbing. Jack confessed that was why he had come to Arran. He was hoping to tackle Goat Fell. 'You're meant to be able to see three kingdoms from its summit,' he said.

'What three kingdoms?' Phil said scornfully.

Jack grinned. 'England, Ireland and the Isle of Man.'

'That's not a kingdom!'

'Don't ever say that to a Manx man.'

Phil laughed uproariously. Jack grinned, a little surprised to find his witticism so appreciated.

'I say, we're awfully late for supper,' Eliot said, pulling out his watch. 'We must go.'

'Won't you join us?' Phil said to Jack. 'Eliot's father won't mind. He's Professor of Art History at Harvard, and so will be most interested to meet an Oxford fellow.'

'Well ...' Jack hesitated, looking at Margot. She looked away, all too aware of the hot colour again surging to her face.

'You'd be most welcome,' Eliot said. 'That is, if you don't have any plans.'

'Oh, no, I'm all on my lonesome,' Jack said. 'Well, if you're sure ...'

Phil and Eliot began to clatter down the steps, talking at the top of their voices.

Jack waited for Margot. 'Are you sure Mr Norton will not mind me joining you?' he asked, offering her his hand to help her down the last few steps.

'I do not know … I do not think so … he's very good-natured …' Margot was very aware of the warmth of Jack's hand through her glove, and felt its absence once he let her go.

It was a merry supper party. Sally and Lily were delighted to have such a handsome young man join the party, and it balanced out their numbers perfectly. After supper there was dancing, and then a walk in the twilight gardens. It was late, but the sky was still flushed with light. Margot saw how the other girls laughed and flirted with Jack, and once again wondered miserably what was wrong with her, that she found even the most casual of conversations so hard.

A plan was hatched to spend the next day exploring the island. Jack had told them all about the King's Cave, where Robert the Bruce was meant to have hidden once, and then a mysterious circle of stones not far away that had been raised thousands of years earlier. Sally and Lily at once cried they must see them both, and Mr Norton indulgently said they might go, as long as Mr Mackail did not mind escorting the party and showing them the way.

The King's Cave was on the other side of the island, a journey of several hours. The caves were inaccessible at high tide, and so they were up early in the morning to be sure to have enough time to explore before the tide turned. The sky was full of thin running clouds and sudden slants of sunlight and unexpected darts of rain; the girls all wore their coats and carried long-handled umbrellas.

'My old nurse would have called this weather blirty,' Jack said. 'I hope it clears, else we'll have a damp walk.'

Mr Norton had hired a pony and cart for them. The pony – a short, stout, shaggy beast with a rolling white eye – needed a great deal of encouragement before it would consent to pull the cart up the very steep mountain road. Margot could not bear it. She seized the whip out of the driver's hands and flung it down. 'You should be ashamed of yourself, whipping the poor beast so!'

She then begged to be allowed out of the cart so that she could walk, and so relieve the poor overloaded horse of her weight. The driver scowled ferociously, but stopped the cart and bent to pick up his whip. Jack jumped down to the road and held up his hand to help her down. The others all scrambled out too, laughing and complaining in equal measure.

'Why did we bother hiring the cart?' Phil said crossly. 'We might as well just have walked the whole way, and saved ourselves the cost.'

Reluctantly he clambered out and walked with the others, as the pony plodded on up the hill, the empty cart rattling behind.

'You are an animal lover?' Jack asked.

Margot turned astonished eyes on him. 'Of course? Aren't you?'

When he declared his undying love for all animals, anywhere under the sun, she told him that her father always said that children must be taught to draw animals. That way, he thought, they would never wish to harm them.

It was a long hard climb, and Margot's legs were soon aching. She would not climb back into the cart, though, until the road at last levelled out and wound its way through brown moorland, patched here and there with bright outbursts of yellow gorse. Then Jack handed her back into the cart to join the other girls, whose resolve had weakened much earlier than Margot's.

'Ye're a douchty lass,' he said admiringly. 'Anyone would think ye were Scots.'

She realised that this was a compliment of the highest order, and flushed.

The road rose and fell, and twisted and turned, and Margot got out to walk every time the poor pony began to labour. Jack always joined her, though the others laughed and teased them both for worrying about a mere horse.

'These Highland ponies are tough, Margot,' her brother said in exasperation. 'They're used to hills.'

She did not reply, but acted as her conscience dictated, as her mother had taught her.

The cart driver dropped them off on the road outside the little village of Tormore, and they walked together through the beech forest. The Norton girls squealed at the sight of a red squirrel scampering up a tree.

The beach was rough with shingle and stones, and many people had built small cairns, which gave the place a strange and magical feeling. The sea pounded on the shore, rushing and retreating, rushing and retreating, rattling all the stones together with a wild kind of music. Jack gave Margot his hand, helping her over the rough shore. Margot saw that Lily was cross to have to ask her own brother for help. The entrance was guarded by an iron gate, but it was not locked and they were able to creep inside, their boots squelching deep in mud.

The roof was high and arched, and on the rocky walls faint drawings of horses and dogs and hunters could be seen.

'They are meant to represent Fingal MacCool,' Jack said, 'a famous hero of legend.'

'Here is a carving of a cross,' Lily said. 'Was this hero of yours a devout man?'

She spoke lightly, teasingly, but Jack answered her seriously. 'I believe the cave was used as a chapel by the Covenanters, when you English tried to force us Scots to worship the way you wanted.'

Lily laughed. 'I'm not English,' she declared. 'I'm American.'

'Well, then, you need not feel guilty here,' Jack answered.

'I'm glad.' Lily held out her hand so Jack could help her across the uneven rocky floor. 'Tell me more about these Covenanters of yours. Did they really worship in a cave?'

On the walk through the rough bracken and birch of the forest towards the road, Margot fell back. She was tired. Her legs ached. She felt an overwhelming sadness begin to engulf her, and did not know why.

Lily was clinging to Jack's arm, laughing and bantering with him. Phil and Sally walked, arm in arm, talking about his plans to be an artist like his father. That left Eliot to escort Margot, but she did not much like the young American. He talked all the time, stridently, about crank shanks and dynamos and solar cells and other such mysteries. He was punctilious in helping her over stiles and warning her against boggy patches, but otherwise delivered a running monologue that Margot soon gave up trying to understand.

The pony and cart were waiting for them, and took them back up along the road to the path that led across the moors to the circle of standing stones. Mist floated in pale wisps over the brown moors. Jack looked across to the mountain, the tip of which was hidden in black clouds. Seagulls called, floating high above their heads in a freshening wind.

'My old nurse always said to beware when the mountain puts its nightcap on,' Jack said. 'Perhaps we should head back.'

'Oh, no!' Lily cried. 'Let us go on. I do so want to see these old stones.'

'We're likely to get wet.'

Lily waved her umbrella. 'I'm no dainty English rose,' she cried, with a quick sidelong glance at Margot. 'I'm American! We don't melt in a rain shower.'

Margot knew she should have a quick riposte, but she could think of nothing to say. Her feeling of dread and misery settled on her as heavily as the clouds wreathing the mountain.

It was a long walk through the moors, a mile at least. Once again Margot trudged along at the back. Jack looked back once or twice and smiled at her encouragingly, but both Sally and Lily were vying for his attention. Phil was worried about the mud and the cow pats and the prickly gorse that snatched at his trousers, while Eliot was now talking at length about attempts to make a gasoline-powered carriage that would chug up and down all these hills without anyone needing to get out and walk.

The mist was thickening, and Margot felt a few sharp needles of rain. She raised her umbrella, but the wind was so strong it threatened to turn it inside out. They passed a ruin of an old stone building, overgrown with blackthorn, climbed over a stile and then came, after a few minutes more walking, to a rough circle of low granite rocks. Not much further along was a double ring of boulders. The six of them wandered about, the Norton girls asking eager questions and Jack doing his best to answer.

'This one is called Fingal's Cauldron Seat,' he said. 'Fingal MacCool is meant to have come here and cooked himself a meal, tying his dog to that stone with a hole in it.'

'What's the mound in the middle?' Lily asked, wandering over to see.

'It's a cist burial, I think. You can find bones in them sometimes, and old weapons and jewellery.'

'So this was like a tomb?' Margot asked, hugging herself against the sharp wind.

'I think so. But not like a graveyard. More like a church that has the graves of important people in it. A king might have been buried here, or a mighty warrior, or a druid.'

Margot wondered what life must have been like for the people who lived here, so many thousands of years ago. It must have been hard, she thought. She imagined a burial procession coming through the moors, flaming torches high, carrying their dead king on their shoulders.

'My father brought me here when I was but a lad,' Jack said in a low voice. 'He thought the druids may have raised these stones, and that they were filled with some kind of magical power. He was a minister, my father, but the wisest and most learned man I ever knew.'

Margot fixed her eyes on his face. 'He ... he's dead now?'

Jack looked up in surprise. 'Yes. He died only a month or so ago. I came to Arran ... oh, as a kind of pilgrimage, I suppose. My mother is dead too, and my sister gone and married. I really am all on my lonesome now.'

Impulsively Margot stepped closer, putting one hand on his arm. 'You can share my mother and father if you like. My mother lost a baby boy who would be only a few years younger than you, she'd love another son to feed and fuss over. And you know my father. He too would find this a place of ancient magic.'

Jack put his hand over hers. 'Thank you. I'd be proud to share your parents with you.'

Margot went red and pulled her hand free, unable to meet his eyes. She went to the edge of the ring of stones, looking across the mist-wreathed moors. She could not think what had made her speak so boldly. Jack would think her very forward.

'There's another circle along here,' Lily called. 'It only has four stones.'

'There were probably more originally. People came and took them to build their houses and walls,' Jack said.

'I wonder they dared.' Margot spoke more to herself than anyone else, but Jack heard her and glanced her way, nodding in agreement.

He led the way along the path. Mist was rising from the ground, veiling the thorn bushes and the standing stones. The mountain had completely disappeared behind cloud.

A little further along the path, three much taller menhirs stood in a triangle. Nearby lay two heavy round stones, a hole bored through the middle.

'It looks like someone tried to carve the old boulders into millstones,' Jack said. 'It's strange that they went to so much effort to carve them into shape, but then left them here.'

'Perhaps something happened to frighten them,' Margot said. 'It is an eerie place. I wonder how old it is.'

'Thousands of years old, I think,' Jack said. He and Margot were alone, the others still exploring the other circles further back along the path.

'Why are they here? What do they mean?'

'I don't know. I have heard, though, that if you come here at dawn, on midsummer's morning, the sun rises right in that cleft between the two mountains. So perhaps it was some kind of sun worship.'

'Mr Mackail!' Lily called.

'Excuse me,' he said and went back to the others.

Margot stood alone among the three standing stones. She laid her hand on one, and then her forehead, shutting her eyes. She felt very insignificant. These stones had seen the passing of thousands of summers and winters. They had seen babies born and ancients die. Perhaps witches had once come here at night, to dance under the full moon. Perhaps blood had been split here.

Tears had most certainly been wept.

It was impossible not to think of her father, who could be the most melancholy of men at times, and yet at other times the most delightfully impish. Margot's mother had once asked her father if he believed in witches. He had answered, 'I should very much like to.' Margot had always wished to believe in them too. She liked to think there was magic in the world, hidden like the wick in the candle wax, but waiting always to flare into light.

Margot realised that she had allowed her own light to be doused. All those long months, curled under the weight of her counterpane, face hidden, heart shuttered.

Her eyes nettled. She put up her hand to scrub them.

For a moment, she thought her vision still obscured by tears. Then she realised that the mist had closed in upon the moor. She could see nothing but swirling white vapour, blowing sideways like a gauze curtain in the wind. She caught glimpses of the tall stones, of a thorn bush, of the fallen millstone. But beyond there was nothingness.

Margot took a few quick steps, looking for the path. She could see nothing. Panic sharp in her chest. 'Phil?' she called. 'Are you there?' Then, more desperately, 'Jack! Jack!'

Her voice was deadened by the mist. She called again, and searched. Another stone looming above her. Margot could not remember which way was east and which was west. No clues to help her. She cast about, eyes on the ground, searching for footprints, a flattened stretch of grass. She cried for help at the top of her voice. Mist all about her, and a fine mizzle of rain that dampened her eyelashes and made it hard to see.

She heard a voice call from what seemed a long distance away. She began to hurry towards the voice, only to find her skirt catching on brambles. She jerked her skirt free and stumbled into a patch of bog. Her boots sunk deep into the brackish water, mud sucking at the hem of her skirt. Margot struggled to free herself. She unbalanced, lurched forward. Fell into a pool of water. Cold as death.

Heavy skirts dragging her under. Margot thrashed towards the shore, trying to grab a branch. It broke. Back she fell. She struggled up, snatched a breath, but sank again, weighed down by all her clothes. Bubbles burst past her eyes.

This is it, she thought. This is when I die.

Then came the thought, sharp as a pin. I don't want to die. I want to live!

She kicked frantically, and felt her foot touch something hard. She pushed off with all her strength. Her head broke through the surface of the water, and she gasped a breath. She managed to catch some rushes in her hand. They sliced open her palm, but she dragged herself high. Her skirts like a millstone tied to her legs. Above her, mist clearing. Light amidst the shadows. She hauled herself towards it.

'Margot! Margot!'

'Jack!'

She heard him panting and scrambling, then his tall figure emerged from the mist. He bent and lifted her. Her skirts dripped icy water.

'Oh my God, oh my God, I thought I'd lost you,' he cried. 'I should never have left you. I'm sorry!'

He carried her all the way back to the cart, his coat about her. Margot shut her eyes, aware only of the warmth of his body, the strength of his arms, the sound of his heart banging hard beneath her ear.

7

Briar Wood
Autumn 1884–Summer 1885

Margot feared she had fallen in love.

What else could it be? The flush of blood in her face, the thunder of her heart, the thrill deep in the pit of her stomach, whenever Jack Mackail was near. She dreamt about him at night and thought of him all day long.

It was agony.

She did not think he could feel the same way about her. How could he? Papa might tell her a dozen times a week how beautiful she was, but Margot knew he doted on her. For Papa, she was his little one, his dearest girl, his beloved.

Margot knew she was just an ordinary girl.

Her father hated the thought of her growing up, leaving home, getting married. Margot did not want to distress him, and so she tried to never allow a hint of her feelings to show on her face when Jack came to visit them. He came often, staying for supper, talking for hours about art and poetry and history with her father.

Papa liked him, she knew.

Her father was hard at work on his big paintings of Sleeping Beauty, which he had been planning for so long. He had almost finished the first in the sequence. A young knight in black armour stood on the far left of the canvas, his bared sword in his hand, looking into the tangle of the briar wood where sleeping knights lay in enchanted slumber, their shields caught in the thorns. Papa had spent a long time researching and drawing the armour of all the sleeping knights, to show that each had come to do battle with the cursed forest at different times over the course of the hundred years.

He was troubled by the thorns in the picture. Jack thought they were wrong. 'I've never seen thorns so sharp and curved, Mr Jones,' he said. 'Are they realistic that way?'

Papa clutched at his head. 'Realistic! Realistic! Mr Mackail, this is the enchanted briar wood that surrounds the castle of the Sleeping Beauty. The thorns have been growing for a hundred years and no knight has ever been able to cut his way through. What does realism have to do with it?'

Jack laughed. 'Of course, you're right, sir.'

But the damage was done. Ned brooded over the thorns day and night, and went out and looked at all the roses that grew in the garden, and fretted himself half to death.

A few days later, he announced at lunch, 'I have written to Lady Leighton asking her to dig around in her garden and find me the thickest, thorniest, hoariest old monarch of the wild rose possible ... one with stems as thick as my wrist with long, horrible spikes on it ... so that I have evidence for my enemies that I am right and he is wrong.'

'Mr Mackail is not your enemy, Papa,' Margot said, her heart quailing within her.

'All you young people are my enemy. You're an unbelieving generation, and your disbelief infects this poor old believer and gets him all in a muddle.'

Mammy laughed. 'Never mind, Ned. I think you can make your thorns as thorny as you like.'

'No, Mr Mackail is right. Everything has to be as real as possible, to make it seem as if the story of the Sleeping Beauty is true. How else will people believe in it?'

'Well, I'm sure Lady Leighton will be delighted to assist you,' Mammy said, with the sarcastic note that she got in her voice whenever she talked about one of Papa's female admirers.

A week later, a box arrived packed full of wild rose briars. Papa was delighted. 'What use they'll be to me! Look at this one, Margot. Have you ever seen a thicker and more terrible specimen? It is all my soul lusted for. I'll invite that Jack Mackail over and wave it under his nose, I shall.'

The thorns aren't like what you drew, though, Papa,' Margot pointed out. 'They are not nearly as sharp and hooked and horrible.'

'True,' he sighed. 'It's a sad disappointment. I shall have to repaint all the thorns.'

'But there must be thousands of thorns in the paintings,' Mammy objected. 'It'll take you days.'

'Weeks, more like. But it must be done. My honour is at stake, and more importantly, so is Sleeping Beauty's.'

So, slowly and laboriously, Papa repainted every thorn, though he took some pleasure in allowing the briars to be as impenetrable as he liked.

The winter passed.

Jack continued to come to the Grange every few weeks, always bringing books for Mammy and Papa, and a new toy for Frill, Margot's cat, so the big Persian had something to play with apart from mice and birds. Sometimes Jack and Margot walked in the orchard, under the bare apple trees. He read her the poems he was writing, or talked to her about his decision not to accept a position at Oxford University, but to join the civil service. 'I want to do some good in the world,' he said. 'Besides, it'll be hard to marry and have a family on an academic's income.'

He had laughter in his voice, but his words made Margot sad. She wondered if he had someone in mind to marry. No doubt she'd be tall, and brilliantly clever, and have golden hair.

Margot found herself sliding down into the slough of despond again that winter, and so too did her father. He was heartbroken at the news that

William Graham, his most faithful patron, was dying of stomach cancer. Mr Graham was not just the most avid collector of Papa's works, but he brought many other clients to his studio and then negotiated much better prices for the paintings they bought.

In May, Mr Graham wrote to Papa to say that he had a dealer interested in buying the Sleeping Beauty sequence of paintings.

'But I've only painted one!' Papa exclaimed, his wispy hair standing up on end, his eyes filled with panic.

'Well, it's a very beautiful one,' Mammy soothed him. 'And if you had a buyer for all four paintings, you'd be more likely to actually settle down and finish them all.'

'But I have so much else to do! So many paintings to work on!'

'Yes, I know, my dear. But think how lovely it would be for you to finish some of them. And it would make dear Mr Graham so glad, to know he's managed to secure some kind of financial security for you. It would relieve his mind very much, I think.'

William Agnew – the most powerful art dealer in London – came to visit the studio in early May. Mammy insisted on cleaning up the studio, which was in its usual state of dirt and disorder, and picked flowers from the garden to put in vases on the table and the mantelpiece. She and Margot cooked raspberry sponge cake and made piles of chicken and walnut sandwiches for afternoon tea. Mammy even made Papa put on a clean painting smock and comb his hair.

'Indeed I do hope this Mr Agnew loves the painting,' Mammy said to Margot, as they set the table out in the garden. 'For I must admit Mr Graham is not the only one to worry about our finances. If only your father was not so particular! He paints so slowly and worries so much. And he exhibits so rarely! How are we to find new patrons when he is so fussy about what he exhibits, and where?'

'He wants his paintings to be perfect,' Margot said.

'Yes, but perfection is not possible. We live in an imperfect world.'

Margot nodded. 'I know. And he knows too. But you'll never persuade him to stop trying.'

Mammy's face softened. She gave Margot a little caress on the cheek. 'Yes, I know. I know all too well. Oh dear, let us just hope this Mr Agnew is not one of those fellows who heaps criticisms on a thing in order to try to drive down the price. If he is, Ned will be devastated and never want to look at it again. I do have to say, Margot, that I have high hopes for these pictures! The story has always been very special to me.'

'He wants me to sit for his princess,' Margot said anxiously.

'I know. That is one thing that makes me hopeful. Ned paints most beautifully whatever he loves most deeply, and you are the dearest thing to him in the world, Margot.' A look of sadness crossed her mother's face.

All went well. Mr Agnew seemed to like the painting, and asked a great many questions about when Papa was likely to be able to finish the other three in the sequence. Papa showed him all his drawings and studies, and the work he had already done on the paintings he called *The Council Chamber* and *The Garden Court*.

'My daughter Margaret is to be the model for the sleeping princess,' Ned said.

Mr Agnew smiled at Margot. 'Then I am sure it will be most beautiful.'

A few weeks later, it was Margot's nineteenth birthday.

Papa gave her a moonstone ring. 'So that you may never know love and stay with me always,' he told her. It was a joke, but like so many of Papa's jokes, it revealed the very true feeling behind it. Margot tried to smile, but it was hard. She wanted to be loved so badly. Papa put his arm about her and said, 'It is rather wonderful to look at, isn't it? So cold and desolate, like looking at the moon.'

Every time Margot looked at the ring, it made her sad but she could not bear to hurt her father's feelings by not wearing it.

The next day, Papa was having a nap on the sofa in the drawing room when a loud ring came at the door. Soon a servant came to say there was a man wanting to tell Papa that he had been elected to the Royal Academy.

Mammy was annoyed. 'That's an unkind joke,' she told the man. 'I will not have my husband disturbed over such a trick.'

He protested, but Mammy showed him out. 'I wonder who it could be, playing such a trick,' she said to Margot. 'If Gabriel was alive, I'd have suspected him. He did love a prank, and of course he was always at loggerheads with the Academy. He used to call Sir Joshua Sir Sloshua, and the Academy "fogey-dom".' She sighed, looking sad, as she always did when she spoke of Uncle Gabriel.

In the morning a letter came from Lord Leighton:

'Dear Ned, an event has just occurred which has filled me with the greatest satisfaction and with real joy. A spontaneous act of justice has been done at Burlington House – the largest meeting of members that I ever saw has by a majority elected you an Associate of the Royal Academy, I am not aware that any other case exists of an Artist being elected who has never exhibited, nay, has pointedly abstained from exhibiting on our walls. It is a pure tribute to your genius.'

'I am flabbergasted,' Ned said, laying the letter down next to his breakfast plate. He said it again, with emphasis. '*Flabbergasted!*'

'What are you going to do?' Mammy asked.

'I don't know. I'm utterly befuddled. To reject such an honour would seem churlish, don't you think? But then, it is fogey-dom. Am I such an old fogey now that they're willing to admit me when they've scorned me and my work for years?'

'Perhaps they have grown wise enough to see your worth,' Mammy said, folding her napkin and rising. She went and dropped a kiss on the top of his head. 'Don't fret yourself into illness over it, Ned.'

But of course Papa did. Letters flew back and forth, between Lord Leighton and the members of the Academy, who begged him to accept, and all his old friends who thought he should scorn it. Uncle Topsy said, 'I don't see why they should force Ned into doing what he disapproves of,' while Mr Graham wrote to Mammy, '*He cannot surrender his independence, I know, and that he will ever feel in the humour to sing … in a gilded cage in Piccadilly, I don't much credit. All the same I am very glad … that they have done it.*'

In the end, Papa accepted but the worry made him sick and melancholy for weeks, and he hardly painted a thing.

On the last day of June, a letter came from Mr Graham. Papa was too nervous to open it, sure it would have news of the negotiations with the art dealer Mr Agnew. He sat at the breakfast table, his hands clenched in his lap, staring at the envelope as if he feared a snake was coiled within.

'Do you want me to open it for you, dear?' Mammy asked.

'Yes … no … I don't know …'

She reached over and took the envelope, slicing it open with her butter knife.

'Stop! I don't want to know. What if it's bad news?'

'Only one way to find out,' Mammy said, and took out the letter and read it.

A look of astonishment crossed her face. She did not speak.

'What does it say, Mammy?' Margot prompted her.

'Agnew hates it,' Papa said with gloomy conviction. 'He thinks it's awful. He'll never look at one of my paintings again.'

'Mammy?' Margot asked again.

Mammy laid down the letter.

'He loves it. He wants to buy it.' Her eyes were glowing. 'Oh, Ned. He's offered fifteen thousand pounds for the four paintings. Fifteen thousand pounds!'

Margot could hardly believe it.

'It must be a mistake,' Ned said. 'You've misread the amount.'

Mammy passed him over the letter. Ned read it, then read it again. He laid down the letter. 'We'll be rich,' he said dazedly. 'Oh, Georgie, what shall I do?'

'Finish the paintings!' she cried.

8

The Rose Bower
Winter 1885–Autumn 1887

As the days turned towards winter, Papa began to paint Margot as the sleeping princess.

'I hate and loathe winter,' he said, gazing out at the dead garden under a lowering thunderous sky. 'I hate the rain, wind, cold, sleet, frost, fog, snow, slush, mud, I hate it all.'

'But what about Christmas?' Margot asked.

'I hate Christmas too. I hate its beef, its balls, its parties, its mince pies, its puddings, its bon-bons, its crackers, all of it.' He was silent for a long while, the only sound the flurry of brushstrokes. 'My father was always unhappiest at Christmas,' he said at last. 'It's hard to rejoice when the world is dead to you.'

Slowly the painting of *The Rose Bower* grew. The sleeping princess lay on her bier, sweet-faced and innocent, dressed all in gauzy white, one hand resting on a green sash that bound her hips. Her face was turned away from the dangerous rose briars that coiled close about her. On the floor, a rug with a peacock motif, a discarded mirror, a crown overgrown with brambles.

'Did you know,' her father said, painting wild roses, 'that God cursed the earth with thorns after the fall? They symbolise the pain of sin.'

Margot lay still, her eyelids closed, listening.

'That is what the tale means, I think. The Sleeping Beauty has an unawakened heart. She has not yet felt the pain of love, the thorn of sin.'

I want my heart to be awakened, Margot thought. But when? When shall I be awakened?

So the year passed.

Margot felt as if she only half-lived. Her melancholy deepened day by day, till she found it hard to get out of bed in the morning. Another birthday passed. She was now twenty. A girl no longer. Her mother hovered anxiously, alternating between cajoling and commanding her.

'Rise and shine,' she'd cry, pulling open the curtains. 'It's a beautiful day.'

But it was the day's beauty that hurt Margot. She could not bear to look.

The summer was spent at Rottingdean, and her father worked away at his book of flowers.

He designed five new pictures: *Love in a Tangle*, *Witches' Tree*, *Grave of the Sea*, *Black Archangel* and *Golden Greeting*. The final little painting showed a red-headed woman bending out of heaven to embrace a dark-haired man on barren earth. 'I wish *Golden Greeting* might be quite true,' he said wistfully.

Papa could not stay long, for he had many commissions to fulfil for the summer exhibition at the Grosvenor Gallery. He was exhibiting a portrait of Margot as well as a large painting of *The Garden of Pan* and a picture of Perseus showing Andromeda the severed head of Medusa. It was an astonishingly beautiful painting of an awful subject, as so many of Papa's paintings were.

Papa had decided to add his middle name to his last name, so that he would be called Edward Burne-Jones, to help him stand out from all the other Joneses in the world. So that is how his name was printed in the catalogues.

'I must admit Georgie Burne-Jones sounds much better than Georgie Jones,' Mammy said with a laugh. Margot liked it too. Margaret Burne-Jones definitely had a more aristocratic ring to it.

Papa wrote to Margot from London: '*The garden looks lovely still – a little sad, except in the first morning hours when the autumn sun shines on it and makes it look divine, but in the afternoon it is given over to sadness and at twilight, it is haunted by spirits, not ghosts – wraith and spectre never entered this dear garden … I long for you back …*'

I am the dearest thing in the world to him, Margot thought. And because he loves me so, he will paint the most beautiful picture ever painted. It is going to make him rich and famous. But he will never be able to let me go …

She felt as trapped as if thorns truly held her captive.

'Why are there only four paintings?' Margot asked her father one day. 'Why don't you show the moment when the prince finds the princess and awakens her with a kiss?'

Papa smiled sadly. 'I want to stop with the princess asleep and to tell no more of the tale. For that is the moment when all is about to change, when the spell is about to be broken, for better or for worse. It's the last moment of innocence, the last moment of the old world. Who knows what they will wake to find?'

Again the world turned toward winter, and still her father laboured over the Sleeping Beauty. He painted the king asleep on his throne, his head sunk into his chest, his long silver beard growing past his lap. He held a quill in his right hand, an unsigned scroll unrolling over his lap, his scribe asleep at his feet with a book in his hand.

The king looked just like her father. He was dressed all in pale colours like the sleeping princess. White, pearl-grey, silver, touches of softest gold.

Margot wondered where the queen was in her father's painting. He had painted the women of the castle sleeping at their looms and their spindles in the garden court. There were six women there, the briars twisted all about them, their dyed hanks of wool hanging above their heads just like they did in Uncle Topsy's workroom. The women were all barefoot, their heads uncovered, their clothes simple.

Perhaps the queen was the woman slumped beside the princess, her hair bound beneath a black hood, dressed in dark colours as if in mourning, a medieval lute cradled in her arm. She had Mammy's chestnut-brown hair, her straight nose. But no crown, no jewels, no cloth of gold, no silver thread. She was as dark a presence as the prince in his black armour at the furthermost end of the paintings.

The prince would need to step over the woman with the lute if he was to bend and kiss the sleeping princess awake.

Margot watched her father paint, and wondered what it all meant.

Slowly each day trickled past, unlike the sand in the king's painted hourglass.

Margot's father liked to talk as he painted.

So Margot lay still, her hands resting gently beside her, her face turned towards him, listening. He was a wonderful talker, her father. It seemed as if he remembered everything he had ever read, and that he had read anything ever worth knowing.

One evening, he told her that a friend had offered to send him a copy of *Anna Karenina*. 'But I begged him not to. I cannot afford to be made unhappy, and I suspect it would. It's Russian, and so I know just what to expect. There would be a beautiful woman in it, with all the best in her of any woman, and she would be miserable and love some trumpery frip, as they always do, and she would die finding out that she had been a fool. It would be beautifully written and just like life, and I couldn't bear it. These books are written for the hard-hearted. They are not meant for the poets but for stockjobbers, to wring iron tears from them for once. That is the use of sorrowful art, to penetrate the thick hide of the obtuse, and I have grown to be such a coward about pain.'

'Why, Papa?' Margot asked.

She heard his brush pause in its work. There was a long silence.

'Because I have been much hurt, I suppose.'

Margot opened her eyes and looked at her father. For months, after seeing her father and Madame Zambaco together, she had felt so sad and hurt, wounded by his betrayal of her mother and for the rupturing of her own childhood innocence. Slowly, against her will, she had found herself forgiving him. He was still her dear old whimsical father, filled with strange fancies and fears, who painted love as an angel with fiery wings lost in a blue mist. She wanted to try to understand.

'Who hurt you so badly?' she dared to ask.

He did not answer for a long time, and Margot worried that she had broken the moment of confidence. Then slowly he began to paint again.

'A woman ... I loved her very much ...'

'But she hurt you?'

'Yes.'

'Then I hate her,' Margot burst out with such vehemence she surprised herself.

She was remembering her father with his lover, his cries as if he were in pain.

'Do not hate her, Margot,' he whispered. 'Some things are beyond our understanding. Hurricanes and tempests and billows of the sea. Love is one of them. It is why ... oh, it is why I hope to keep you safe. I could not bear for you to be so hurt.'

I would not mind, Margot thought. I'd rather love with all my heart and be hurt than to never know love at all.

She thought of Jack. It had been a long time since she had seen him. She wondered where he was, and if he still wrote poetry, and if he had married that girl with the golden hair and had the children he wanted. The thought hurt her, like a fragment of something sharp pressing into her heart.

When her father was packing away his brushes and paints for the day, Margot rose from the studio bed and walked back to the house through the garden. It was autumn, but heavy-headed roses still bloomed here and there, petals loose and shaking free in the evening wind. She gathered a few, wincing as their thorns snagged in her skin. All the time she was thinking of what her father had said.

She took the roses into the kitchen, looking for a vase. Her mother was busy helping the cook prepare supper.

'What lovely roses, darling. They'll soon be finished for the season. It's always so sad to see the last petals blow away. How is the painting coming along?'

'He'll be finished soon,' Margot said. 'If nothing happens to upset him.'

'The closer he gets to the end, the more easily he'll be upset,' Mammy said. 'He'll grieve for it when it's done.'

Margot busied herself arranging the flowers in the vase. 'Mammy, have you ever wondered why Mr Mackail doesn't come and visit us anymore?'

She said it lightly, as if on a passing whim, not looking at her mother.

Her mother laid down her wooden spoon.

'I didn't know that you cared to see him. You were always so ... so cool.'

Margot bit her lip. 'Was I? I did not mean to be. It was just ... well, he always seemed more interested in talking to Papa than me, anyway. I just thought ... Papa must be missing him.'

Mammy picked up the spoon again. 'Indeed, yes. I think your papa has been lonely these past few years, with Topsy so busy with his new causes, and so many old friends moved away or died. Perhaps I should write and ask Mr Mackail to tea.'

'I think Papa would like that.' Margot carefully slid another rose into the vase.

'I'll write this afternoon. I'm sure he'd be interested to see how the Sleeping Beauty paintings are coming along.'

The next day, a letter arrived from Jack thanking them for the invitation and arranging a time. Margot felt flushed and feverish all day. She did not know what to wear. She put on her best dress, then thought better of it, and put on an old frock, only to change again. In the end she settled on a loose pale dress with a blue sash that brought out the colour of her eyes.

Papa was very pleased to see Jack, and the talk ran merrily between them all tea-time. Margot found herself without a word to say. She caught him looking at her once, but he looked away and did not speak to her. Margot looked down at her tightly entwined fingers. Perhaps it was too late. Perhaps he had never cared for her.

As Mammy began to clear away the cups and saucers, Jack said, 'I've a hankering in me to see the garden. It must be looking so beautiful. Miss Jones, would you mind …'

Papa looked up. 'Oh, I can do that. We can stretch our legs and have a smoke.'

'I need you here for a moment, Ned,' Mammy said.

He looked cross. 'Oh, but … why? Not when we have guests, Georgie.'

'It'll only take a minute, dear. And I'm sure it'll do Margot good to stretch her legs too.'

'Oh, very well,' Papa said. 'I will take you down to the studio in just a minute, Mr Mackail.' He followed Mammy into the house.

Side by side, so close that her sleeve sometimes brushed his, Margot and Jack walked into the garden. She could think of nothing to say, and so they walked in silence. They came to the mossy spot under the oak tree where dozens of crosses made from sticks marked the graves of small animals.

'Buried any mummies lately?' Jack asked.

Margot had to laugh. 'No! Will you tease me about that forever?'

'I hope so.' His voice was grave.

She looked up at him in surprise. There was an intent look in his grey eyes, and his jaw was stiff with tension.

Margot did not know what to say. She took a deep breath and tried.

'What about you? Are you still writing poetry?'

'I've not had much to inspire me recently. Perhaps poetry is only for the young and naïve.'

'I don't think so,' she said. 'I think we need poetry whatever our age. Perhaps we need it more when we get older.'

'Perhaps I've just not had the heart for it.'

'You've been ... unhappy?'

He nodded, not looking at her.

'I have also. I don't know why. My mother calls it the slough of despond, and says our family has a fatal tendency to fall into it. My father says it is the Celt in our blood. Something wild and dark and fierce and always longing for something it does not have.'

'Then I must have the same blood for that is what has been wrong with me.' At last he met her eyes. Margot put out her hand and took his, drawing him to sit beside her on the little seat under the gnarled old apple tree.

'Tell me.'

His fingers twisted in hers, holding her fast. 'I've found things hard. My father dying ... having to try to make my own way in the world ... wanting things I cannot have.'

Margot's heart began to beat faster. 'Like what?'

'Like ... ' He made a helpless gesture with one hand. 'Well, like a house like this, with apple trees and roses and forget-me-nots in the garden, and tapestries of angels on the walls, and stained glass glowing with the light behind it, and old bits of furniture that have been loved and used for centuries. And a place where I might work, uninterrupted, at something I love ... at something that makes the world a more beautiful place ...'

'Like poetry.'

'Yes, like poetry! But poetry doesn't sell, you know, and if I want the house of my dreams ... and the girl I want ... well, then, I must find some way to make money.'

'Must you?' she said wistfully. 'Is that what she wants? The girl you want?'

'I don't know. I don't know what she wants. That's why ... that's why I've found things so hard. She's like a princess in an old tale, and there's no way through to her.'

Her heart gave a weird little thump. Surely he could not be talking about some other girl, when his hand was holding hers so tightly and he was gazing at her with such a look in his eyes?

'Perhaps she's just an ordinary girl,' Margot said. 'Too afraid to open her heart.'

'Margot ...' he said.

He leant towards her. Greatly daring, she leant towards him. Somehow, their mouths found each other.

His hand stole around her waist. She nestled closer, her arms linking behind his head. Closer and closer they entwined, till both were breathless and shaken.

At last they parted. Margot dropped her head to his shoulder.

'Margot ... I need to tell you ... I think I'm rather awfully in love with you.'

'I know that I'm in love with you,' she whispered.

Jack caught her close. 'Are you? Truly?'

He kissed her again before she could answer. Margot could not get close enough to him. His hands traced the soft curves of her body.

'We need to be careful,' she whispered. 'My father ...'

He drew away. 'I assure you my intentions are entirely honourable,' he said stiffly.

She laughed. 'I'm glad! I don't think my father will be, though. He ... he cannot bear partings. We will have to live close to him.'

'I think we can manage that.' Jack kissed her again.

'And see him as often as we can.'

'I'll find us a house next door.'

'And you'll have to not mind if he hates you for a while.'

'As long as you love me, he can hate me as much as he likes.' Jack's mouth pressed against the pulse beneath her jaw.

Margot sighed. 'And we'll have to wait a while ...'

His mouth paused in his downhill journey. 'What? Why?'

'We need to wait for the painting to be finished.'

'Really? Must we? I don't want to wait.' He resumed his exploration of her skin, his hand clumsily undoing a few buttons to help him slide lower.

'It's only for a little while,' she whispered. 'A few months. Maybe a year.'

His head came up. 'That's too long!'

She kissed him. The whole world faded away. There was only his mouth, his hands.

Margot heard herself cry aloud in joy. It rocked her for a moment. So close to the sound she had heard her father make. For the first time she understood the delirium of love.

'Margot …' he murmured against her hair. 'Don't make me wait too long.'

She caught his hands, kissed each palm.

'I won't,' she promised.

9

A Premonition of Light
Winter 1888

'I have a very bad feeling,' Ned said. 'I shall die before I ever finish the Briar Rose paintings. Georgie, I need to make a will. I shall leave everything to you. My estate must be worth at least twenty-seven pounds, four shillings and three tuppences. It will all be yours.'

'Thank you, dear,' Georgie said, darning the heel of one of Ned's socks. 'But you need not worry. I shall not let you die anytime soon. I have plans for that fifteen thousand pounds you are owed.'

Ned looked up from the stained-glass cartoons he was drawing. 'Do you, indeed? And what may they be?'

'I'd quite like to buy the house next door to ours in Rottingdean,' Georgie said. 'So we have room for …' She had been about to say 'Margot and Jack', but caught herself up, saying quickly instead, '… guests'.

Ned did not seem to notice her hesitation.

He nodded and shrugged. 'Why not? If we can afford it. Is it for sale?'

'No,' Georgie said. 'I'm just thinking ahead.'

'Well, I shall buy you a new hat,' Ned said. 'That old bonnet of yours is a disgrace.'

Georgie shrugged. 'It keeps the sun out of my eyes. Is that not what it's for?'

'It's one of the things it's for,' Ned said severely. 'But not the only thing. Things should be beautiful as well as useful, you know. Or so Topsy tells me. And if Topsy tells me a thing, I generally know that it's true.'

'It's only a bonnet, Ned.'

'Yes, but why wear an ugly bonnet if you could wear a beautiful one?'

All adornment is vanity, Georgie's father used to say. And the Devil finds work for idle hands. When she had been a little girl, if he had ever found one of his daughters unoccupied, he would insist on an impromptu prayer meeting. All the girls would be made to kneel on the ground around him, their heads bowed, their hands folded before their faces, as he prayed over their heads. 'Nothing tries my temper more than to see anyone about me idle,' he would say. 'An idle person tempts the Devil to tempt him. We must rise early and be at our work till late, and always zealous about our duty, and doing the work of God so that the Devil cannot find a chink of time in which to whisper to you and lead you into temptation.'

Georgie had long ago put away her father's sermons and her mother's homilies. She had not been inside a church for many years. Yet here she sat, defending her right to wear an ugly bonnet and darning socks when she could have been playing her piano.

'You are right,' she said. 'I suppose that I have always thought I shouldn't spend any money on something so frivolous, when there are always so many bills to be paid.'

'Beauty is not frivolous,' Ned said, carefully drawing angel wings. 'I intend to spend the rest of my life loving beauty with all my heart. I shall have no time left over for hatred or unkindness or for trying to force people to do what they don't want to do. I want people to like what they like.'

Georgie put her needle into the heel of the sock, and put it back into the basket. 'Wise words,' she said, half-mockingly. She rose and went to her piano, and opened the lid.

'You know what I have realised?' Ned said. 'People are *like* what they *like*. The splendid like splendour, and the glorious like glory, and the tender like tenderness, and the frozen like brass ...'

'I'd have thought you would say the frozen like ice,' Georgie interjected, playing a few notes with one finger. It had been so long since she played.

'No,' Ned said firmly. 'The frozen like brass, and the timid pretend they like brass. The nasty like nastiness, and the vague like vagueness, and the clean like cleanness, and the mean like worthlessness ...'

'And so what of you?' Georgie pulled out her tattered old music books and began to ruffle through them.

'I like beauty,' he said simply. 'I want to make things beautiful. I have no politics, and no party, and no particular hope. I only know that beauty is very beautiful, and softens and comforts and inspires and rouses and lifts up and never fails.'

'You are missing Topsy,' Georgie said.

Ned looked sad. 'Yes. I am. Those damned Socialists have their hooks in him and he has no time for art anymore. He wants to start a revolution, and fill the streets with rivers of blood.'

'He wants to change the world for the better.'

'I know.' He drew a long sweeping angel feather. 'I think I am afraid the world will be changed for the worse,' he whispered after a while.

Georgie took a deep breath. Perhaps this was the chance she had been waiting for, the opportunity to prepare him for the knowledge that his little girl had fallen in love and wanted to leave him. 'Everything must change in time, Ned. It's the nature of the world.'

She thought of all that had changed since she had met Ned. Match-girls were striking against their employers, slums were being cleared, and all children had to go to school. Even girls.

And women were now permitted to own property, and earn a living.

The Queen had celebrated her Golden Jubilee. Fifty years on her throne, most of the last two decades spent in the slough of despond. Georgie wanted to shake her awake. *Look out the window! Your people are restless. They're throwing off the shackles, they're demanding changes to the world. Women want the vote, the Irish are rebelling, India is no longer the stolen gem in your empress's crown. Wake up, you fat old woman! Can't you smell the fresh wind blowing?*

Ned mumbled something, his attention on drawing a perfect halo.

Georgie tried again. 'Without change, there'd be no growth. Without winter, there'd be no spring. And without darkness, there'd be no light.'

He looked up, his attention caught. 'Yes. That's right.'

Without another word he put down his pencil, caught up his hat and coat, and went out into the snowy night, head bowed under the force of the icy wind. Georgie watched him anxiously from the back door until she saw the distant windows of the studio kindle with lamplight, and knew he was safe.

Then she went to her piano and played till her fingertips were sore.

Ned did not come to bed. The next morning she braved the snow and took her husband some hot coffee and fresh bread rolls for breakfast. He lay on his studio couch, asleep, looking so tired and thin she did not have the heart to wake him. She examined the paintings curiously, wondering what new inspiration her words had sparked. It took her some time to find the change.

There was no sense of depth of perspective in any of the four huge paintings. The strong arabesques of the interlaced briars, the heavy looped curtains and the dark, shuttered windows all created a sense of almost stifling enclosure, as if no world existed beyond that of the enchanted castle. But Ned had, in the night, painted three small windows in the sleeping princess's room, allowing just a glimpse of open air beyond the thick, guarding branches of thorns.

A premonition of light.

Still Margot said nothing to her father.

Georgie wondered why she hesitated. To her eyes, it was clear that Margot was radiant with happiness. It was as if she had found the missing part of her soul. She could not understand how Ned had not guessed, as she had.

But all of his awareness was focused on the Briar Rose paintings. Nothing else mattered.

One evening, in the last days of winter, Georgie said to her daughter, 'Darling, I think you should tell him. The longer you go without telling him, the harder it will be.'

Margot gazed at her mother in astonishment. 'You know? About Jack?'

Georgie nodded.

'We thought we were doing such a good job of keeping it secret.'

'Not from a mother's eyes,' Georgie said with a smile. 'I'm so happy for you, darling girl. He is just the man I would have chosen for you.'

'Is he?' Margot cried in delight. 'Why?'

'Because he is so kind,' Georgie said. 'And because he loves you.'

She felt a pang as she said the words. Georgie had thought Ned the gentlest man alive, and their love preordained from the beginning of time. And yet he had hurt her so cruelly. So much that she had hated him for it.

Georgie pushed the thought away. 'Would you like me to tell him?'

Margot hesitated, but then shook her head. 'No. I'll do it. At least ... I think Jack and I should do it together.' She bit her lip, looking down at her hands. 'Will he ... will he be very sad?'

'Yes,' Georgie said. 'But also so very glad for you both.'

Joy, sorrow. Love, hate. Kindness, cruelty. Beauty, ugliness.

What a mysterious world we live in, Georgie thought. Mysterious but miraculous.

So Margot and Jack stood together before the fire one evening, fingers entwined, to tell her father that they planned to be married.

Ned sat very still, looking from one to the other. 'That's ... that's wonderful. Congratulations.' He stood up stiffly, shook Jack's hand and kissed Margot on the cheek.

Margot put his arms about him. 'I shall always be your little girl, Papa.'

'I know, I know.' He tried to smile. 'This calls for a celebration! If only your mother allowed us a wine cellar. It shall have to be tea.'

The evening passed with much merriment and the making of plans. Margot only wanted a small wedding. Jack had but one sister, and no mother and father, and she did not want his side of the church to be empty while hers was full. 'I told him once that I would share my parents with him,' she said, laughing.

'I told her it would be an honour and a pleasure,' Jack said.

He was a grave young man, but that evening it was as if something had been unlocked in him, allowing him to grin and laugh, and tease Georgie and Ned, and mock himself. 'I made such a fool of myself the first time I saw her,' he said. 'Up on the podium, reading aloud my ridiculous poem, and then I see her, gazing up at me with those great blue eyes of hers, and next thing I know I'm blushing and stammering like a schoolboy.'

'And then Papa said Jack seemed like a nice chap and was going to come and see his studio. And I, of course, was hoping that it meant he wanted to come and see *me*.'

'I have been greatly deceived,' Ned said. 'I thought you a most learned fellow who came because you wished to converse about books. It did not occur to me that you came because you wished to steal away my daughter.'

There was an edge to his voice.

'I'm sorry, sir,' Jack said. 'I promise you I won't take her far away. Margot wants to find a house as close to you as she can get.'

'Yes, but she still won't be *here*,' Ned said. He took a deep breath and composed himself. 'It's just that I am used to having her about. The house will seem very empty with you gone, my blue-eyed damsel.'

'I know,' she said and put her arms about him, pressing her cheek against his. 'But you'll find something new to paint and then hardly notice I'm gone.'

'I'll always know you're gone,' he said mournfully. 'I don't know how I'll do without you.'

'You'll just need to rely on me,' Georgie said, getting up and tidying up the cups. 'Look at the time! Jack, will you mind if we draw the evening to a close? Ned has been so unwell again this winter. I don't like him to be up too late when he's had a long day in the studio. And Margot needs her beauty sleep.'

Jack stood up at once and said his farewells, and Margot walked him to the front door. Ned sat, back hunched, staring into the fire. Georgie came and put her hand on his shoulder. 'Well done,' she said quietly.

He nodded, and got up and went out. She could hear his slow heavy footsteps on the stairs.

Margot came back in, bubbling with joy, and Georgie went up with her to her bedroom, to brush out her hair and talk some more. 'Papa did not seem to mind at all,' Margot cried, as she changed into her nightgown and bounced into bed.

'See, I told you. Now go to sleep, if you can. We will talk more in the morning.'

'I'm so happy, I'm afraid,' Margot said.

Georgie felt such a thickening of the tissues of her throat she could scarcely breathe. 'If there is only one gift I could give you,' she managed to say, 'it would be to have the courage to love him with all your heart. Just love him. That's all that matters.'

'I know,' Margot said. 'I will, I promise.'

'Good night, darling.' Georgie gave her daughter one last kiss. 'I'll see you in the morning.'

She went quietly about the house, blowing out candles and putting the guard in front of the fireplace. Outside, the wind rattled through bare branches, and an owl was hunting. The sky was clear, but few stars could be seen. The glare of London was too close for that. She went to her own room, and slowly undressed and unpinned her hair. A few silver hairs glinted amongst the brown. She did not look in the mirror, but washed her face and cleaned her teeth.

She did not climb into her own bed, but went as quietly as she could along the corridor to Ned's room. It was lit only by the glowing coals in the fireplace. He lay in his bed, curled up on his side. His breath was raspy and uneven. Georgie took off her dressing-gown and slippers, and climbed into bed beside him. She put her arms around him.

'It's all right, my darling. I'm here.'

His chest heaved. A few tears fell on to her wrist. She kissed his shoulder. 'You did so well. I'm so proud of you. Sssh, now. They'll be happy, I promise you.'

Gradually his sobbing breaths calmed. One of his hands found hers, and returned her clasp. She kissed him again, and soothed him with her voice.

'What shall I do? How shall I bear it?' The words came with great difficulty.

'You must,' she said. 'Don't think of it as an ending, but as a new beginning.'

He took a deep shuddering breath. 'You know, if I ever see my mother again … in heaven, you know … she will be such a young thing … she was just Margot's age when she died. So young. Too young.'

Georgie crept a little closer to him, and he turned to face her. 'Margot has her life ahead of her,' she whispered. 'She's running to meet it. Let her go, Ned. Let her be happy.'

'I … I want her to be.' His voice shook. 'It's just … I'm so afraid. Of her being hurt … or her dying …'

'I know. But you can't save her from any of that. You shouldn't want to try. Life is for living, Ned.'

They lay together in silence for a long time, then Ned gave an abrupt nod. 'You're right. I know it. I'll try to be happy for her.'

'Perhaps they'll have little ones,' she whispered. 'You'll be a grandpapa and I'll be a grandmama.'

He laughed and sobbed together. 'I'm not old enough for that!'

'I'm afraid you are. You'll be fifty-five this year, and I'll be forty-eight.'

'I don't want to get old.'

'No-one ever does.'

He had shifted towards her, so that she no longer embraced his back but lay in the crook of his elbow, her head on his shoulder, one arm across his chest. How familiar it felt to her, and yet how strange. It had been a very long time since they had shared a bed.

'To think I liked him,' he said.

'You'll like him again. Give yourself time.'

He sighed. 'I suppose I should have seen it coming.'

She smiled and looked up at him, even though she could see him only dimly in the low light. 'Margaret did not want to upset you. She did her best to hide it from you.'

'I hope he's good to her. I'll wring his neck if he hurts her.'

Georgie caught her breath, and turned a little away from him. So long ago, and yet still he had the power to wound her.

Ned shifted so that he could look at her. 'I just hurt you then, didn't I? I'm sorry. I didn't mean to.'

She could not speak.

He drew her closer. 'I am sorry. About … well, about it all.'

'I know,' she managed to say.

He bent his head and kissed her cheek. 'It just happened. And then … I couldn't stop. I wanted to, and yet … oh, she wasn't who I thought she was. But by then things had got out of hand … and I realised I'd ruined everything.' He pressed her a little closer. 'I've been sorry about it for a very long time.'

'But … you kept going back to her?' This was something Georgie had wanted to ask him for a long time.

'She's the very Devil,' Ned said, in a tone of wonderment. 'The harder I tried to escape, the tighter she would cling. But then, when I followed her, she would laugh at me and tell me I was a fool. And so I would go away … and then she'd come again … and throw herself at my feet and cry and tell me her heart was broken … and I couldn't bear it, I just couldn't bear it.'

Georgie tightened her arms about him. He drew her closer, kissing her temple, and then her cheek. Georgie could not help pressing her nose into his skin, inhaling his scent. She had always loved the way he smelt. His mouth found hers. Something melted within her. She could not bear for him to lift his mouth away, and caught hold of the back of his neck, pulling him closer. His hand slipped down to her breast, hidden behind good sensible flannel, and then found the edge of her neckline and slid within. Georgie sighed at the feel of his hand on her bare skin. One of her feet found his.

'You're cold,' he whispered. 'Let me warm you.'

He pressed both of her small feet between his own, his hand drawing up her nightgown, then edging between her knees. Georgie sighed, and lifted herself so he could reach her more easily. They kissed, gently, tenderly.

Georgie thought she had stifled all desire. She thought she had left all hunger far behind.

She had been wrong.

10

All the Treasure
Winter–Spring 1890

Margot's daughter was born on a snowy winter's night in late January.

As she heard the baby's first gasping wail, a thrill went through her.

I have looked death in the face now, she thought, and I have beaten it.

The midwife passed her the tiny white bundle. Margot looked down at her daughter's face, soft as a rose petal, and gently touched her cheek. 'Your daddy and I, we made you. We gave you life.'

The big dark eyes looked up at her. One small hand grasped at the air.

'So you make sure you live a good one,' Margot whispered.

Mama stroked Margot's sweat-dampened hair away from her face. 'Well done, darling,' she said. 'You had a hard time of it but you won through. How do you feel?'

Margot tried to find the word.

'Exultant,' she said at last.

Mama smiled and nodded. 'I know it happens every day, all over the world, but it really does seem a miracle, doesn't it?'

Margot nodded, surprised to find tears leaking from her eyes and running down her face. 'I don't know why I'm crying. I'm so happy.'

'You can cry from joy as much as from sorrow,' Mama said. 'Here, let me mop your face for you. Can I bring the men in now? They've been beating a path in your carpet downstairs.'

Margot nodded. She could not look away from her daughter's face. She wished that she could capture this moment forever. Sharp within her was a sense of terror at the hurt the world might do to this tiny, vulnerable creature who she had carried within her for so long. For the first time, she understood some of her father's fierce love – and fear – for her.

The door opened and Jack came in. He was white-faced and haggard, but smiling in joy and relief. 'Hello, you,' he said to his daughter. 'Welcome to the world.'

He kissed her tiny hand, and then kissed Margot. 'Thank God you're safe,' he whispered. 'I was so afraid.'

She smiled at him wearily. 'Me too. But we won through in the end.'

Then Papa was bending over her, kissing the damp little curls on her daughter's head.

'Georgie, can you believe it? We're grandparents.'

'What are you going to call her?' Mama asked.

Margot looked down at the baby nestled in the crook of her arm. 'Angela. For she's as beautiful as any of Papa's angels.'

Carriages clogged the road all the way down to Piccadilly Circus.

So many hundreds of people milled outside Agnew's Gallery, policemen had been called to keep order. They stood in rows, truncheons at their belts, the badge on their blue helmets glittering in the bright sunshine, ordering the crowd into a long queue that snaked away down Old Bond Street. Street-sellers strolled up and down, selling hot elderberry wine and roasted chestnuts in paper cones. Despite the bright blue sky, the day was chilly, and people in the queue stamped their feet and tucked their hands inside muffs or coat pockets. A girl was riding about on a bicycle, flaunting her shapely calves.

'Can you believe it?' Georgie marvelled. 'There must be a thousand people here.'

'It's like a fair day,' Margot said. 'Papa, come and look.'

'I don't want to look,' Ned answered. He was sitting on a low chair by the fire, Angela in his arms. He dangled a silver rattle above the baby's face, and she cooed in delight and reached for it with tiny hands.

Georgie and Ned and the rest of the family had come to see the opening of the exhibition of the 'Legend of Briar Rose' painting, but had been so trampled by people that they had retreated to Mr Agnew's sitting room on an upper floor. Ned had bought Georgie a new hat for the occasion. It was the most frivolous thing she had ever seen, frothing with pink roses like a summer garden. It gave Ned great pleasure to see her wear it, though, and so she had bravely pinned it in place, and was surprised to find she enjoyed everyone's compliments.

Ned, however, looked thin and old and stooped. He was utterly done in, Georgie thought. It had been an immense task, finishing the four paintings of 'The Legend of Briar Rose', the title Ned had finally chosen for the story cycle. Topsy had written four lines of verse for each painting, which had been engraved on the golden frame beneath each of the giant canvases. Georgie knew each verse off by heart.

The fateful slumber floats and flows
About the tangle of the rose;
But lo! the fated hand and heart
To rend the slumberous curse apart!

The threat of war, the hope of peace,
The Kingdom's peril and increase
Sleep on, and bide the latter day,
When fate shall take her chain away.

The maiden pleasance of the land
Knoweth no stir of voice or hand,

No cup the sleeping waters fill,
The restless shuttle lieth still.

Here lies the hoarded love, the key
To all the treasure that shall be;
Come fated hand the gift to take,
And smite this sleeping world awake.

Georgie thought 'The Legend of Briar Rose' was the most exquisite work Ned had ever done. And it seemed the rest of the country thought so too. The newspapers were all full of glowing reviews. *The Times* spoke of Ned's 'exuberance of fancy', and *The Magazine of Art* said the four vast canvases were 'equal to anything that has ever been done since painting began'. Many spoke about the simplicity and purity of *The Sleeping Princess*, and wondered why Ned had not painted the moment in which she was awakened with a kiss.

Ned refused to read any of the reviews, or to answer any of the curious questions. Only once had he tried to explain his purpose in the paintings, when he had wearily said, 'I just want to tell people something.'

There had been talk of sending the paintings on tour to America, but Ned had shaken his head. He wanted them to be part of the free Easter exhibition at Toynbee Hall, where anyone who wanted to could see them, and then to be hung in their final resting place at Buscot Park. He planned to paint intersecting panels of entangled rose briars to connect the four paintings together.

Georgie looked back down at the crowded street, at the queues of people lining up to see her husband's paintings, and shook her head in disbelief. After so many years of poverty and struggle, after so many years of being torn apart by critics and ignored by the establishment, this ecstatic response just seemed impossible.

She thought of a young girl who had visited Ned's studio just that week, to watch him painting *The Star of Bethlehem*.

'Do you believe the story's true?' she had asked in her sweet, piping voice.

He had answered gravely, 'It is too beautiful not to be true.'

Part V

Wake, Dearest
1896–1899

Not until his fifth-seventh birthday in August had come and gone did he tell anyone what he then confessed, that for years he had been filled with premonitions and forebodings that he would never live to see it. 'I had it strongly as the time drew near, and very potently the night before. And that's why I hurried so to finish Briar Rose.'

Lady Georgiana Burne-Jones

Memorials of Edward Burne-Jones, Volume II

1

No More Kings
Summer 1896

'Where's the baby?' Judy shrieked.

'I have had the saddest o' misfortunes, my dear,' Punch said sadly, in his funny high-pitched voice. 'It's just … the baby was so terrible cross, I throwed it out the window.'

All the children laughed, except for the little boy on Ned's knee who shrank away in terror. It was his birthday, and also his mother Margot's birthday. Denis was very like her, Georgie thought, being delicately made with huge blue eyes and soft brown hair. He was a sensitive little chap too, prone to night terrors just like Margot had been. Georgie hoped that the Punch and Judy show would not inspire any nightmares that night.

'Oh, no, the baby, the baby!' Judy rushed about the tiny stage, weeping, then snatched up a cudgel and whacked Punch hard.

Punch snatched the stick away and began to beat her around the head.

'I'll go to the constable, an' have you locked up!' Judy cried.

'Go to the Devil. I don't care where you go!' As Judy rushed off stage, Punch began to dance about, singing raspily:

As I was walking
down the street

a pretty girl I chanced to meet,
hi ho hi ho hi ho!

The audience began to sing along, and six-year-old Angela piped up in her sweet voice, looking up to her grandfather's face every now and again to make sure he was singing too. After a moment, little Denis joined in and Ned took his hands and clapped them together, inside his own much larger ones.

Just then a puppet dressed in the blue coat, white gloves and tall hat of a policeman crept on to the stage, a truncheon in his hand.

'Watch out, Punch!' Ned shouted. The children took up the cry. 'Watch out! Behind you!'

Punch whipped around and struck the policeman hard over the head with his slapstick. The policeman fell over.

Ned guffawed so infectiously that the whole room erupted into uproarious laughter. Even little Denis laughed, clapping his small hands together joyously.

The play went on in all its vital silliness, Punch gleefully beating down the lawyer, the hangman, and then the Devil in turn, and throwing the baby out the window whenever it made an unexpected appearance.

Georgie watched quietly from a chair under the apple tree. Margot sat beside her, smiling as much at her children's delight as at the puppet show itself. Angela in particular was beside herself with delight, dancing about and pretending to punch and whack the air.

'Aren't they enjoying it?' Margot said. 'It's strange. Angela doesn't seem frightened at all. I used to be terrified of Punch.'

'I don't much like it myself,' Georgie confessed. 'But your father loves it so much, I haven't the heart to ban it.'

'I suppose he never saw it as a child,' Margot said.

'No. But then I never did either. We were never permitted to see any kind of theatre, not even a puppet show. I first went to the theatre in Paris, with your father and Mr Ruskin, when Phil was only a little fellow. We went to the ballet, and I was so shocked!'

Margot laughed. 'The costumes or the closeness of the embrace?'

'Both! I'd never seen the like.' Georgie mimicked her own mother's shocked tones at anything she thought unseemly.

Margot smiled at her. 'But you go to the theatre all the time now.'

'Oh, yes. But not with your father. We have very different tastes. He loves comedy, while my taste runs more to tragedy.'

'Yet you are always so cheerful and even-tempered, while Papa is the one who struggles with melancholy.'

'I know. Your papa always says he cannot bear any story about heartbreak. He says such stories are only for the hard-hearted. And he, of course, is the softest-hearted of men.'

Georgie sighed, thinking of her husband's new infatuation with May Gaskell, the beautiful and desperately unhappy wife of a rich but aloof military man. Ned could never resist beauty and misfortune. And he loved the kind of intense romantic friendship that allowed him to pour out his heart to a sympathetic listener, and have them utterly charmed and bewitched by his whimsy. Georgie had known him far too long to be so bedazzled. In a week it would be their thirty-sixth wedding anniversary. Though Ned told everyone it was their one hundred and thirty-fourth anniversary, which made Georgie laugh.

She did not mind Ned writing little love-notes, and meeting Mrs Gaskell for tea, and painting her daughter, and going to stay with her in the country. She knew there was no harm in it; indeed, it seemed to help both Ned and Mrs Gaskell, who had the same kind of wistful sadness about them. You should never want anyone to be everything to you, Georgie had realised. It placed too much of a strain on them. Far better to love and be loved for who you truly are, and turn to others when you needed more.

It was the same with friendships. Ned had been greatly saddened by the rift that had opened between him and Topsy over his passionate zeal to change the world. Yet Ned had, in time, filled that rift with other close relationships. Including, most interestingly, Georgie's nephew Rudyard Kipling, who had just published the most enchanting work for children called *The Jungle Book*. Georgie could not help a little pang at its success.

Once upon a time she had dreamed of writing a book, and illustrating it herself, but such dreams had been put away long ago.

There is only room for one genius in any family, she had told herself.

Topsy was still very dear to Ned, of course. Indeed, Georgie thought their friendship had been strengthened and warmed by Ned's eventual willingness to let his friend go. Topsy came to breakfast every Sunday morning, demanding vast quantities of tea and eggs and ham, and entertaining them all with his crazy outbursts of rage and enthusiasm, and his quite dreadful language. Georgie pretended to be greatly shocked by all the oaths that flew from his mouth, but in truth she wished that she could sometimes let herself go and stamp about, shouting, 'Damn blast it all to bloody hell!'

It must be very soothing.

Topsy was just as radical as ever, despite having been arrested once for knocking off a policeman's helmet at a court hearing. Yet in recent years, he seemed to have calmed down a little. He and Ned had spent many long hours together, working on a magnificent illustrated edition of *The Works of Geoffrey Chaucer*, with eighty-seven wood-cut illustrations. Ned said it was like a little cathedral, so beautifully and carefully was it made. He had given one of the first editions to Margaret for her birthday just that morning, wrapping it up in great quantities of brown paper into such a strange shape she could not possibly guess what it was.

Georgie smiled to herself again. Her old fellow was still the funniest man she'd ever met.

'Thankin' you ever so much, my lady. It was a pleasure, it was, puttin' on the show for your littlies.' An obsequious cockney voice interrupted her thoughts, and she looked up. It was the puppeteer, holding his greasy hat in his hand, smiling at her hopefully. She had her purse ready with his payment, and counted out the coins carefully, with an extra tip in thanks for amusing Ned so well.

The puppeteer's voice slipped into the high, shrill tones of Punch. 'That's how you do it!'

'However do you do his voice?' Ned asked, coming up behind him.

'Now that, sir, is a punchman's secret. Can't ever tell that, on pain o' death,' the old man answered, with an exaggerated wink. 'Thank you again, my lady.' He waved his hat and gathered up his barrow of puppets and striped tent, and wheeled them away, whistling.

Georgie stared after him. She just could not get used to being called 'my lady'.

Who would ever have guessed that ordinary Ned Jones from Birmingham would end up being named a baronet?

The baronetcy had been created for him by the Queen two years ago. Ned had then applied for a royal licence to change his name officially to Burne-Jones, which meant – rather comically – that his full name was now Sir Edward Coley Burne Burne-Jones. Not that anyone called him that, of course.

Georgie felt uneasily that Topsy was disappointed in Ned for accepting the title. It would have been such a good opportunity for him to make a public declaration of the hollowness of all such honours. But Ned was far too polite to do such a thing, and was actually secretly pleased. Their son Phil had been very publicly pleased, since he would inherit the title eventually. And it seemed so hard to make Phil happy these days, Ned thought it better to gracefully accept.

It still gave Georgie a little start when letters arrived for her addressed to Lady Burne-Jones, however. She had been plain Mrs Jones for so long, she felt a little guilty opening the envelopes as if she was prying through someone else's mail.

A lot had changed in recent years. Motor carriages could be seen shoving their way through the crowded city streets, startling the horses with their high-pitched beeps. There was talk of founding a women's suffrage union, and – much to Georgie's surprise and pleasure – she had been elected a parish councillor in Rottingdean. 'You should have seen her,' Ned had crowed to Topsy. 'She's marching about and rousing the people – she's like a flame, going through the whole village.'

He was exaggerating, of course, but Georgie had high hopes of establishing a nursing service for the village, setting up a system to drain the cesspools and clean the streets, build new houses for the workers, and educate them so they could have some hopes of bettering themselves. If she had her way, every labourer in the village would be reading Topsy's socialist newsletters. It was a struggle, there was no doubt about that, but Georgie relished the challenge.

They lived in wonderful times, she thought. The world had changed so much already. What other changes would they see in the next fifty years, the next hundred?

Margot brought her a slice of cake and a fresh cup of tea, then went to Jack's side, winding her arm through his. He was talking in his serious way to a few of their neighbours about a new ballet said to be taking Europe by storm. It was inspired by Sleeping Beauty, just like Ned's famous painting, and the score was written by a controversial composer called Pyotr Ilyich Tchaikovsky. Jack smiled at Margot and pressed her arm a little closer, and she joined in the conversation eagerly.

The children ran about the garden, screaming with delight as they chased each other with sticks. Ned came to sit next to Georgie. 'I really do think Punch is the noblest play in the whole world. He's such a fine character, so cheerful and good-natured, and such a poet. It's such a shame he has such a shrew of a wife, and that the world keeps breaking in on him.'

Georgie knew he was teasing her. In answer, she pointed to where Angela had just whacked Denis across the back with her stick. The little boy was crying, and his sister was defending herself loudly. 'We was playing Punch, Mama. You can't play Punch without whacking!'

'And quite right too,' Ned said, but got up to swoop on Denis, and hang him upside down, and march with him around the garden. Angela chased after them, demanding to be carried too. Soon the little boy was laughing hysterically, his face crimson, his lashes damp and spiky with tears.

The next day Topsy came for breakfast as usual.

'I say, old boy,' Ned cried. 'We had a Punch and Judy show here yesterday. You'd have loved it!'

'Yes.' Topsy wearily leant his tousled white head on his hand. 'I do like Punch.'

After he had gone, Ned came to Georgie, looking frightened. 'Did you see Tops leaning on his hand? He never used to do that. I'm afraid, Georgie. He doesn't look well.'

She comforted him, but was worried too. Topsy was looking so thin and bent. And she knew that he had been forced to miss many of his Socialist meetings, his daughter May reading out his speeches for him.

Topsy grew sicker as the year passed. A sea journey to Norway did little to help, and at the end of August they were all horrified to hear that he had tuberculosis of the lungs and did not have much longer to live. Ned wept in Georgie's arms, and she had difficulty in hiding her own grief. It was like a fist punch to her diaphragm, making it almost impossible to breathe.

On the first of September, Topsy wrote to Georgie in a shaky hand, *'Come soon, I want sight of your dear face.'*

When she came into the hall of Kelmscott House, Janey met her, looking thin and haggard. Grey streaked her abundant black hair. 'Oh, Janey, how is he?' Georgie cried. Janey turned from her, and pressed her face into her arms against the wall. Her shoulders shook.

Georgie patted her in wordless comfort, then went slowly down the corridor and into Topsy's room. He lay in his bed, wheezing. He smiled when he saw her, though, and took her small hand in both of his huge, bear-like paws.

They sat together in silence for a long time.

Topsy died a month later, at eleven-fifteen in the morning, as gently as a babe falling asleep. Both Ned and Georgie were with him, as well as Janey and May and a few other dear friends. Ned fell to his knees by the bed and sobbed. 'I am alone now. Quite, quite alone.'

Georgie hugged him close. 'I know, my dear. I know.'

Topsy was buried in the churchyard in Kelmscott, on a wild and stormy day that lashed the mourners with rain and hail, as if Topsy's spirit was in one last rage. His coffin was of a simple oak, covered with one of his ancient tapestries instead of a pall, and surrounded with all the flowers he most loved, the wild flowers of the meadow and hedgerow. It was carried to the church on a two-wheeled farm cart lined with moss and entwined with willow leaves and vines, with the roan mare that pulled the cart wearing blinkers made of leaves.

'It's so beautiful, it just breaks my heart,' Ned said, leaning against the wall as if he had no pith left in his limbs to hold him upright. 'It's the funeral procession of an old pagan king … and once he is buried, there'll be no more kings. The last of the great ones is gone.'

2

Starting Afresh
Summer–Winter 1896

Janey was unutterably lonely without him.

The house was so quiet. No bellowing of rage, no gales of laughter. She could hear the ticking of the grandfather clock in the hall, the susurration of leaves in the garden. Lying on the sofa, her embroidery lying limp in her hands, Janey would have given anything to hear Topsy roaring her name.

A discreet knock on the front door surprised her. Janey was expecting no visitors. Perhaps it was someone who did not know Topsy had died. According to his wishes, she had not hung the door knocker with crepe, or drawn the drapes, or even dressed in mourning. Topsy had hated what he called 'that mumbo-jumbo'.

The door opened and the parlour-maid bobbed her head. 'A visitor for you, missus.'

It was Mr Blunt. A handsome man in his late fifties, he had thick dark hair, a gingery beard and sardonic hazel eyes. He had been – for a while – her lover, but in recent years their ardour had cooled to an intermittent friendship. She did not want him here now, when her grief was so raw and her loneliness so heavy.

Janey stumbled to her feet, one hand on the sofa arm to steady herself. He came straight to her, put his arms about her and kissed her.

She drew herself away.

'I came as soon as I heard the news, Mrs Morris. I am so very sorry. He was a great man. A genius!'

She turned away, trying to compose herself. 'After all this time, don't you think you might call me Janey?'

He smiled and shook his head. 'Oh, no. I like to think of you as Mrs William Morris. "Famous for her husband, a poet, and most famous for her face; so let this picture of mine add to her fame".'

Gabriel had inscribed those words on the first portrait of her that he had painted so lovingly, so long ago. Sometimes Janey thought that Mr Blunt had only seduced her because she had been the lover of the two men he admired most in the world.

Janey clasped her hands together. 'Why are you here, Mr Blunt?'

He smiled and took her hand, stroking her palm. 'In my experience grief is a sharp spur to desire.'

Janey drew her hand away. 'What makes you think I am grieving? I am not unhappy ... Topsy is at peace now and no longer in pain.' Her voice was cool.

'Do you feel nothing at his death?' he asked with avid curiosity.

She could not look at him. 'Well, of course it is a terrible thing. I have been with him for such a long time ... since I first knew anything of the world. I was just eighteen when I married him.'

And now I am fifty-seven, she thought. With grey in my hair and lines on my face. Fifty-seven and all alone.

Tears sprang to her eyes. She moved across to the window, and looked out into the garden.

'So you never loved your husband?' Mr Blunt was avid with curiosity.

'No,' she lied.

Once Mr Blunt had asked her – as they lay drowsily in each other's arms – if she had ever given herself quite so completely to Gabriel. She had said 'no' to him then too.

Janey did not want to reveal the deepest secrets of her heart to the world.

Mr Blunt came to her side, taking her cold unresponsive hand once more. 'Let me comfort you, Mrs Morris. You can tell me anything, you know that. You can unburden yourself to me. Let me look after you. Come and stay with me. My wife won't mind.'

Janey shook her head.

'You could come to Egypt with me,' he said. 'Escape the London winter. See the Sphinx, climb the pyramids.'

That caught her attention. 'You mean it? Come to Egypt?'

'If you like.' Her sudden interest unnerved him, and he drew back a little.

'Very well, I'll come,' she said. 'But only if I can bring May.'

So, three days after her husband's funeral, Janey and her daughter went to stay with the man who had once been her lover.

He lived in a lovely Jacobean manor house in Sussex. Peacocks strutted across velvet lawns, displaying their brilliant plumage, and gleaming horses with manes like silk looked out from spotless stables. As always the house was filled with aristocratic ladies in white bell dresses and impoverished poets in sack coats and floppy bow-ties. Janey was glad to walk in the gardens with May, and listen to music in the evenings in the grand drawing-room. Mr Blunt offered her a pansy once – a secret invitation to his bed – but Janey smiled and shook her head. Ruefully he wandered away and offered it to a bored-looking noblewoman with a wasp waist and leg-o'-mutton sleeves, who took it with a discreet smile and tucked it in her buttonhole.

It was such a relief to be away from the gloomy house at Hammersmith. Once so full and noisy. Now so empty and quiet.

Bought to provide a haven for Jenny, the huge old house no longer fulfilled that function. Five years earlier, Jenny had been committed to an asylum, after going mad one day and trying to throw herself out a window.

They had to tie Jenny to her bed, till the doctors came to take her away. It had felt like a death blow. Topsy had broken down afterwards and taken to his bed, and Janey felt he had never truly recovered from the shock of it.

May, meanwhile, had fallen head-over-heels in love with a young playwright named George Bernard Shaw. They acted in dramatic theatricals together, marched in Socialist rallies, and fought over the suffragettes' cause. May was fiercely independent. She had become head of the Firm's embroidery department at only twenty-three, and believed passionately in the need for women to work and earn their own living.

Mr Shaw had blown hot, then cold, then hot again, only to fall for an alluring actress and break off their affair. On the rebound, May had married a weak-chinned Socialist called Henry Halliday Sparling, who let her order him around as she pleased. Janey had been horrified. Her beautiful bright daughter, throwing herself away like that! She and Topsy had argued with May, to no avail. In the end Topsy had cut her off. May had proudly struggled to live on only a few pounds a week, refusing to admit she had made a dreadful mistake.

Then, most shockingly, Mr Shaw moved in with May and Henry. It was meant to be temporary, while his lodgings were refurnished. But he stayed and stayed and did not leave. Soon the three of them were living in a far more open and scandalous ménage-à-trois than Topsy, Gabriel and Janey had ever shared.

Unsurprisingly, it had ended in catastrophe. May had thrown her husband out, in the hope Mr Shaw would stay with her. Mr Shaw, however, tasting the first dazzle of success with his plays, had taken up with yet another actress.

It had been one hard blow after another for May, and Janey hoped that a complete change of scene would be healing for them both.

A few weeks of idleness in Sussex, and then they set sail for Egypt. Janey was more excited than she cared to admit. She had been fascinated by the land of the Pharaohs ever since seeing the Egyptian Gallery at the British Museum. She had always wished to travel the world, but apart from trips to Germany and Italy had been greatly confined to England by her husband's work, the need to care for Jenny, and her own ill health.

Egypt was as fascinating as she could have wished. Miles of wind-ruffled red sands. The enigmatic gaze of the broken-nosed Sphinx. The mysterious pyramids. Endless mazes of souks and alleyways. Fragments of ancient embroidery sewn before Christ had been born.

Janey and May rode out into the desert, Janey's horse being led by a tall man in sand-coloured robes. May joked that Mr Blunt should procure a camel for her, and wondered why it was that Janey had never learned to ride when she had grown up in a stable.

'The horses weren't ours to use,' Janey explained, and – for the first time – shared a little of the truth of her childhood with her daughter.

May was slowly coming back to life in the warmth of the Egyptian sun. She liked to watch the native jewellers at work in their tiny huts, and bought herself heavy, intricate jewellery which she then pulled apart and put back together in different patterns. She sketched an embroidery pattern that she called 'An Eastern Garden', inspired by the stylised drawings of birds and flowers they saw on vases and platters, and sewed an embroidered robe for herself inspired by traditional Arab robes called 'djibbahs'. Janey was so glad to see her daughter working again. May was so like Topsy, she was only happy when she was doing something with her hands.

On their last night in Egypt, Janey and May walked out into the old quarter of the city, quietly accompanied by one of Mr Blunt's servants. The crooked narrow streets smelt of strange spices and the heavy fragrant smoke of tobacco saturated with molasses. Hawkers shouted their wares, singers beat their hands on their drums and wailed in high-pitched voices, veiled women in long black robes fingered bright-coloured silks, hawkish bearded men in white turbans dragged along overladen donkeys, and barefoot ragged children ran and played with shrieks of laughter. It was like they had wandered into a story from *One Thousand and One Nights*.

Janey and her daughter found a high vantage point and watched the sun go down over the domes and minarets of the mosques. As the sky darkened, the eerie call of the muezzin calling the faithful to prayer rose into the hot dusty air.

'So, back to normal life now,' Janey said with a sigh.

May turned to her mother and burst out, 'I don't know what to do!'

'About Henry?' Janey asked, after a long moment.

'I thought if I turned him out … if I ended our farce of a marriage …'

Janey took a deep breath. 'You thought Mr Shaw would …?'

'Yes. But it seems he does not want me.' May's voice was bitter.

'I always thought Mr Shaw was a dolt.'

May turned to her, half-shocked, half-laughing. 'But Mama! Everyone thinks he's brilliant.'

'Which is why he sleeps with the window open in the depths of winter, and refuses to eat meat, and wears those awful sanitary woollen suits.'

May's laughter broke free. 'They are rather awful.'

'Exactly.' Janey smiled at May. 'He is a dolt, though, darling girl. He had his chance to have you, and he threw it away.'

'I can't go back to Henry.'

'You don't need to. The laws have changed now. You have the right now to keep your own property, and earn your own income, and divorce a man if you don't love him. You can start afresh if you've made a mistake.'

May heaved a great sigh. 'But … what will everyone say?'

'Who cares?' Janey said. 'Not me.'

May looked at her in astonishment, a smile quirking her finely cut lips.

'We could go to Kelmscott Manor for a while,' Janey said. 'Till the scandal blows over. Jenny could come and stay. She's always calmer at Kelmscott. We could read the Brontë sisters, and walk by the river, and sew, and tell each other stories …'

'It sounds heavenly,' May said, leaning on her mother's shoulder.

'Then that's what we'll do,' Janey said, and kissed the top of her head.

3

Awakening the World
Summer 1898

'I don't mind how much I work, I'd like to kill myself with it,' Ned told Georgie.

'You will do so if you are not careful,' she said, bringing a blanket to drape around his shoulders. 'Come to bed, my dear. Avalon will still be here in the morning.'

'But I might have lost the dream,' he said. 'I might wake up and it'll be gone, and then the painting will be no good.'

'You're tired. You'll paint better when you've had a rest.'

'I really don't want to rest. I'm afraid I will die before I have a chance to finish, and then what will happen to my poor painting?'

'You'll have plenty of time to finish the painting, my dear. There's no need to worry.' She took the brush out of his hand and stuck it in one of the many jars of turpentine that crowded the table and shelf.

He let her lead him through the dark garden, the lantern swinging from her hand. It was a beautiful summer's night, with faint stars above the apple trees, and the scent of flowers all around them. He pulled at her hand as they reached the terrace, and halted, looking up at the thin paring of the moon. His beard was white and his face lined, but his pale grey eyes were as full of light as when she had first met him, in her pinafore with her hair in plaits down her back.

'I think the painting is too sad,' he said. 'King Arthur is not dead, he is just sleeping. Will you pick me armfuls of summer flowers, Georgie? I want to paint his garden full of flowers.'

'That's a lovely thought, Ned. I'll pick you as many flowers as you like.'

She tried once again to lead him inside, but once again he resisted her pull.

'You know, Georgie, there are only two types of women. Those who take the strength out of a man and those who put it back in.' He kissed her brow. 'You're the kind that puts the strength back in, Georgie.'

'I'm glad,' she said simply. 'Now will you come to bed?'

Ned had been working on his immense painting of *The Last Sleep of Arthur in Avalon* with the same kind of obsessive intensity that he had brought to the painting of 'The Legend of Briar Rose'. Georgie worried about him. He was sixty-three years old now, and buffeted by endless bouts of influenza. Sometimes she brought him his tea, and found him lying down, his hands draped over his chest. 'It's just the thumping of my heart,' he told her.

Georgie never knew if his heart pounded because he was ill, or because he was anxious. The two things were so closely entwined in her husband.

Ned wanted to be nowhere in the world but in Avalon. When Georgie went to Rottingdean for a few days, he wrote her little notes every day, and named his address as 'Avalon' instead of 'The Grange, Fulham'. Often he said to her, 'No, I cannot go out tonight, I wish to go to Avalon tomorrow.'

Georgie raided the garden for columbines and irises and forget-me-nots, and he took great pleasure in painting them in the foreground of King Arthur's bier.

The ninth of June was their thirty-eighth wedding anniversary. Georgie woke to find a little square of paper laid on the pillow next to her cheek.

It was a page from his secret book of designs, in which he worked to wring secrets from the mysterious names of flowers.

Drawn in the centre of the page was a circle, like a kind of magic mirror. Within the circle, thorns and wild roses entangled two figures. A knight in dark armour bent over the forget-me-not blue bed of a sleeping princess. The shield on his back looked like wings. He had lifted one of the sweet-faced maiden's hands to his heart. His other hand tenderly stroked her hair, the same chestnut-brown as Georgie's.

In the corner of the page Ned had inscribed, in neat block letters, 'Wake Dearest'.

Eight days later, Ned called to Georgie in the middle of the night and she ran to him.

'My heart,' he croaked, clutching at his chest. 'My heart.'

She called for help, and sent urgent messages to Phil and Margot and the doctor, but they did not arrive in time.

Ned died at the bluest hour of the night.

What a kindness, she thought, to let him die alone in my arms.

There was much to do. Ned was to have a memorial service in Westminster Abbey, the first artist to be so honoured. His remains were cremated and then buried in the church at Rottingdean, where Margot had been married.

Georgie brought only a small wreath of heartsease to lay on his grave.

'I am so very sorry,' Janey said to Georgie.

She answered simply, 'We must pay for the wine we have drunk.'

Georgie did not want to go back to London. She wanted to stay in Rottingdean, where she and Ned had been so happy. She could walk across to the grave, and bring him wildflowers, and think of him anytime she liked. London was so dirty and noisy now, and the Grange much too big for her now she was alone.

'But what shall you do down there, all by yourself?' Margot asked her anxiously.

Georgie smiled and patted her hand. 'Do not doubt that there is work for me as long as I am left on this earth,' she answered.

Packing up the Grange, she took care to save every letter Ned had ever written to her, every notebook in which he had scribbled down his thoughts and dreams. She asked all their friends to post her their memories, and any letters Ned might have written them. She set up a study for herself, and began the long and difficult task of resurrecting the past.

All my dear Ned ever wanted to do was awaken the world with beauty, she thought to herself, looking at the last little painting of the Sleeping Princess that he had painted for her.

That is what I must tell.

Author's Note

When Edward Burne-Jones was painting his series of small water-colours inspired by the names of flowers, he wrote, 'it is not enough to illustrate them – that is such poor work: I want to . . . wring their secret from them'.

This is what I hoped to do with this novel about the women of the Pre-Raphaelite circle. I wanted to wring their secrets from them.

I have been fascinated by the Pre-Raphaelites ever since I was a young university student. I was living out of home, and so poor I often had to choose between eating or paying for the bus fare home. I saw a poster of Dante Gabriel Rossetti's painting of Jane Morris as Proserpina in a newsagent's window. I loved it so much I bought it. I was living in a student squat, with an old mattress on the floor and not much else. I stuck the poster up on my wall, so I would have something beautiful to look at every day.

A few weeks later, I bought a biography of Rossetti at a second-hand book sale. It cost me $17, a huge amount for an impoverished student. I was so fascinated by the painting, however, I wanted to know more about it. That was the first time I read about the tangled lives of the Pre-Raphaelites. As time went on, I read everything I could find, bought more artworks, and even began to dress how I imagined a Pre-Raphaelite poetess would look.

Years passed, and I became a university student again, undertaking a doctorate in fairy-tale studies. I wrote a chapter on William Morris and his 'Rapunzel' poem for my exegesis, which reignited my interest in the lives of the Pre-Raphaelite circle. I began to think about their work reimagining other beloved fairy-tales. A trail of crumbs led me to the story of Edward Burne-Jones's lifelong obsession with 'Sleeping Beauty'. I knew at once I had to write a novel about it. I began to explore and read and research and imagine. Two years later, I finished what proved to be the most fascinating and challenging book I have ever written.

Along the way I read hundreds of books, biographies, journal articles, poems and letters – far too many to list here. I am most indebted to the work of Judith Flanders, Lucinda Hawksley, Jan Marsh, Fiona McCarthy and Wendy Parkins – and, of course, to *The Memorials of Edward Burne-Jones* by Lady Georgiana Burne-Jones.

In regards to understanding Edward Burne-Jones's paintings of Sleeping Beauty, I am grateful to the research of Kirsten Powell, 'Burne-Jones and the Legend of the Briar Rose', in *The Journal of Pre-Raphaelite Studies*, Volume 6, 1986; and 'Smite this Sleeping World Awake: Edward Burne-Jones and The Legend of the Briar Rose' by Andrea Wolk Rager in *Victorian Studies*, Spring 2009.

Thanks also to my guide at Red House, Dharshan Thenuwara of Morris Inspirations Tours, who patiently answered so many questions for me; Rachel Barnes who took me on a private tour of Tate Britain's Pre-Raphaelite art and stayed talking with me long after her time was up; Nick Powell, the Visitor Experience Manager at Highgate Cemetery who showed me Lizzie Siddal's grave on a day just as gloomy and atmospheric as I could have wished for; and the knowledgeable and helpful staff at Kelmscott Manor and Buscot Park, who let me stay and gaze at 'The Legend of Briar Rose' as long as I liked.

I am so grateful to the modern-day Pre-Raphaelite sisterhood of writers and bloggers who cheered me on and never tired of helping and supporting me – in particular, Stephanie Graham Pina, Kirsty Stonell Walker, Kimberly Eve, Essie Fox, Kris Waldherr, Joanne Harris, Terri Windling and – although she does not know it – Grace Nuth, whose blog *The Beautiful Necessity* was the first place I read about Edward Burne-Jones's obsession with 'Sleeping Beauty'.

And a big shout-out to Colin Smith from Royal Tunbridge Wells, who thought up the title of the book when I cried out for help on Facebook.

As always, thanks to my family and friends who let me rave on about the Pre-Raphaelites for hours and never let on if they were bored; to Susie Stratton for the world's most expensive cup of tea in the Hotel Meurice in Paris, where Georgie and Ned stayed with John Ruskin; to my long-suffering husband who let me refurnish our house with William Morris cushions galore; and an especially heartfelt thanks to my brilliant and wise mother, Gilly Evans, who first bought me the Grimm Brothers' fairy-tales.

To Tara Wynne, Cheryl Pientka and Alice Lutyens, my wonderful agents, and Meredith Curnow, Patrick Mangan and the rest of the team at Vintage, thank you so much for having such faith in me and this book, and for all your insight and wisdom. You made the book so much better than I could ever have managed on my own!

To my dear readers, thank you for reading my books – you have made all my dreams come true!

If you would like to know more, you can download a Reading Group Guide at my website – www.kateforsyth.com.au.

Finally, I thought I would share with you one of the eerie serendipitous discoveries I made while writing this novel.

From the very beginning, I imagined Georgie Burne-Jones as the queen who wished for a child in the 'Sleeping Beauty' fairy-tale, and her daughter Margot as the princess who pricked her finger and fell asleep for a hundred years. What would the world be like, I wondered, when she awoke?

So imagine my feelings when I discovered that Margot Burne-Jones was born on the 3rd of June 1866, exactly one hundred years before I was born …

About the Author

Kate Forsyth wrote her first novel at the age of seven, and has since sold more than a million copies around the world. Her books include *Bitter Greens*, a retelling of Rapunzel which won the 2015 American Library Association Award for Best Historical Fiction; *The Wild Girl*, the story of the forbidden romance behind the Grimm Brothers' famous fairy tales, which was named the Most Memorable Love Story of 2013; and *The Beast's Garden*, a retelling of 'The Singing, Springing Lark' set in the underground resistance to Hitler in Nazi Germany. Recently voted one of Australia's Favourite 15 Novelists, Kate Forsyth has been called 'one of the finest writers of this generation'. She has a BA in literature, a MA in creative writing and a doctorate in fairy tale studies, and is also an accredited master storyteller with the Australian Guild of Storytellers. Read more about her at www.kateforsyth.com.au.

HIBERNIAN

Official

All-Time Greats

MIKE WILSON

g

Lomond Books
A Grange Publication

g Published by Grange Communications Ltd., Edinburgh, under licence from Hibernian Football Club.

Printed in the EU.

Photographs supplied by D. C. Thomson & Co. Ltd.

ISBN: 1-84204-002-2

CONTENTS

INTRODUCTION

It arose in conversation while researching this book. Just how many players have pulled on a Hibs jersey? It was a question that, while not impossible to answer, would tax even the most dedicated of Hibs historians. A thousand? Twice as many? Not as many as a thousand? All that can be said with any certainty is that since Hibernian FC was founded in 1875, a lot of people have been bestowed a unique privilege. The very act of running on to the park as a Hibs first-team player ought, by definition, to confer hero status. They tread where the rest of us can only dream. Of course, we know the truth to be different. There have been some players we would rather have not played for the glorious Hibernian.

The task of picking the fifty-odd players who constitute this celebratory book was more pain than pleasure (managers, chairmen, etc have been deliberately omitted).

Many of the players speak for themselves. No collection such as this could be without the Famous Five, Joe Baker and Pat Stanton. The bulk of the early 1970s side represent pretty much an open and shut case. There are stand-outs from the pre-war era, even from the 19th century. Players such as Willie Harper, Harry Rennie and Willie Groves.

If, however, your personal favourite is missing, it might be that - in the tangle of justifications whether to include or exclude - they just missed out. Or, because they were from a dim and distant era where the documentation of players' exploits was not so lavish or is not so readily available. Fear not, if your favourites are not here, they remain locked in the best place anyway: your heart.

Fifty-plus players are enough to be going on with. We salute you, every one.

Mike Wilson

The author would like to thank Kenny Barclay, Leigh Edwards, Brian, Mark and Rikki Raginia for their help.

BOBBY ATHERTON

ibs have had over 50 players capped for Scotland whilst playing for the club but only one for England, Joe Baker, and one capped for Wales, Bobby Atherton. Bobby joined Hibs from city rivals, Hearts and made his debut in 1897, against St Bernards. Soon enough, he was elevated to the club captaincy and helped guide Hibs to their Scottish Cup win over Celtic in 1902 and their League Championship victory the following season. His last game for Hibs was in 1903, after which he played for Middlesbrough. Tragically, he was killed in action during the First World War, when the submarine in which he served was lost in the English Channel. Records show he made 77 league appearances for Hibs, scoring 27 goals. He won nine Welsh caps.

BERNARD 'PAT' BRESLIN

Lanarkshire-born Bernard Breslin was not only a member of the Hibs team that lifted the Scottish Cup in 1902. He was a player who was with Hibs right at the start of their renaissance after having briefly closed down in 1891. Joining Hibs soon after their resurrection, Bernard - otherwise known as Pat - was a long server, remaining at the club until 1906.

In the days when the popular playing formation was 2-3-5, he played in the half-back trio. On the right side. And, folklore has it, he tackled like a man possessed. What he lacked in pace, he made up for in determination. Newspapers of the day described him as 'hard but fair'. His tragic death at the age of 39, just five years after his retirement from playing, prompted the following obituary in the local Edinburgh newspaper: "He never sought to take unfair advantage of an opponent."

As well as helping the turn-of-the-century Hibs team net the league title and the Scottish Cup, he was there when Hibs won the Second Division titles in 1893/94 and 1894/95 (promotion being denied Hibs the first time around because the step up was by invitation rather than performance).

Sad to say, he was also in the side that lost the Scottish Cup final to Hearts in 1896, with one newspaper report describing how he and fellow half-backs Bobby Neil and John Murphy "were all at sea."

Records show Breslin made 231 league appearances for Hibs, scoring nine league goals. He left Hibs for Celtic, but it was only for the briefest of spells before he gave up playing in 1908.

STEVE ARCHIBALD

Steve Archibald's best days were arguably behind him when he joined Hibs but with a pedigree that began with Clyde and continued to include Aberdeen, Tottenham Hotspur and then Barcelona, he was still an impressive acquisition. He arrived at Easter Road at a time when the club was thinking big. It is not known whether he arrived in a Rolls-Royce but it would not have been untypical of the former motor mechanic to have announced his entrance with such a theatrical flourish. It was almost written in the stars that he should score twice (within six minutes) in a 3-1 defeat of Celtic at Easter Road, at the time when Hibs were ambitiously going to be floated on the Stock Exchange.

A man of considered and strong opinions and something of a dressing room lawyer, Archibald - born on September 27, 1952 - joined Hibs in 1988, sporting a hatful of honours. Along with his Scottish Cup and FA Cup winner's medals, he had an UEFA Cup winner's medal from 1984 plus a runners-up medal from the 1986 European Cup Final. He had already earned the last of his 27 Scottish caps.

Such experience went a long way towards helping Hibs secure a place in Europe at the end of season 1988/89 by finishing fifth in the Premier Division. He made his competitive debut in a League Cup match, a 4-0 win over Stranraer on August 17, 1988.

It was on the European stage, however, that signs of strain between Archibald and manager, Alex Miller, became evident. Infamously, Miller omitted Archibald from the team that lost (after extra time) to FC Liege in the second round, second leg of the 1989/90 UEFA Cup. It would not be long after that the mystery deepened with Archibald's departure. He left many memories, not least a goal at a rain-soaked Tynecastle that helped a ten-man Hibs team (following the sending-off of Gordon Rae) to their first away victory over Hearts in ten years.

Records show that he played 44 league games for Hibs, scoring 15 goals.

JOE BAKER

Joe Baker played in some memorable derby matches in his time with Arsenal and Torino. But one of the greatest moments of his career was in the Edinburgh derby when he scored all four goals in a 4-3 Scottish Cup defeat of Hearts on March 1, 1958.

When it came to scoring goals, Joe was a genius. He might not have picked up too many winners' medals in his career but he was one of the biggest names of his era. And to this day, he must rank among the top ten players ever to grace the green and white.

Joe made his Hibs debut at the age of 17 and was to enjoy two spells at Easter Road, the first seeing him score 159 goals. In season 1959/60 alone, he scored 42 league goals, to create a new club record. Briefly, he formed an impressive partnership with Bobby Johnstone, one of the Famous Five, who was with Hibs for a second time after four years at Manchester City. Another club record is Joe's nine goals in one game, against Peebles Rovers in the Scottish Cup.

In 1960, he scored five goals in a Christmas Eve demolition of Third Lanark that ended 8-4. He also scored the first of Hibs' three goals in one of the club's greatest-ever nights, the second leg tie against the mighty Barcelona in the 1960/61 Fairs Cup, which ended Hibs 3 Barcelona 2 (7-6 on aggregate). His good looks and sense of fun cast him as a truly rock 'n' roll footballer.

At a time when transfers abroad were almost unheard of, his move to Torino was foisted upon him. A demand for a small pay rise (£5 per week) was met with Hibs happy to cash in their prized asset, with various big-name European clubs starting to enquire about Joe. The transfer fee was £65,000.

At Torino, Joe was joined by 'fellow' Scot Denis Law. He was, however, seldom paid the £100-a-week 'fortune' he was meant to be earning, partly because of the number of silly fines he was required to pay, for example when he missed a chance in front of goal. His taste of Italy came to an abrupt and almost tragic halt when he was involved in a serious car accident in which he was lucky to survive.

His return to the UK began with Arsenal (for whom he scored over 100 goals in four seasons), continued with Nottingham Forest and Sunderland and entered its twilight with a return to his beloved Hibs. His first game back was at Easter Road, against Aberdeen and it was a notable return on two counts. First, Aberdeen goalkeeper, Bobby Clark, conceded his first goal in just over 12 league games. Second, Joe - who scored the second goal in a 2-1 win - sported a pair of (then unusual) white boots.

Records show that - over two spells - he played 137 league games for Hibs.

GEORGE BEST

It's a sad fact but restrospectives of George Best tend to overlook the eleven eventful months spent by the maverick genius at Easter Road. The Irishman was signed by Hibs Chairman, Tom Hart, in November 1979, in a bid to stave off relegation. He was reputed to be on £2,000 per appearance and though his arrival failed to prevent Hibs dropping into the First Division, he brought colour and flair to what was a fairly drab era in the club's history.

Making a scoring debut in a 2-1 defeat by St Mirren at Love Street on November 24, 1979, Best actually remained with Hibs for a short period when in the lower division. His last game was against Falkirk on October 11, 1980, when Hibs won 2-0. He had joined Hibs from Fulham. His first home appearance was against Partick Thistle and the crowd of 20,622 was four times the size that would ordinarily have turned up. The fans were rewarded with Hibs' first win in 14 weeks, a 2-1 victory, partly helped by the penalty of Hibs' goalkeeper, Jim McArthur.

Records show that he played 17 league games for Hibs, scoring three goals.

Team-mates reflect wistfully upon Best's presence in the dressing room. Despite his fame and fortune - particularly when he, Denis Law and Bobby Charlton helped guide Manchester United to the 1968 European Cup - they testify to a friendly, easy-going personality who, of course, liked the odd party.

Infamously, he was briefly sacked when he failed to show for a Scottish Cup match against Ayr United that was scheduled for a Sunday. It soon emerged that he had been partying the night before with the French rugby side who, the previous afternoon, had played Scotland at Murrayfield. His reinstatement included a public declaration that he had a drink problem and was taking positive steps to combat it.

He left Hibs for San Jose in the USA, leaving behind him a trail of mostly happy memories. For example, against Rangers on December 22, 1979 - a game Hibs won, 2-1 - he reacted to a nasty, two-footed challenge by handing the perpetrator, Derek Johnstone, the ball. In that same game, he jokingly picked up a can that had been thrown at him from the Rangers fans in the away end of Easter Road and motioned to drink from it.

JOHN BLACKLEY

John Blackley acquired his nickname, 'Sloop', because of a song by the Beach Boys but, funnily enough, there was something about his smooth, composed style of play that made the nickname doubly appropriate.

He was an elegant sweeper, sometimes arrogant and sufficiently skilled to win seven caps for Scotland and represent his country in the first of Scotland's three games in the 1974 World Cup finals in West Germany.

Born on May 12, 1948 near Falkirk, he joined Hibs in 1965 and in fact enjoyed two playing spells at the club. In time, he would become coach and manager. He played in the Hibs sides that won the League Cup in 1972 but lost the League Cup Finals of 1969 and 1974, as well as the 1972 Scottish Cup Final. He was well known for his superstitious insistence on being the last to appear on the pitch and kicking the ball into the Hibs net before kick-off.

Though Newcastle United had been interested for some time in signing him, it was not until October 1977 that they finally got their man, in a deal costing £100,000. A year after Blackley joined the Magpies, Hibee, John Brownlie, did likewise. After Newcastle, Blackley joined Preston North End.

Records show that he played 276 league games for Hibs, scoring six goals.

Before moving into the management side of things at Hibs, he was briefly player-manager at Hamilton, staying at Douglas Park for a few months before taking the assistant manager's post at Easter Road, under Pat Stanton. That was in 1983.

In October 1984, he succeeded Stanton as manager and though he had money to spend, not all his buys were astute. Gordon Durie (bought from East Fife for £65,000, sold to Chelsea for a reported £400,000 - with East Fife getting a slice) was a superb purchase; less so were the likes of Mark Fulton, Stuart Beedie, Billy Kirkwood and Mark Caughey. He resigned the manager's position in November 1986 but unlike many, he did not disappear into obscurity.

At time of writing, he is Paul Sturrock's assistant at Dundee United, previously having been so at St Johnstone. Before St Johnstone, he managed Cowdenbeath and was coach at Dundee.

CRA
RD'S

DES BREMNER

As a team, Hibs went close to reaching the final of the European Cup in season 1955/56. Over the years, there have been individual Hibs players who have either gone on to pick up an European Cup winner's medal with another team, or joined Hibs having already won a winner's medal. In the latter group, players such as George Best, Bertie Auld and Frank Sauzee feature. In the former, Des Bremner and Ronnie Simpson. Bremner - born on September 7, 1952 - was in the Aston Villa side that won the 1980/81 English League Championship and went on to defeat Bayern Munich 1-0 to lift the European Cup the following season.

He signed for Hibs from Highland League club, Deveronvale and found himself slotted into the right-back role following the tragic leg break suffered in January 1973 by the regular occupant of the number two shirt, John Brownlie. In time, he moved forward into the midfield.

It was with Hibs that he won his only Scottish cap, versus Switzerland in 1976. He played in the Hibs sides that lost the triple-headed 1979 Scottish Cup Final to Rangers. He also played for Hibs in the League Cup Final of October 26, 1974, lost to Celtic, 6-3. He joined Villa in 1979.

Records show that he played 199 league games for Hibs, scoring 23 goals.

DAVIE GIBSON

Davie hailed from the small West Lothian village of Winchburgh which has produced more famous footballers than seems appropriate for its size, players such as Willie Harper - the Hibs goalkeeper from the 1920s, Willie Thornton - of Rangers and Scotland fame, Bobby Murray - a Scottish schoolboy cap in the 1950s and a player with West Bromwich Albion and John Gorman - of Celtic and Spurs fame who later became assistant to England manager, Glenn Hoddle.

Davie Gibson made his Hibs debut in 1958. He was a classy inside-forward who might have prospered even more had he been just a shade stockier. He had tremendous vision.
He won seven Scotland caps, albeit while playing for Leicester City whom he joined after his stint at Easter Road. He played in the Scotland side that - in front of a crowd of 94,596 at Hampden Park - was involved in an infamous match against Austria on May 8 1963. With Scotland 4-1 up, the game was abandoned after 79 minutes because of on-field violence by the visitors.

MATT BUSBY

t was a typical piece of opportunism from Hibs manager, Willie McCartney, that he snapped up Matt Busby when the Scottish international's war-time commitment as a physical training instructor with the army took him to Edinburgh.

Busby had earned just the one cap for Scotland but he had personal qualities that McCartney thought would prove valuable for his young players to be exposed to – qualities that were to take Busby to the pinnacle of football as manager of Manchester United from February 1945 to July 1971 (with an 18-month spell in the capacity of administration manager while Wilf McGuinness was nominally manager).
During his time at Old Trafford, he produced two outstanding teams, the second winning the European Cup in 1968, partly in honour of the first - the 'Busby Babes' - which was cruelly dismantled on the very brink of greatness, following the disaster at Munich airport on February 6, 1958.

Though Matt played for other teams during the war, he played in the Hibs side that lifted the 1941 Summer Cup, following a 3-2 win over Rangers. He began his career as an inside-forward but made his name as a player when he moved into the half-back line, where he was known for his composure and accurate distribution of the ball. In 1958, he was awarded the CBE; in 1968 he was knighted. He briefly doubled as Manchester United and Scotland team manager during the 1958/59 season.

JOHNNY HALLIGAN

Johnny Halligan may not have been as prolific a goalscorer as some of his forward colleagues, but with over 400 league appearances to his name, he was integral to the smooth-running of the machine. His attachment to Easter Road continued after his playing days when he became caretaker manager - succeeding Bobby Templeton - of the club in 1935.

Records show he made 411 league appearances for Hibs, scoring 48 goals. His league debut for Hibs was on September 20, 1920, against Celtic. His last game was 13 years later, against Falkirk.

His first goal came two months after his debut, in a 2-0 home win over Dundee. His loyal service - which included leading Hibs out of the Second Division after they had been relegated at the end of season 1930/31 - saw him granted a testimonial game long before he finally hung up his boots.

JOHN BROWNLIE

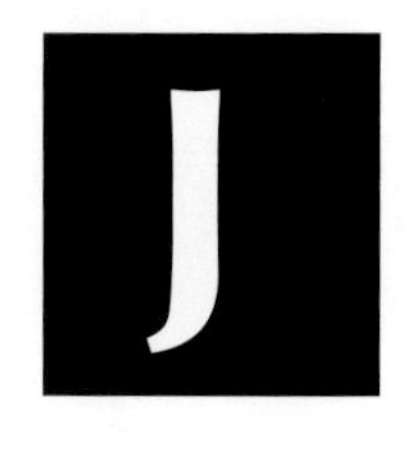

ohn Brownlie's glorious career at Hibs began in the role of sweeper. But the position he made his own was that of right-back - or, to be more accurate, overlapping right-back. He got his chance in a game against St Johnstone, at Muirton Park, in August 1971. Coming on as a substitute for the injured Chris Shevlane, he created two goals in a 3-1 win and the rest, as they say, is history.

So effective was he down the right flank, that he won the first of his seven Scotland caps at the tender age of 19 years and 95 days. It was against the USSR. He was born in Caldercruix, Lanarkshire, on March 11, 1952. Like fellow Hibee, John Blackley, he was to leave Easter Road for Newcastle United. From there, he enjoyed spells at Middlesbrough, Hartlepool United, Berwick Rangers and Blyth Spartans. On the face of it, he enjoyed a long career but it was a career cruelly divided in two, when his leg was broken in a tackle in January 1973. A week before, Hibs had gone to the top of Division One with a famous 7-0 rout of rivals, Hearts, in a never-to-be-forgotten Ne'erday fixture. On January 6, Easter Road fell silent when Brownlie, aged just 20, clashed with the Methil side's Ian Printy.

It could not have come at a worse time for player and club. Hibs' fluidity and rhythm were severely affected by his absence. Matters were not helped by an eight-week suspension slapped on midfield play-maker, Alex Edwards, following a booking picked up in the same game. By the end of the season, Hibs had slipped to third in the league. John missed 50 league matches before embarking on his comeback.

He signed for Hibs under manager Bob Shankly but truly made his name under Eddie Turnbull. One of his most memorable moments was scoring against Rangers in the semi final of the 1972/73 League Cup, a trophy that Hibs were to go on to win, with a 2-1 victory over Celtic. John collected the ball on the half-way line, hurdled a couple of tackles and found the space to crack the ball into the net. A low point was missing a penalty against Liverpool in the 1975/76 UEFA Cup. He had scored from the penalty spot the previous Saturday against Ayr United. But against Liverpool, with the opportunity of extending Hibs' first leg advantage - following a goal by Joe Harper - he fluffed. In the return, Hibs lost 3-1 (3-2 on aggregate).

Brownlie was in the sides that lost the 1972 Scottish Cup Final and the 1974 League Cup Final. But he was away just before Hibs played their marathon Scottish Cup Final in 1979 against Rangers. He had played 341 games for the club. His move to Newcastle involved a player swap, Ralph Callachan travelling north from Tyneside.

PADDY CALLAGHAN

hese days, the one-club player is something of a rarity. But even a century ago, the idea of a player staying with a single club for fifteen years was considered remarkable. Paddy Callaghan was just such a player, joining Hibs in 1899 - from Glasgow junior club, Jordanhill - and not leaving until 1914.

He was mainly a number ten, playing at inside left. But given the length of his career at Hibs, he played in most positions going. He even turned out in goal against Dundee, when it was realised regular goalkeeper, Willie Allan, had missed his rail connection. Sad to say, Hibs lost 4-1 to the Dens Park side. Paddy was known as something of an 'artful dodger', with or without a ball at his feet.

The story goes that he was deaf in his left ear until struck by the ball in a game against Kilmarnock, at which point his hearing was fully restored. The story also goes that he was selected to represent the Scottish League against its Irish counterparts, for no better reason than that only he could understand what the opposition were saying.

Part of the turn-of-the-century Hibs side that netted the league title and the Scottish Cup, Paddy won a single cap for Scotland, against Ireland on March 3, 1900.

Between the First and Second World Wars, he was a Glasgow licensee. Records show Paddy made 270 league appearances for Hibs, scoring 66 goals.

His Hibs debut was on February 25, 1899, against Leith Athletic in the East of Scotland Shield. His last game was against Hearts, on August 26, 1914. By coincidence, Leith and Hearts were the opposition in two benefit games staged for Paddy, the first in 1907 (against Hearts), the other in 1911 (against Leith).

JOHNNY CUTHBERTSON

One of Johnny Cuthbertson's greatest claims to fame is scoring for Hibs in the first post-war Scottish Cup Final, that of 1947 between Hibs and Aberdeen. He wasted no time getting his name on the scoresheet, netting within one minute. Unfortunately for Hibs, it proved not enough, as the Dons scored twice to win their first Scottish Cup. Cuthbertson was a prolific goal-scorer for Hibs, though, oddly, he was often a reserve team rather than first-team player.

During five years as a pilot - flying Hudsons with Coastal Command - he was stationed at Leuchars in Fife and would require a 48-hour pass to play for Hibs. He finished his career with Third Lanark and Stenhousemuir.

JOE DAVIS

For a left-back, a total of nearly a half century of goals is no mean feat. For Joe Davis, the truth of the matter is that almost all of his strikes came from the penalty spot. Often, the penalties were awarded following a surging run into the box from team-mate, Eric Stevenson. Signed from Third Lanark in 1965, Joe rarely missed from the penalty spot. Sadly, one of the few times he did miss was against Hamburg in the third round of the 1968/69 Fairs Cup, which Hibs lost on the 'away goals rule', 2-2.

His very first miss was in a 2-1 defeat by Hearts in the Scottish Cup, played at Tynecastle.

Records show that he played 156 league games for Hibs, scoring 35 goals.

JOHN COLLINS

n the modern era, there are few players considered more professional than John Collins (pictured right). On the field, he gets on with the game without resort to dissent, feigning injury or ill temper; off the field, he is equally modest and gentlemanly. He has worked hard at improving himself as a footballer and as an athlete.

One of the first signs of his maturity was his decision to extend his stay at Hibs for two years longer than anyone anticipated. In time, he would move on but not before being persuaded that an extension to his contract would be good for his football education.

There is no telling what an earlier move away would have done to his career; suffice to say, the decision to remain has not prevented him becoming a successful footballer and a wealthy man.

Records show John made 166 league appearances for Hibs, scoring 16 goals. His league debut was versus Aberdeen on August 10, 1985, while his last game was against Dunfermline on May 5, 1990. He joined Celtic in the middle of July that year for a fee of one million pounds. At time of writing, he is with Everton (recovering from a lengthy injury), whom he joined from Monaco after the 1998 World Cup finals.

TONY HIGGINS

Tony Higgins - the thoughtful, long-time secretary of the Scottish Professional Footballers' Association - likes to tell the odd story against himself. The time, for example, when he nipped in ahead of proven goal-scorer Alan Gordon to head a cross agonisingly over the crossbar during Hibs' nail-biting UEFA Cup match against Leeds United in October 1973.

But with every self-depricating tale, there is a flip side. In that same Leeds match, for instance, he was awesome against the midfield threat of Billy Bremner.

And so too there was light and shade in the Scottish Cup final of 1979, which went to two replays after the first and second matches ended goal-less. In that second replay, Higgins netted Hibs' second. Higgins made his Hibs debut in 1973. Records show he played 102 league games for Hibs, scoring 23 goals.

BOBBY COMBE

History cruelly dictates that J. Robert Combe (pictured right), better known as Bobby Combe (the 'J' stood for James), was the sixth man of the Famous Five line up of Gordon Smith, Bobby Johnstone, Lawrie Reilly, Eddie Turnbull and Willie Ormond - the Hibs forward line of the late 1940s and early 1950s that is considered to be one of the most devastating strike forces in the history of the Scottish game.

Leith-born Combe - born on January 29, 1924 - was a Hibee through and through and though the Famous Five ought really to be known as the Sensational Six to include him, the fact that he could play pretty much anywhere on the park probably counted against him, as far as being seen as part of the Hibs' forward line is concerned.

He enjoyed, however, the consolation of being club captain, giving sixteen years' loyal service to Hibs, during which time he made 354 peacetime appearances, scoring 67 goals. During the Second World War, in 1941, he scored four goals in an 8-1 rout of Rangers.

He began his career in 1941 and retired from playing in June 1957. Afterwards, he was assistant trainer at Easter Road. And for an even shorter spell, he was manager of Dumbarton in the late 1950s.

As well as gaining three League Championship medals with Hibs, he won three caps for Scotland: in 1948, against England, Switzerland and Belgium. He was in the initial Scotland squad for the 1954 World Cup finals but did not travel, because Scotland decided to limit the pool of players they took to thirteen.

ARCHIBALD GRAY

A stocky right-back who joined Hibs in 1899 and stayed at Easter Road for five years. An uncompromising defender on the field, a modest man off it. Born in 1883, in Govan, Glasgow, Gray won one cap for Scotland, against Ireland on March 21, 1903. Following Hibs, he played for Woolwich Arsenal, then Fulham. He was a member of the Hibs team that won the Scottish Cup in 1902 and the League Championship the following season.

PETER CORMACK

Peter Cormack has had some career. As a youngster at Hibs, he scored with a left-foot volley against the mighty Real Madrid in a friendly organised by then Hibs manager, Jock Stein, in which Hibs won 2-0. As a 19-year old, he starred for Scotland against a Brazil side that included the peerless Pele. With Liverpool, whom he joined from Nottingham Forest (who took Peter from Hibs in an £80,000 move in March 1970), he was twice a Football League champion and once an UEFA Cup winner.

In his time, he has been assistant manager at Easter Road. He has also managed in Cyprus and at Firhill. And he fondly remembers an African Nations Cup tie between Botswana and Malawi, watched by 36,000 people, won 2-0 by Botswana, of whom he was briefly in charge.

Born in Edinburgh on July 17, 1946, Peter had actually been on the groundstaff at rivals, Hearts, when Hibs manager, Walter Galbraith, signed him in 1962. It wasn't long before he won the first of his nine Scotland caps (under five different managers!).

A winner but also extremely cool under pressure, Peter actually enjoyed two spells at Easter Road, returning to Hibs in February 1980 after a spell at Bristol City. Curiously, while playing for Bristol City in an Anglo-Scottish Cup tie against Hibs, he got sent off.

His first game back was against Dundee United, at Tannadice, on February 23. Hibs lost, 1-0. By December, he had retired from playing. His hopes of being installed as successor to managers Eddie Turnbull and Willie Ormond were dashed by the appointment of Bertie Auld.

Records show that - over two spells - he played 203 league games for Hibs, scoring 71 goals.

His travels thereafter - including three years as manager of Partick Thistle and a couple of years as assistant at St Mirren - appeared to make him the ideal candidate to work as assistant to Hibs manager, Alex Miller. For a while, the relationship worked well. But in 1990, after three years at Easter Road, there was something of an acrimonious split between the pair, with Cormack the one having to go.

ALEX CROPLEY

Frail, prone to fractures and full of flair, Alex Cropley (pictured right) is one of many Hibees who - even with a big-name club desperate to sign him - would have happily remained at Easter Road.

Nicknamed 'Sodjer' (he was born in the military town of Aldershot on January 16, 1951, the son of Aldershot player, John Cropley), Alex was a classy left-sided midfielder and key to the success of the 1970s side managed by Eddie Turnbull.

But despite the player's own reluctance to move, Hibs sold Alex for £150,000 to Arsenal in December 1974. After Arsenal, he joined Aston Villa; after Villa, he played for Portsmouth.

If only he hadn't kept suffering serious leg breaks, he would surely have found the consistency required to build on the two caps he won for his country. Despite his birthplace and because of his parentage, his country was Scotland. His caps were won against Portugal and Belgium.

Cropley scored in Hibs' 7-0 win over Hearts on January 1, 1973. He had picked up a League Cup winner's medal a few weeks earlier. Success came early in his career, maybe too early for the player to fully appreciate. There were some memorable European ties, not least against Leeds United at Elland Road in the 1973/74 UEFA Cup, in which Hibs were unlucky to come away with only a goalless draw. With the likes of Billy Bremner and Johnny Giles for competition, Alex dominated the midfield.

Records show that he played 125 league games for Hibs, scoring 28 goals.

ROBERT GLEN

Robert Glen - born on January 16, 1875 - was something of a child prodigy, becoming a Scottish Cup captain (for Renton) at the tender age of 20, having made his league debut (again for Renton) four years before. He was principally a left-back but often played at left-half and was in the Hibs side that won the Scottish Cup in 1902. He won three Scottish caps.

TRAVEL ANYWHERE
The

ARTHUR DUNCAN

The story about the hare and the tortoise is about speed versus perseverance. Arthur Duncan was both. His pace down the flanks was a trademark of the famous Hibs side of the early 1970s (the team dubbed 'Turnbull's Tornadoes') and his commitment to the Hibs cause saw him make a staggering 446 league appearances, a club record. An evergreen, indeed.

He signed from Partick Thistle in January 1970 for a fee of £35,000. The manager at the time was Willie Macfarlane, who succeeded Bob Shankly. And though Arthur - born on December 5, 1947 - was more of a winger than a striker, he did have his goal-scoring moments.

He scored 112 goals for Hibs and was the club's leading scorer in season 1975/76, with 16 goals.

He scored twice in Hibs' 7-0 rout of Edinburgh rivals, Hearts, in the Ne'erday game of 1973. The previous season, on October 23, 1971, he scored four against Falkirk. His first hat-trick came in November 1975, during the inaugural season of the Premier Division. In season 1972/73, he, along with Messrs Gordon (Alan) and O'Rourke (Jimmy), scored 100 goals between them.

Unfortunately for Arthur, he also scored one of the most infamous own-goals, in the second replay of the 1979 Scottish Cup Final. Rangers won 3-2 after extra time and the third goal came from the head of the hapless Hibs player, following a Rangers corner.

Six caps were won for his country, the first against Portugal on May 13, 1975.

His days at Easter Road finally came to an end during the close season of 1984, though he didn't travel far to continue playing at senior level, joining nearby Meadowbank Thistle. Qualifying as a chiropodist, he has kept a steady involvement in football, for example, with Livingston, on a part - time basis.

ALEX EDWARDS

Every Hibs fan knows about the 7-0 drubbing of Edinburgh rivals, Hearts, on January 1, 1973. And most Hibs fans are aware that, in the following game, tragedy struck when right-back, John Brownlie - an integral part of Hibs' fluidity - suffered a broken leg against East Fife. Not so many fans are equally aware that, in that same game against East Fife, midfielder, Alex Edwards (pictured right), received a caution that was to have almost the same devastating effect on Hibs' title aspirations as the injury to Brownlie. Edwards was a midfield genius, who had a fragile temperament to match. The result of his caution against East Fife was an eight-week suspension. Just at the time when the side needed his accurate passing most.

Edwards was signed in October 1971 by manager, Eddie Turnbull and was one of the buys of the decade. He was signed from Dunfermline, for whom he made his debut against - coincidentally - Hibs, at the tender age of 16.

And why was Edwards cautioned that fateful day, January 6, 1973? East Fife - managed by former Hibee, Pat Quinn - were obviously on a mission to shackle Hibs by fair means or foul. Brownlie had his leg broken and Edwards threw the ball away in a fit of temper, after having been fouled for the umpteenth time.

Records show that he played 111 league games for Hibs, scoring five goals.

JOHN KENNEDY

With Parick Murray, John Kennedy formed an exceptional Hibs' right wing, the two players noted for their rapid interchanging of positions. He won one cap for Scotland, against Wales on March 20 1897, a year after having played in the Hibs side that lost the Scottish Cup final to Hearts. John Kennedy was the scorer of the first league goal against Hearts and also the scorer of the first hat-trick against them. After Hibs, he joined Stoke.

JOHN FRASER

In his time, John Fraser was both a player and a coach with Hibs, his playing career beginning as a centre-forward signed from local club, Edinburgh Thistle. Soon enough, however, he swapped the number nine shirt for the number seven and in time, he moved into the right-back berth. As a number seven, he famously scored against Rangers in a Scottish Cup semi-final replay, helping Hibs through to the 1958 final against Clyde.

He played right-back, three years later, against Barcelona in the Fairs Cup and occupied the same position a further three years later, in 1964, when Hibs - then under the management of Jock Stein - won the Summer Cup, defeating Aberdeen in the final.

Without doubt, one of his finest moments was when he supplied the cross for Willie Hamilton to head Hibs to a late 2-1 win over Rangers in the Scottish Cup on March 6, 1965. Indeed, there is a counter-claim that Hamilton did not get his head to Fraser's cross at all, meaning the credit for breaking Rangers' 23-game unbeaten run in the Cup (lasting four years) goes to the reliable defender, not the mesmerising forward.

His coaching days were under Eddie Turnbull.

JIMMY KERR

A goalkeeper who became a Hibs director and one of the best goalkeepers never to have won a cap for his country. He was also one of the youngest goalkeepers to have played for Hibs. Again, a player whose career was cruelly interrupted by the outbreak of the Second World War. That said, he made the odd wartime appearance for Hibs. He kept goal, for example, for Hibs during the 1941 Summer Cup final, when Hibs defeated Rangers 3-2 (after Hibs were two-nil up at one stage). He played in the first post-war Cup final, the 1947 final, against Aberdeen, which Hibs lost 1-2, despite Johnny Cuthbertson putting the Easter Road side ahead as early as the first minute. He saved a penalty in that game. A one-club player, he eventually had his day, picking up a 1947/48 championship medal.

Records show that he played 102 league games for Hibs plus various wartime fixtures.

JOHN 'JOCK' GOVAN

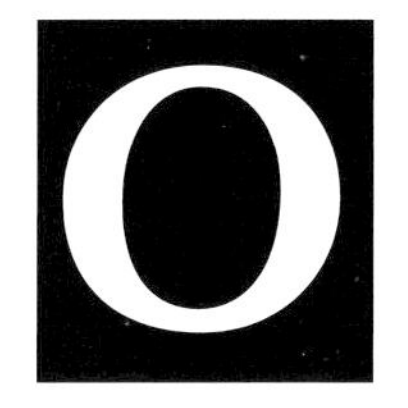

ften described as the first overlapping full-back, Jock Govan won six full caps for Scotland in 1948 and 1949, having signed for Hibs in 1942. He left for Ayr United 12 years later, having collected three League Championship medals with Hibs. He retired from playing in 1955. Records show that he played 163 league games for Hibs but scored no goals. Tall, he linked up particularly effectively with Gordon Smith, of Famous Five fame.

JIMMY DUNN

'Ginger' Dunn's Scotland career involved the winning of six caps and the spanning of three years - between his debut against Wales on February 14, 1925, and his final game, against Wales again, on October 27, 1928. And there is no doubt what the high point will have been. On March 31 1928, Scotland travelled to Wembley to take on England as part of the annual series of matches against the home countries. They came away with a thumping 5-1 win, earning themselves the epithet, 'Wembley Wizards'. Dunn - born on November 25, 1900 - was one of the Wizards' forward line.

He signed for Hibs from Glasgow team, St Anthony's, for £20. And as well as being a prolific scorer, he was infamous for his practical jokes.

Along with fellow Hibee, Harry Ritchie, he headed south for Everton, where he teamed up alongside Toffee's legend, Dixie Dean. With Everton, he won a League championship medal and an FA Cup winners' medal. His move to Exeter City in 1935 was for a then club record fee.

Records show he made 268 league appearances for Hibs, scoring 92 goals. A tiny figure on the park but with heart of a lion, Dunn's last game for Hibs was against Raith Rovers, on April 14 1928, eight years after having made his league debut for them, against Airdrie. He appeared in the Hibs side that contested the 1923 and 1924 Scottish Cup finals.

ANDY GORAM

ndy Goram is the anti-hero to most Hibs fans but it far from diminishes his attraction as a footballer and a personality. Some elements of the media seem intent on pillorying him and he may be his own worst enemy at times. However, get him on a football field (or at the crease of a cricket wicket) and there are few people more focussed.

An all-round sportsman with an incredible capacity for concentration, Andy joined Hibs from Oldham Athletic for a fee reported to be £325,000. He was born in Bury, Lancashire, on April 13, 1964, and had fate dealt a slightly different hand, he might well have been playing first-class cricket instead of Premier Division football with Hibernian and Rangers and at the of writing, Scottish Premier League football with Motherwell. His father, Lew, was, like Andy, a goalkeeper. Also like Andy, he played for Hibs. It was through Lew that Andy qualified to play for Scotland. He was shattered not to play in the 1990 World Cup, despite having represented his country a handful of times before. Thereafter, he was pretty much first-choice, though his main rival for the job, Jim Leighton, did an impressive job staking his own claim, especially when Andy was out of action through injury.

He has had his ups and downs, has Andy. But where there is chaos off the field, there is karma on it. Just before the 1998 World Cup in France, he pulled out the Scotland squad for reasons not wholly connected with football. It wasn't the first time he had taken such drastic action.

Hibs fans will fondly remember him for, among other things, the goal he scored from a kick-out against Morton at the end of season 1987/88 (on May 7, 1988). They will remember him for the penalty he scored against Clydebank on August 22, 1989 during a League Cup penalty shoot-out. They will remember the string of world-class saves in a match against Hearts at Tynecastle that had everyone in the stadium - Hibs and Hearts fans alike - applauding his performance.

Then he went and joined Rangers, with whom he won every honour going in the Scottish game.

Records show that between seasons 1987/88 and 1990/91, Andy made 138 league appearances, registering 47 shut-outs in the process. His league debut was in a 4-0 win against Dunfermline on October 10, 1987. His last game was away to St Mirren on May 11, 1991. He joined Rangers in July that year for £1,000,000.

FRANK

ALAN GORDON

e was elegance personified and the subject of a now infamous rebuke by his manager, Eddie Turnbull: "The problem with you, son, is all your brains are in your head." Alan Gordon wore the number nine shirt in the 'Turnbull's Tornadoes' side of the early 1970s and his speciality was scoring goals with his head.

He was signed on January 20, 1972 from Dundee United for a modest fee, bought to replace the injured Joe Baker. His league debut was against Motherwell in a game that, unfortunately, ended in a 2-1 defeat.

His first goal for Hibs came in the Scottish Cup and it was to help launch a run that went all the way to the final. Alan scored in the final, for Hibs' only goal of the game. Their opponents, Celtic, replied by scoring an astonishing six goals.

Thankfully, the disappointment was not allowed to fester for long. In the pre-season curtain raiser, the Drybrough Cup, Hibs met Celtic in the final and Alan was on hand to help Hibs win 5-3 (after extra time). As it happened, he also scored in the following Drybrough Cup, twelve months later, again against Celtic, this time finishing 1-0 in Hibs' favour.

Records show that Alan played 84 league games for Hibs between seasons 1971/72 and 1974/75, scoring 51 goals in the process. His 13 appearances in the Scottish Cup netted seven goals, his 24 appearances in the League Cup resulted in ten goals and his 13 appearances in European competition saw him plunder a respectable eight goals. In other words, 138 appearances in all competitions and 76 goals, an average of more than one goal every two games. Alan's last game for Hibs was at East End Park, against Dunfermline. Typically, he scored, the game finishing one apiece. Though he was never capped for Scotland, he was conferred the honour of playing for a Rest of the World Select against Hamburg SV in a 1974 testimonial for Uwe Seller.

He was replaced by Joe Harper, whose £120,000 move from Everton set a Scottish transfer record. Remarkably, he played for both Hibs and Hearts as well as Dundee and Dundee United, his move to Dundee following his stint at Easter Road, his spell at Hearts including a two-year sojourn in South Africa. While Joe was struggling to win over the fans' affections, the popular Gordon went on to pursue a career in chartered accountancy.

JOHN GRANT

In the immediate wake of the demise of the Famous Five, the Hibs side was a mix of attacking flair - not least through Joe Baker - and defensive weakness. To illustrate the point, while Hearts won the league title at the end of season 1959/60, Hibs - finishing seventh - actually scored more goals (Hibs' 106 against Hearts' 102). John Grant was the exception to prove the rule.

A rugged and dependable tackler, he eventually ended up as a right-back, though he had also played inside-forward, centre-half and wing-half. Indeed, on March 1, 1958, in Hibs' 4-3 win over Hearts in the quarter final of the Scottish Cup (a game in which Baker famously scored all four of Hibs' goals), Grant played in midfield. Nicknamed 'The Duke', he made two appearances for Scotland - against Wales on October 18, 1958 and against Northern Ireland on November 5 the same year. After Hibs, he joined Raith Rovers.

Records show that he played 224 league games for Hibs, scoring two goals.

JOHNNY MacLEOD

Small, tricky and at home on both the right or the left wing, Johnny MacLeod's career included - like that of another Hibs hero, Joe Baker - spells at Armadale Thistle, Hibs and Arsenal.

MacLeod signed up at Easter Road from Armadale in 1957 and left for Arsenal in June 1961 in a £40,000 move. It means he played in the Hibs side that lost the 1958 Scottish Cup final and, on a happier note, was part of the demolition squad that took Partick Thistle apart 10-2, at Firhill, in December the following year, doing his bit by scoring a hat-trick.

He won four Scottish caps, making his international debut for Scotland in the infamous 9-3 defeat by England in 1961. He also played for Scotland in three World Cup qualifiers, in the unsuccessful campaign to qualify for the 1962 World Cup finals.

Scotland - dripping with talent in the likes of Denis Law, Pat Crerand and Ian St John - failed to make the finals in Chile after failing to defeat Czechoslvakia in a play-off. Records show that he played 85 league games for Hibs, scoring 27 goals.

WILLIE GROVES

In some people's eyes, he was perceived as a traitor. But Leith-born Willie Groves, in most people's estimation, could do no wrong, even when he joined the ranks of Hibs players to defect to the newly-founded Celtic in Glasgow.

His abiding quality was his close ball skills, displayed to the full when he dribbled his way through the heart of the Dumbarton defence to score the winner for Hibs in the 1887 Scottish Cup Final, the first time Hibs won the Cup, thanks to a 2-1 victory.

Mind you, Hibs were almost stripped of that same Cup win because of Groves, on the rather flimsy pretext that he had been paid money for time off work - in strict contravention of the amateur code that persisted at the time.

Fortunately for Hibs, the stunt (Hibs' Irish immigrant roots meant they were not fully accepted by sections of the Scottish football establishment) failed to succeed.

He won three caps for Scotland, one while at Hibs: the 5-1 demolition of Wales, played, coincidentally, at Easter Road, on March 10, 1888. He scored in that one.

The following year - this time as a Celtic player - he scored a hat-trick against Ireland. From Celtic, he was meant to have joined Everton but instead arrived at West Bromwich Albion.

At WBA, whom he joined in October 1890, he moved from centre-forward to left-half. His three Scottish caps did not prevent him representing the English League once. He picked up an FA Cup winners' medal with WBA and went on to become a Football League champion with his next club, Aston Villa.

His final years were spent in poverty and ill-health. Indeed, he was already quite ill when - in his mid 20s - he joined Hibs for a second time, prompting concerns that he should never have been picked at all to play in the all-Edinburgh Scottish Cup Final between Hibs and Hearts on March 14, 1896, in which Hearts won.

Ironically, given the affection in which he was held - his nickname was 'Darlin' - he died, from heart disease, aged just 39, on Valentine's Day 1909. Following his death, an article in the local newspaper, The Evening News, descibed his style thus: 'When he got the ball at his foot, forward went his head, up went his shoulders, threading his way through a maze of opponents, feeling his way, for he worked by instinct and certainly not by sight.'

WILLIE HAMILTON

Hibs, like many clubs, has its fair share of players who have won one cap. And by the same token, its fair share of one cap players who deserved more. Willie Hamilton won his single Scottish cap against Finland on May 27, 1965, at the age of 27. In some ways, he may have been lucky to scale that particular height. But his mercurial talents also deserved more. He was that classic mix of frustrating genius, a player of great skill who appeared to know only how to squander it. He joined Hibs from rivals, Hearts, in October 1963, signed - for just £6,000 - by Walter Galbraith. But it was Galbraith's successor, Jock Stein, who tempered Hamilton's tendency to self-destruct, so much so that it was under Stein that Hamilton received his Scotland call-up.

Hamilton drank pints and pints of milk to ease the discomfort of a stomach ulcer. He was also reputed to drink too much of other types of beverage. Stein - on his arrival from Dunfermline in April 1964 - applied the necessary discipline. In response, Hamilton began to shine on the park, not least against the star-studded Real Madrid side brought to Easter Road for a glamour friendly on October 7 that year. He memorably scored the late winner in a 2-1 win over Rangers in the Scottish Cup on March 6 the following year, the first time Rangers had been defeated in the competition for over four years (there is a debate whether Hamilton's faint header on John Fraser's cross actually connected but there is no debate about how inspiring a figure he was).

The shame for the player and the club was that Jock Stein left for Celtic with the season nearing its climax, with Hibs in the hunt for both the title and the Scottish Cup. With Stein gone, the team spirit seemed to go with him. In the end, Hibs finished fourth in the league and lost to Dunfermline in the semi final of the Cup. And though Hamilton remained with Hibs as they undertook a lengthy tour of Canada and the USA (there is a story that a silver salver, presented to Hamilton for scoring seven goals in one game in Ottawa, was bent in two by the player so that it could fit in his small travel bag), he was soon to be soon back playing in English football, with Villa. He was transferred in August 1965 for £25,000 by Stein's successor, Bob Shankly, to Aston Villa; probably - said one journalist - so the manager could sleep more soundly at nights.

He died little more than a decade later, on October 22, 1976, from a heart seizure. He and his family had by then settled in Calgary, Canada.

JOE HARPER

n many people's eyes, not an obvious candidate for a Hibs hero, given that his arrival at Easter Road on February 1, 1974 was followed by the departure of favourites such as Alan Gordon and Jimmy O'Rourke. Joe could hardly be blamed for a managerial decision like that. An additional problem, though, was the weight of expectation.

Hibs had shelled out a record fee (£120,000) for a Scottish club and the fans - not best pleased with his arrival in the first place - were in no mood for excuses, a foretaste of the cool reaction of many Scots fans to Joe's inclusion in the 1978 World Cup squad, then at the seeming expense of Aston Villa's Andy Gray.

At Hibs, it didn't help that, during his first matches, Greenock-born Joe was not fully match fit. His debut was in a 0-0 draw at Falkirk. But it should not be forgotten that Joe had some impressive moments: a hat-trick against Celtic in the 1974/75 League Cup Final; five goals in a friendly against Dutch side, Nijmegen, in August 1974.

Before Everton, he had been at Aberdeen and before that, Morton and Huddersfield Town. From Hibs, he returned to Aberdeen, maintaining a strong connection with the north-east of Scotland even when his Aberdeen days were over – for instance, by playing, coaching and managing in the Highland League.

Records show that he played 69 league games for Hibs, scoring 26 goals.

ROBERT NEIL

Robert Neil spent two years at Hibs, during which time he played in the 1896 Scottish Cup defeat by Edinburgh rivals, Hearts. Born in 1876, he played for his country twice, once while at Hibs, the other time when he was at Rangers. In between Hibs and Rangers there was a stint at Liverpool, whom he joined from Hibs in May 1896. At Rangers, he won four League championship medals.

GORDON HUNTER

There is a line in the programme for the Testimonial Match of Gordon Hunter (pictured right), against Coventry City, which took place on September 9, 1996: “Seldom has a servant of Hibs deserved to be rewarded with one as much as Gordon.” It was written by the chair of his testimonial committee and showed the regard in which he was held at the club.

Gordon - born in Wallyford, East Lothian, on May 3, 1967 - was much admired for his wholehearted defensive displays and will be remembered for his close-range shot that broke Hearts’ 22-game unbeaten run against Hibs. The date: August 27, 1994. Sixty-two minutes into the game. His Hibs’ debut had been over eleven years before, in 1983, against Kilmarnock in the League Cup.

Records show that he played 340 league games for Hibs, scoring seven goals. At time of writing, Gordon was playing in Australia.

PADDY MURRAY

When talking about the first few years of Hibs, a distinction has to be made between two quite separate eras. For the first fifteen years following their founding in 1875, the club operated an exclusively Irish signing policy. That was to change when - after temporary closure - the club was re-formed along non-sectarian lines. The collapse of the club was in 1891, caused mainly by the creation of Celtic in Glasgow and a sizeable defection of Hibs players to join the new venture.

There was no better symbol of the new era than Edinburgh-born Paddy Murray, the first of the ‘New Hibs’ to be capped by Scotland. The first of his two Scottish caps was won on March 28 1896, against Ireland; the second on March 20 the following year, against Wales. He played mainly at outside right, though there were times - for example, against Wales - when he took the inside-right berth.

Records show that, following his league debut for Hibs - against Glasgow Thistle on August 19 1893 - he was to make a further 117 league appearances for the club. By the time he stopped playing for Hibs - in season 1900/01 - he had scored 37 league goals for them.

1875

WILLIE HARPER

There are few Hibs players more deserving of the tag, 'legend', than Willie Harper, a giant of a man in more ways than one. Continuing an already rich tradition of excellent goalkeepers to play for the 'Cabbage', Harper stood between the sticks for Hibs. Likewise for Scotland, too. He played for the country eleven times, his debut being against Ireland on March 3, 1923. The West Lothian-born custodian was aged 26 when he first represented Scotland.

In four games against England, Harper was never on the losing side. A physically imposing man, Harper was a blacksmith to trade and in his time, a heavyweight boxing champion while serving with the Scots Guards. During World War One, he served in the Royal Flying Corps. He signed for Hibs in 1920. He joined as Hibs - under manager Davy Gordon - struggled to regroup after the War.

It is believed he was spotted by then Hibs director, Barney Lester, who is said to have remarked that Harper was the best goalkeeper he had seen since Harry Rennie, of the turn-of-the-century Hibs' vintage. His debut was on September 1, 1920, against Airdrie.

He was known for his feats of daring, as a player and as a fashionable young man. While at Easter Road, he started a new craze in goalkeeper's tops when he turned out for a Scottish Cup tie against Queen's Park wearing a yellow top instead of the grey or brown that was the norm. During a close season tour of Austria in 1924, he even wore a yellow top and violet pants, though it is not clear whether he was making a fashion statement, or improvising, after the club's kit had gone missing in transit. According to records, he made 173 league appearances for Hibs, enjoying 60 clean sheets in the process.

In November 1925, he left Easter Road for Arsenal, for what is believed to have been a world record fee for a goalkeeper. Herbert Chapman, the most famous of the Highbury managers, signed him for £4,500. With Arsenal, he was a Football League champion in 1931. His Arsenal days included a short stint playing in the USA.

Harper's longest spell, however, was with Plymouth Argyle, whom he joined in December 1931. Following his retirement in 1935, he stayed on with the south Devon club, beginning as a trainer and going on to occupy most roles, including that of groundsman.

HUGH HOWIE

Arguably, Hugh Howie's greatest moment came in one of the longest-ever Scottish Cup matches. It was Hibs versus Motherwell. The game - a semi-final tie, on March 29, 1947 - took two hours and 22 minutes to complete, with Hibs eventually winning 2-1. With the teams locked at 1-1 after ninety minutes and unable to score during the following 30 minutes of extra time, the game simply continued until a goal was scored. Howie lobbed the winner from long distance.

Equally arguably, however, his greatest moment may have been winning a cap for Scotland, against Wales on October 23 1948, in a 3-1 win in which he scored. It was his only cap, just as Hibs were his only senior club. Mind you, he was three times a League champion with Hibs - in 1948, 1951 and 1952.

He retired from playing in 1958, taking up journalism. Four years later - nearing his 34th birthday - he was tragically killed in a car accident.

Records show that he played 132 league games for Hibs, scoring no (league) goals.

DUNCAN URQUHART

Born in 1908, Duncan Urquhart joined Hibs in 1928/29 and left for Aberdeen in September 1935. He was a left-back whose tenacious tackling made up for a lack of pace and was rewarded with a single cap for Scotland, against Wales on October 4, 1933.

RAB WALLS

Born in Leith in 1928, Rab Walls played for Hearts and St Bernards before Hibs signed him in 1932. He helped Hibs win the Second division flag in season 1932/33. Stayed three seasons and scored 28 goals, from 93 games. He was transferred to Aldershot and also played for Cowdenbeath.

DARREN JACKSON

Darren Jackson made his competitive Hibs debut against Aberdeen on August 1, 1992, and was one of manager Alex Miller's best-ever buys during his ten-year reign at the club. Bought from Dundee United, Jackson - born on July 25, 1966 – seemed to have a particular likeness, during his first couple of seasons at Easter Road, for scoring spectacular goals against Dundee United. Few who were there will forget the tearing apart of 'The Arabs' - newly-crowned Scottish Cup holders - on the first day of season 1994/95. Darren and another former United player - the skilful Michael O'Neill - ran riot during a 5-0 slaughter. Darren even pitched in with a couple of goals, while O'Neill also got his name on the scoresheet. The date was August 13, 1994.

Dissent was an initial problem for Darren at Hibs. But if he sounded off a little too often for referees and opposition fans, it was because he so disliked losing or letting himself down. On the advice of, among others, John Collins, Darren was converted to the benefits of working out in the gym. It might have been relatively late on in his career but the effects became obvious. The extra pace and strength he developed turned him from a player on the fringes of the Scotland set-up to a regular. Records show that he played 173 league games for Hibs, scoring 50 goals.

He could not have scored his first Scotland goal in more spectacular fashion. It happened on October 5, 1996, away to Latvia, in a World Cup qualifier. Scotland were already one up and 77 minutes were on the clock. Jackson intercepted a pass in the centre-circle. By eluding two Latvian defenders with a combination of bravery and quick-thinking, he found himself with a 40-yard open run on goal. From just outside the box, he drilled an impressive, low shot.

Throughout that World Cup build-up, Jackson steadily began to endear himself to the Scottish public. He worked tirelessly and formed a profitable partnership with Kevin Gallacher.
Jackson eventually signed for Celtic. A few months afterwards, his life was endangered by fluid on the brain. Happily, the surgery he had to undergo was a success. Celtic, however, were a club just outwith Darren's reach; he was never guaranteed a first-team place. He spent a couple of months on loan to Coventry City and he rejected a possible move to China. In the end, he joined Hearts (there is a photograph of him having been a Tynecastle ball boy). He was signed by Hearts manager, Jim Jefferies, to ignite a flagging 1998/99 season that was threatening to end in relegation. Darren's arrival refreshed his own career and that of his new club.

Carlsberg

BOBBY JOHNSTONE

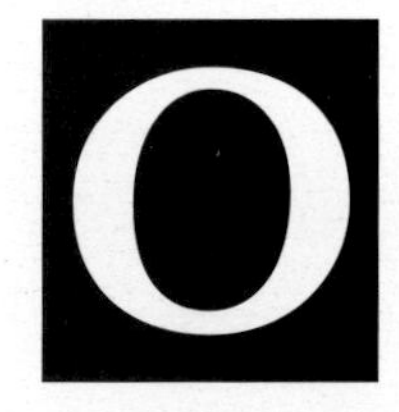

ne of the Famous Five. Need any more be said? Bobby Johnstone - born in Selkirk on November 7, 1929 and winner of 17 Scottish caps - was the creative cog in the combination, the main supplier to Gordon Smith who, despite being posted on the right wing, was so abundantly blessed with skill he could score goals as well.

Johnstone made his Hibs debut in an 'A' Division game on April 2, 1949. He was the last to make his debut and the first to leave, taking his dandy good looks to Manchester City in March 1955, transferred for £22,000. And though he was to return to Hibs for a second spell in September 1959 in a £6,000 deal - to provide a young Joe Baker with the ammunition to score goals - it is his first six years at Hibs that are the most cherished.

Though manager, Willie McCartney, died before seeing the Famous Five properly come together, he is rightly credited with being its creator. Hugh Shaw, McCartney's assistant, took over from McCartney and fulfilled the plan. It was under Shaw that the Famous Five made its debut, firstly in a friendly in April 1949 - against Nithsdale Wanderers, in Sanquhar - then competitively, six months later, against Queen of the South on October 14.

The great irony is that the Five came together for its competitive debut that October as a result of a reshuffling of the half-back line, which had performed poorly the previous week as Hibs lost to Dunfermline in the semi final of the League Cup.

Though one League Championship - that of season 1947/48 - had been won without the Five being in existence; and though the Five really only performed as an unit for six years, the successes achieved by Hibs at the time - three titles in five seasons - are synonymous with them. That is not to diminish the efforts of the rest of the team, class players like Bobby Combe and Jock Govan, themselves international-quality players.

With Manchester City, Johnstone scored 42 goals in 142 appearances, scoring in both the 1955 and 1956 FA Cup Finals, the first lost 3-1 (to Newcastle United), the second won 3-1 (over Birmingham City). He joined Hibs in 1946 from junior side, Newtongrange Star. After his second stint at Hibernian, he spent a short time at Oldham Athletic, whom he joined in October 1960 for a reported £3,000 transfer fee.

One of Johnstone's most important goals for Hibs was a cheeky free-kick in the quarter final of the 1951 Scottish Cup. In front of a huge crowd, Hibs won 3-2 and Johnstone's accuracy in spooning the ball over the Rangers defensive wall, provided the winner. Described as the perfect cup tie, it took place on February 10, 1951, at Ibrox.

PAUL KANE

Paul Kane is one of that select band of players whose father also played for Hibs and there is no question where Paul's allegiances lie, even if it is now some years since he has played for Hibs and even though he has since worn the shirt of at least two other top-flight Scottish clubs, Aberdeen and St Johnstone.

He is also one of that select band of Hibees who scored on their league debut (Paul's moment coming against Dundee) and at Easter Road into the bargain. It was a dream start for the youngster, signed from Salvesen Boys Club in 1982.

Records show that between seasons 1983/84 and 1990/91, Paul made 245 league appearances, scoring 33 goals in the process, season 1987/88 being his most prolific, when he netted ten league goals to make him the club's top scorer that season.

There is no doubting the place in his affections for at least one of his goals: In 1987, Paul scored one of the two goals (Eddie May getting the other) that ended a ten-year victory drought over rivals, Hearts. Almost as importantly, in November 1988, he scored the opener for Hibs against Hearts at Tynecastle, getting his head to an Alan Sneddon cross. Not satisfied with that contribution to what would be another historic victory, he released team-mate, Stevie Archibald, to make it number two, in what turned out to be a 2-1 win.

He was transferred to Oldham Athletic in 1990.

JAMES MAIN

Jimmy Main, a brilliant full-back who represented his country, had his life tragically cut short when he died as a result of an injury sustained while playing against Partick Thistle at Firhill on Christmas Day, 1909. He died four days later, aged 23.

He was capped for his country once, against Ireland. How it might have been more. Records show that his six seasons at Hibs - he made his league debut for the club on September 17, 1904 - totalled 135 league appearances and four league goals.

FRANK
GRAHAM
GROUP

JAMES LUNDIE

During the early years of association football, James Lundie - born on April 20, 1857 - must have been considered something of a pioneer. As a contemporary of his remarked: "Not of big build, he was a brainy player, thoroughly understanding the value of positioning himself and studying his opponents' tactics." Lundie played at right-back. He joined Grimbsy Town from Hibs but not before picking up a single cap for Scotland.

JIM SCOTT

Eight seasons at Easter Road speaks for itself. Jim Scott arrived at Hibs in season 1958/59 and his loyalty to the club was rewarded with a healthy 76 goals, mostly scored from the outside-right position, though there were moments when he was pushed inside to take up the centre-forward role, including against Real Madrid in a friendly lined up by then Hibs manager Jock Stein.

Unlike his brother, Alex, who also played for Hibs (after having played for Rangers and Everton), Jim was not a speed merchant, but he had craft.

He was a member of the Hibs side that won the Summer Cup against Aberdeen in 1964. His one Scottish cap was against Holland in 1966, in the same match that fellow Hibee Pat Stanton made his international debut.

Jim's finest goal was in an Edinburgh version of the English Charity Shield, which was played as a season curtain-raiser during the 1950s and 1960s, when a Hibs-Hearts Select took on a top English team. In this particular game, played at Easter Road, Newcastle United were the opposition. Scott gathered the ball on the half-way line, embarked on a mazy run upfield and finished in style by walking the ball around the bemused Newcastle goalkeeper.

It was reckoned that a Jim Scott bodyswerve sent half the crowd the wrong way. Records show that he played 143 league games for Hibs, scoring 40 goals.

PETER KERR

long-server in many ways, Peter Kerr - born in Prestonpans, in East Lothian - joined Hibs in 1910 and stayed with the club until May 1926, at which point he joined rivals, Hearts. His last Division One game was in season 1930/31, by which time he was well past 40 years old. He played at right-half, possessed a lethal long-range shot and after his playing days were finally over, managed Leith Athletic. In all that time, he won a single Scottish cap - against Ireland on March 1, 1924. Sad to say, he never won a Scottish Cup winner's medal, though he played in three finals - 1914, 1923 and 1924 - each time with Hibs.

BOBBY KINLOCH

Forever remembered as the man who scored the winner in a nail-biting end to Hibs' second round, second leg tie against Barcelona in the 1960/61 Fairs Cup. Hibs had performed heroics to come away from the first leg in Spain with a 4-4 draw. But despite a whirlwind start to the return at Easter Road, the half-time scoreline was Hibs 1 Barcelona 2.

With Hibs cranking up the pressure in the second half, they faced the agony of three penalty claims being turned down. It was not until the game had entered its final quarter of an hour that Tommy Preston headed home an equaliser, by which time it was the turn of the opposition to get anxious. With five minutes remaining, having tried to disrupt Hibs with a string of fouls, Barcelona's antics eventually forced the referee to blow for a penalty after Johnny MacLeod - released by Joe Baker - was pulled down inside the box.

Kinloch had to wait at least five minutes - an eternity in such a pressure situation - before taking the vital spot kick. So vociferous were the Spanish protests at the referee's decision, the police had to intervene. Kinloch drove the ball low and to his right. Hibs won 3-2 on the night, 7-6 on aggregate.

It was during the second leg of the next round - the semi final - against AS Roma, that the Hibs management team pulled off the masterstroke of putting Kinloch in Joe Baker's number nine shirt and Baker in Kinloch's number eight. As the Italian defence kept a tight rein on whom they believed to be Baker, the real 'Baker Boy' was given the space to score twice in a 3-3 draw (Kinloch getting the other). With the scores locked 5-5 on aggregate and because there was no 'away goals' rule in operation at the time, a play-off was arranged, which Hibs lost.

RUSSELL LATAPY

He has just signed e new contract with Hibs, but Russel Latapy (pictured right) has been the subject of enquiries from clubs in the English Premiership. That is not much of a surprise, given the impact he had on Hibs during his first season at the club. Signed on October 23, 1998, the Trinidad and Tobago internationalist arrived as something of a mystery. Not to his compatriots back home, who laud him as much as they do their other famous sons, footballer, Dwight Yorke and cricketer, Brian Lara. No doubt it is partly because Latapy has not lost his feeling for his country, despite having played a number of years in Portugal before moving to Hibs (he joined Hibs from Porto). Latapy has set up a foundation back home to provide educational opportunities for disadvantaged children. If that alone was not grounds for hero status, his silky displays for Hibs have held people in awe. His Hibs debut was against Ayr United on October 24, 1998 (Hibs drew 3-3). He made the number 10 shirt pretty much his own soon after.

ARTHUR MILNE

Arthur Milne was an early indication of manager Willie McCartney's astuteness. The story goes that Milne was meant to be signing for Liverpool from Dundee United. But since neither Dundee United nor Liverpool had properly registered the player's name, the shrewd McCartney nipped in to lure the player to Easter Road. Milne made his league debut for Hibs on August 13, 1938.

He was a prolific goalscorer and would have surely added considerably to his total had his career not been interrupted by the outbreak of the Second World War. Records show he made 44 league appearances for Hibs during seasons 1938/39, 1939/40 and 1946/47, scoring 26 goals in the process. His wartime record involved 76 'league' games and 46 'league' goals.

A stocky player with a cheerful but determined personality, one of Milne's early strikes for Hibs was against Hearts in the Ne'erday derby of 1939.

He played a big part in Hibs' famous 8-1 win over Rangers in September, 1941. Milne got the show on the road with a goal after just seven minutes. He added another goal later. At the end of the war - with new Prime Minister, Clement Atlee, in attendance at Easter Road - he scored the crucial goal against Partick Thistle in the 1946 Victory Cup, a tournament Hibs were to finish runners-up in (losing the final 3-1 to Rangers).

Carlsberg
Mitre

JIM LEIGHTON

For years, Jim Leighton was a goalkeeper at the top of his game. With Aberdeen, he was twice a Scottish League champion and four times a Scottish Cup winner. He played in the Aberdeen team that won the Cup Winners' Cup in 1983 and the European Super Cup soon afterwards. With Scotland, he was the regular number one. When his former Aberdeen manager, Alex Ferguson, issued an invitation to join him at Manchester United, no longer could English pundits heap ridicule on Scottish goalkeepers, as they had done for years. Leighton was a star. Though it was not the best of opening seasons at Old Trafford, he could not have been prepared for the stinging criticism he would receive following a miserable 3-3 draw against Crystal Palace in the FA Cup Final at the end of that first season, 1989/90. Leighton was blamed for at least one of the goals and was sensationally dropped for the replay (which United won).

Suddenly, his career at Old Trafford was going nowhere. Since confidence is vital to a goalkeeper, nobody else was prepared to take a gamble on him. He found himself in the Dundee reserve side. Then Hibs' manager, Alex Miller, decided to take a chance and just as quickly as it had nosedived, Leighton's career was back on the rails again. He made his league debut for Hibs against Partick Thistle in a 0-0 draw on August 7, 1993 and during the four seasons he spent at Hibs, he handsomely repaid Miller's faith in him. He left in June 1997, following the arrival of former Dundee manager, Jim Duffy and returned to Aberdeen. While at Hibs, he had been good enough to reclaim the goalkeeper's jersey for Scotland. He retired from international football in late 1998.

Records show that he played 151 league games for Hibs.

PETER MARINELLO

ad Peter Marinello not missed a relatively easy chance during his first weeks playing for Arsenal, he might easily have fulfilled his promise as the 'Scottish George Best'. Whether he actually had the skills to match Best is a different matter but he certainly had the haircut.

As far as Hibs were concerned, it was a good piece of business selling him to the Gunners for £100,000 in January 1970. He hadn't been a regular first-team player at Easter Road but he had youth and - undeniably - talent on his side. Arsenal had spotted something. But he was not a success with them.

Stints at Portsmouth (from July 1973), Motherwell (from July 1976), Fulham (from December 1978), Phoenix Inferno in the USA, Hearts (from October 1981) and Partick Thistle (from March 1983) followed. At time of writing, he was living in Bournemouth.

COLIN STEIN

Yet another Hibs player to have been schooled at Junior club, Armadale Thistle, in West Lothian, Colin Stein's main claim to fame was that he was the first player to be transferred between two Scottish clubs for a six figure sum, his £100,000 move from Hibs to Rangers taking place in October 1968, three years after having joined Hibs.

Like another number nine with an Armadale Thistle background, Joe Baker, Stein could score goals. He famously scored Hibs' fifth goal in their 5-0 rout of Napoli in the 1967/68 Fairs Cup. In fact season 1967/68 was full of rich pickings for Stein who finished as Hibs' top scorer for the season, with 29 goals. Not bad for a player who started out as a left-back.

Of course, it had to be the case that when Stein lined up against Hibs in the colours of Rangers, he goes and scores a hat-trick.

Records show that Stein played 75 league games for Hibs, scoring 41 goals.

NEIL MARTIN

Hibs have been relegated three times in their history and been close a few times more. One such touch-and-go season was 1962/63 and having escaped the drop by the skin of its teeth, the club went in search of a striker to spark a revival of fortunes. They came across Neil Martin, with Queen of the South but on the verge of giving up the game to become a lorry driver. With the Dumfries club, he had netted 30 goals during the course of the season; earlier in his career, at Alloa Athletic, he had scored 32 goals in season 1960/61. He was signed by manager, Walter Galbraith, in return for a transfer fee of £6,000. It was to prove a great signing for man and club.

Neil made his debut for Hibs in a League Cup tie, against St Mirren, at Love Street. The date: August 10, 1963. He was three months short of his 23rd birthday. He scored. And throughout the season, he didn't really stop, scoring 38 goals in all competitions, 20 in the league. Hat-tricks were something of a Martin speciality and in the space of three seasons at Hibs, he scored ten, five in the league, the remainder in other competitions. One of the league hat-tricks was against Celtic on March 22, 1965. If 38 goals in his first season at Easter Road wasn't enough, he hit the fifty mark the following season, 25 of them in the league.

The next again season - 1965/66 - he managed to score eight goals in two games, four against his former club, Alloa, in the League Cup on September 22, 1965; and another four three days later, against Falkirk, in the league.

A month later, in October, he was off to Sunderland in a £45,000 deal, going on to join that select band of players to have scored at least 100 goals in both the Scottish and English leagues. As well as Sunderland, he played for Coventry City, Nottingham Forest, Brighton & Hove Albion and Crystal Palace. After his playing days were over, he enjoyed a spell in Kuwait as assistant manager to Arabic Sporting Club. In 1981, he became co-manager at Walsall, becoming sole manager a few months later, until June 1982.

His Hibs record shows that in barely two-and-a-half seasons, he scored 53 goals from 65 league games.

WILLIE McCARTNEY

ot the Willie McCartney most Hibs fans have heard of. Not the Willie McCartney of elegant suits and the vision to form a team that would go on to win three League Championships in five seasons. Not the Willie McCartney who tragically died barely four months before the first title win - at the end of season 1947/48 - had been secured. This Willie McCartney was involved in a different League Championship but as a player, not as a manager. Though a broken leg ruled out this Willie McCartney from Hibs' Scottish Cup win of 1902, he had recovered in time to help then win the League Championship the following season.

This Willie McCartney also won a Scottish cap, against Ireland, on March 1, 1902.

HARRY RITCHIE

There can be few clubs who, like Hibs, have appeared in successive Cup finals with exactly the same line-up. But that is what happened during the 1923 and 1924 Cup finals. The Hibs team on both occasions, lined up as follows: W Harper, W McGinnigle, W Dornan, P Kerr, W Miller, H Shaw, H Ritchie, J Dunn, J McColl, J Halligan, J Walker.

Though Hibs lost both finals they were a formidable side. In fact, it used to be said of the forward line of Harry Ritchie, Jimmy Dunn, Jimmy McColl, Johnny Halligan and Johnny Walker that they were the 'First Famous Five', a precursor of the blistering attack Hibs had at their disposal in the late 1940s and early 1950s.

Perthshire-born Ritchie played outside right, wearing the number seven shirt and was the possessor of a fierce shot. He had been signed from Perth Violet, a junior club. He made his league debut for Hibs on September 9 1919, against Albion Rovers.

With Jimmy 'Ginger' Dunn, he was part of a highly-regarded wing duo.

Records show Ritchie played 276 league games for Hibs and scored 75 league goals. Ritchie was capped twice for Scotland, against Wales on March 17 1923 and Ireland on February 25, five years later. After Everton, he had spells at Dundee and St Johnstone. He died in July 1941, aged just 42.

ALLAN McGRAW

llan McGraw is probably better known as 'Mr Morton', given his many years of sterling service to the Greenock club. But his association with Hibs is deeply-held, taking on a generational aspect when his son, Mark, played for Hibs in the early-to-mid 1990s. It comes as no surprise that Allan joined Hibs in 1966 from Morton.

For a man who can barely walk because of the mis-application of pain-killers to keep him playing when he was younger, he is fondly remembered by Hibs fans for the bravery he showed in a League Cup semi-final match against Dundee, held at Tynecastle. Allan had gone off injured – but not for long. Though limping, he returned to the field to play on the wing. Not only that, he scored the winner in the last minute.

JAMES McLAREN

One of the original group of Hibs players poached by Celtic during their formation in 1888, James McLaren was, nonetheless, popular enough at Hibs for the club to agree to playing a testimonial match on his behalf a few years later. Known as the 'Auld General' for the way he could control a game from his position as left-half, McLaren won three Scottish caps (between 1888 and 1890) and with Hibs, was a Scottish Cup winner in 1887. He held the distinction of scoring the winner for Hibs against Preston North End in the game billed as the 'World Club Championship', held on August 13, 1887.

He played in an impressive Hibs half-back line consisting of himself, James McGhee and Peter McGinn. Born in Ayrshire, he was brought to Hibs by co-founder, Michael Whelehan. His arrival helped break a rule being operated by the Edinburgh Football Association, that only local players could turn out for local teams.

He was on the brink of being called up to play for Scotland as early as season 1884-85 but the Scottish Football Association initially believed he was Irish, not Scottish. In April 1912, he emigrated to British Columbia, Canada, where he ran a ranch until his death in 1927.

ALLY MacLEOD

t is not often that players get to score four against Rangers but Ally (short for Alexander) MacLeod - when at St Mirren, his first senior club - is one such player. Scoring goals was something that came easily to MacLeod, who joined Hibs not from St Mirren but from Southampton, whom he joined in May 1973, aged 22.

His arrival at Easter Road was in December 1974 and he immediately set to work at becoming the goal-scorer supreme, finishing each of the five seasons from 1976/77 to 1980/81 as the club's top scorer (please note: in all competitions – in two of these seasons he was not the top league goal-scorer).

In the end, he scored a total of 99 goals for Hibs and for many years held the Premier Division record for the longest run of goals scored in consecutive league games. It began on March 11, 1978 with a 5-1 win over his former club, St Mirren, in which he scored once, from the penalty spot. It continued thus: March 15, Motherwell 2 Hibernian 4 (scored twice); March 18, Clydebank 0 Hibernian 3 (scored twice); March 22, Hibernian 4 Ayr United 2 (scored once, from the penalty spot); March 25, Hibernian 3 Dundee United 1 (scored once); March 29, Hibernian 1 Rangers 1 (scored once, from the penalty spot); April 1, Hibernian 3 Partick Thistle 1 (scored once); and April 5, Celtic 2 Hibernian 1 (scored once, from the penalty spot). To add to the achievement, immediately before the St Mirren game, MacLeod scored in a Scottish Cup match on March 7, which Hibs lost 1-2, away to Partick Thistle.

Come 1984/85 season, MacLeod's record would be equalled by Aberdeen's Frank McDougall. Come season 1997/98, it would be beaten by one, by Rangers' Marco Negri.

MacLeod's scoring feats failed to secure a Scottish cap but he did represent the Scottish League in a match against the Irish League, held in Belfast in 1980. He scored Hibs' second goal in the second replay of the 1979 Scottish Cup Final against Rangers (which Rangers won 3-2, after extra time).

Ally's career at Hibs ended with a free transfer to Dundee United in the summer of 1983. Sadly, he was never to play for United, a practice game injury to his knee forcing him to retire from football. His last days at Easter Road failed to live up to the billing of him and emergency signing, George Best, together producing magic to save Hibs from relegation to the First Division at the end of season 1979/80.
Of the many goals he will be remembered for, one of the sweetest was executed against Dundee in front of the television cameras. From a free-kick, he popped the ball into the net, only to have the goal disallowed by the referee, who ordered the kick to be re-taken. Unperturbed, MacLeod stroked the ball into the net in a repetition of his first attempt, this time the goal being allowed to stand.

MURDO MacLEOD

At time of writing, with less than six months to go before the turn of the century, only two Hibs captains have lifted a trophy this century at Hampden Park: Pat Stanton, when he lifted the League Cup on December 9, 1972, and Murdo MacLeod, when he lifted the Skol League Cup on October 27, 1991. Though Hibs won the Scottish Cup in 1902, the game was played at Celtic Park. And other trophies, such as the Summer Cup, various wartime cups and the Drybrough Cup, don't quite register on the same level of importance.
MacLeod arrived at Easter Road from Borussia Dortmund, whom he joined from Celtic. From midfield, he provided determination and an eye for a good pass. Suprisingly, for a player who rattled in long shots on a regular basis for Celtic - including one during a title decider between Celtic and Rangers on May 21, 1979 - he wasn't a prolific scorer for Hibs.

Murdo went on to manage Dumbarton and Partick Thistle before becoming assistant manager to Wim Jansen at Celtic during season 1997/98, which ended with a League Championship but the two men also leaving Celtic Park.

Records show that he played 78 league games for Hibs, scoring two goals.

JACKIE McNAMARA Snr

hen someone as legendary as Jock Stein says of a player: "[He] could be as good if not better than [Kenny] Dalglish....he has all the skills...he's just a slow developer," you have got to take notice. The player in question, Jackie McNamara, has been grabbing headlines ever since, not necessarily for his football; for example, in the build-up to the elections for the new Scottish Parliament, he publicly supported the Scottish Socialist Party.

Jackie - born on September 19, 1952 - certainly required the courage of his convictions when he arrived at Easter Road from Celtic. Jock Stein may have rated Jackie but it was not to work out as hoped at Celtic Park and in exchange for Jackie moving to Easter Road, Stein took the much loved Pat Stanton in the opposite direction.

That Pat was already toying with the thought of moving from Hibs, did little to diminish the sense of loss among the Hibs fans. Nor the fact that the relationship between Pat and Hibs' manager, Eddie Turnbull, had reached a point when Pat's departure was only a matter of time. It goes without saying that 'Jackie the Red' - so-called for his political beliefs - was not an immediate hit at Easter Road. But to his eternal credit, he persevered, finally winning over the Hibs support with his desire to do well. Sometimes it boiled over. He was famously told to make his own way back to Easter Road from training by an irate Bertie Auld, Hibs manager during the early 1980s.

In a match against St Mirren on November 6, 1982, he threw his shirt at referee, Joe Timmons, after being ordered off, claiming he hadn't even committed a foul. He was suspended for four games and then ordered to pay a £50 fine for bringing the game into disrepute, which he refused to do, claiming he was being punished twice.

Jackie was signed by Eddie Turnbull and to this day, rates Eddie as one of the best-ever managers. He began at right-back but struggled with the position. It was only when he became a sweeper - taking over from John Blackley, who had been transferred to Newcastle United - that the tide began to turn in his favour. He was helped by the fact that his first competitive game as sweeper was against Aberdeen, for whom former Hibee, Joe Harper, was playing. Keeping Harper quiet changed the attitude of many of his critics.

At Morton he began as a player-coach, going on to become assistant manager. Later, he was an assistant at Berwick Rangers. Arguably, however, the high point in his coaching career was at Easter Road itself, when he was assistant manager to Jim Duffy from January 1997 until the end of Duffy's reign on February 2, 1998.

Bukta

JOHN McNAMEE

ikes winning, hates losing. John McNamee was a big guy, with a big heart and a pretty massive temper. He was signed from Celtic in April 1964, by then Hibs manager, Jock Stein. At Celtic, for whom he signed in preference to Manchester United, he played as a centre-half, often alongside Billy McNeill.

Even during those early years, he had discipline problems. After breaking a curfew when Celtic were in Ireland, he was sent home. In a reserve match, he was booked after arguing with his own goalkeeper, Frank Haffey.

At Hibs, there were other tales of woe. He got sent off in the semi-final replay of the 1965 League Cup, against Celtic, which Hibs lost 4-0. Not only that, he came close to grabbing the referee, Bobby Davidson, by the neck, until common sense prevailed.

Yet, he was also a tower of strength. He played, for example, in the Hibs team that defeated Aberdeen to win the Summer Cup in 1964.

Two years later, however, he was gone, transferred to Newcastle, mainly to make a fresh start. Records show that he played 77 league games for Hibs, scoring four goals.

MATTHEW PATERSON

ee pictures of Matthew Paterson and he was a sight to scare the living daylights out of opposition strikers. He was a hard-looking centre-half and just the player Hibs needed during the pre-First World War era, when the club was going through a difficult patch, not least financially, which meant the calibre of player at Easter Road was not as high as it might have been.

TOMMY PRESTON

There are some players who struggle to find favour with the sometimes fickle Hibs fan. In recent years, the likes of Joe Tortolano; before him, Ally Brazil and John Baxter. In the 1950s, the subject of much barracking was Tommy Preston. And yet, like so many players before and since, the criticisms were unwarranted. Here is a player who scored four in Hibs' record away league win against Airdrie in 1959, a match that finished 11-1. Here is a player who scored in both the away and home legs of Hibs' massive win over Barcelona in the 1960/61 Fairs Cup. Here is a player who scored 49 times for Hibs, including a hat-trick in October 1957, at Tynecastle. Mind you, just his luck, the game against Hearts was not a league match. Instead, it was a friendly to mark the first switching on of the Tynecastle floodlighting system. Mind you, a win is a win and Hibs won 4-2, the other scorer being Joe Baker. Records show that he played 229 league games for Hibs, scoring 34 goals.

WILLIAM ROBB

A big, imposing goalkeeper, one of William Robb's most notable achievements was that, in the course of five consecutive seasons at Rangers - between 1920/21 season and 1924/25 - he did not miss a single league game.

He joined Hibs in April 1926 and was at Easter Road for four years, after which he moved south. He didn't retire until 1939, by which time he was aged well over forty.

Records show he made 134 league appearances for Hibs, 24 of which were shut-outs. He won two Scottish caps, both against Wales - on October 31, 1925, and on October 29, 1927.

WILLIE ORMOND

illie Ormond was once quoted as saying that if his right foot had been as good as his left, Brazilian legend, Pele, would not have been heard of. He might have been so one-footed that the other was merely for balancing, but he didn't do too badly by becoming a football institution. As part of the Famous Five, he won three Scottish League Championships and six Scottish caps. What's more, his name is commemorated in three Scottish football grounds. There is the Ormond Stand at St Johnstone's McDiarmid Park; there is the hospitality lounge at Stenhousemuir's Ochilview Park, where his kindly face bears down from a mural and there is the Famous Five Stand at Hibs' Easter Road stadium.

Ormond was awarded the OBE in 1975, partly in recognition for managing Scotland during the 1974 World Cup finals, held in West Germany. Though Scotland did not get beyond the first round, they returned with their heads held high, undefeated in three games.

Ormond made his playing debut against Queen of the South on December 7, 1946. It was an 'A' Division fixture, simply because the classification, 'Division One', was still some ten years off. His trademark was to push the ball ahead and chase after it, before cutting in to unleash a shot. He was brave, too, having his legs frequently chopped by frustrated defenders, with the result that he suffered more than his fair share of leg breaks, in total, three, one while playing against Aberdeen in a Scottish Cup tie.

From Falkirk, where he had a spell as assistant trainer from 1961, he became manager of St Johnstone, where he led the club to a famous victory over SV Hamburg in the 1971/72 UEFA Cup. From St Johnstone, it was the Scotland job, appointed in January 1973. His Scotland record read: P38 W18 D8 L12. After leaving the Scotland job - making way for Ally MacLeod - he briefly managed Hearts. He then took the short journey back to Easter Road, initially as assistant to Eddie Turnbull and then - a month later, in April 1980 - full manager, when Turnbull and Hibs finally parted company.

His managerial stint at Hibs began with a 1-1 draw at Aberdeen but there was never enough time to stave off the relegation that had been threatening since long before he arrived. The following autumn, following a bright start to the promotion drive, he gave up due to ill health and to concentrate on running his public house. He died on May 4, 1984, aged 57.

JIMMY O'ROURKE

For young fans watching Hibs during the 1970s, the elegance and fluidity of the side meant little compared to the cheeky nose for goal which belonged to Jimmy O'Rourke. In a side of arresting skills and complementary talents, O'Rourke was its vital spark. It helped that he was a Hibs fan.

It helped also that he was blooded young. He made his debut at the tender age of 16, against Utrecht in the Fairs Cup during season 1962/63, making him the youngest Hibs player to play in Europe.

Sadly, a leg break the following season set back Jimmy's seemingly meteoric rise. But while it took much longer for Jimmy's form to return than his fitness, he had his moments to savour. Scoring twice as Hibs went into a 4-0 lead against Hearts within just ten minutes of the kick-off, was certainly one of them. That was on September 18, 1965.

The arrival of Eddie Turnbull as manager helped turn Jimmy into a better player and a regular. He scored in Hibs' 2-1 win over Celtic in the 1972 League Cup Final. He was in among the goals when, less than a month later, Hibs were cuffing Hearts 7-0 on January 1, 1973.

His partnership with fellow striker Alan Gordon delivered mountains of goals.

It was a partnership that was not allowed to go its full course. Turnbull began to break the side up, too early, most people will now agree. O'Rourke was among the first to go, partly to make way for Joe Harper, bought from Everton for £120,000, the biggest fee paid by any Scottish club for a player at the time. Jimmy joined St Johnstone. The great irony is that his career was brought to an end because of a broken leg, suffered while playing for the Perth side at Easter Road and inflicted by Hibs' defender, George Stewart. George - another big Hibee - was a good friend. Indeed, both Jimmy and George later became assistants to Pat Stanton during his managerial stint at Easter Road during the mid 1980s.

Records show that he played 197 league games for Hibs, scoring 77 goals.

TROL ICI

GORDON RAE

Gordon Rae may have gone on to play for Partick Thistle when his playing days at Easter Road were over but in the minds of many Hibs supporters, he was really a one-club man, a Hibee who served his club through thick and thin. Starting off as a centre-forward and ending as a centre-half, Gordon signed professional forms in 1975. His Hibs debut was, unfortunately, not the most propitious, Hibs losing 2-1 to Queen of the South in the League Cup on August 17, 1977. However, the disappointment was soon to turn to joy, when Hibs lined up against Rangers three days later in the Premier Division.

Not only did Hibs win, 2-0, but Rae scored the opener, with just four minutes on the clock.

Gordon spent thirteen seasons at Easter Road, playing in Scottish Cup Finals, European ties and relegation dog fights. Sadly, he missed the League Cup Final of 1985 through suspension and his towering presence was sorely missed as Aberdeen won at a canter, 3-0.

He was part of the team that won promotion to the Premier Division at the first time of asking, in 1981. He was Hibs' leading scorer in seasons 1981/82 and 1982/83 with (in all competitions) twelve and ten goals respectively.

Undoubtedly, one of the highlghts of his career will have been scoring the winner against rivals, Hearts, in the quarter final of the Scottish Cup in 1979 (that run was to end at the hands of the Rangers, in the final, after two replays).

Another highlight will have been the testimonial game granted to him in recognition of his long service. The opposition was Manchester United and though the game got off to an unfortunate start - with Hibs defender, Joe Tortolano, sent off in the first minute for a rash tackle on United's Gordon Strachan - it was a night to remember, in front of 15,000 grateful fans.

Records show that he played 347 league games for Hibs, scoring 47 goals.

Gordon's spell at Partick Thistle has been followed by a coaching post at East Fife and management stints at Gala Fairydean and Edinburgh City. He is coaching again, and this time at his beloved Hibs.

P&D
WINDOWS

LAWRIE REILLY

hen the cry was raised in the main stand at Easter Road, “Gie the ba’ tae Reilly”, it was for a reason. Reilly could score goals and though he would modestly counter any praise heaped on him by saying he was merely finishing off the hard work of his illustrious colleagues, his was an impressive form of finishing off.

For club and for country. As the centre point of the Famous Five forward line, he scored - between seasons 1950/51 and 1956/57 - 23, 27, 30, 15, 15, 23 and 16 league goals, making him the club’s top marksman each season. For Scotland - for whom he is Hibs’ most capped player, with 38 caps - his strike rate eclipsed that of Denis Law and Kenny Dalglish, who share the record for most goals for Scotland. Reilly scored 22 goals from 38 appearances, a better strike rate than Law’s 30 goals from 55 appearances and much better than Dalglish’s 30 goals from 102 appearances. Throughout his Scotland career, he did not go more than four internationals without scoring. He acquired the nickname ‘Last Minute Reilly’ after twice scoring late in a game against England in 1953 that resulted in a 2-2 draw (his second - scored in the last minute - thanks to just beating Alf Ramsay to the ball). He was something of a lucky charm: Reilly’s first dozen games for Scotland each ended in victory. With Scotland, he sometimes played outside-left.

Illness, injury and arrogance denied him the World Cup stage he surely deserved. By the time of the 1958 World Cup in Sweden, he had retired from the game, having to call it a day because of cartilage problems on the eve of Hibs’ Scottish Cup Final appearance of that year (his last game was against Rangers a week before the final, against Clyde).

Born in Edinburgh on October 28, 1928, he was a Hibs fan before he was a Hibs player. He didn’t present any difficulties when asked to sign and he made his debut on October 13, 1945, in a Southern League fixture against Kilmarnock. He was aged 16. His youth kept him mostly out of the side that won the Scottish League Championship during season 1947/48. There was no doubt about his presence when Hibs again became League Champions 1951 and and 1952.

Famous goals? Lawrie is remembered for many. Against Falkirk, he headed a cross from Eddie Turnbull with such perfect timing, the ball screamed into the net. Against Motherwell, he collected the Motherwell keeper’s kick-out on the half-way line, nodded the ball over their centre-half, took the ball for a run past nearly half-a-dozen players, before walking it round the bemused goalkeeper for a tap-in. Records show that he played 253 league games for Hibs, scoring 185 goals.

HARRY RENNIE

ibs have long boasted some of the best goalkeepers of their day. In modern times, the link between club and country has been particularly strong via the likes of Alan Rough, Andy Goram and Jim Leighton.

Harry Rennie - born on June 1, 1875 - was considered the best goalkeeper of the Edwardian era. He made 13 appearances for Scotland, which, given the infrequency of international games at the time, is some achievement. He made his Scotland debut against Ireland on March 3, 1900 and it was against Ireland again that he made his final appearance, fourteen years later.

He pioneered many new goalkeeping techniques, not least marking out his area so he could better judge the angles that needed covering as opponents converged on goal. By today's standards, some of his ideas may have bordered on the eccentric; there is many a newspaper report describing how Rennie was expertly lobbed because he was standing closer to the half-way line than his own goal-line. There was nothing eccentric about the way he joined Hibs, though, presenting the club with his contractual terms before signing.

Certainly, he was respected enough to be given, after his playing days were over, the opportunity to coach three generations of goalkeepers, including Scotland international, Jimmy Cowan.

Born in 1873 in Greenock, he began his career with Greenock Volunteers, followed by Bellgrove Ramblers. From there he joined Morton and then - for the sum of £50 - Edinburgh rivals, Hearts. It was while at Hearts that he won his first two caps. Thereafter, his international appearances were during his career at Hibs, where he stayed for eight years. It is believed his move from Hearts to Hibs was prompted by a refusal by the Hearts committee to increase his weekly wage by ten shillings.

His 'scientific' approach to goalkeeping included looking out for what he called 'the shooting gesture' in an opponent's positioning of their feet. Records show that, from August 25, 1900, when he made his league debut for Hibs (against Celtic), to his last game in season 1907/08, Rennie clocked up 196 Hibs appearances, registering 55 shut-outs in the process. He played in the Scottish Cup-winning Hibs side of 1902 and picked up a Scottish League Championship with the club the following season. After Hibs, he played for Rangers and Kilmarnock. He died in 1954.

ALAN ROUGH

lan Rough had won all but two of his 53 Scotland caps when he signed for Hibs. He had already been voted Player of the Year by the Scottish Football Writers' Association. He was moving into the autumn of a career that previously had only been with Partick Thistle. Yet he proved to be an inspired signing when Hibs manager, Pat Stanton, brought him to Easter Road in November 1982 for a reported fee of £60,000.

As had always been the case when he was at Partick Thistle, 'Roughie' was hardly ever flustered. For years, he had heard people question his abilities and doubt his ambitions. He had a poor World Cup in 1978 and his critics were instantly on his back, questioning his positional sense and asking rhetorically why no big club appeared especially interested in signing him.

It was that same calmness that made him instantly popular with the Hibs support. He was steady and more than that, he saved the club valuable points with some outstanding stops.

He remained at Hibs for five seasons until the signing of Andy Goram from Oldham. He was freed on April 19, 1988, aged 36. But it wasn't long before he was back, this time in the colours of Celtic - for whom he made seven appearances as emergency cover. His return was warmly applauded, particularly since Hibs won. Spells thereafter at Hamilton Academical and Ayr United were followed by a move into management, with Ayrshire junior club, Glenafton.

Records show that he played 175 league games for Hibs.

KEITH WRIGHT

Keith Wright used to organise a supporters' bus to go to Hibs games but for long enough it seemed his dream to play for his favourite club would not be realised. His career began by signing for Raith Rovers in 1983. From Starks Park, he moved to Dundee, forming an impressive strike partnership with Tommy Coyne. But still, the call to move to Easter Road failed to materialise. When it eventually did - the transfer fee of £450,000 partly coming from the sale of Paul Wright to St Johnstone - he made his debut in a pre-season friendly against Chelsea in August 1991, the game finishing one apiece. His league debut was soon after, against St Mirren, in a 4-1 win.

What a start he made to his Hibs career! During those first few months, Hibs were riding high in the league and doing even better in the Skol League Cup. Keith was at the heart of it all, scoring - for example - in every round of the League Cup, including the final, which Hibs won, defeating Dunfermline 2-0. He scored the only goal in the colossal battle with Rangers in the semi final and he scored the clinching second goal against the Pars in the final.

Not surprisingly, he ended that first season as Hibs' top scorer, with seventeen goals and with his goal-scoring, came recognition at international level. A squad player for three European Championship games, he finally got the call to play for his country in a friendly against Northern Ireland. Though it proved his only cap and though opposition defenders started to learn how best to shackle Keith's attacking, he still had his moments, finishing season 1993/94 as Hibs' leading goalscorer, with 19 goals.

Keith finally bid farewell to Hibs in 1997, joining his old club, Raith Rovers. From Raith, he moved to Greenock Morton, where, at time of writing, he still is. Even at a distance, Keith helped out Hibs, his decisive goal for Morton against Falkirk paving the way for Hibs to clinch promotion to the Scottish Premier League against Hamilton on April 3, 1999.

However, as is often the way with former stalwarts, Keith has had the chance to put one over his old club. In January 1998, First Division Raith travelled to Easter Road to take on Premier Division Hibs in the third round of the Scottish Cup. Though Keith did not score, he was instrumental in a shock 2-1 victory.

Mitre
1875
Hibernian
FOOTBALL CLUB
Edinburgh

JIMMY McCOLL

immy McColl holds the special distinction of having scored 100 league goals with one Scottish club - Celtic - before repeating the feat with another - Hibs (for whom he scored 139 goals).

Talk about prolific. But he didn't arrive at Easter Road straight from Celtic. The story goes that because he was so good and brave as a striker - he was not known as 'Sniper' for nothing - Celtic did all they could to ensure he didn't return to haunt them wearing the colours of another Scottish club.

However, by selling him to Stoke City, it appears the club had not reckoned about the homesickness being suffered by Jimmy's wife. So, in no time at all, he was back in Scotland, with Partick Thistle. For reasons that are not known, it did not work out at Partick Thistle, either. Hence, he arrived at Hibernian and the rest, as they say, is history.

Remarkably, he was never capped for his country. Alex Maley - brother of Celtic manager, Willie - was manager when he joined Hibs and is said to have described McColl as "the best boy I ever signed." McColl scored his first league goal for Hibs on October 21, 1922 - against Raith Rovers and rarely missed from that day on. In one game - against Hamilton Accies - he scored four goals in a 5-2 win. Born on December 14, 1892, and a contemporary of Harry Ritchie and Johnny Halligan, McColl was a member of the Cup losing Hibs sides of 1923 and 1924. His last game for Hibs was against Falkirk in 1931 and his coaching travels soon took him to Northen Ireland, where he managed Belfast Celtic.

He returned to Easter Road two years before the outbreak of war to act as assistant to trainer Hugh Shaw. He was upgraded to trainer in 1948 when Shaw was upgraded to manager. He was therefore trainer to three championship-winning sides.

Over twenty years later - on August 2, 1971 - he was presented with a gold watch from all the members of the Famous Five for services to Hibernian - as a player, trainer and general assistant. He died in 1978, aged 85.

RONNIE SIMPSON

onnie Simpson enjoys worldwide fame because of his days at Celtic and in particular, some nifty footwork shown during Celtic's European Cup win over Inter Milan, when he left his box to dribble the ball past one of the opposition. But that is not to deny him a quite extraordinary career with other clubs, including Hibs, for whom he performed heroics to stave off the threat of relegation at the end of season 1962/63.

It is a career that began with a league debut aged just 14 years and 304 days. A career that neared its end with the first of five Scottish caps being earned at the grand old age of 36 years and 196 days (in Scotland's 3-2 Wembley win over World Champions, England, no less).

Ronnie joined Hibs in October 1960 for a fee of £2,100 and left four years later, in the September of 1964 (reports of the fee vary from £1,000 to £4,000). It was not until 1970 that he retired and not before being conferred, in 1967, the title Player of the Year. Between October 1971 and September 1972, he managed Hamilton Academical. Records show that he played 128 league games for Hibs.

DAVY SHAW

Davy Shaw was the Hibs captain from an impressive football family, his brother, John, having played for Rangers under the colourful soubriquet, 'Tiger'.

While Davy played left-back for Hibs, 'Tiger' played left back for Rangers. Davy won eight caps for Scotland - his first against Wales on October 19, 1946, his last against Northern Ireland on November 17, two years later - while 'Tiger' won four.

Davy was a hard tackler and a man who quickly earned the respect of his peers. His team-mates used to call him 'Faither'.

Records show that he played 86 league games for Hibs, plus various wartime fixtures.

Born on May 5, 1917, Davy joined Hibs in 1939 and stayed at Easter Road until 1950, leaving to join Aberdeen. When his playing days finished in 1953, he moved into coaching, then management and back into coaching - all at Aberdeen. He retired in 1967 and died a decade later.

GORDON SMITH

It is said Gordon Smith was as good as the legendary English winger, Stanley Matthews. Some say he was even better. Certainly, there appears to be unanimity among those privileged to see him play. He was the best ever. For Hibs. For Hearts. For Dundee. With each club, he won a League Championship medal. With each club, he played in the European Cup. A record that begs the question: why did Hibs let him go when he had a few years of his career left?

The answer may be that the club thought imminent ankle surgery was not worth paying for if there was little chance of the player making a recovery. In the end, Smith persevered, went ahead with the surgery and made the desired recovery.

But that is a small sour note. Smith played for Hibs for a long time and the memories are mostly happy ones. Including his testimonial match - a classic - between Hibs and Manchester United, which ended Hibs 7 Manchester United 3, even though Hibs were 3-2 down at half-time.

Smith was born in Edinburgh on May 25, 1924. He grew up in Montrose. If anything, he was a Hearts supporter. He came to the attention of both Edinburgh clubs when, at the age of 16, he played for a junior select against a Hibs/Hearts select and scored three times. The newspapers the following day claimed he was heading for Hearts. Hibs manager, Willie McCartney, had other ideas and travelled to meet the youngster face to face. His debut was against Hearts, as it happened, on April 30, 1941 and he scored a hat-trick. In total, he made over 500 appearances (in all competitions) for Hibs - the pretext for the testimonial. During the war he made 139 'league' appearances, scoring 96 times; after the war, he made a further 314 league appearances, scoring 127 times. In all competitions, he scored 364 goals - a club record. He was at Hibs for 17 seasons, an average of just under one season per Scottish cap. With Willie Waddell often preferred to Smith for the outside-right berth, Smith won only 18 caps. Just as he captained his club, he also captained his country.

He famously scored five goals in an 8-0 rout of Third Lanark. He scored twice in Hibs' 8-1 win over Rangers in September 1941. He was the club's top scorer between 1943 and 1950. He was also the sort of player capable of juggling the ball along the touchline on his head before volleying spectacularly into the roof of the net (actually, on the occasion he remembers trying it, instead of volleying the ball into the net, he headed it wide instead). He retired later that year. He was never anything but a gentleman perfectionist, no matter which position he played.

PAT STANTON

The biggest Hibs hero of them all? Some might argue that it was Gordon Smith, others Lawrie Reilly. But there is no doubt about the place Pat Stanton occupies in the affections of Hibs fans. Up there in the top three? No question about it.

For one thing, he was a brilliant player. Born in Edinburgh on September 13, 1944, he was signed by Walter Galbraith and made his Hibs debut aged 19. He ended his career at Celtic, where - under manager Jock Stein - he won the League Championship and Scottish Cup winner's medals that had so eluded him at Easter Road but which were definitely his due. He won 16 Scottsh caps, an inadequate reflection of his true worth. Later, having assisted Alex Ferguson, manager of Aberdeen and managed himself at Cowdenbeath and Dunfermline, he took on the manager's job at Hibs. Had the club not been so strapped for cash, Stanton's eye for a good player would have reaped even greater dividends. He was Hibs manager from September 2, 1982 to September 16, 1984 - including a two-day spell in the middle of 1983 when he resigned but was persuaded to return.

He was not the most demonstrative of managers, typical of his nickname, 'The Quiet Man'. He certainly did not have the gruff style of Eddie Turnbull, who managed him during the latter part of his career at Hibs and with whom he had the odd fall-out, not least after an embarrassing defeat by Montrose in the League Cup, which saw Pat being dropped for the UEFA Cup match in season 1975/76 against Liverpool - a decision which rebounded, as Liverpool's John Toshack took full advantage of Pat's aerial presence being absent.

There is no doubt Hibs failed to convert their talent into trophies during the early 1970s. Apart from a couple of Drybrough Cup wins, there was only the League Cup, won in 1972. Pat scored Hibs' second and as captain, became the first Hibee in too many decades to mention, to lift a major piece of silverware.

Pat's league debut - against Motherwell in October 1963 - was a scoring one. But Hibs lost, 4-3. In all, he made 399 league appearances for Hibs and scored 50 goals, one of his more famous being an injury time equaliser in an Edinburgh derby at Tynecastle, when he towered over the Hearts defence to head home powerfully. He also scored in a 5-0 hammering of Napoli in the 1967/68 Fairs Cup to reverse a 4-1 first leg deficit. A sadder moment was when he missed during a penalty shoot-out against Leeds in the 1973/74 UEFA Cup, his effort rebounding agonisingly off the post.

At Celtic, he made 44 appearances in all competitions, making his debut in an Old Firm match on September 4, 1976, having signed three days before. Two seasons later, he did not want to take any risks with an injury and called it a day. His standing in the game was such that over 20,000 fans turned up to pay tribute at a testimonial game between Hibs and Celtic held in April 1978 at Easter Road.

ERIC STEVENSON

Eric Stevenson returned from a trip to Wolverhampton - after having visited the football club who were keen on signing him - to find, to his surprise that he had been registered as a Hearts player. As far as he was concerned, he was a schoolboy player for them but wanted to sign for Hibs. He got his wish, Hearts were punished for acting improperly and Hibs fans had found a new hero to worship. He arrived at Easter Road at the start of season 1959/60. He left for Ayr United just as Eddie Turnbull was about to become manager in 1971. He played on the wing and was handy with the odd goal, including two against Hearts as Hibs went 4-0 up within the first ten minutes of a derby match in 1965. He was a player who loved life and football. Records show that he played 257 league games for Hibs, scoring 60 goals.

JAMES McGHEE

When Hibs' very future was thrown into jeopardy by the defection of a substantial number of players to Celtic - formed in 1888 - James McGhee was one of the Hibees who refused to be seduced by the new Glasgow outfit. As it turned out, his resistance proved in vain as Hibs folded and Celtic began in earnest.

Only when Hibs' was forced to close - fortunately for just a few months - did he succumb, joining Celtic in December 1890, seven years after having joined Hibs. A plasterer to trade, he was considered one of the best right-halves of his generation. He won one Scottish cap and skippered Hibs to victory in the 1887 Scottish Cup final.

GEORGE STEWART (1)

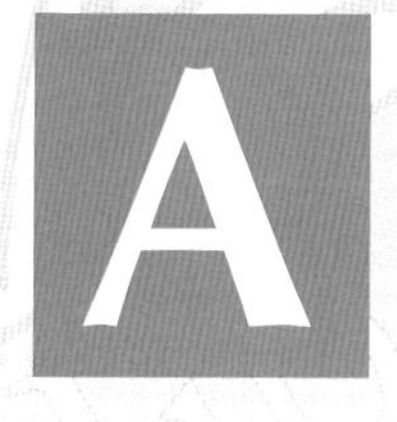
n outside-right, known as a lovely crosser of the ball. He was part of the Hibs team that won the League Championship in season 1902/03. He won four Scottish caps. After Hibs, he joined Manchester City, with whom he won a Division Two winner's medal in 1910.

GEORGE STEWART (2)

A Hibee through and through, George Stewart was kept on tenterhooks for most of his career before he could join his beloved club, not joining Hibs until he was 28 years old. Once one ambition was achieved, it was written in the stars that he would captain the club, doing so during the 1979 Scottish Cup Final. Remarkably, with both Hibs and his previous club Dundee (where he was for 13 years), George was never on a losing side at Tynecastle. It was against Hearts - albeit at Easter Road - that George scored a fine header from a Ralph Callachan corner to help Hibs to a 2-1 quarter-final win on the way to the 1979 Cup Final.

During the mid-eighties, George was part of the 'dream management team' at Easter Road, with Pat Stanton the manager and George, plus Jimmy O'Rourke, as his assistants. Before Hibs, George and Pat were in partnership at Cowdenbeath and Dunfermline.

George's passion for the club saw him become heavily involved in the 'Hands Off Hibs' campaign that successfully repelled a take-over attempt in 1990 by the then chair of Hearts, Wallace Mercer.

Records show that he played 109 league games for Hibs, scoring two goals.

EDDIE TURNBULL

Perhaps the unsung hero of the Famous Five? There are few people more inextricably woven into the Hibs fabric than Eddie 'Ned' Turnbull. First, he played in the most potent strikeforce the club - and arguably, the country - has ever seen. Second, he was - along with Willie McCartney - one of the club's most important managers. He had a thunderous shot as a player and a thunderous temper as a manager. But no-one could dispute his contribution as a player (he was the first Briton to score in European competition) or his tactical genius as a manager.

During the early 1970s, when his 'Turnbull's Tornadoes' were chasing Celtic - under Jock Stein - for everything, Turnbull's tactical genius won admirers throughout the game.

He was born in Falkirk on April 12, 1923. He won eight Scottish caps. With Hibs - his only senior club as a player - he was three times a Scottish League champion, in 1948, 1951 and 1952. One of the longest serving of the Famous Five, he played in Hibs' Scottish Cup Final appearances of 1947 and 1958. Before managing Hibs, he was a coach at Queen's Park and then a highly successful boss at Aberdeen. He retired from managing Hibs, after almost a decade in charge, in April 1980. He made his Hibs debut as a player in an 'A' Division game against Third Lanark on November 2, 1946. He played his last game against Real Gijon on May 31, 1959, during a four-game tour of Spain.

Records show that he played 321 league games for Hibs, scoring 141 goals.

MICKEY WEIR

For a born and bred Hibee, whose love of club was such that, when he left Hibs for Luton Town, he just had to return, Mickey Weir's Hibs' debut is one to forget. Not necessarily for his own performance but for the result and the aftermath. Mickey's debut was at Easter Road against Dumbarton in September 1983 and the 3-2 defeat by the Sons was the final straw for Hibs boss, Pat Stanton, who that night tendered his resignation.

Weir (pictured right) was a pocket dynamo, who worked hard in training and thought deeply about his game – the more so when, towards the end of his Hibs career and during the early part of his spell at Motherwell (whom he joined from Hibs in March 1997), he was sidelined by injury for, effectively, three years.

Among Mickey's many high points, the Skol Cup Final win of 1991 is especially memorable. It was during the semi final against Rangers that Mickey latched on to a punched clearance from Rangers' goalkeeper, Andy Goram, to coolly drop a cross on to the head of Keith Wright for the only goal of the game.

In the final itself, which ended 2-0 for Hibs over Dunfermline, Mickey was brought down for a penalty, from which Tommy McIntyre put Hibs ahead. Mickey also had a big say in Hibs' second, timing his pass perfectly to set up Keith Wright to score. After both the semi final and the final, Mickey came away with the Man of the Match awards.

Records show that he played - over two spells - 206 league games for Hibs, scoring 30 goals.

MICHAEL WHELEHAN

Hibs were formed in 1875 at a time when clubs were founded and folded on a regular basis. They were an exercise in self-improvement and owed a lot to the support of the Church. Also to the perseverance of individual players, such as Michael Whelehan, co-founder and captain and an ancestor of another Hibs hero, Pat Stanton.

ERICH SCHAEDLER

hen people think of the attacking football Hibs became famous for in the early 1970s, it is no surprise that Hibs' two full-backs, John Brownlie and Erich Schaedler, often spring to mind. Both were thoroughly attack-minded. And even if Schaedler was not the most skilful, he was one of the most committed.

Records show that he played - over two spells - 292 league games for Hibs, scoring two goals.

He was good enough to win a Scottish cap; and being the son of a German father who once played for Borussia Moenchengladbach, it was a nice coincidence that he should represent Scotland against West Germany. Indeed, he was a member of the Scotland squad that travelled to West Germany under the management of Willie Ormond for the 1974 World Cup. Had Scotland not been graced by a world-class left-back in the shape of Danny McGrain, more caps would surely have come Erich's way.

He made his Hibs debut in a friendly against Polish club, Gornik, on December 8, 1969. Legend has it that his first touch of the ball was a poor one, leading to team-mate, Peter Cormack being badly injured. As well as being a tenacious tackler, he was an expert at the long throw-in.

Erich enjoyed two spells at Hibs, re-signing for them from Dundee in 1981. Tragically, personal problems led to his untimely death, on Christmas Eve four years later.

TOMMY YOUNGER

Known by many as a gentle giant of a man, Tommy Younger was lots of things to lots of people. For some, he was the Hibs goalkeeper who travelled back and forth between Easter Road and Germany, where he was stationed while doing National Service. For others, he was a player of considerable renown, winning 24 caps for Scotland and - unusually for a goalkeeper - captaining his country during a World Cup - the 1958 staging, held in Sweden. For others, he was the man who - having played for Hibs, Liverpool, Stoke City and Leeds United - rose through the ranks of the Scottish Football Association to reach the very top of the game, as SFA president and able football administrator.

He was born on April 10, 1930 and with Hibs he won a League Championship in 1951 and 1952. He had signed for Hibs in 1948 and became first-choice goalkeeper at the start of season 1949/50, replacing George Farm, who went on to win ten Scotland caps while playing for Blackpool. It was during that first season that Tommy must have thought he was due his first piece of silverware in senior football. Hibs had reached the final of the League Cup and were to play Motherwell, whom they had comfortably defeated at Fir Park a fortnight previously, scoring six goals in the process. They were on form and it looked like it would be a formality. Motherwell won 3-0, with Younger responsible for the victors' third, following a poor clearance.

That was on October 28, 1949. By the following June, his commitment to the Hibs cause was put to the test, when National Service took him to Germany, albeit as a League champion. Instead of throwing in the towel, he spent the weekend travelling back and forth between Scotland and his base. In total, he made 76 round trips, in other words flew 150,000 miles, at a cost of £3,000 - a lot of money in those days. The reward was another League Championship.

His first Scottish cap was won on May 4, 1955, against Portugal. A hankering to sample English football was finally granted when he joined Liverpool in 1956 for a fee of £9,000. Thereafter, it was a spell at Leeds, a coaching stint in Toronto and a shot at management at Falkirk.

But in time he was to return to Easter Road, this time in the capacity of director, having built up a tidy business supplying vending machines. From his position on the board, he built up influence at the Scottish Football Association, his step up from vice-presidency to presidency involving a hectic schedule of representing the Association throughout the world. His bonhommie made him a welcome visitor.